waiting for

walker

robin reardon

IAM Books
www.robinreardon.com

WAITING FOR WALKER

The events and characters of this book are entirely fictional. Any similarity to events or people, living or dead, is entirely coincidental.

Praise for *Throwing Stones*

"There is always something to expect from a Reardon novel and she never disappoints. If you are not sure how I feel abut this book, I am giving it a rave and I doubt anyone will have any trouble understanding why."
—Amos Lassen, "Reviews by Amos Lassen"

"*Throwing Stones* is filled with magnificent characters, each with their own flaws, but also some brightly shining lights. This story has left me hopeful and uplifted; I hope it will do the same for you. An easy 5 out of 5 stars."
—Gay Guy Reading Reviews

It's all well and good to throw out the saying, 'One person can make a difference.' But what Robin Reardon has accomplished here is to show us what that looks like, and in a completely credible way."
—Love Bytes Reviews

*For intersex individuals everywhere,
and for the people who love and support them*

We can't direct the wind, but we can adjust the sails.

~ Thomas S. Monson, 16th president of the Church of Latter Day Saints

Foreword

"There are countless reasons for reading, but when you're young and uncertain of your identity, of who you may be, one of the most compelling is the quest to discover yourself reflected in the pages of a book." —Michael Cart

Waiting for Walker is a captivating novel from page one. Woven into this story are myriad issues germane to our youth of today: socio-economic disparity, familial loss through military service, divorce, Christian and Muslim dynamics, and a more subtle message, but no less important—being intersex is not a new phenomenon.

Intersex people have existed throughout history. At times revered, at times reviled, the treatment of intersex people is profound. It wasn't until post-World-War-II environs gave way to genuine research that intersex individuals began being viewed as human beings. Still and yet, it wasn't until 2006 that laws began being enacted in the United States to give intersex individuals rights—*human* and humane rights—civil liberties that those who are born within the binary genders enjoy from the day they are born. While the United States has come far, there remains a long road ahead and, largely, throughout the world, intersex people have no rights.

Walker is a beautiful, confused, vulnerable human being with the tensile strength of steel. Micah is wonderful; down-to-earth with a noir bent, he is an average gay teenager who is falling hopelessly in love with Walker. He is loyal, protective, supportive, and understanding of Walker's, at times, precarious emotional state. More importantly, Walker and Micah wend their ways through the complicated labyrinth of their relationship to find, in the end, they are meant for each other. Walker's and Micah's parents also add a positive message to this story: not all people reject intersex youth.

Superb, courageous, and finely tuned to realism, Robin Reardon creates extraordinary characters. She puts Walker boldly and unconditionally forward as an intersex character and shows us but a fraction of what he endures in coming to terms with his sexuality, his sexual identity, and most crucially, *who he is determined to be*. A master storyteller with a rare talent for grounding stories in everyday reality, Ms. Reardon breathes new life into the fragile notion that we are all equal. She shows us that financial and marital status, religious beliefs, familial loss, and our genetics are only parts of us—that *what we say and do speaks to who we are*.

The elements contained in this story can be polarizing, and I don't want to give the impression Ms. Reardon minimizes them. The reader clearly understands what Walker has gone through, and goes through, and at times, it is heartrending. But Ms. Reardon doesn't render Walker with a blunt instrument; she renders him with finesse. This coming-of-age story is one of discovery, love, hope, and healing.

Waiting for Walker is an important story. Please read it, and discuss it with your family and friends. Librarians and teachers, please share this story. Beautifully written, it stays with you long after you have turned the last page. Please join me in lauding Walker and Micah. May their legacies endure and inspire youth for generations to come.

Thank you for reading this book.

Cody Kennedy
Los Angeles, California
May, 2017

WOULD YOU LIKE TO KNOW MORE ABOUT BEING INTERSEX? TAKE A LOOK AT THESE RESOURCES

What's It Like to be Intersex?
https://www.youtube.com/watch?v=cAUDKEI4QKI

InterACT
http://interactadvocates.org/

Differences of Sex Development (DSD)
http://aisdsd.org/intersex-faq-interact-mtvs-faking/
http://aisdsd.org/fact-check/

Intersex Society of North America
http://www.isna.org/

National Institute of Health - U.S. Library of National Medicine
https://www.ncbi.nlm.nih.gov/pmc/articles/PMC3176412/

OII - Organization Intersex International
http://oii-usa.org/about/our-intersex-mission/

American Library Association
http://www.ala.org/glbtrt/sites/ala.org.glbtrt/files/content/pr ofessionaltools/IntersexResources.pdf

Chapter One

It was dead. Perfect.

Almost immediately, I was deep in that zone I get into when I'm shooting—where nothing matters except the shot, because nothing else exists. My problems don't exist. Even I don't exist, in a way.

With my camera attached to the mini tripod and hovering over the seagull, I hunched my entire body so I could zoom in as far as the focus would let me. I wanted to capture the little maggotty things I could barely see between the barbs of the wing feathers' vanes. Then I zoomed out a little and shot different parts of the lifeless body—the leathery feet, the limp neck, eyes sunken a little into the skull—and finally I took the camera off the tripod to get the whole bird.

The way it was stretched out on the rock, wings open and out to the sides, it almost looked like it was flying.

Standing again, I was examining my last image, trying to decide if I wanted more zoom shots of the head, when I heard this voice.

"Did you kill that bird?"

The voice shocked me out of my concentration so suddenly I almost gasped. Now I could hear the little waves lapping against the tiny strip of sandy shore at the water's edge. Now I could feel the wind off Long Island Sound, chilly for late June. Now I could feel the painful tightness in my left leg from how I'd had to balance on the rock surface as it sloped down toward the shore, while I took my shots.

I stared at the guy who'd spoken, the guy who'd brought the real world crashing back in on me. The intruder was in a sailboat, as close to the shore as he dared get, probably; I know nothing about sailing. The boat was gorgeous: pure white where it met the water, then a thin, red line separating the white from the shiny dark blue above. The afternoon sun from behind the guy in the boat lightened his already blond, curly hair, giving him a kind of halo effect. But he was more like a devil to me. He'd destroyed my mood.

"Yeah," I lied. "What of it?"

He stared back for a few seconds. I couldn't see his face very well because of the sun being behind him, but I guessed he was about my age. Then he said, "Did not."

That pissed me off further. Ignoring him, I folded the tripod and put it back in my pack.

But he wouldn't stop. "What kind of camera is that?"

As I hefted my pack onto one shoulder I heaved a long-suffering sigh. "Canon PowerShot." I turned to walk away from the shore. Away from him.

"Is not. My dad has one, and it doesn't look like that."

Head half turned toward the water, I said, "I don't give a fuck what your father has."

Before I'd taken seven steps, I heard, "Why so hostile, anyway?"

I turned around to face him, and now that I was higher up on the hump of rock, looking down toward the water, I could see him better. Yeah, my age. Sixteen, maybe seventeen. He wore a pale yellow IZOD polo shirt and khaki shorts, and he was very blond and very tan, even this early in the summer. He'd grabbed a long tree branch that stuck out over the water, one foot on the edge of the boat, using the branch to hold the boat in place. On that foot was a light brown shoe, raised stitching around the toes, with a bright white sole. I was pretty sure he was wearing what's called boat shoes.

2

Like so many stones, I threw these words at him: "Why do you care?" I didn't want an answer. I turned and walked away, fast.

"Wait!"

Again, I ignored him. All I wanted was to be alone again, and to find something else to shoot, find something else—anything else—to get me back into the zone he'd stolen. I decided to walk farther east along the shore where it would be easier for me to get to the edge of the water. I still needed a shot I could double-expose with the whole seagull to make it look like it was underwater, a dead swimmer.

An hour later, with several shots of water that wouldn't work because they were too opaque, I gave up and pedaled home. I locked my bike to the metal stand around the side of our unit, the motel manager's apartment where my mom and I lived, and as I took my helmet off I had a brainstorm: Take a shot of the pool water! That would be clear, and there was still enough sun left in the afternoon to light it up nicely.

I ignored the odd stares from the family with three kids who were already using the shallow end of the motel's pool. I hate families. They make me angry, all that togetherness and camaraderie. Too bad for me; lots of them came to stay at the motel.

Legs hanging over either side of the puny diving board at the deep end, I managed to take a few shots when the stupid kids weren't splashing around too badly. Then the biggest kid, maybe eleven, swam toward me.

Treading water made his voice waver with his efforts. "What are you taking pictures of?"

I gave him an evil, sideways glance. "Sharks."

He nearly looked around, I could tell. And then I saw his arm get ready to fling water, so I pulled my camera out of the way of the splash and scooted off the diving board.

Inside our unit, Mom was at the kitchen table hunched over her laptop, surrounded by paperwork and cigarette smoke, bottle-blond hair pulled into a messy nest in the general direction of the back of her head. It was a shade she'd had since just after New Year's, and although she didn't seem to know it, it wasn't her friend.

A glass with something clear in it was within reach. Didn't look like water. Or, it wasn't in a typical water glass. I guessed it was her usual: gin. That was something else that had changed in the last year or so; she never used to have more than a gin and tonic before dinner on the weekends. She's insisted that she's not an alcoholic. Says she could stop any time. I've never challenged her on it.

She didn't look up as I came in. "Where've you been, Micah? I need you to pick up a few things. Nick isn't here today."

Nick Dowd. The motel manager's assistant. Mom's assistant, in other words. Nick was a local kid home from college for the summer who, although I didn't much like him, was obliging enough when he had a chance to earn a little money. He was short and kind of funny-looking, with twisted teeth that were too easy to see because of how often he smiled. He was one of those people who are always asking if they can help you but you aren't really sure if they mean it, which is why I didn't like him. Also, it seemed like he was never around when I needed him to be.

"Can I take the car?"

"You can not." She scowled at me. "I don't have time to go with you, and you can't drive on your own yet. You know that. What's wrong with your bike?"

I did know that, yes. I'd asked mostly to hear her talk some more so I could gauge how much she'd had to drink. It was a good thing to know generally, and also if she'd had enough, she wouldn't care that I wasn't yet legal to drive alone. But she was sober enough to be practical. So I said, "Depends. How much stuff do I need to carry back?"

4

"Nothing you can't fit into a backpack. Here." She pushed a few papers around, picked up something with pencil scrawls on it, and flapped it in my general direction, eyes back on her paperwork. As I took the list from her hand, I glanced over the rest of the mess on the table. Looked like she was working on financial stuff for the motel, so it was a good thing that she didn't sound too drunk yet. I tucked the paper into a pocket, grabbed some bills from the stash she keeps in a box on the counter, and headed out again, not even glancing toward the kid in the pool who shouted something at me.

At my laptop after dinner, I had just put the final touches on the image of a dead seagull "swimming" in crystal blue water when the sounds of Mom crying cut through my focus. Ordinarily I do my best to ignore her crying, partly because it happens so often, and partly because I just don't want to know about it.

She never used to be like this. Once upon a time, she was a normal mother, and we were a normal family. She cried sometimes when something made her happy.

Now when she cries, it's almost always for one reason. She misses Dylan, and she pulls out the box of his stuff that she saved from our old house—the one we lived in before she and Dad split, the one we all lived in before Dylan was killed in Afghanistan—and paws through his few worldly possessions as though he might appear at the bottom. But his Army dog tags are in there, and they wouldn't be if there was any hope.

I really didn't want to see her doing that. For one thing, it's pathetic. But also it made me feel… Shit, I don't know. It made me feel like shit. Like, she was the only one who missed him? Okay, so he was her son, but he was my brother! So it pissed me off.

But that's not the worst feeling. Hell, no. The worst feeling is that I have something of his that she really, really wants, something I'd bet she's looking for every time she goes into that box. And she doesn't know I have it.

The next day, Saturday, was a weekend with Dad, and I got to leave that sad motel unit haunted by Dylan's box. Dad lives in Warwick. It's not a big city or anything, but at least there are things to do. Dad always had something planned. It was a challenge, though, to get Mom moving in the morning, and she needed to drive me to the parking lot of the Big River Management Area, half-way to Warwick, where Dad always picked me up. He'd get pissed if she was more than fifteen minutes or so late, and it would spoil some of my time with him, which would piss *me* off. Today I was lucky, and we hit the road only about ten minutes behind schedule.

Dad was there in the parking lot, waiting in his blue Chevy pickup, arm hanging out of the window and tapping in some regular beat that no doubt matched the music he was playing. He likes "oldies."

Mom didn't get out of the car. "You make sure he's got you back here by six tomorrow night, Micah. I don't wanna have to ruin dinner on his account."

On *his* account? More likely he and I would wait in the parking lot, mostly just hanging out, for maybe half an hour before she showed up to get me. Without me to light a fire under her backside, the only thing she seemed able to rouse herself for were her regular visits to Madam Alberta Halliday, the medium who'd been picking our pockets since January. One of Mom's New Year's resolutions, which started around the same time as the change in hair color, was to connect with Dylan, and she believed this charlatan was doing that. I didn't buy it.

Whatever. I grabbed my duffle bag and dashed over to the pickup, threw the bag behind the seat, and climbed in beside Dad. He grinned at me, and I grinned at him. He looked great. The skin around his blue-gray eyes crinkled, and his dark hair—the same color as mine, the same color Mom's used to be before she rejected it—was tousled and hanging a little over his forehead. His face was ruddy from working outdoors on construction sites.

He held up his right hand in a loose fist, and I bumped it with mine, exploding our fingers at the same instant.

"You all set?" he asked, which I knew meant did I already have my swimming trunks on under my jeans, as he'd texted me to do.

"All set. Where are we going?" Wherever it was, I hoped it would be someplace other than the ocean, maybe a lake someplace. But I didn't want to say that to Dad.

He turned his grin toward the windshield and started the truck engine. "You'll see."

We drove south for maybe forty minutes, mostly in silence. And unfortunately, south was where the ocean would be.

Dad did ask a little about shooting; he'd given me the camera for my birthday last August, and he'd been pretty tickled when I took it to shop class and constructed a wooden housing for it that made it look like the Rolleiflex that Vivian Maier used when she took all those shots of New York City. This explains why that sailing boy didn't believe me; his father's camera would look very different from mine, given my modifications.

"What are you shooting these days, Micah?"

I was tapping the roof with my right hand, elbow propped on the door, window open, my head nodding in time with the music. It was old stuff, but it had an okay rhythm. "Took a cool series of a dead seagull yesterday." I described in as few words as possible how I'd made it "swim" in the pool water.

Dad chuckled. "When you said you wanted a camera, I figured you'd shoot people. And I sure never thought you'd shoot dead birds." He laughed, a sound I loved. "You're full of surprises, boy."

I didn't respond to that. I could give him a really big surprise and tell him I'm gay, but I wasn't willing to risk pushing him even further away than Mom had already done.

Eventually we left the paved road and followed a track for a bit. I could hear the surf and smell the salt of the ocean better every minute. Damn. Dad pulled the truck in beside several other vehicles in an area that didn't look like any kind of official parking lot.

We were still on the Rhode Island side of the border with Connecticut, where Mom and I lived. I'd never been to this spot before. "Special beach?"

Dad laughed again. "You have no idea. Just you wait."

We got out, and from the bed of the truck Dad pulled a large cooler and a tote bag. With each of us holding one handle of the cooler, he led the way through some bushes, down a narrow path toward the water, and then down the beach for maybe five minutes.

"Just how far are we going, Dad? This thing is heavy."

"Don't be a wuss, Micah." His own breathing was a little labored. "And it'll be worth it, I promise. You're nearly seventeen. Old enough to appreciate this place."

I focused on the sand, willing myself to keep moving despite the difficulty of walking on the shifting stuff, so when Dad said, "Okay. Here we are," I hadn't seen what or who was around us.

I could tell Dad was watching me for some kind of reaction as we stripped down to our swim trunks. And when I did finally take stock of the surroundings, what I saw said worlds about why Dad had wanted to come here, and why he'd thought I'd want to come here. There weren't a lot of people on this narrow stretch of beach, but most of the women were not wearing the tops to their two-piece bathing suits.

Almost under his breath, just loud enough to be heard above the surf, he said, "Well? Worth it?"

I didn't have the heart to disappoint him, or to see that broad grin turn into a grimace, which is what I was sure would happen if I told him why this sight was more "meh" than "wow" for me.

"Amazing." I hoped that would get me by.

While we spread the blanket he'd brought in the tote, he told me how this was one of the few places in Rhode Island where people did this. "They used to go totally nude, men *and* women, over at Moonstone Beach. But that was a while ago. There was too much resistance from residents in the area."

Now, *that* might have interested me. "So people all have to wear the bottoms now?"

"Yeah. But topless girls? That's what I'm talkin' about. That's enough."

He pulled beach towels out of the tote and tossed them onto the blanket. "Race you to the water!"

And we were off, sand flying behind us as we swerved around the half-naked women, crashing into water so cold it took my breath away. But I was also breathless for another reason. I hated being in the ocean.

I stopped—as I always do—not far from shore, at a depth where it was waist-high between waves, and already I could barely breathe. Already the blood pounded in my head, my vision blurred, and I felt dizzy. Dad swam out farther and gestured, but I stayed put, arms waving in the water at my sides, gasping for air long after it was the cold that made me do that.

My foot hit something under the water, and I nearly lost consciousness. But it was just a rock, not a horseshoe crab or anything that was going to attack me. That had happened once already, and I had the scars to prove it.

It had happened when I was twelve, when we were still a family, when Dylan was still alive, still with us. My folks had rented a tiny cabin on the shore in North Carolina for a week that summer. It had seemed like heaven: long, lazy days on the beach, fried clams and french fries for dinner, body-surfing in the ocean, flying kites with Dylan, playing Frisbee with Dylan and Dad and Trapper. Trapper was Dylan's dog, but I really loved him, too. He rode down to North Carolina in the car with us, and boy, did he love the water. And Frisbee. He was part shepherd and part something else, with a lighter coat than most shepherds have, and he was super smart. Dylan and I had both taught him lots of tricks, and he'd always seemed as entertained doing them as we were watching him.

Anyway, one evening over dinner I must have been doing something that annoyed Mom, because I got scolded, so I got sulky. I wanted to be alone, so I headed down to the beach. The sun had set, but it was still barely lighting a few high clouds with deep shades of peach.

I walked down the shore, kicking at the surf, then back toward our cabin, but I wasn't ready to go back. I turned and watched the water for a bit as the tide went out, the white surf almost all I could see. For some reason, I walked into the water. I didn't want to swim, I just wanted to feel the water surround me, to feel the sand move under my feet. I was maybe fifteen feet from the tideline, water halfway up my thighs. And then something slammed into my left calf. Something sharp. Very sharp.

You always see TV shows where people get totally surprised by something, and they scream. I don't think most people would do that. I think most people would do what I did, which was to take a sudden, painful gasp of breath into my body. I tried to pull away from the pain in my leg, which was getting worse by the second, but it moved with me. I reached down with a hand and felt something firm and slimy. All I could see was churning water. Then I felt something warm, the churn turned darker, and I knew it was my blood. That's when I found my breath. I screamed.

The next thing I was aware of was something crashing through the water from the shore. It was Trapper. He didn't make a sound, just dived toward my leg. He must have bitten the shark, because it let go suddenly. I was barely aware that someone was calling my name, and then Dylan was beside me. He lifted me out of the water and laid me onto the dry beach. Mom appeared next and wrapped something tight around my thigh and something soft around my calf. I don't remember anything after that.

Later, in the hospital, I woke up to throbbing pains in my leg and my head. There were umpteen bazillion stitches in my calf, and a doctor who came in told me that there would always be a a scar and a bit of an indentation in the muscle where the shark had made off with a piece of me.

"It's actually not too bad," he told me, his southern drawl reminding me of where I was. "The size of the bite indicates that it must have been young. I'm pretty sure it was a black tip shark. It left a tooth in you. Here it is." He opened his hand, and this small, white, serrated triangle fell onto the table beside the bed. I still have it.

My shark bite wound got me a lot of cred when I went back to school in the fall. I tried to make like I hadn't been terrified, but that was a lie. At sixteen, I was still terrified. And I hated going into the ocean.

So I couldn't bring myself to follow Dad out farther into the water. He was still gesturing to me, so I half turned away so pretend I didn't seem, but I kept him in my peripheral vision in case he tried to sneak up on me. He'd done that once last year, trying to get me to "buck up" and stop being afraid, about to drag me by force farther away from shore, and in my total panic to escape I'd given him a black eye. It was not something I wanted to repeat, and it made me not trust him.

After maybe five minutes that felt like an eternity, I headed back to shore, forcing myself to move casually. I sat on my towel, arms wrapped around my knees, and tried like hell not to be pissed at Dad. Maybe he thought that I'd be so distracted by the semi-nudity that I'd forget to be afraid of the water. Or of what was in the water.

Before long, Dad headed back toward the beach and dripped his way toward our blanket. Standing over me, hands on hips, he said, "One of these days, Micah, you're gonna have to get over this."

I didn't look at him. "Why?"

"If you don't master your fears, they master you."

"Think I'll let this one get away with that."

He toweled off a little and sat beside me, both of us looking out to sea. "Bet you didn't know I'm afraid of heights."

That got my attention, and I turned toward him. "How can you be afraid of heights with your job?" I pictured him high on one of the in-progress office buildings with his construction crew, defying death with every step.

"I mastered my fear. That's what you'll have to do."

Arguing would get me nothing; I didn't reply. Dad was silent, too, until a particularly attractive woman came into view and walked toward the water, her boobs bouncing just like the fat they were full of. Dad poked me with an elbow. "Wouldn't mind getting to know that one, if you know what I mean."

"She's a little young for you, don't you think?" I had intended my tone to be joking, but that's not how it came out.

Dad looked at me. "Fine. You go talk to her, then." He pushed at me with both hands.

If I had resisted, things would have gotten ugly. So I stood, but I walked away from Dad in the opposite direction from the bathing beauty who'd attracted his attention.

"Micah!"

I ignored him and kept walking, keenly aware that the skin around my shark bite pulled with every other step.

Why *couldn't* I just accept that I'd never again be attacked by a shark? Why couldn't I go into the water like a normal person?

Sometimes I hated myself.

Dad and I were pretty quiet as we ate our sandwiches a little later, and although we walked together along the shore after that, it felt pretty tense. After Dad took another swim—alone this time—we packed the truck up to leave, a little less pissed at each other by that point. It helped that he let me drive.

We stopped at a grocery store on the way to his apartment, and by the time we left the store we were okay again. We were in total agreement over what dinner should be: hamburgers, fries we'd heat in the oven, and just enough lettuce to say we'd had some green food, then ice cream after.

Dad's place was on the third floor, the top floor, so there was no balcony above his. Even though it was against the rules, he had a little hibachi out there where we cooked and then ate the burgers. He handed me a bottle of beer, and we sat in webbed lawn chairs, slapping at the occasional mosquito, watching the sky darken and the city's lights come on. We'd each finished a second burger when he opened another beer for himself, and somehow I knew he had settled in to talk about something specific.

"Micah, tell me about this Madam Whoever your Mom's spending so much money on. What do you know about her?"

I shrugged. "Madam Alberta. I don't know much about *her*. All I know is that Mom thinks she's putting her in touch with Dylan."

Dad took a slug of beer. "What do *you* think?"

"I think it's a bunch of crap. I mean, I never go with her, so I never see what it is Mom thinks she's seeing or hearing or whatever, but she comes back crying, kind of sad-slash-happy, convinced Dylan has nothing better to do in the afterlife than talk to her."

Silence. Then, "What does he tell her?"

"Dad, don't tell me you believe in that shit, too."

"No, no, I just mean, you know, what kinds of things does she *think* he tells her?" He sounded a tad defensive, like maybe he did believe it, at least a little. Or maybe it was just that he wanted to.

"I don't ask her. A couple of times she's said that he's watching over us, you know, like he cares about what happens to us. She thinks that means he's manipulating things in our favor, like he was God or something. Once I asked what he thought about her drinking."

"Oh, Micah..."

"I know. Dumb, huh? Won't do *that* again."

"Um, just how bad is it? The drinking, I mean."

I lifted a shoulder. How was I supposed to gauge that? "I just do my best to figure out how far gone she is at any given time so I'll know how to act."

He shook his head slowly. "So, does she feed you okay? Do laundry, that sort of thing?"

"Sometimes I have to help. But it's not that bad, really. She keeps up with the motel management and all. We're not getting kicked out, or anything."

"So she's functional."

"Yeah, I guess." I polished off the last of my beer. "Can I have another?"

"I think one's enough for you. There's some soda in the fridge if you want."

I didn't even really want another beer. I just wanted to change the subject. As much as I liked being with my dad, I didn't think I'd want to come live with him. I liked doing my own thing, coming and going however I wanted, and with Mom I could mostly get away with that. If Dad thought her drinking was bad enough, he might revisit the custody arrangement, and I doubted he'd be so easy-going to live with. Plus I didn't want to change schools again, like I'd had to after Dylan died and my folks split. And this coming year I was going to be photographer for the school paper. Mostly I don't hang with anyone, but my guidance counselor said I had to get involved in something. And I was kind of looking forward to this assignment.

To make sure the subject got changed, I got up and went to fetch my camera. The colors of the dying coals in the hibachi were calling to me.

Lost in that zone I get into when I'm shooting, I was surprised when Dad spoke again. "Got a girlfriend yet, Micah?"

Here we go. He'd been totally confused when I hadn't wanted to go to junior prom, and every so often he'd ask me about girls. And every time he did, I thought about telling him the truth. And instead, I'd hidden that truth, which was feeling like a bigger and bigger lie every time the subject came up.

"No, Dad. No girlfriend." I went back to my lies and to the coals, hoping that would be an end to it.

"But you date, right?"

If it's possible to sigh and clench your jaw at the same time, that's what I did. I gave up on the shooting and sat in my chair. My brain froze. I didn't know what I was going to do. I wanted so badly to tell him who I was, to be honest with him, to trust that he'd love me anyway, but the risk was so huge.

I must have been quiet for too long, because then Dad said, "Micah?"

Something in his tone, something almost pleading, got to me. I came so close to blurting out the truth, just dumping it out there onto the gritty surface of the balcony floor.

"Look, kid," he went on, "this is another one of those places in life where you have to face your fears. And, I mean, what's the worst that can happen? If you don't have a favorite girl, then just ask someone you think is okay. If she says 'No,' you've lost nothing and you've had a little practice. You'll see that the sky didn't fall, you're still fine, and you'll be able to ask someone else."

That was it? *Really?* He was thinking that the idea of asking girls out was like going into the ocean? It also sounded like he had a pretty old-fashioned idea of how kids hang out these days. I suppose I could have tried to explain how things had changed, how asking girls out on dates wasn't the be-all-and-end-all of a boy's teen years any more. But that semi-nude beach had pushed me closer than ever toward who I really was, which meant further than ever from what Dad *thought* I was. Or what he wanted me to be. The lies, or near lies, were pushing me farther from shore, and I felt sure that if I let Truth open its mouth, its razor teeth would sink into my heart and tear it to shreds.

When I said nothing right away, he took a breath like he had more to say on the subject. I stopped him in his verbal tracks. "That's not it, Dad. It's not that I'm afraid of asking girls out." Deep breath. *Master your fears, even if it means going into deep water.* "It's that I don't *want* to."

Even though I was gazing off into the distance, letting the city lights blur in my vision, I knew he was staring at me. Neither of us spoke for, maybe, half a minute.

"What are you saying, Micah?" His voice was low, more of a warning than a threat in the tone.

I lifted my empty beer bottle up and tilted a couple of drops onto my tongue, jerking my hand up and down to hide the fact that it was shaking. "Not 'saying' anything. I just don't want to."

"Why the hell not?"

I wheeled toward him. "Why've I gotta have a reason? Can't I just be who I am? Christ!" I started to get out of the chair, hoping to escape inside, but Dad stood quickly and caught my arm. I jerked away and landed back in the chair so hard it thumped against the outside wall of the apartment.

I wouldn't look at him. I couldn't. But I could tell he already knew. He must have known, on some level, before he even asked me about girlfriends five minutes and several eons ago. There was no going back, and both of us knew it.

"Look, Micah, what you're not saying is just something you think is true because it's easier than facing growing up. Easier than putting yourself out there and maybe getting rejected."

I stood up and faced him, angry now, arms moving in emphatic gestures as I yelled. "Are you fucking kidding me? You think this is the *easy* way out? You think for one fucking second that this is something I *chose*? That's it's even something I *could* choose? Christ, Dad! You sound so dumb right now."

He took a step forward and I stepped back, scared of him for the first time I could remember. He grabbed my arm again and practically dragged me inside.

In the kitchen, I yanked my arm away once more and rubbed it where his grip had been.

"Do you want the whole world to hear you, boy?"

We stared at each other, me doing my best to look defiant, him scowling and breathing hard through his nose. We were roughly the same height, but it didn't feel like that at the moment. I couldn't speak; inside my head a voice told me, "He's ashamed of you."

Finally he turned away, hands clenching into fists at his sides, like he was trying really hard not to hit me. Then he turned just the side of his head toward me. "Don't you ever say that word to me, do you hear? The word that you're thinking is you. Don't make me deal with it."

He grabbed a pack of cigs and his keys and left the apartment, slamming the door behind him.

I stood still for a couple of minutes, breathing hard and struggling not to scream. Then I grabbed anything that I'd taken out of my duffle and stuffed it back in, shouldered the bag, and left.

I thundered down the first flight of stairs but then realized I didn't know where Dad was or even if he'd gone all the way down, and I didn't want him knowing I was leaving. So I took the next flight quietly. Didn't see him anywhere, and the spot where he'd parked the truck earlier was now empty. The apartment complex wasn't very far from the highway, so I made my way toward it through the dark.

For sure I didn't want to go home; I didn't want to have to explain anything to Mom. My plan was to pick up some water and food from a Dunkin' Donuts I knew of near the Big River area and then camp out someplace in the woods until Sunday afternoon, when Mom would come get me.

Hitchhiking on the highway is probably illegal, but I did it anyway. I'd never hitched before, and I felt like an idiot, not even sure whether anyone could see me. But after about twenty cars had gone by, an SUV with two girls in it pulled over and came to a stop on the shoulder ahead of me. I ran to catch up.

One girl leaned out of the passenger side window, a cigarette dangling from her fingers. "Where ya goin'?"

"Just to Hopkins Hill Road." Closer, now, I could tell it was a roll of pot, not tobacco, in her fingers.

She blinked. "That's, like, in the middle of nowhere."

I nodded. "Suits me fine at the moment."

She shook her head, puzzled. "Hop in, then."

I climbed into the back, and the smell of weed was strong enough I thought I might get high on that alone. But then the girl who'd invited me in turned around toward me, grinning and holding the joint out.

She had to shout over the music playing, something I didn't recognize. "I'm June. Have a hit."

"Micah. Thanks." I'd never smoked pot in my life. Hell, I'd never smoked anything. And I'd never hitched. And I'd never come out to anyone. It was a day of firsts.

I inhaled as best I could, fighting the coughing fit that threatened to give my inexperience away. I knew you were supposed to hold onto the smoke as long as possible, and for me that wasn't very long.

June laughed. "Ever done this before?"

I gave up, coughed for a few seconds, and grinned back at her. "No."

The girl who was driving spoke up. "You're a virgin no longer, Micah!" Her laugh was more like a high-pitched giggle.

June reclaimed the joint and turned back toward the front. No one spoke again, and somewhere in the ten minutes it took to get to Hopkins Hill, I could barely hear my cell phone ring. I figured it was Dad and ignored it.

As she pulled off the highway onto the side road, the driver asked, "Where you going for real, kid?"

"There's a Dunkin' Donuts just ahead."

"K." And she drove me right to the store. "Here you go, then. You'll be okay?"

"Yeah, fine. Thanks." I hopped out before she could ask me any more questions.

The place was still open, at least for another fifteen minutes. They had a few sandwiches left. I bought two that had no mayonnaise in them and stashed them in my duffle. I didn't like coffee, and all the cold drinks were sold in lidded cups, so I was gonna have to carry whatever liquid I wanted very carefully, but I figured I didn't have far to go. I got a large iced green tea and asked for a large cup with just water, too. A half-dozen donuts in a bag, along with the sandwiches, went into my duffle.

19

It was awkward, for sure, carrying two cups of liquid with my duffle bag slung around me, but I managed to work my way back along the road toward the highway, in the direction of the Big River area. I came to a dead stop on the side of the road where it headed into a short tunnel, the underpass for Route 95.

There was no shoulder on the road inside the tunnel. It wasn't a long tunnel, but I couldn't run with these cups, and I couldn't get out of the way of any car or truck or whatever might be about to run me down.

And if that wasn't enough, it was super dark in there. What if there were bats? What if there were spiders? What if someone attacked me in there? What if there was some kind of bridge troll living in there?

I could feel my heart racing. My pulse pounded in my ears and my breathing got shallow. I tried to tell myself this was nothing like not being able to see below the surface of the ocean. It didn't help.

Get a grip, Micah! This is what Dylan used to say to me when I'd get scared by something. Like Dad, he'd always tried to get me to stop being afraid, to show some courage, to be a man. *Get a grip.* So I did my best. I took a deep breath. And another. Should I make noise in there, or should I be as quiet as possible? I closed my eyes for a second and, like the coward I was, nearly fell over. I stared into the tunnel, reminding myself it would lead to the other side.

Now.

I held my breath without meaning to, and as soon as I got through the tunnel I let it out with a long rasping sound. I wanted to stop and rest, but I was still way too close to that tunnel. Wobbly knees or no, I had to keep going.

The edge of the park was right there on the other side of the tunnel. Using the light of the moon, which was just past full, I turned to my left and toward the woods as soon as I could, moving slowly now so I wouldn't trip over anything.

Of course it got darker as the trees blocked the moonlight. I set down the duffle and the cups someplace where I knew I could find them again and went just far enough into the woods to find a place to crash for the night, pretty quickly coming across a large rock under some pine trees with space for me to sit or lie down. With my phone lighting the way now, I retrieved my stuff, found the rock again, and did my best to settle in.

I figured the worst I had to fear in the woods was a skunk, or maybe ticks, or a rabid raccoon, or a coyote, or— *Get a grip, Micah!*

It wasn't cold, but it wasn't super warm, either, and I was kind of wishing I'd gotten something hot to drink. Even though I wasn't actually hungry, having had dinner just a little while ago, I pulled out my bag of donuts. Holding one in my hands, I stared down at it, noticing that it looked colorless in the dark. I stared, and I stared.

It was just starting to sink in that my dad had basically said he didn't want to know me. He'd left me there, in pain from what he'd said, because if he'd stayed he would have beaten me senseless. I was sure of that.

My hands dropped onto my lap, and as my head fell back I felt a jab from a pointy part of the boulder I was leaning against. It hurt, but I left my head there. Maybe it was supposed to hurt. Maybe that was my lot in life, to be hurt.

I'd never been good at much of anything. Okay, I was good at photography, something Dylan had never been interested in, but so what? I'd never been as good at anything else as Dylan. Neither of my folks had ever loved me as much as they loved him. And if that wasn't enough, it was my fault Trapper had died.

Trapper. He was the best dog ever! And he'd saved me from that shark. And how did I repay him?

Dylan had been in Afghanistan for maybe a month when it had happened. He'd made me promise to walk

Trapper, and to play with him, so the dog wouldn't miss Dylan too much. Not as much as Dylan would miss Trapper, anyway. So I promised. And I did walk him, but I wasn't very good at that, either. Before long Trapper figured out that I wasn't really leading him—not the way Dylan had done—and he started leading me. He was the brave one, after all, not me. So I decided I'd had enough, and I began just leaving him outside in our fenced back yard instead of walking him.

But one day I didn't check to make sure the side gate was shut. Trapper got out. He was hit by a car right in front of our house.

He didn't die right away. Mom had me sit in the back seat of her station wagon, and she set Trapper along the seat, his head on my lap. The vet clinic wasn't far, but the news was bad. Trapper had too many broken bones, and one of his internal organs—I forget which—had been damaged. Mom sent me out to the waiting room while they put him to sleep. On the way home, the only thing she said was, "How are we going to tell Dylan?"

She might not even have been talking to me. She might have been talking to herself. But her words tore through me like sharks' teeth.

At home, she got out of the car quickly, no doubt to go inside and cry in private. I decided to stay in the car and cry there. I got into the back seat where I'd held Trapper's head, curled myself into a ball, and sobbed. At some point I opened my eyes, and my gaze fell on Trapper's collar, on the floor of the car. Mom must have saved it as some kind of token and then dropped it in her rush to get away from me. I grabbed it.

When Mom told Dylan about Trapper, he specifically asked her to save the collar for him. And I remember the panic she flew into when she couldn't find it. She asked me if I'd seen it, and I said I thought I'd seen it once on the floor of the car, which was true. What I didn't tell her was

22

that I'd claimed it. At the time, I told myself I was keeping it for Dylan, like he'd asked.

Now, I'm just keeping it.

Tears seeped out from behind my closed eyelids, my chest hurt from the sobbing gasp that came next, and my head jerked forward and then landed back on that rock with a painful stab. I pulled my head forward and threw it back onto the rock. And again. And again. And again, until I was nearly unconscious from the pain. Donut forgotten, I fell onto my side. I didn't cry. I wailed. I was alone. I would always be alone. No one could hear me wail. No one cared if I wailed.

No one cared if I died.

Chapter Two

Maybe an hour or so after I stopped screaming at the trees, I felt around for my donut. I'd eaten about half of it, forest floor grit included (what else did I deserve?), when the sounds of a man's voice cut through my gloom. I stopped chewing on the grit so I could hear it better. What if someone found me here and—I don't know, beat me up, or something? But that was crazy; that kind of person wouldn't be calling out for anyone. So, then, who—

"Micah!"

Dad. And he was closer, now. But Jesus Fucking Christ, how had he found me here?

"Micah! I know you're here. 'Friends and family,' remember?"

The app! I'd forgotten about it, and I hadn't turned my phone off.

I could hear his footsteps now, crunching leaves and twigs. I tried to gauge how directly he was coming in my direction. Just how good was that app? I was willing to risk that it wasn't good enough for him to pinpoint my position very accurately, and I kind of liked the idea that he would search the park for me and come up empty.

From the sounds he was making, it seemed like he was just wandering around. I could make out the beam of a flashlight, seeming to flicker on and off as he swept it from side to side and trees came between me and the light. He went past me, deeper into the woods, and I lost sight of the light. The noise stopped; he must have been standing still, probably looking at his phone. Then he must have turned, walking again, and the beam of light came closer. Then he stopped again.

"Look, Micah," he said into the darkness, his voice pitched to carry, "I'm sorry, okay? You caught me by surprise."

Bullshit. I knew—I was *positive*—that he'd known. Or at least that he'd suspected. Otherwise, why quiz me about girls all the time? Today had not been the first time that had happened.

"Micah? Come on, son. Let's talk about this. Can we at least do that? Will you talk to me?"

Why? I almost said it aloud. *What's gonna change?*

For no apparent reason, the back of my head stabbed at me. I hadn't hit the boulder again, so...? I reached a hand back, and three things happened at once. One was that I felt, for the first time, the caked blood from the wound I'd mostly inflicted on myself. Another was that I hadn't known the bump would be so big, so I misgauged the placement of my hand and landed right on the worst of it, and it hurt like hell. The third was me saying, "Shit!" just loud enough for Dad to find me.

I heard his footsteps coming closer. There was no way to pretend not to be there. I stood, and the flashlight beam glanced off of my face.

"What do you want?" I'd been going for angry, but it came out more like sulk. "You ran out on *me*, remember?"

"And you ran out, too."

"What the fuck did you expect me to do? Wait there for—how long—until you decided to come back and yell at me?"

He didn't speak until he was right in front of me. His voice was quiet. "I didn't yell at you, Micah. And I'm not yelling at you now. So, let's go back. We can talk about this."

"Can I say the word 'gay?'"

25

I could see him flinch, even in the dark; the flashlight beam gave it away. "If you have to."

"If I have to? If I fucking *have* to?"

"How about if we don't use words like 'fucking,' eh? It just makes us dig ourselves in deeper, makes everybody angrier."

"Fine. And, yeah, I have to. Because that's what I am, Dad. I'm gay. And if that's too much for you, then just leave me here and go home."

He was quiet for too long. So I said, "See? You can't take it. It makes you sick, and it makes you hate me, and it makes you—"

"No." I barely heard him. With a start, I realized he was trying not to cry. "I don't hate you, Micah. You're my son. My only son. I just want what's best for you."

"And that would be, what? Being just like you? Just like Dylan?"

As he sighed, his head fell forward and shook slowly side to side. Then he looked up at me. "Oh, Micah." So soft. His voice was so soft.

I felt my face crumple, and I held my breath so I wouldn't cry. Then I saw the beam of light sweep out and around me, leading the way for his arms.

He held me. And I held my breath. I figured he'd let go any second. But he didn't. And the longer he held me, the harder it was to hold my breath. And when I finally let it out, it was a sob.

We stood there, in the woods, in the dark, until I wasn't sobbing any longer. Then, without a word, he shone the flashlight on the ground and started to pick up the things I'd strewn around. I watched, unable to move, as he dumped out the green tea and the water, crushed the cups so they'd fit into the Dunkin' Donuts bag, and packed all of it into my duffle. He picked up the duffle and looked at me. Barely nodding, he turned and walked away. I followed.

I hunkered down in the truck's passenger seat to present as small a target as possible. As we drove back toward Warwick, Dad asked, "Have you told your mother?"

"No. I haven't told anyone."

"You told me."

"Yeah, well. You kind of forced my hand."

Nothing but road noise for about a minute. Then he asked, "How long have you known?"

How long... what a question. How could I pinpoint the day—or even the year—when I managed to identify this feeling that had always been there, this feeling that there was this unspeakable difference between me and Dylan, between me and other boys? It was unspeakable at first because it crept up slowly and wouldn't identify itself, and unspeakable later because of what it said when it did speak: GAY. But when *did* it tell me what it was?

"I dunno. Maybe a couple of years. It's not something that makes an announcement."

He was quiet a long time, and I figured he was trying not to say all the things he wanted to say, about what a disappointment I am, about what this will do to Mom, you fill in the blanks. And at first, I thought I was right.

"So have you *ever* liked a girl? You know, that way?"

"No." It wasn't quite as simple as that, but almost, and I sure didn't want to give him any hope.

When he spoke next, I had to reassess his reaction to me. "Micah, I don't pretend to understand this thing. And maybe if you'd told me five years ago, I would've... Let's just say I think everyone needs to get with the program. I mean, there are gay people out there, they aren't going away, and every one of them is related to someone. And as it happens, one of them is related to me."

Too stunned to speak, I waited for him to go on.

"I don't understand it, Micah. But I don't want to make your life miserable, either. I know this isn't exactly a rousing cheer or anything, but we're a family. Divorced or not, we're a family because of you."

"Not because of Dylan?"

He took a deep breath and let it out slowly. "Dylan's gone, son. And losing him is part of what happened to make your mom and me split. We couldn't figure out how to help each other through that. It was like something about her grief set me off, and probably vice versa. We didn't grieve together."

He paused, and then, "Hell, I don't know. It still makes no sense to me. But one thing I'm sure of. I won't lose you, too. So you and I, we've got to work together on this." He glanced at me and then back to the road. "You with me?"

"Yeah." It was quick, with no feeling in it, but I meant it.

When we got back, I used the fact that I had to pee really badly to get into the bathroom fast so I could wash the blood out of my hair. If Dad had seen it, maybe it would have been enough to say that I'd accidentally hit that rock, but it was still really clear in my mind that I'd deliberately made it worse. And in my current vulnerable mood I didn't want to have Dad notice the blood.

That night I had a weird dream. It was kind of good, because I really got off, made a mess and everything. But it was weird.

It was about that guy in the sailboat, the one who'd ruined my mood. God, was that just yesterday? Seems like eons ago. Anyway, he and I were in his boat, out at sea, wind all around us and fluffing his golden hair. For some reason the image of his shoes was really strong—white soles, weathered brown leather with stitching all around the front, leather thong laces. We smiled at each other, and something electric happened. I couldn't take my eyes off of his, even though the water was getting all white-capped and scary around us. And then we were on the floor of the boat, making out, kissing, groping—and in a way I can't describe, it was somehow different from anything I've ever felt before. And when we came, the ocean calmed down, and the sun came out, and I realized I hadn't even noticed that there had been no sunshine up to that point. I lay back and gazed up at the blue sky as the boat rocked gently.

And then I woke up.

I didn't even know that guy's name. Or whether I'd ever see him again. Or why the image of his shoes stayed in my head.

Next day, before breakfast, I did a quick internet search on the term "boat shoes." I wanted to know if what I'd seen on the kid in the boat was really a thing. It was. I found an article about the origins of these shoes saying that the reason for the white soles is so there won't be dark scuff marks on the white surfaces of sailboats.

Dad and I were mostly quiet until about half-way through breakfast, when he asked, "Anything in particular you'd like to do today, Micah?" I shrugged, looking down at my plate. "Anything you need at the mall?"

That made me look up from pushing a piece of bacon through the yolk of a half-eaten fried egg. The mall? "You think because I'm gay I wanna go shopping?"

His surprise looked genuine. "What? No, of course not. We all need stuff. We don't have to do that, but it's supposed to cloud over and rain before noon, so the mall seemed like a good idea. Forget it."

"Well, no, wait. I might like something. Um, I could use a pair of boat shoes."

"Boat shoes? What on earth for?"

Good question. And I had no idea what for. But once
I'd said it, I had to come up with a reason. So I said, "I
know this guy who has a boat, and he has these cool shoes.
They're white on the bottom. It's so they don't mark the
boat."

"And you need shoes like that why?"

Another shrug; I didn't want to come on too strong.
"He said he might take me out on the water. Maybe even
teach me to sail." Yeah, that was likely.

Dad made a face like, *Are you kidding me?* But he went
exactly where I wanted him to go. "You'll be able to do
that?"

"Facing my fear, like you said."

But then he went someplace I hadn't anticipated.
Should have, probably.

"And this 'guy.' Is he someone… y'know…."

Took me a couple of seconds. "Oh! No, Dad. No way."
Despite the dream, I really didn't see myself even liking
this guy, let alone falling for him. We were from different
worlds; his had money and privilege, mine didn't. He lived
the sort of life where he could just assume that if he spoke
to some random person, not only did he have the right to do
that, but also that person would be glad to talk to him. Me?
I don't assume anybody particularly wants to hear what I
have to say. And it wasn't like I wanted to be in his world.
Hell, no; I don't really like the people of that world. So I
was sure I didn't "like" the guy. I just wanted the shoes.

If I had those shoes, then every time I looked at them I
could feel that dream. I'd feel like I'd felt in the dream, like
what that guy and I did in the boat was natural and perfect
and right. Like kissing another guy was *supposed* to feel
great. It didn't need to be that guy in particular.

I had to have those shoes.

Dad drained his coffee mug and pushed his empty plate
aside. "How much do they cost, anyway?"

I had no idea. Dad earns a lot more money than Mom, but I know he gives her money for me every month. So I try not to ask for too much. And I hadn't considered the cost factor. I pulled out my phone and did a quick search.

"Looks like when they're not on sale, they're mostly under a hundred. Some are more. I don't need those."

I waited while he tapped his fingers on the table, obviously thinking. "I suppose we could look. No harm in that. But I'm not spending an arm and a leg, Micah."

It was actually kind of fun shopping with my dad for boat shoes. We had a goal, and as long as I kept his wallet in mind we didn't hit any real snags. Some of the shoes that called themselves boat shoes had white around the edges of the soles but not on the bottom. Mostly, they were the cheaper ones, which was too bad, because of course Dad leaned toward those. But they weren't right, for my purposes, or for that boat I'd never see the inside of.

We discussed the choices over a late lunch of burgers (yeah, more burgers; what can I say? I love burgers) at Red Robin. As it turned out, the hardest part was deciding whether to get a pair like that kid had, in a medium brown, or go with navy or dark brown or light tan. I ended up with a medium gray pair that I figured would go with lots of stuff, and the white showed up really well against the leather. They were even on sale.

As we headed back to the car, shoes safely in one of those plastic bags with a cord that I slung over my shoulder, I brought up something that had been in the back of my mind since last night. "Dad, I don't want you to tell Mom. About me, I mean."

"But you'll tell her, right?"

"Yeah. Soon." So he agreed.

Back at Dad's apartment, I packed up my duffle and threw the new shoes in there. I couldn't wear them now; I didn't want to have to explain them to Mom, and if they just kind of quietly appeared on the scene at some later time and caught her attention, I could sort of imply that maybe she forgot about them, with a glancing shot at her drinking. I was just about to pick the bag up and tell Dad I was ready to go when he surprised me.

He'd been leaning against the kitchen counter, waiting for me to finish packing, but when I turned away from the couch I slept on whenever I was there, he was right behind me. And for the second time that weekend, he did something I don't think he'd done since I was a little kid. He wrapped his arms around me.

It was a quick hug, a "guy" hug followed by a couple of slaps on the back, and neither of us said anything. We didn't need to.

True to form, Mom was almost half an hour late meeting us at the Big River parking lot. "That's my Abbie," Dad said, but he didn't sound affectionate.

We sat in the truck, rain bouncing off the roof, while he played an old CD, singing away with the band—Derek and the Dominos, of all the stupid names for a band. Some of it was kind of lame, some of the music sounded sort of country-western, and Dad said some of the numbers were in the style of the blues. I kind of liked those. But I really liked one I'd heard somewhere before: "Layla."

The desperate feeling that came through the guy's singing—Dad said it was Eric Clapton—and the wailing of the guitars really slayed me. It sounded like the singer was beyond desperate because of wanting this woman. I wondered if I would ever want someone as much as that.

After it ended, Dad told me the song was about this love affair between Clapton and the wife of one of the Beatles (George, I think?). She and George got divorced, then she married Eric, but then she divorced him, too, and married someone else she ended up staying with.

At first I wasn't paying a whole lot of attention to what Dad was saying, but when he got to the part about that third marriage, the one that took (as it were), his voice changed somehow. When I looked at him, I could see there was something behind his eyes, wanting to get out, maybe not sure about whether it was a good idea.

Just then, a car horn honked. We both looked. It was Mom. Whatever he was going to say stayed behind his eyes.

Dad watched as we drove off. I know, because I was looking at him.

What was it he almost said to me?

I was glad I hadn't worn my new shoes. Mom was actually sober; she'd been late because she'd spent a lot of time putting a nice meal together. It just wasn't for a reason I liked.

Smiling, she set a plate in front of me with roast chicken, baked potatoes, and mixed vegetables that come frozen and cut into little bits, orange cubes of carrot standing out like beacons. I wracked my brain but couldn't think what might be going on. It wasn't anyone's birthday—not even Dylan's—so that wasn't it. I decided to take a risk and ask.

"Special occasion, Mom?"

"As a matter of fact, yes. I think so." She sat across the small table from me, her plate and a glass of water— nothing alcoholic—in front of her. Still smiling.

"Do I get to know what?"

She opened her napkin across her lap, and said, "Madam Alberta gave me some very interesting news today." She picked up her fork but didn't do anything with it. "About your brother."

Duh. What else would it be? "Oh?"

She set the fork down again. "He's still alive, Micah."

I needed to be very, very careful here. Did Mom believe this? Obviously. Did I? No. What would happen if she knew that? All hell would break loose. I limited myself to one word: "Wow."

"Can you believe it?" She didn't want an answer. She picked up her fork and knife and dug into her meal, which didn't stop her talking. "She's not sure what happened, and she doesn't know where he is, but he's alive. She was very surprised!"

Well, sure, I was thinking. *She'd better be. She's been telling you a different lie all along.* What I said was, "So who was it she's been connecting with all this time?"

"Micah, don't be a smarty-pants. It was Dylan. He just wasn't dead. Madam Alberta was channeling the energy of a live person instead of a dead one."

"And she didn't know?"

She shot me a glance that told me to shut the fuck up.

Did I want to encourage her? I did not. However, to do anything else at this point would be suicidal. So I said, "Okay, so what did he tell her this time?"

"Don't be silly, Micah. He never actually *said* anything before. Madam Alberta picks up intention. Or feelings. Or something. Anyway, this time was different. She just senses it. She says this doesn't happen very often, but she had a feeling something was up. So she used a different technique."

"What technique?"

"Oh, I don't know; she's very mysterious. But she sat still for the longest time, and then her eyes flew open. Micah, I wish you could have seen it! I knew immediately that something important was happening."

I didn't hear anything else she said. I was too busy fighting this anger that got hotter by the minute. Madam Alberta must have run out of messages to relay and had come up with this new approach to keep the money rolling in.

At some point I tuned back in, about when Mom started talking about all the things she'd need to buy for Dylan's homecoming. I nearly lost it when Mom started going on about what things would be like when he got back. She had it all figured out: I'd go live with Dad, and Dylan would come live here. At first this bothered me because I'd already decided I didn't want to do that, didn't want to move in with Dad. And then, after I remembered that Dylan wasn't really alive and I'd never be required to move, it bothered me that she'd toss me out, just like that. Didn't even need to think about it, let alone discuss anything with me.

Fortunately, her mood was high enough for three people, so she didn't really notice my lukewarm response to this "news."

In my room after dinner, poking through my photos and not really seeing them, I debated in my mind whether to call Dad. He'd already been a little concerned about her reliability, because of drinking. What would he think about this?

Speaking of drinking, Mom hadn't had a drop of alcohol from the time she picked me up, when she'd been sober, right through dinner. Was she drinking now?

I got up and wandered into the kitchen, grabbing a couple of cookies as cover. She had the TV on, but the sound was off. She was writing in a notebook, a cigarette beside her sending up whitish-gray curls of smoke. The writing took so much of her attention that she didn't seem to notice me. A glance around told me there was nothing liquid in sight.

Back in my room I shoved my earbuds into my ears and brought up something to watch on my phone. But I couldn't concentrate. *Call Dad? Don't call Dad?*

If he knew what Madam Alberta had said, he'd probably worry about the same things I worried about. What would Mom do to prepare for this non-existent homecoming? How much money would she spend? That is, waste? How long could Madam Alberta keep her believing this lie? And what would happen when she lost hope?

If I didn't tell him, and Mom started spending money and getting all weird, he'd be mad that I hadn't told him. He might think he could have done something to make her see reality before she wasted more money than she was already spending on Madam Alberta. But I didn't think he could do anything that would lead to even a vaguely good outcome.

Finally I decided I'd wait and see how things went.

Monday morning, Mom was still flying. Over breakfast, talking mostly to herself, she said things like, "If only I hadn't given away his clothes! He's probably lost a lot of weight. I don't know what to buy for him. Micah can take the sheets and towels and things he's been using with him. I'll get new ones for Dylan." And on and on.

I waited until she took a mouthful of toast. "Mom, you'll have plenty of time. I mean, you don't even know where he is, let alone when he'll come home."

She nodded, swallowed. "True, but I don't want him showing up on the doorstep, and me with nothing prepared."

It was an effort to walk through this mine field, to figure out what to say and what not to say. After all, I wanted him to come home, too, so I would love to have believed Madam Alberta. But I knew she was a fraud, and she was leading Mom down some garden path. The problem was that I had to pretend to believe something I knew to be false but very much wished could be true.

I had to get away from this scene, which felt like a play by Molière we'd studied in school last year. But I was a little afraid to leave Mom on her own; would she go out and spend our month's budget on things for Dylan's homecoming?

So as I helped clear the table, I asked, "Got plans for today, Mom?"

She sighed and mumbled something about having messed up last week's records for the motel, so I figured our bank account was safe. And so was I; there was no way I could help with this accounting fix—or, no way I wanted to start getting involved in it. I grabbed my camera, unlocked my bike, and pedaled off.

Once I was safely away from the motel, I stopped to decide where I'd go. I'd been meaning to wander through Stonington Cemetery, only a few miles away from the motel. Mostly I stayed away from there unless I really wanted to visit Dylan's grave; Mom went there a lot, and I really didn't want to run into her.

She wouldn't be there today, though, and I wanted to snag a photo of one of the older gravestones there as a background for this cool poem I'd found on the internet:

Look, blooming youth, as you pass by.
As you are now, so, once, was I.
As I am now, so you must be.
Prepare for death and follow me.

I wanted to superimpose the poem over the image of the stone, replacing what was actually engraved, though I hadn't yet figured out how to make the letters in my poem look like they were engraved. One step at a time.

I spent a few minutes at Dylan's grave. There wasn't much in there. There hadn't been much that they'd found to send home. He'd been in an MATV—Military All Terrain Vehicle—that had hit an IED. There had been piles of rocks in the road to force vehicles to one side so the only way forward was over the bomb. Insurgents hidden nearby had shot anyone not killed in the blast, and between that and the fire from the bombed MATV, there hadn't been much left of anyone. Another guy who'd been there was still MIA, and it wasn't clear whether he was really missing or if there just weren't enough remains to account for all the bodies.

I suppose, if we're being honest, it's entirely possible that the bits and pieces they sent back to us aren't even Dylan, and someone else has his bits and pieces.

Like I said, I didn't come here a lot. Part of it really was to avoid Mom. But the rest of it was that I didn't know what to do here.

The stone just had Dylan's name and dates, nothing else. Mom and Dad had argued like mad about what else to put on it, like a saying or something, and in the end they put nothing. So I stared at the stone, little spots of mica in the granite catching my eye from time to time as I tried to think what to say to Dylan. To myself. To God. To anyone.

Nothing came to me. I sighed and turned my back on Dylan Jackson Jaeger.

Given that I wanted to stay away from home, it took me too little time to find the perfect stone for my own project: one of the oldest ones, for some girl who'd died at nineteen, in 1850. It had curlicues all around the edges of the stone, though you could barely make them out, the stone was so old. It was even in the shade, which was good because there weren't any shadows on it to mess up the contrast and make the photograph harder to work with. I spent another thirty minutes or so looking around and shot another few stones, but nothing else was as perfect as that first one.

When I'd pretty much exhausted the place, I headed home to grab a sandwich and a can of soda. Mom barely noticed that I came in, and I worked around her as quietly as possible. I threw lunch and a handful of cookies into a bag, put it all into my backpack with the camera, and headed out again.

And, somehow, my bike decided to head toward the ocean, to that rock under some trees where I'd seen the guy with the boat on Friday. The guy with the boat shoes. So I sat in the dappled shade on that rock—not too close to the dead bird, which was almost gone but looked disgusting— and ate my lunch while gazing out over the water. There were some boats out there; it was summer and a sunny day, though I couldn't tell whether one of them might be the one I'd seen Friday. Then, drowsy, I lay back on the rock, head carefully turned to one side to avoid that bump I'd mostly inflicted on myself, and dozed.

I woke up when a seagull landed beside me and started to peck at the remains of my lunch. I shooed it away and packed everything up. Just before leaving, I scanned the water once more.

And there he was. At least, I was pretty sure. It was a sailboat, probably about the right size. It was too far out to be positive, but I did see a blond guy in it, looking in my direction through binoculars held with one hand. The sails were fully out, or whatever the right sailing term is, and they were so big I was amazed that one kid could control the boat. But he was definitely alone.

I decided to bring Dylan's old binoculars next time. I'd just have to sneak them out of that box of his things that Mom worships.

While Mom was in the shower the next morning, I went into her room and pulled Dylan's box out from under her bed, grabbed the binoculars, and tiptoed back to my room. They were in a black case, which I put in the bottom of my backpack, camera and tripod on top of it.

But I didn't see Blondie or his boat that day, even through the binoculars. It was overcast, but not rainy. It was also very still, with no wind. Maybe that's why he wasn't there? For sure, there weren't as many sailboats out there as there had been on Monday, and the ones that were there weren't exactly hauling ass.

On the ride home, I kept asking myself why I had even wanted to look for Blondie. I never heard an answer.

Still with no reason in my head as to why it was so important to see Blondie again, I was glad Wednesday was sunny and breezy. I sat or stood on that rock all morning, scouring the water with the binoculars, listening to some music from time to time. I even downloaded "Layla."

After I'd eaten my packed lunch, I watched the water for a while and then decided I was being totally ridiculous. But I couldn't talk myself into leaving. I couldn't even talk myself into going someplace to shoot. I did manage to take my eyes off the water long enough to lie down and doze, like I had before.

"Hey! What the fuck!"

Something wet and floppy had hit the side of my face. I sat bolt upright as the sound of cackling laughter made me look toward the water. It was Blondie! He half watched me and half paid attention to the job of pulling in these oblong white things hanging over the edge of the boat, probably bumpers that kept the boat from banging against the rock; there was no sandy strip today because the tide was higher.

Blondie laughed as he pushed away from the rock with something long, and then he started up an outboard motor to coax the boat back into more open water. I stood, knowing I should be furious, trying to work up a froth and not quite succeeding well enough to shout anything at him. When the boat was well out of danger of hitting anything on shore, Blondie killed the motor and let the current take over, his smiling face still turned toward me. We watched each other until he opened up those huge, tall sails, moving west and out of my line of sight behind the trees on the shore. For some reason, today those triangular shapes—white though they were—made me think of a shark's dorsal fin, cutting through the waves.

On the ground at my feet was a wet rag. I sat down and poked at it and a crinkling sound came from inside. The rag was tied around a plastic bag. And inside that plastic bag was a note.

Tomorrow, Angry Gull Cafe, Sailaway Marina, outdoor tables, 2:00. Be there or be square.

It wasn't signed. Not that it needed to be, but I couldn't exactly call him Blondie to his face. That's if I even went. Maybe I'd rather "be square."

And anyway, what did he want? What *might* he want? I mean, we'd exchanged only those few words, the day of the dead seagull, and they hadn't been nice words. At least, mine hadn't. So I had no clue why he wanted this meeting.

What about me? What might *I* want? I'd told Dad I had no interest in the guy. But if that was true, why had he been in that dream? Why had being with him in that imaginary boat been so wonderful? Why did I keep coming back to this rock? And why, for fuck's sake, did the guy's friggin' *shoes* stay with me the way they did?

What did I have to lose if I did meet him? And what did I have to gain?

If I did go, and we talked like normal people instead of the way it had been last week, I might find out that he's not even gay. After all, it was pretty unlikely that he would be; there are lots more straight people in the world. Would that ruin the dream for me? Or if he was gay but I didn't like him, or he didn't like me, would I lose the dream that way? Because at this point, it was all about that dream. But whether he was gay or not, if we liked each other—even just as friends—then that would be a really great thing. And maybe I *would* like to go out in his boat.

On the other hand, if I didn't go, I still had the dream. And I still had the boat shoes Dad had bought for me. But I'd still have all that if I did go. Except, possibly, the dream.

And, like I said, it was all about the dream. So I figured probably I shouldn't go.

Oh, hell. I'd go.

Two o'clock was what the note said. But I was there by one. I'd downed a peanut butter sandwich, knowing I didn't have the money to buy lunch, and then dithered for maybe fifteen minutes about what shoes to wear. I could wear my new boat shoes, of course. But—was that too on the nose? Was it like asking for the boat ride I'd told Dad about? I decided against them.

Next question was what T-shirt. I chose a black one with a meaningless design on it, a vertical column with swirled rainbow colors beside two circles to the right, one above the other, touching the column, also with swirled rainbow colors inside. I'd picked it up at a used clothing store in Warwick a few months ago, and I wasn't sure why I liked it, but I did. For jeans, I chose the rattiest ones I owned so Blondie wouldn't think I was trying to look neat.

Mom didn't ask any pointed questions as I was leaving, like she usually doesn't unless she needs me to do something. And even though her usual reason for not noticing me—that is, drinking—had taken a back seat to this "news" about Dylan, the news was at least as much of a distraction for her. I couldn't help wondering how long that would last. But, for now, I planned to take full advantage of it.

I was a nervous wreck on the ride over, going back and forth for the twenty-eleventh time between what I might lose and what I might gain. And what was rising to the surface, as a complete surprise to me, was the possibility of making a friend. Even if he wasn't gay, and even if we were from different worlds, we might still be friends.

Right?

But why did I care? I'd prided myself on not having friends. Not needing friends. It had been easy after the divorce, after I'd had to change schools. Living in that motel management unit... well, that wasn't something I wanted to share with a whole lot of people. And the easiest way to avoid sharing it was just not to be with people.

I had friends once. Well, a few, anyway. Before the move. Before Dylan died.

The marina was only a few miles from the motel. I locked my bike to a railing where I was sure it would be out of the way. With the camera around my neck, I felt protected from these people, these rich boat owners. The camera was something between a talisman and a shield, and because of the way it's configured in that housing I'd made, you look down at it to frame your shot. You don't have to hold it up, which means you're not looking directly at your subject in any way that lets them know you're taking their picture.

I located the cafe and then wandered around, mostly back and forth on the floating walkways where boats were tied to some of the moorings. I was focusing on one of the boats, named *First Million*, enjoying the sloshing and sucking noises the water made against the hulls of the boats, when this man came up to me.

"Hey, there," he said, not outright threatening, but definitely wanting me to know he'd noticed what I was doing.

I looked at him. Typical rich sailor, I thought; ruddy skin on his face, lots of crinkles around his eyes, light blue knit shirt, khaki slacks. I forced myself not to get defensive, not to act like maybe I wasn't supposed to be there, not to act like he had any reason to wonder why I was there. And I couldn't exactly tell him I was meeting a mysterious blond boy whose name I didn't know, for reasons that weren't clear to me.

"Hi. This your boat?"

He glanced at *First Million* and then back at me. He didn't answer my question. "I know it isn't yours."

"Nope." I held up my camera. "Working on an article for my school paper."

He looked like he didn't believe me. And, after all, I had lied. "What school would that be?"

"Stonington High."

He looked even less like he believed me, now. "Okay, but classes are out for the summer."

I smiled. "Yeah. But in the fall, I'll be on the school paper. I gotta have some material to work with right away." I didn't, but he couldn't know that.

The man nodded, like he'd thawed a little. "Well, don't you get too close. Sometimes the water pushes the boats against the docks, and you could get hurt. And don't you go onto any of them."

"For sure." I gave him as sincere a grin as I could muster and watched as he turned and walked back toward the main part of the marina.

Pretty soon it was nearing the time to head over to the cafe. As I got closer, that magical summer smell of fried seafood floating on warm wafts of air on top of the aroma of salt water grew stronger. I scoured the outdoor tables with my eyes; was Blondie there yet? Maybe he'd been there for a while and had eaten lunch already. But I didn't see anyone who even vaguely resembled him.

A few tables were open. I chose one off to the side where I could keep an eye on anyone approaching, set the pack with my camera in it on the ground dead center under my chair where I wouldn't kick it, and ordered a ginger ale. I almost told the woman who'd said she was my "server" that I was waiting for someone, but what if he didn't show up?

Chapter Three

But he did show. At quarter of two. Or, that's what time I saw him. He maneuvered his sailboat (sails furled, or whatever the term is) toward one of the floating docks with a skill that impressed me, tied it up, and jumped onto the dock. As he started toward the cafe, he saw me, smiled hugely, and waved an arm high over his head like we were friends who hadn't seen each other in a year. I raised my chin in acknowledgement but that was it; I still didn't know what he wanted.

Still grinning, he flopped into the chair across from me. "Hey."

"Hey." I figured that was noncommittal enough.

It was difficult not to stare. The kid was gorgeous, even pretty. His eyes were a deeper color than most blue eyes, and his blond hair, just a little darker toward the roots, framed his face in soft curls. He was wearing those boat shoes. And that smile! That smile was so infectious I nearly smiled back. But it was way too early for that.

He said, "Fancy meeting you here."

Wow. Okay, not much of an opener. I shrugged.

"My name's Walker. What's yours?"

"Micah."

"Nice. I like it." He nodded, like he approved, which got my back up. "That's a cool T. Plan B makes some fun stuff."

I glanced down at my chest, and suddenly the design on my T-shirt made sense. That column with the two stacked circles was kind of an artistic capital B. As in, Plan B. "Yeah, I guess. I just kind of threw it on."

He changed the subject. "Do you sail?"

I held his eyes for just a minute, wondering if he was having me on. Before I could think how to respond, the woman who'd brought me the ginger ale was there, holding out lunch menus.

She smiled at Blondie. "Hi, Walker."

"Hey, Toni. I'll have the fish and chips, extra tartar, as usual. Cole slaw. And a Coke."

"Sure thing. And you?" She turned toward me.

I love fish and chips, so I glanced at the menu. Sixteen dollars! I sure as hell couldn't pay that. I shook my head. "Could I have another ginger ale?"

Walker spoke before she could answer. "Really? Wouldn't you like something to eat?"

"I had a sandwich earlier."

He looked at Toni. "He'll have the same as me, only—what was that, a ginger ale? Another one of those."

"Wait! I—I didn't bring enough money."

Walker waved a hand. "It's all going on Dad's tab, anyway. No worries!"

I sat back in my chair and shrugged again. As long as I wasn't paying, I figured—you know—he was the one who'd set up this rendezvous, after all.

He handed the menus back to Toni. "Thank you, Antoinette. We'll await your next appearance." He grinned, and she beamed back. Either she genuinely liked him, or she was hoping for a good tip.

He turned that grin, that open face, those twinkling eyes my way again. "Where were we? Oh, yeah. I was asking whether you sail."

I picked up my glass and slurped the last quarter inch of liquid through the straw. I couldn't have said why, but for some reason I wanted to lie. I wanted him to think I was at least somewhere near his level in life. In reality, I knew I was completely outclassed. It made me ashamed and then angry that I was ashamed.

I tried a distraction. "Really? You're starting there?"

"Whaddya mean?

"Well, we didn't exactly start out great, with you pestering me about the dead bird and me swearing at you, and then you throwing a wet rag at me."

He laughed. "But you're here."

Couldn't argue with that.

Toni set our drinks on the table and left with my empty glass.

"Fine," I said as soon as Toni was out of earshot. "I've never been in a sailboat."

"Oh, wow, I can't get my head around that. I was in a sailboat for the first time before I could speak. I got a Sunfish when I was twelve, and for my birthday this year, Dad bought me the Cape Dory Typhoon. They don't make them any more, so we had to get a used one, but she'd just been refurbished. She's a 1984 Weekender. And, man, can she sail!"

He paused long enough to drink some of his Coke, keeping his eyes on my face.

Instead of saying, *What makes you think I know how a Cape Dory Typhoon is different from a Sunfish or any other friggin' sailboat?* I said, "Must have cost a pretty penny."

"Twenty-five large. Yeah. There were a few that were cheaper, but this one was in great shape. And I really love the colors, don't you?"

I stirred my ginger ale with the straw to stall for time. I hadn't meant for him to actually tell me how much the thing cost. But now that he had? Let's just say "outclassed" doesn't come close to how I felt. "Yeah. Great color."

"That red line really makes it, you know? Wouldn't be nearly as special without it. I wasn't gonna get the outboard, but Mom made me. It's easier to dock with it.

And she doesn't want me getting stuck someplace, caught in the doldrums."

Whatever doldrums were....

He went on. "But it's only a six horsepower. Wouldn't get me back from Block Island, but that's not an option in this boat, anyway. It wouldn't get me *to* the island, either!" He grinned like that was some kind of joke.

After Toni set plates before us and left, I said, "Your folks let you go out alone in that thing, then?"

He laughed. "Oh, sure! All the time. I was born to be on the water."

"Ever see a shark?"

"From my dad's boat, yeah, once in a while. Some guy caught, like, six of them by accident at Long Beach last summer, and that's practically in Manhattan. They had to close a couple of beaches near there after some shark sightings."

I remembered that. It had scared the willies out of me. Not that I ever went very far into the water, but still....

Walker waited while Toni set our plates down and made sure we didn't need anything else immediately, but he wasn't done.

"There's a Block Island shark fishing competition every summer. All these people go out with rods and reels. They can enter only one shark at a time, and only some types... Threshers? Makos? I forget what else. We almost never see anything like a great white. Well, I've never seen one. Anyway, Dad hates that tournament. He says the ocean needs those predators right where they are. Some species are in real trouble, actually. Not the ones the tournament accepts, though."

I wanted to shift him off of sharks; I had not expected him to be so full of information that told me there were many more sharks in home waters than I would ever have guessed. "So, you keep your boat here?"

He swallowed a mouthful. "Depends. We can moor both the Cape Dory and Dad's yacht at the house, because there's a long enough dock, and it's reenforced. But we're on Jasper Island. We can trailer the sailboat, but not the yacht. So we need a slip for the yacht someplace on the mainland. I'm using it now, because the yacht is at home."

"Your dad has a yacht." Man... Where did this kid come from?

"*Magic Spell*. It's a forty-four foot Carver."

Another name that meant nothing to me. He seemed like he was about to say more, but he stopped short and gave me a look like he wasn't sure what he wanted me to know. Or, maybe, he wasn't sure what I wanted to know.

I'd had about enough of a description of his gold-plated life. "Look, I don't want to be unfriendly or anything, but what are we doing here?"

His hand stopped halfway between the plate and his mouth, a french fry sticking out between a finger and the thumb. The hand dropped back down. His face, which until now had been cheerful and smiling, froze into something that looked like uncertainty. He dropped the fry and sat back in his chair, eyes looking down at nothing as far as I could tell. There was something going on inside his head, and it didn't look like fun.

Finally, he said, "Okay, look, I just thought it might be fun to make a new friend. The kids I know from the homeschool support group I go to are all right, but there aren't very many of them. So when I saw you—"

I interrupted him. "Wait... your 'homeschool support group?' What the heck is that?"

"Yeah, well... I have a tutor. And—"

"You *what?*" This was the end. The kid was so rich he had his own private teacher?

He shrugged. "It's just homeschooling, really. Only it's not one of my parents doing the schooling." His voice got really quiet. "That's all."

I wasn't exactly angry, but somehow that's how I must have sounded. "Homeschooling? Why? I mean, if you're too good for public school, why didn't your folks just send you to some private academy?"

His face took on a stony look, like I'd struck a nerve and he didn't want to admit it. "There are reasons."

Oh, very mysterious, I'm sure. I sat back and crossed my arms over my chest.

His voice changed, and he sounded almost challenging. "Do you want to know, or not?"

"Know what?"

"I was about to answer your question about what we're doing here."

"Fine. Yeah. Tell me."

He exhaled loudly like he was trying to remain calm. "When I saw you shooting a dead bird, I thought, 'Okay, he's different.' And, like I said, my circle of friends is a little limited."

"I wasn't very nice to you, though."

He smiled, but it wasn't the same open, friendly smile from earlier. "No. You weren't."

"So what made you think I'd want to be your friend?"

"Truth?" he asked, and I nodded. "The truth is that I kind of liked that you tried to put me off. It made me think about you. See, mostly the kids who try to be my friend just want the benefit of hanging out with me because my parents are rich. They want to go sailing with me, get rides on my dad's boat, come stay on the island, use my PlayStation, get invited places. Thought I'd take a chance and see if you were different in that way, too."

I shook my head, mystified. "But—you just spent several minutes talking like you *wanted* me to know you're rich. Like you wanted to let me know just how good you have it."

"No, I—" His voice was small and uncertain. "I wasn't trying to impress you or lord it over you. This is just what my life *is*, you know?"

"You mean expensive boats, and fancy properties in exclusive places?"

He looked a little confused at first, but sounded more confident as he spoke. "Yeah, I guess. I mean, sure, I know not every family has a yacht. Not every kid has a sailboat, especially one like *Dare Ya*. But—well, I do. And I won't pretend I'm someone I'm not, even to get a new friend." He paused, and then added, "I'm willing to take a risk. Are you?"

I froze for just a second. Was I pretending, in my own way? Was I trying to hide the gulf between his financial status and mine? And if so, why? Did I want a new friend, and was deception any way to get one? Maybe it was time to be honest. Or, maybe, just a little more honest. We'd have to wait and see about the friends question.

I knew I was avoiding his challenge, and probably he did, too. But I took a risk of my own. "Okay, so before you take this risk, you might want to know a few things about me. No, I don't sail. The only boat I've ever been on was a tour-the-lagoon kind of thing in North Carolina. My folks are divorced, and I live with my mom in the manager's unit of The Afterdeck Motel. I have a bike but no car. My dad lives in a one-bedroom apartment in Warwick. He drives a two-thousand-nine pickup truck and manages a construction crew. And this T-shirt you like?" I plucked at it and let it settle again. "Bought it at a used clothing store." I stopped, at first hoping I hadn't sounded angry, then hoping I had.

Walker's face hadn't changed. He left a little space after my rant before he said, "You finished?" I shrugged. "Because none of that makes any difference to me. Here's what I care about. You have a standard camera you've done something odd to, and you shoot unusual subjects. When I sailed right up to you in a gorgeous boat, you didn't oohh and aahh and smile at me like you wanted a ride. Instead, you snapped at me, I guess because I interrupted your art. I think you want to be seen as dark and moody. That's there, sure. But you came back to that rock and looked for me, out on the water. I think you want a new friend, too."

I'd barely moved. Even my face was frozen in my effort not to let on that he was right on all counts. Especially the last thing he'd said.

He sat back in his chair and grinned at me, with an expression on his face that reminded me of the name of his boat: *Dare Ya*. Then, with just a touch of facetiousness in his voice, he said, "What d'you think about going sailing sometime?"

His right hand toyed with the fork, turning the tines in one direction and then another on the plate. He looked at me and then at the fork, at me and then the fork a couple of times, while my mind raced. The first thing it said to me was *YES!* and then *Whoa, wait just a minute...* and then *Well...* and then *Why not?* And finally I felt a kind of shaking shudder in my gut that told me I was going to do it even though just the idea terrified me.

And why was I going to do it? How much of it was what Walker had said, that I wanted a new friend? Did I think that sailing might actually turn out to be fun? How much of it was so I could tell my dad I'd done it? How much of it was to prove I wasn't a coward?

And how much of it was just that I loved looking at Walker, talking with Walker, being with Walker, despite some stubborn determination not to like anything about him? And what would happen when he found out I was gay?

Of all the things I could have said, this is what came out. "I have boat shoes."

His face lit up. "See that? I *knew* it! I knew this would be a good idea." He dug back into his fish and chips.

Eventually it dawned on him to ask, "So, if you've never been sailing, why do you have boat shoes?"

Because of a dream I had about you and your shoes. Because I want to keep that feeling of being with someone who makes me feel fantastic.

I couldn't say any of that. I shrugged like it wasn't important. "Just like the look of them."

"Do you have them with you?" I shook my head, not sure if I was more thrilled or terrified about what I was sure he'd say next. "That's okay. It's not a great sailing day, anyway. But what about tomorrow? There should be a light breeze. Good day to take your maiden voyage, as it were."

Okay, this was getting real. Suddenly it hit me that there was this huge gulf between thinking it might be fun to go sailing and actually doing it. Mentally I searched for something to keep the reality at bay.

"Um, well… the thing is…" *The thing is I'm terrified of the water. Or of what's in the water.* I wasn't convinced that Walker's little boat would be big enough to keep me safe if we did encounter a great white shark. I mean, I knew *Jaws* was't real; what happened in that movie wasn't ever gonna happen. Still….

Walker was waiting for me to finish. For some reason I panicked; something in my gut told me to back-paddle. Fast. "The thing is, I can't swim." And just like that, I was back to lying. Because I *can* swim. I can swim really, really well. Just not in the ocean.

He blinked like I'd told him I was from Pluto, which isn't even really a planet any more. "Why not?"

I shrugged as if to say, *No reason.*

Walker waved a hand in the air. "You can wear a life vest. Not to worry."

And suddenly this whole idea took a nasty turn in my mind. I saw the two of us, a capsized boat nearby as we waved our arms in the freezing water, bobbing helplessly by the grace of our orange vests, as sharks circled, their triangular sails—I mean, dorsal fins—looming larger as the circles shrank.

I started to speak but had to clear my throat. "What if… um… what if the boat capsizes?"

From the expression on his face, I might as well have asked what language he was speaking. What he said was, "A Typhoon? I'm not sure what you'd have to do to get it to capsize. Destroy it, probably. I don't go out onto the open ocean, so even if we fell in for some weird reason, we wouldn't be far from shore."

"A storm wouldn't do it?" I'd seen *The Perfect Storm*, too.

His head shook quickly back and forth. "No way. First, the Typhoon is an incredibly stable boat, even in rough water. Second, if it looks stormy, I don't go out. And like I said, I don't go very far from shore, so we could get back fast if a storm came up suddenly."

It was my turn to say something, my turn to suggest another problem, but I couldn't think of anything. Walker was watching me closely.

"Micah, are you afraid of the water?"

I picked up my glass, shook it so the melting ice clinked and swished around as I stared down at it, took a sip, set the glass down. This gave me just enough time to decide what to say. Because as long as bobbing in the water as shark bait wasn't going to happen, then maybe I'd be okay. And, in fact, it wasn't the water itself that terrified me. I looked up. "No."

He tilted his head a little, eyes narrowed. "Are you sure?"

"Positive." I held his eyes as I took another sip.

He sat back. "Okay then." He popped the last fry into his mouth with one hand, held the other toward me, and changed the subject abruptly. "Can I see your camera?"

My camera. My alter ego. My shield, my permission-giver, my validator. Why had he thought about it at all? It was completely out of sight. "How do you even know I have it with me?"

"I can't imagine you without it."

That stunned me. It was the first time I could remember someone saying something that got so close to the heart of who I am. My dad had come close by giving me the camera, but he hadn't seen what Walker had just put his finger on. *I can't imagine you without it.* He'd just compared my camera's importance for me to the importance of sailing for him.

Even so.... "Why d'you want to see it?" It sounded more pointed than I had intended, but I was actually a little freaked out.

Walker didn't seem fazed. "I know how to use my dad's PowerShot. I won't hurt it, promise." And he grinned.

He waited as I stared at his face, at the open friendliness of it, the trust, the gentle presumption that of course I would do as he asked, because someone like him always got exactly what he wanted. Something in me wanted to deny him. Something else wanted to make sure he would always turn that sunny grin my way, and it made me want to give him whatever he asked for. Frozen with conflicting feelings, I hesitated.

He withdrew his hand and sat back. "It's okay. Never mind. I know it means a lot to you."

I felt like an idiot. All the guy wanted was to look at my friggin' camera. He knew how to take care of things; he had a sailboat worth twenty-five thousand fucking dollars. If he damaged my camera, he'd probably buy me one twice as expensive. I shrugged, leaned over, and gently fished it out from its hiding place in my pack. Before I held it out, I cradled it in my palms.

Walker took it gently, carefully, placed the strap behind his neck (just as I would have done, in case it fell for some reason), and examined the housing I'd made. He looked at the camera itself and nodded, like he recognized the features.

He looked up. "Did you do this? This case, whatever?"

"Housing. Yeah, in shop class last year."

"Why?"

"Well... It hangs better on the strap. It's more stable, even if I set it down someplace. It's easier to mount on a tripod."

Eyes back on the camera, he nodded like that all made perfect sense. Lifting the strap off his neck, he handed the camera back to me. "What kinds of things do you shoot? Besides dead birds, that is."

He could have previewed my shots; he said he knew how the camera worked. But he hadn't done that. He hadn't invaded my territory. I told him about the gravestone I'd shot, and the poem that I would superimpose onto it.

"Grim," he said. "Along the lines of a dead bird, I guess." Then, "So are we on for tomorrow?"

I didn't give myself time to think. Or feel. "Okay." Couldn't have said why, but suddenly I needed to leave. It meant not quite finishing my fish and chips, but it was a sacrifice I had to make. I pushed my chair back as Walker reached into a pocket and pulled out his phone.

"Meet here, eight-thirty. Number?"

I froze in my seat. "What time did you say?"

"Eight-thirty is almost too late to get the best morning sun. I'd say let's get started even earlier, but as it is I'll need to trailer the boat here from the island, 'cause I'm sailing back there now. We can sail from here to the island and have a late lunch at my house and drive you back from there. What's your phone number?"

My brain wouldn't function beyond giving him a string of numbers. My phone rang, I answered it, and he said, "Now you have mine, too."

I felt numb. *His house?* His house that was probably bigger than the entire motel my mother managed? His house with a dock long enough to moor a sailboat and a yacht? His house that probably had servants and sculptures in the garden with bushes trimmed to look like animals?

"Who… um… who all will be there?"

"Mom will probably be home. She might eat with us. Dad often works from home, especially in the summer, but he'll be in his office. If Paige¬—she's my sister—is there, she'll be hiding in her workroom. Or her bedroom. She's twenty, home for the summer from college. RISD. Rhode Island School of Design. She won't bother us."

Christ. Would I have to wear anything special for a lunch with these rich people? But that was stupid; both Walker and I would have been sailing.

Me! I will have been sailing! I will have been sailing in a boat that cost more money than I knew how to count. It was too much. But I didn't know how to back out of anything. No, that wasn't it. I didn't *want* to back out of any of it. Plus, I figured, if I changed my mind, I had Walker's number.

I stood. "Thanks for lunch. Or, thanks to your dad, I guess."

"Sure you don't want some ice cream or something?"

"I, uh, I have to get back."

"Okay." And he gave me one more of those beautiful grins. "Later, dude."

Dude. Who says that? I was maybe ten feet away from the table when I heard, "Wear your boat shoes, and bring a hat! And sun glasses!" I didn't need to turn and look at him to know he was grinning. At me. At the prospect of sailing. Together.

On the ride home, I didn't allow myself to think. I was afraid that if I did, if I gave any thought at all to what I'd committed myself to… well, I didn't know what might happen, but I didn't really want to find out. Not yet. For now, all I wanted to do was focus on the idea of being on the water in a beautiful (I had to agree with Walker, there) sailboat, on a sunny summer day, with our destination a huge (no doubt) oceanfront home on Jasper Island, the very lap of luxury.

That mixture of pleasure was heady enough. But on top of all that, I'd be with Walker—Walker the gorgeous, the friendly, the entitled, the generous. The gay? If only. But— was it out of the question? And did I have anything to go on other than his beautiful face? No; not much, other than the fact that I wanted him to be gay. I decided I'd hold off on any revelations of my own, maybe indefinitely. Maybe forever.

Forever. Would I be waiting forever to be myself? Waiting for myself to be ready to start my real life?

I shook myself mentally.

I didn't allow myself to focus on the parts of this adventure that had the potential to scare the shit out of me. Instead I wondered just how much older than me he was. If he could drive alone already—legally, that is—he had to have been seventeen for at least six months. I wouldn't be seventeen until August. Just one more thing he had over me.

Mom wasn't home when I got there. Nick would be in the office, but I didn't have any reason to talk to him. I threw on swim trunks and went to the pool, which had no one in it at the moment. This was one perk of living here, and I was sure there were no sharks in this water. Plus, I could see all the way to the bottom.

I'd told Walker I couldn't swim. That wasn't true, thanks to an after-school program I'd taken during the time when my folks were fighting. It had kept me away from home with a good excuse.

I took several laps back and forth: Australian crawl, backstroke, sidestroke, even breaststroke. I hadn't ever tried to swim in the ocean because… well, because sharks.

So I didn't know how much different that would be. But I figured I could at least tread water if necessary; I wouldn't drown, though I might die of heart failure for other reasons.

I'd just finished dressing after my swim when I heard Mom coming in, the sounds of shopping bags rustling loudly as she struggled with the door. I went out to help, afraid of what I would see, and—sure enough—the bags were full of sheets, towels, God knew what else.

Mom, flushed with the heat of her efforts, gave me a big smile. It was a smile the likes of which I hadn't seen on her face in more time than I could remember.

"Couldn't resist. At least this much will be ready!" I watched her, speechless, as she pulled things out of the bags. "Oh, and I located a new bed I want to order. You can take yours with you."

Evidently she'd forgotten that Dad's place had only one bedroom. If I'd reminded her, I knew what would've happened next as clearly as if it were really happening. She'd call Dad, tell him about Dylan being alive, inform him that he needed to find a bigger apartment because I was coming to live with him, and generally talk as though everything had been decided. So I said nothing. But I decided it was time for *me* to call Dad.

All through dinner, Mom chatted about what she'd bought and why, how hard it was to wait on other things (like clothes) that didn't make sense to buy until Dylan was home, and how knowing he was alive had put joy back into her life. She drank iced tea with dinner.

I just sat there and let her ramble on; I don't think she even noticed that I said nothing to encourage her, that I said nothing about Dylan at all. It was like she'd gone manic. And under all of it for me was the question of whether her joy would be as great if I had been the one who'd died and then been resurrected.

I was pretty sure it wouldn't.

As soon as I could escape after dinner, I grabbed my phone and went outside. I walked all the way to the other end of the motel, into the parking lot of the drugstore next door, before I called Dad.

His reaction was pretty much what I'd expected. "This has to stop. Bad enough that she's delusional, but she has to stop spending money. And that bitch, Madam Whoever-the-fuck, is going to hear from me. Tell me again what her name is, Micah."

I was afraid to tell him. "Maybe you should just talk to Mom first? Get her to hold off spending any more money? Then when Dylan doesn't show up, she'll come down from cloud nine again."

In the silence that followed, I could hear him breathing loudly through his nose, no doubt trying to control his temper. Then he said, "Micah, do you want to come live with me? I could get a bigger place."

In some ways, it did seem like a good idea. It was getting freaky living with Mom. But when she wasn't manic, she was manageable. This was the only time I'd seen her like this. It couldn't last, could it? And any change would mean lawyers, or at least arbitrators.

Also, I was kind of afraid to leave her on her own. If Dylan were going to show up for real, that would be one thing. But he wouldn't, and she would get more and more anxious waiting for him, and despite Madam Alberta's best lies, someday Mom was gonna crash. I couldn't leave her alone.

And like I said, I didn't wanna have to change schools again. Plus there was Walker, whatever that might turn out to be. It was at least likely to be fun, and I could sure as hell use a little of that.

"How about this, Dad. I'll keep an eye on her, see if I can get her to calm down. You are gonna talk to her, right?" I waited until he said he would. "If she really goes off the deep end, then we can rethink things. But let's give it a little time."

"You keep me up on things, then. Because if she doesn't stop this soon, I will take action. Maybe put my child support payments into escrow, or something, so she doesn't spend it on…you know."

Yeah, I knew; it was so she wouldn't spend it on her dead son instead of her living one.

"Micah, are you okay? Be honest. How freaked out are you?"

"Not too freaked, really. It's just kind of hard listening to her go on about it, but—well, she'll know I called you. So she might chill for that reason alone."

"You check in with me every day, boy. At least for a while. If I don't hear from you by nine on any given night, I'll be arriving in person as quick as I can get there."

This gave me a warm, fluttery feeling that I couldn't quite identify. What it left behind was knowing he really did love me. A bit of a pain, calling every day, but I'd do it, if only because it meant he had my back if this got really bad.

"K. I better get back, now."

"I'll call her as soon as we hang up. And, Micah, don't you spend your life looking out for her. That's not your job. You got any friends?"

Not something he'd ever asked me; just girlfriends, that's all he'd cared about in the past. "Actually, I'm going sailing tomorrow with that kid I told you about. I'll be wearing those boat shoes you got me."

His voice changed noticeably, and although he didn't say the words, I knew he was thinking that maybe I was finally mastering my fears. "That's great, kid. What's his name, by the way?"

For some reason, I didn't want to tell him. But I was the one who'd opened this door. "Walker."

"Don't think I know any Walkers in the area. Where does he live?"

Walker. Dad thought that was a last name. And with a start, I realized I didn't know Walker's last name. I decided not to correct him. "Jasper Island." I held my breath; would he want to know more than I could tell him? Would he try to stop me from going?

"Must be rich, living there, having a sailboat and all."

"I guess. I've never seen their house."

"Big boat?"

I was *not* mentioning the yacht. "My friend can sail it on his own, so not very. We won't be far from shore."

He laughed. "Good thing. You won't be able to help him. Listen, you wear a vest, Micah. I know you can swim and all, but even close to shore, it's not like the pool."

"Yeah, I figured. No worries."

More silence, without the audible breathing this time. "You have fun, then. And don't forget to call me."

Whew. "You got it. And, Dad? Thanks."

"You bet."

I could hear Mom's voice before I got close enough to open the door from outside. And it was obvious it was Dad she was yelling at.

"I don't care what you think of her! But I'm getting a damn good picture of how much you don't love your own son!" I knew she meant Dylan, not me.

Um, Mom, he does love his own son. The only one he has. This was not something I could say, of course. I shut the door loudly enough to announce my entry. Mom looked toward me but didn't seem to see me, exactly.

"Dylan is alive. He's coming home. And that's an end to it!"

She jabbed at her phone as though he'd be able to tell how hard she'd hit it. I expect hanging up on someone was much more satisfying when there was something hard to slam down onto another hard thing.

She glared at me. "You had to go and tell your father, didn't you?"

The best defense being an offense, I said, "I can't believe you didn't tell him yourself. Maybe you don't really believe it." *Stupid, Micah. Stupid Micah.* But it didn't quite give away that I didn't believe it, and it distracted her from yelling about Dad.

Her arm shot into the air, pointing in the general direction of my room. "Get out of my sight!"

Standing close to my closed bedroom door, from inside the room I listened hard to see if I could tell what she did next. And what I heard was a sequence of sounds I knew too well. She was into the gin. And she was crying.

I distracted myself for the rest of the evening on stuff I could watch on my phone while propped up on the bed, back against the wall: Youtube vids, scraps of TV shows I didn't have to pay much attention to in order to follow them, that sort of thing. Eventually I opened a link I'd saved from Discovery Channel's annual Shark Week feature. It was a full week of show after show of sharks. Sharks and the people who studied them. Sharks and the people they'd eaten.

I muted the audio and leaned back, not really watching the flashing images on the screen. I loved and hated Shark Week. The images of massive great white sharks leaping head-to-tail out of the waters of False Bay in South Africa while brave idiots like the amazing photographer Chris Fallows lay on one-man floating sleds dragged behind boats, way too close to the fake seal decoy that was intended to tempt the monsters to attack, were the stuff of nightmares for me, and yet I devoured the shows every summer. I could probably name more different kinds of sharks than anyone else I knew, and for most of them I could describe sizes, habits, and favorite prey.

Sometimes I saw vids where someone had a shark attached to some part of their body, and they punched the shark on its oh-so-sensitive nose to get it to let go. But punching anything underwater is kind of a dud, so this approach was by no means foolproof. One image that scared me silly but that I somehow wanted to keep in my head—probably because it seemed to work every time— was something I saw Fallows do if he was in the water and needed to break the bite of a shark. With the heel of one hand, he'd press up hard on the underside of the shark's nose. It didn't need to be a punch, just a determined push. The shark would open its jaws, releasing whatever it had hold of—though I didn't remember seeing anyone do it on a fully grown great white.

I remembered one show in particular I'd seen last summer, where these divers were trying to figure out whether there were predictable behaviors, shapes, or colors that might attract sharks. They were able to conclude that one thing to avoid was anything large that was yellow. Most colors fade radically under water, so the temptation for divers is to wear something that other divers could see if someone needed help. But guess who (what) else can see yellow better. Sharks were so attracted to that color that the divers referred to it as "yum yum yellow."

Despite all the times I'd heard that sharks don't really like people as food, it didn't make me feel any better to know that. After all, the sharks figure this out by taking a bite and deciding they don't like human as much as they like seal. And it takes only one exploratory bite from a great white to do a person in. I was living proof that a shark's "exploration" was hardly harmless.

But Walker had said he didn't see great whites anywhere near shore, right? In fact, hadn't he said he'd never seen one at all? That's what he'd said, wasn't it? I didn't even own anything yellow, anyway. But there were other sharks out there. It didn't take a great white to kill you, and it hadn't been a large shark that had made off with some of my leg.

Whatever.

I set my alarm and fell asleep with my earbuds firmly in my ears playing a loop of a mountain stream on my phone.

Chapter Four

I rejected three T-shirts before I settled on one of my favorites, with large color blocks of black, gray, and white—not too much white, or the sharks might see that. I figured there was nothing a shark would see as food that had odd-shaped color blocks on it. What else had Walker told me to bring? A hat, right? I grabbed my black baseball cap with the red sailfish embroidered on it, another used clothing store find; that seemed appropriate. What else? Sun glasses. Right. Did I even have any?

Dylan had had some. They were in that box. Which was under Mom's bed. Great.

Her door was cracked open just enough for me to hear soft snoring. If she'd had enough gin last night, this should not be a problem. I cringed as I inched the thing out from under her bed; I'd forgotten how much noise the box made just sliding over the floor. But Mom never woke up.

I threw a sandwich of bread and cheese slices together, tossed that and a can of ginger ale into my backpack with the camera and the binoculars, scribbled a note saying I'd be out all day, and tiptoed out.

Defying all rules of safety, I strapped my helmet behind the bike seat so I could eat my sandwich as I pedaled, and then I opened the ginger ale and drank that. I found a trash bin near where I locked my bike up and then headed in the direction of the cafe.

Walker was at our table from yesterday, finishing breakfast, the sun's slanting rays making him look warm and fresh at the same time. He had on dark sunglasses, so I wasn't sure he'd seen me until he smiled that gorgeous smile at me.

"You came!"

"Did you think I wouldn't?"

Avoiding my question, he drained his coffee cup and held it up. "Want some?"

I shook my head. "I hate coffee."

"Wow. Okay, something else, then? I'd like one more cup. Ginger ale?"

I shook my head. "Is it a good idea to drink so much? Won't we be on the water for a while?"

He laughed. "Don't know about you, but I plan to piss overboard if that becomes necessary. Whales piss in the ocean; I think it can handle mine."

Duh. And, of course, sharks. "Ice water, then. Thanks."

It wasn't Toni this morning, but the fifty-ish woman today also knew Walker. They exchanged a few sentences I didn't pay much attention to. I was getting more nervous by the second about what was going to happen. Walker hadn't been wrong to wonder whether I'd show. I was almost ready to walk away right now. When my ice water arrived, I had to will my fingers to let go of their desperate grip on the edges of my chair seat, praying that my hand wouldn't shake when I reached for the glass, repeating *Don't be a wuss don't be a wuss don't be a wuss* over and over in my head.

Walker drank maybe half of his fresh cup of coffee right away. "Is there anything you want to know about sailing, or anything like that?"

I hadn't considered this. I'd asked him yesterday the question that had been at the top of my mind, about sharks. "Don't know what I would ask. I don't know anything."

"Do you want to?"

"You mean, do I want to learn how to sail?" I shrugged. "Let's just sail today, okay? Then I'll see."

He nodded and drained his cup. "Think I'll take a proactive piss. Be right back."

Alone at the table, with no one to hide it from, my anxiety hit a peak. I stood and paced back and forth in front of the cafe, then around to the side and back, sat down, took several deep breaths and fished out Dylan's sunglasses as Walker approached the table.

"All set? Did you want to finish your water?"

Willing myself to stand slowly, I shook my head, noticing that I had a couple of inches on him, height-wise. "All set. Lead on."

Walker led the way along one of the floating docks to the place where he'd moored *Dare Ya* yesterday, talking as we went.

"There's a whole list of things to check before you set sail, but I already did that. There's also a post-launch checklist. I'll go through that as we leave the marina and tell you what I'm doing. Just in case you're interested. Most of it's for safety, and since you've never been sailing, my guess is you'd like to know what the safety checks are." His voice gave me no feeling of being patronized, and I was listening carefully for that.

"By the way," he added, "I see you've worn jeans." Walker's choice had been khaki shorts.

"I don't have any other kind of pants, except slacks." Shorts showed my left calf to the world.

"That's fine; but if something happens and you end up in the water, ditch them. They're super heavy and stiff when they get wet." Then, laughing like of course it was a silly question, he added, "You are wearing underwear, correct?"

I was, but I didn't answer.

The boat was tied sideways to the dock, with ropes holding it in the front, the back, and the side, and there were a couple of those white bumper things keeping it from hitting the dock. The—slip? is that what Walker called it?—was large enough to handle a much bigger boat, like his dad's yacht. *Dare Ya's* sails were all wrapped up, or whatever the right term is. Furled, I think?

Walker stood beside his boat, beaming at me. "Gorgeous, isn't she?"

"Sure is." What else could I say?

"You get onboard first, one foot forward. But don't leave your back foot on the dock; she's tied well, but you don't want the boat pushing down or away with you hanging over the water. I'll untie us and jump on once you're secure."

The small gap between the boat and the dock looked huge. Must have been all of a foot. I did as I'd been told and nearly collapsed once I was on board, my knees were shaking that hard.

"Okay, now sit on the—that is, along the side—and be sure you're low enough that the boom won't hit you."

I was sure there was some term for "along the side" that he'd decided not to use. Fine. But I had to ask, "Boom?"

"The low bar that holds the bottom of the larger sail. It can swing from side to side."

I hunkered down and watched as Walker untied the ropes. It took mere seconds for him to start the motor, the smell of burning fuel floating on the air. I watched as he tilted the engine, turned it, changed the throttle, and steered the boat away from the dock and out of the marina. Once we were far enough away, he walked me through his post-launch checklist as he did it, which involved making sure no water was coming in, things like that. Then he killed the engine, tilted it up out of the water, and pulled in the white bumpers.

He moved around the boat in smooth, knowing motions, and opened first one sail and then the other, the wind catching them in the unmistakable (even to landlubber me) snap that only sails underway can make. It's a clean

70

sound, a fresh sound, and for some reason it made me feel calm. Or maybe what I felt was excited in a good way.

With a couple of ropes tied behind him on the rear deck holding the far end of the boom in place, Walker sat across from me, not quite in the stern, one hand on this long, wooden stick thing that must have been the rudder control, and the other hand holding one of the umpteen ropes all around the boat.

"What I'm doing now is called trimming the sail. It means you let the wind fill the sail until its front edge is in line with the wind. Then you give it slack until it starts to flap and then pull it back until the flapping stops. And then you fly!"

He watched the sails until they caught wind the way he wanted them to. And we were off.

It took my breath away, in a good way—not in the way it had happened at that semi-nude beach Dad had taken me to. Despite the sunglasses, I had to squint my eyes nearly shut against the wind. It was like magic. *Dare Ya* skimmed over the water like it couldn't wait to get into wide open spaces and fly. Walker moved the rudder in smooth, easy motions that were completely mysterious to me, the rope he'd been holding now wrapped around some metal thing to hold it in place.

At first I tried to watch Walker's face, the uplift of his chin, the gentle smile, the way the wind lifted his curls and flattened them again. But pretty soon I became almost hypnotized by the motions of the boat and the sunlight as it danced off the water. I faced ahead of the boat and closed my eyes.

Gone were all my misgivings. This was the most fun I could remember having since Dylan died. I let the wind massage my face, I let my body float on its own in sync with the boat, and I let this feeling of euphoria lift me out of all my cares.

We'd been underway for maybe ten minutes when I felt the boat slow just a little. I opened my eyes and then heard Walker's voice.

"Under the deck there's a couple of storage lockers. Can you reach me the red backpack from the one on the right, and open it for me?"

Keeping down to avoid that boom, I moved forward, crawled along the cushion-covered benches that met in the front of the boat, and opened the only thing under the bench on the right that might be storage. I pulled out the pack.

"The other side has life vests. You should probably wear one, yeah?"

I moved back to my seat and handed Walker the pack. "I don't know why I told you I couldn't swim. I can swim really well. Just haven't done it in the ocean."

"So you could tread water. But what if you get hit by the boom, and you're not conscious enough to tread anything?"

"You're not wearing a vest."

"Um, hate to point this out, but I know what I'm doing. If the weather were to turn, I would put one on. But—up to you, Micah." He did something with the ropes, and we slowed down. He fished through his pack and came up with a cap. I decided to fish mine out of my pack as well. Then he pulled a tube of sunscreen from an outside pocket of the red pack, massaging the white ointment into his face and onto the back of his neck, and when he handed me the tube I did the same.

"Put this back for me?" He pushed the red pack toward me with a foot. "Yours could go in there as well."

While I was up there, I decided to pull a life vest out of the other side and hang onto it, just in case. But I didn't put it on.

The boat picked up speed again as Walker tightened that rope and moved the rudder, and we headed in a mostly southern, partly eastern direction, in a kind of slow zig-zag pattern that Walker described as tacking, which he said was to get the most power out of the wind. Other than that, neither of us spoke for a good fifteen minutes. The water was the deepest blue, throwing itself into white splashes that almost seemed to laugh where they hit the boat.

I looked back toward the shore. Mistake. It seemed so far away. I wasn't at all sure I could have made it back if I'd had to swim. And just like that, the wonderful feeling of freedom and joy no longer existed anywhere in the universe. My stomach gave a little heave.

Walker looked at me and then nodded his head in the direction of something a little to the right ahead of us. He had to raise his voice to be heard over the wind in the sails and the sloshing of the water against the sides of the boat.

"That's Fisher's Island over there. And over to the left in the distance is Block Island; can't quite see it. Montauk is farther out toward the right. It's super clear today; ten mile visibility."

"Um... how far out are we going?"

He grinned. "Is the name of the boat any clue?" I'm sure the look on my face was what made him laugh. "I'm turning soon, or we wouldn't make it home in time for dinner, let alone lunch. And 'dare ya' is not a challenge I'll take with the tides and currents we'd hit farther out."

I pointed toward a spit of land off to the left side. "What's that?"

"Napatree point. It's the extreme edge of Westerly. That's as far west as Rhode Island goes. Okay, here we go. Hold on."

Walker did something to change direction, playing with the rudder and the ropes until the sails could catch enough wind to move us west, and the boat leaned way over on its side, forcing me to lean into the center of the boat for dear life. I swear one side of the boat was completely out of the water. I couldn't breathe.

As Walker evened the boat out I took a couple of deep, shuddering breaths and tore my eyes away from the water near the boat, where without even realizing it I'd begun to scour the unknowable depths for dark shapes.

Walker must have seen the shudders. "It's a little chilly out here, yeah? In where the packs are is a blue bag. Wanna fish that out?"

I had to will myself to move, I was that glued to the solid feel of where I'd been sitting, of where I'd been hanging on for dear life. I crawled toward the cabinet or whatever he'd called it earlier—storage locker?—and pulled out the only blue bag I saw.

"There are a couple of windbreakers in there, one for each of us."

I pried open the gathers that kept the nylon bag closed and pulled out two windbreakers.

They were both yellow.

Visions of those divers barely escaping the business ends of curious sharks attracted to yum yum yellow flashed through my panicked brain. I barely heard Walker speak.

"Slide back this way for a sec." Somehow I did as he asked as he let slack out on the rope again. "I've got us in a stable position. Here; take hold of the tiller while I put one of those on."

Take hold of the tiller? ME???

You're not afraid of boats, idiot. You're not afraid of wind. You're not even afraid of water.

Walker must have seen that I was struggling. "Just hold it in place. In fact, you don't actually need to hold it; we're not really going anywhere. I just thought you might like to."

I looked down at the wooden stick, brown grain lines curling around the end where it showed under Walker's hand. I had to fight a sudden surge of arousal as a flashing image of his hand like that on my dick hit my brain. My own hand, moving slowly forward, came into view, fingers wrapping around the tiller/dick as his hand withdrew. I didn't know where to look or even whether I should be looking at anything in particular, so I stared at the tiller. What would happen if I jerked it hard in one direction or another? Might something break? And then where would we be? Before I could form a full thought around that idea, Walker had slipped into the windbreaker and reclaimed control of the boat.

"You wanna put yours on?"

I moved back to where I'd been, the yellow shark beacon at my feet. "Maybe later."

He shrugged, his gaze back on the horizon. "Suit yourself. But it'll also keep the sun off your arms. Prevent burn, you know?"

Fuck. Shit. Damn it to hell. My mind went through a series of swear words as it led me toward a feeling of throwing all caution to the winds, as it were. I picked up that yellow jacket, put it on, and turned toward Walker.

Master your fear, Micah. "Lifting half the boat out of the water... I dare ya to do that again."

He cocked his head a little sideways and then grinned.

Within minutes, because of my newly found courage/determination/whatever it was, I was having the time of my life. Walker made that boat fly, moving us in different directions and catching wind in those snapping sails, throwing splashes of frothy water up on one side, then another, until I was in some altered state and covered with a light mist of sea water. Once or twice I laughed out loud as Walker pulled some surprising maneuver.

Eventually he evened things out and asked me to fetch a water bottle from his red pack. We took several gulps each, and then we headed toward the north side of Fisher's Island. As we got a little closer, I heard him say, "See that castle-looking thing? That's Simmons Castle. It's really a house. Built by the mattress people."

"Mattress people... Oh, I get it."

He sailed west along the north shore of the island, but I didn't see any more houses. I said, "Doesn't anyone else live there?"

"We're going past a golf course. There are two of them on the island."

Within a few minutes, we did start to see some houses, no doubt worth millions and millions apiece. "Would your folks ever consider living out here?"

He laughed. "No way. Boring, for one thing; it's not set up for activities other than golfing and boating. But the people who live there wouldn't let us get out of the boat."

I turned away from the conspicuous consumption to look at Walker. "What do you mean?"

He lifted his chin toward the island. "Serious, serious, heavy-duty Republican enclave. My folks tend toward the liberal side of social issues, but even though they're fairly conservative when it comes to finance, we'd be tossed into the ocean if we tried to set foot there. Not to mention, we don't have that kind of money."

Walker was keeping the speed down somehow, I supposed so I could get a good look at that rich and famous playground. Staying close to shore, we'd put about half of the island behind us when I heard a helicopter. Ahead of us to the west, the whirlybird descended toward the far end of the island.

"Private copter," Walker said. "Lots of the residents get on and off the island with them, or a small plane. There's an airfield at the end of the island."

I noticed the boat slowing more and more, and I looked at Walker. "You're not, um, daring them to let us on land are you?"

He looked at me with most evil grin you can imagine on a face as gorgeous as his. "I have another dare in mind." His voice changed, pitched higher to carry, with a heaviness that implied a fake innocence. "You know what, my friend, we've been out on the water for a long time, and I do feel a need to piss. How about you?"

He pulled his sunglasses down long enough to wink at me and stood, facing the snobby island. One second I couldn't believe what he was about to do. The next, I had jumped up to join him.

We unzipped and let our streams flow, though I noticed that mine was a much higher arc than his, which barely cleared the boat even though he was practically leaning against the side. He watched the nearest house along the shore. I pretended to do that, instead trying to sneak a glance at his dick, but—no joy. All I could see was that he was hunkered down a little farther than I needed to be, and he was using his hands in some way I didn't understand.

As Walker finished, he let out a long, relieved sigh and said, "Oh, I feel so much better. Don't you?"

He laughed like a maniac, zipped up, and got us out of there as quickly as possible, working some kind of magic with ropes and cranks, and we headed in what I guessed was an east-northeast direction, not directly at the mainland, and once we were moving fast he set the sails so that we were leaning fairly far over to one side.

It was... man, it was exhilarating! We flew over the water, the little boat holding steady in that leaning position. If *Dare Ya* had emotions, it—she—was delighted with life. I turned toward Walker, and he looked at me and grinned, and I laughed out loud.

The time had gone by so quickly, once I got over my terror, that it was nearly two o'clock when we started a slow approach to what must have been Jasper Island. I'd never been on it at all, even though there's a bridge that goes out to it over a spit of water maybe five hundred feet across. For sure, I'd never seen it from the ocean side. But it was clear that's where Walker was pointing us.

I took a deep breath and let it out slowly. "Man. That was maybe better than sex."

Walker said nothing, and when I looked at him there was no grin. There was not even the hint of a smile. It was almost like I'd said something wrong. Finally, not looking at me, he asked, "Have you done that, then?"

"What? Sex? Well... no. I mean, except alone. You know." He nodded, his gaze toward the island. I asked, "You?"

One side of his mouth pulled in, not in a smile. It was more of a smirk. "Nope."

Neither of us spoke again as we passed a few docks, some with boats, no doubt belonging to other wealthy people on Jasper Island. Then Walker maneuvered the boat around a point of land to the left and close to a very long dock, with me doing nothing except trying to figure out what had gone wrong between us, and where all this tension had come from suddenly. That, and—oh, yeah— trying to keep my jaw from dropping to my waist at the sight of the yacht tethered to one side of the dock. I now understood completely all those "friends" who'd cozied up to Walker hoping for a ride on that thing.

That boat was unbelievable. There were at least three levels—a little hard to tell from the outside—and it had one of those covered perches on the top, where I'd guess the captain would sit when the boat was underway. There were long, narrow, windows along the sides, and they came to points toward the front, giving the boat a look something like evil glee. It looked like there were two different places for passengers to sit or stand and enjoy the ride, one just above water level in the back that was open, and another a level up, below the captain's perch, that looked like it could be covered if needed. And then there was the perch itself, which looked big enough for at least a few people besides the captain. Other than the floating docks at Sailaway, I'd never been this close to anything like it. And, unlike *First Million*, I did know who owned this yacht.

I watched as Walker threw some bumpers over the side of his boat, did something to get the front sail to curl itself up electronically, then lowered the big sail and somehow tied that all up into a roll around the boom. I pulled his pack and mine out from the locker and then watched in ignorance as he stabilized the boat so we could climb up the few steps of a kind of wooden ladder that led to the top of the dock. Then he let the line out a lot more than he had to, in terms of the distance between the boat and the dock.

"What's with all the slack?"

"Tide's coming in. The boat will rise with it, of course, and the line will be longer than it needs to be. But when the tide goes out again, the boat will fall with it. It'll need the longer line to reach down to the low tide water level."

Oh. Right. I felt like an idiot, but it wasn't because of Walker's attitude.

It wasn't until we were on dry land again and approaching the back yard of his house that I realized I'd never taken my camera out of the pack, which was now slung over one shoulder.

The expanse of tough grass sloped down gently to the left, toward a bit of an overhang that fell sharply to the water. There didn't seem to be any beach, just a lot of huge, tumbled rocks (boulders, really), but it wasn't low tide at the moment.

To get to the huge, fieldstone house we walked across a large area paved with flagstones and then around a kidney-shaped pool. Several lounge chairs were positioned on the house side of the pool, facing the ocean and the afternoon sun. There were plantings all around the house, but they weren't sculpted (which was how I'd pictured them yesterday), and off to the far left was a flagstone-paved path that led away from the house to something I couldn't see through the trees and shrubs.

"What's over there?"

Moving ahead of me, Walker turned his head just enough for me to hear. "The garage is on that side of the house. Past that, off to the side, are the guest cottages. There's no one in them this week."

Cottages. Plural. OMG. What had I gotten myself into? And did "this week" mean they frequently had visitors? "Who stays there?"

"My grandparents, sometimes. Or, that is, just Gramma, now; Grampa died last year. Or my mother's brother and his wife, or my aunt on my dad's side. Divorced. She comes here a lot, unfortunately with my cousin Cameron."

Great, I thought, another guy in this family with a last name for a first name. And as Walker was about to open the door to what looked like a huge three-season porch, I said, "Wait! I... um, I don't know your last name."

"Oh my God! That's right. And I don't know yours." He grinned in a way that let me know he was being facetious, like last names didn't matter.

"But—"

"Don't worry." He stepped inside the porch, which was partly screens and partly glass, with lots of comfy-looking furniture around, white painted metal with flowered cushions in pastel colors, a few fluffy throws here and there for when the evenings grew chilly, I supposed. He had me set my pack down beside his on a bench just outside the doorway into the main part of the house.

We went through a small entrance room with a bench on one side and cupboards that probably held boots and brooms and things, past a doorway on the left that led into what looked like a TV/video room, and then into a huge kitchen. A woman on the far side of it turned toward us.

"There you are! I was about to send out the Coast Guard." She had Walker's hair, his blue eyes, and her own beautiful smile. She wiped her hands on a towel and moved toward us. "You must be Micah." She held her right hand out, and I took it without thinking. Evidently, Walker had told her I'd be sailing with him today.

"Micah, this is my mother, Mrs. Donnell."

"Do you have a last name, Micah?"

"Yes, ma'am. Jaeger." I pronounced it carefully, as though it began with a Y instead of a J.

"I've always loved that name! German. It means hunter, yes?"

I had no idea what it meant; I'd always just wanted it pronounced correctly. "I think so."

She moved back to where she'd been working on something when we came in. "Are you boys ready for lunch, late though it is? I've had mine."

"Thanks, Mom. I'm famished. Can I help?"

"You can get the two of you something to drink. Want to sit at the island?"

I made my way to one of the stools at the long, curved island in the middle of the room and was immediately transfixed by the countertop: massive swirls of deep blue in some kind of cream stone with flecks of something coppery scattered through it. A look around the room revealed that all the counters had this stone on them.

"D'you want ginger ale, Micah? I'm having that."

"Sure. Thanks."

Mrs. Donnell put blue placemats for us on the counter, along with forks and pale blue napkins. Cloth ones. By the time Walker had set our glasses down, Mrs. Donnell was bringing over a huge green glass bowl, white on the inside, with something green in it, and then she brought a clear serving plate with sliced hard boiled eggs and tiny little tomatoes sliced in half. Walker fetched a couple of the whitest plates I've ever seen, and from the green bowl he scooped pasta in some unusual curly shapes that had been tossed with whatever the green stuff was. I watched as he piled my dish high, noticing little fragments of what looked like potato and chopped green beans. But most of the green was from the dressing, or whatever it was. And, whatever it was, it smelled wonderful.

"Hope you like pesto," Walker said. "Mom is convinced it's ambrosia from the gods. We have it so often in the summer, I swear it's turning my skin green."

"You silly bear," came his mother's voice across the room. "It's not as if you don't love it."

He grinned as he piled his own plate high. Then he handed me the plate with the eggs and tomatoes. "There's no protein in the pasta. And take however many grape tomatoes you'd like."

Pesto. I'd heard the term, but I had no idea what it was. The mouthwatering smell was driving me crazy, though, and my stomach very much wanted me to just tip the plate into my mouth and swallow. Something told me to wait until Walker's plate was ready. It seemed like the polite thing to do, whether it was expected or not. As soon as he picked up his fork, I did the same.

I stabbed just a couple of pasta bits at first; things that smelled good didn't always taste good. And what I learned that day was that pesto tasted even better than it smelled. I also learned where it came from.

"Mom fell in love with the way they serve it in Cinque Terre, with potato bits and beans. We were there last summer. That's where pesto got its start, actually. And you won't believe this. There was one place along a harbor where they had a vending machine full of little bottles, all with pesto in them!"

Not a place I'd ever heard of. "Where's Cinque Terre?"

Walker's mouth was full, so his mom said, "It's on the Ligurian Sea, on the north end of Italy's western coast. Let's see... Vernazza, Manarola, Corniglia, Riomaggiore... shoot. I always forget that fifth one."

"Monterosso al Mare," Walker finished for her with a much more convincing Italian accent than I could have faked. "Cinque Terre means five lands, or in this case little villages, kind of perched on the ocean with the mountains rising up really steep, right behind them."

"Well," I said, "I might go for the scenery, but I'd stay for the pesto if it's anywhere near as good as this."

They both laughed, which really surprised me; I wasn't used to people finding what I said to be funny. Maybe I'd never been to Italy, but I wasn't a total loss.

At some point I'd had just enough food to take the edge off my hunger, and that's when I noticed the fork in my hand. It didn't look or feel quite like any metal fork I'd ever used.

Walker and I took bowls of pistachio ice cream—green was a theme for this lunch—out to the porch and sat in those comfy chairs. For a few minutes we just ate and watched sparkles of sun dance off the water. Then I noticed that the spoon was made of the same stuff as the fork, which made sense.

"What's this metal? It seems different somehow."

"Yeah, that's sterling silver. Most flatware is stainless steel."

I set my empty bowl onto a glass table to my right, wondering just how much more costly silver flatware was than stainless. Still watching the sparkling water, I said, "Man. I can't believe you live here." I turned to look at Walker, who was watching me intently. "D'you, like, take all this for granted?"

He shrugged. "I guess you do get used to things, you know?" He set his own bowl down. "So, wanna see my room?"

"Sure." We carried our bowls back to the kitchen, where Walker rinsed them and the spoons and put all of it into the dishwasher. I thought, *At least he's not waited on.*

He led the way through the middle of the house, giving me a quick tour: dining room (huge), living room (huger, cathedral ceiling, stone fireplace all up one side of the room to the point of the ceiling). A short hallway lead to a closed door he said was his father's study, and another door stood open to the video room (I'd been right). Another closed door hid what he said was Paige's workroom; evidently she was into fashion design.

The stairs were almost a whole room to themselves—a broad, curving sweep starting across from the fireplace and curling up and along the side of the two-story living room. At the top of the stairs, a kind of open hallway curled back toward the fireplace side of the room and ended near the top of that chimney. Walker's room was the last room along that curl, so he had a corner bedroom.

The room was monstrous for a bedroom. To the right was the bed, head against the right wall. The left side of the bedframe kind of nestled against a low, wooden structure, with lots of drawers along the left side of the bedframe. The foot of the bed and the right side were open, and a gorgeous quilt with splashes of oranges and blues and browns covered the bed. Pillows with the same colors were thrown across the head of the bed, and over that, on the wall—this was so cool—was this mural of wide open ocean under a peachy-colored sky (evidently a sunset, though you couldn't see the sun), and in the distance, off to the right, was a huge sailboat with cream sails, catching just a hint of the peach.

Everywhere I looked there was more to gawk at, from the unusual lamps to the rough board ceiling to the overhead black fan with three twisted blades to the dark blue rugs to a wooden desk. And there was another desk, behind the door to the left, where there was a TV and the PlayStation Walker had said everyone wanted to use. I carefully avoided taking any notice of it so he'd keep thinking what he'd said to himself about me: "Okay, he's different."

I walked over to the large window across from the door, which looked out over the water. I could actually see Fisher's Island from here.

"Wanna check out the games? I just got the PS4 with the dual shock wireless controller. It came with *Uncharted: A Thief's End.*

Was he testing me? I turned and looked at him, not the PlayStation. I shrugged. "If you want, sure. I don't have anything like this, so I don't even know what all that meant." I grinned, hoping it didn't look as deliberate as it was. "Guess it's not something I've ever cared about." Not entirely true....

I stood there, waiting to see what he'd do. About five seconds went by. "Maybe some other time, then. Wanna help me wrap *Dare Ya* up for the night?"

My next grin was genuine. "I don't know what that means, either, but I'd love to."

He beamed. "Come on, then."

On the way back through the kitchen, Walker filled a plastic pitcher with ice water, handed me two plastic cups, and we went back down to the boat. The tide was higher now, so the boat was closer to the top of the dock. Walker had told me this would happen, but for some reason it surprised me anyway.

He set the pitcher and cups on the dock, talking as he descended the ladder stairs. "It's kind of like when you have a horse. After you ride it, you need to brush it down, make sure it has water and hay, oats, whatever. It just means you care about it enough to take care of it. Hand me down the pitcher, will you?"

I carried the cups down in one hand and we stood side by side in the middle of the boat, the water gently rocking us. It was hypnotic.

He looked at me, squinting against the sun. I could still smell the suntan lotion on both of us, but there was something else, too. Some aroma that was all Walker. What was it? Rope, maybe? I liked it. I really liked it.

"Do you have time to help me do a real check?"

I looked at my watch: four-ish. "Sure." Maybe they'd feed me dinner here, too? I'd need to call Mom....

"We'll be done just about in time to get you back to your bike by five thirty or so."

Oh, well... As he'd said about the PlayStation, maybe some other time. "So this is more than the usual brushing down?"

His grin had something sheepish in it, and something else, too. Something devilish, maybe? "Right. Plus, it's more fun to do it with a friend." The feeling I got was as good as if he'd said, *I want to keep you here a little longer.*

I helped unwrap the sails and keep them from catching wind as we checked them for tears or rips. He rolled them back up, and then we went over every rope on the boat, looking for frayed spots, talking as we worked.

"You didn't get your camera out. Did you even think about it?"

"Actually, I didn't. Think about it, that is. I guess sailing took all my attention. Usually I see things and think, 'What kind of a shot would that be? How could I use it?'"

"But not today."

"No."

"You did seem to be having a good time."

I stopped what I was doing long enough to look at him. "I had a really, really good time today. Thanks."

We worked silently for a minute, and I wondered if he might be waiting to see if I asked for another sailing day. It was a bit of an effort not to keep looking at his boat shoes, and then mine, and then his... I kept my mouth shut and focused hard on my task. Then, "Here. Is this a bad spot?"

I held out the part of the rope I'd been examining.

"It is. And it's bad enough I'll need to replace it. Thanks, Micah. Sharp eyes."

He ducked under the front part of the boat where the storage lockers were and pulled out another gathered bag, orange this time, and he brought out a roll of bright orange tape. He tore a piece off and wrapped it tightly around the frayed bit I'd found.

After another short silence he asked, "What's it like for you at home, Micah? I mean, living in a motel. If you don't mind my asking."

I told him more than I would have thought I'd be willing to say about what was left of my family. I told him about Dylan being killed in Afghanistan, about where Mom and I had to live now and why. I told him about visiting with Dad. I didn't mention Madam Alberta or her recent vision, and I didn't mention the gin, but for some reason I told him about last Sunday, when Dad and I had been waiting in the truck for Mom to show up. I mentioned the song "Layla."

He said, "I know that song. Mom loves it."

"It's a cool song." I hesitated, not sure whether I should go on, but nothing stopped me. "It's about this guy who's in love with someone else's wife. There's one divorce, and then another, and then happy ever after."

I stopped my task and stood straight ahead for a second, gazing at nothing. "When Dad was talking about it, it seemed like he was about to say something really important. But... well, something else happened and he didn't have a chance."

Walker stopped what he was doing, too, and looked at me. "Okay, this might be way off base. I wonder—never mind." He shook his head and bent back over the outside of the boat, checking for cracks or weak spots.

"Never mind? You can't just stop like that. Spit it out."

He stood again. "I just didn't want to freak you out or anything. Maybe it wouldn't do that. But I wonder if he was about to tell you he'd met someone."

I blinked like and idiot, staring right into Walker's eyes without seeing them. "Fuck."

"Really? Would it be bad? Were you hoping your folks would get together again?"

I sat down hard on the same spot where I'd been for our sail earlier. "Um, I—Jesus, I don't know. I mean, they kind of fell apart after Dylan was killed. Dad said it was like they couldn't grieve together."

My dad's words, that we were a family because of me, suddenly seemed like a lie. How would we be a family of any kind if he was going to marry someone else? At least it wouldn't be me wrecking everything.

I glanced up at Walker, whose face showed some combination of concern and curiosity. His voice soft, he asked, "Are you okay?"

I nodded, looked away. "Yeah. I guess I just never thought of that. Stupid, really. Why the hell shouldn't he get married again?"

"He might have been going to say something else, you know."

"I suppose." I took a deep breath and let it out slowly.

"Look, it's after five. And we've drunk all our water, anyway." He grinned like he was trying to cheer me up. "Let's go back to the house and find someone to drive us back."

"I thought you could drive."

"Yeah, but I trailered the boat to Sailaway this morning. My car's still there."

"Oh. Right." His car. He has a car. Of course he does.

"Come on." He grabbed the pitcher, I grabbed the cups, and we headed up the even shorter ladder—just one step now—and back to the house.

There was a towel on one of the lounge chairs at the pool, and a glass of what looked like ice tea, almost empty, beside an upturned paperback. Mrs. Donnell must have been out here for a while, was my guess.

She was in the kitchen now, though. "How's the boat?"

Walker let himself fall into a chair at the kitchen table. "Micah found a bad rope. Now I'll have to replace that before I can take her out again. Think Dad would be willing to help?"

"Maybe over the weekend. Right now he's not in a very good mood, having some kind of confrontation with someone over the phone."

"So not a good business day."

She chuckled. "You never know. I'm fairly sure he sometimes puts on a deliberately surly act to cow people into submission."

This kind of messed up my image of Mr. Donnell, who might not be the friendly, doting father I'd pictured.

"Guess we can't ask Dad to drive us back to Sailaway, then. Can you?"

"Sweetie, I've just started working on dinner." She held up a piece of raw chicken. "Get your sister to do it. She's been holed up in her room all afternoon. Her bedroom, that is, not the workroom. Probably reading a novel cover to cover. While texting."

"Oh, man!" Walker made a noise of disgust, or something, and shrank farther down in the chair. "She won't do it. She wouldn't do anything I asked her to."

I couldn't tell whether Mrs. Donnell agreed with Walker, or whether she despaired of getting him to do what she'd suggested, but she glared at him as she washed her hands. Grabbing a paper towel, she left the kitchen and climbed maybe halfway up the staircase before calling, "Paige? Come downstairs, please. Now."

Walker, hunched into his chair, played with a metal napkin ring that had been on the table, staring at it as his fingers turned it one way and then another. I could tell that something between Walker and his sister seemed wrong, or dark, beyond what one might expect between a teenage boy and his college-age sister. Whatever he was feeling translated into anxiety for me.

"Paige! I said *now*."

A few seconds went by before I heard a distant, "I heard you!" Then there was a thump, like maybe she'd rolled off of a bed, and an upstairs door opened. "What is it?" She sounded not just irritated, but irritated in a way that gives you the impression it was her right to be irritated.

"I need you to run Walker and his friend Micah over to Sailaway. It will take you all of ten minutes. I think you can spare that."

There was a noise of exasperation from Paige loud enough for me to hear it, and Mrs. Donnell reappeared. "There. It shouldn't be more than fifteen minutes now. You really do need to learn how to fight your own battles, Walker."

In my head were my Dad's words: "Don't be a wuss, Micah." "Buck up."

The three of us said nothing as we waited—Mrs. Donnell back at the sink with the chicken, Walker toying distractedly with the napkin ring, me wondering what had gone wrong, and all of us in this emotional fog that kept us separated as if for our own safety, like boats that would be damaged if they collided on this unsettled sea.

I found myself marveling—and not in a good way—at the change in Walker ever since his mom had mentioned Paige driving us. All day, he'd seemed self-confident, capable to an impressive degree, sure of what he was doing and why he was doing it, and, to all appearances, happy within himself.

Now? Not the same guy at all. He'd kind of pulled into himself in a way that made me think of what a snail on the beach might do if you poked at it with a stick. Only Walker didn't have a shell to protect him, so all I saw was a surprising vulnerability that confused me.

Waiting for Paige seemed like an eternity, but it was probably about seven minutes later that a tall, slender girl appeared, jet-black hair pulled into a ponytail, a pink halter top over denim short-shorts, pale blue flip-flops on her feet, a slim, navy shoulder bag in her hand (strap dragging on the floor), and an expression of long-suffering righteousness on her narrow, almost-pretty face. If the hair hadn't been enough to make me wonder about her relationship to Walker, there was her skin; she was tanned, no doubt, but so was Walker, and he was nowhere near as dark as she was. If I'd been impolite enough to ask about it, I felt sure she would have skewered me in one way or another and left me bleeding on the floor.

Her body language mirrored the expression on her face, and she hunched there in an attitude implying impatience, as though she'd been the one waiting for us to get our act together. "Well?"

Walker shifted a leg, and that must have been enough for her. She nearly stomped in the direction of the back porch. Hurriedly I thanked Mrs. Donnell for introducing me to pesto and then grabbed my pack as Paige opened a door I hadn't noticed off that inner room. On the other side of the door was the biggest garage I'd ever seen, inhabited by the most expensive cars I'd ever been close to. First there was a pale blue Lexus sedan, then a black Mercedes sedan, and then a bright yellow BMW, which Paige led us to. She got behind the wheel, and Walker opened a rear door and got in. I didn't know whether I was expected to sit beside the Fury in the front, and I was massively relieved when Walker scooted across the rear seat to leave room for me there. It didn't occur to me until I heard the garage bay door closing behind us as we backed into the driveway to wonder where Walker's car lived when it was at home; there were only (only!) three garage bays.

No one said a word all the way to Sailaway. As we approached the parking area, Paige hesitated for a second, and I thought Walker would tell her where he had parked, but he said nothing. The car jumped forward as Paige's eyes landed on her target. She came to a sudden halt, and

Walker and I scrambled out, doors barely shut when the car leapt forward in a cloud of gritty dust.

I looked at Walker. He wouldn't look at me, just fumbled for his key fob and headed for the Jeep Grand Cherokee in front of us, the late afternoon sun showing up the pearly aspects of the deep red color. It was parked along the side of the lot, the trailer that had towed *Dare Ya* over here this morning attached.

Walker climbed up and into the driver's seat without saying good-bye, so I figured maybe he wanted to talk for a minute before I went to find my bike. By the time I climbed into the passenger seat, he was leaning back against his seat, eyes closed, face looking strained. I left my door open, my pack on the ground.

I didn't want to open with something directly related to Paige; not sure why not. So I focused on the vehicle, which was a little overwhelming. To me, anyway.

"Your car... it smells new."

"Yeah. It is. I had a 2014 model, but it had that stupid e-shift thingy where you weren't sure if you were in park, and if you weren't—let's just say we heard about a lot of accidents, like Anton Yelchin, that actor who was in the Star Trek movie. My folks decided they didn't want to have to worry about my car running me over like that. And Dad drives my car sometimes, too. So he got me a 2016 right after they came out."

Nothing. I had nothing in response to that. So I gave it a bit of space and then asked, "You okay?"

He let out a long breath. "Sorry about that. It's always like this with her."

"What's her problem, anyway?"

I heard a low chuckle. "She'd kill me if she knew I was telling you this. Which is partly why I'm telling you." Head still leaning against the headrest behind him, he turned a wry smile my way before facing front again. "She was adopted."

"I knew it! Or, that is, I knew something. She doesn't look anything like you or your mom."

"Or my dad, as it happens. My mom had trouble conceiving, and my folks really wanted a kid. So they gave up hoping for one of their own and adopted Paige. I came along as a surprise a few years later. She's half Pakistani."

"And what's the reason she's such a bitch?"

Walker laughed, a good, relaxed laugh that released something in him. "Oh, God, but I wish she could hear you call her that!" Then, more sober, he added, "I called her that once a few years ago and she slapped me until I cried."

"You're saying you wanna see her slap me?"

He turned toward me again. "Maybe I'd like to see her try. Somehow I think you'd stand up to her better than I do."

I almost asked why he thought that, but I decided I'd just bask in the glory of it—at last, someone who didn't see me as a coward. Besides, there was no way I wanted him to know I'd noticed the transformation in him from self-confident to cowering, so I didn't want to dwell on the issue.

When he spoke again, he sounded more like himself. "So it's gonna take me a couple of days to check the rest of the ropes and replace the one you found, plus this weekend will be a little crazy—July fourth, and all that. You wanna sail again Tuesday? I'd ask you to stay for dinner, but you'd have to put up with Paige."

My turn to chuckle. "Yeah, I don't know that I'm ready for that. But, sure, sailing sounds great. And, you know, I can bike out to Jasper Island. It's only about four miles or so from my house." I felt the need to amend that; there was no house. "From where I live, I mean."

"Better still, why don't I just drive over and pick you up? It's The Afterdeck, right?"

Honesty about my living situation was one thing. Having him actually see the place, maybe even meet my potentially gin-soaked mother, was something else altogether.

Think fast, Micah. "My guess is that if you could have avoided having me meet Paige today, you'd have done that. Right?" I waited for his shrug. "I guess I'm not ready for you to meet my mom."

He kept looking at me. It was a warm look, his lips in a slight smile. "You're passing every test, you know that? Some I think you're aware of. Others, not so much."

So I'd been right. "What tests? And what do you mean, others not so much?"

"Okay, well, for instance, you helped me do that boat check. That's not much fun, just standing in the boat at the dock and scouring every surface and length of rope for problems. But you seemed glad to do it."

Had I known that was a test? Don't think so; I'm pretty sure I'd been too willing to spend more with him, whatever we were doing, to pick up on any agenda. It hadn't mattered that it was a chore. But I couldn't exactly tell him that. Also, did that mean that his reason for asking me to do it was not that he'd wanted more time with me?

I said, "I don't much like that you're testing me."

He let out another long breath. "I can't say I blame you. Sorry. I'll stop, if you're okay with getting together again."

So he really did want to spend time with me. I looked at him kind of sideways, my head cocked in what I hoped was a teasing look. "I will if you ask me nicely."

He laughed again, a rich, joyful sound I loved. And I knew that if we got together many more times, I was gonna fall hard for him. The real him, not the dream version. And I didn't have any reason to think he could or would feel the same about me.

Chapter Five

I stood and watched as Walker maneuvered that red monster, boat trailer included, as smoothly as he'd handled his sailboat. He waved in his rear view mirror as he pulled away.

It was after five-thirty, but I wasn't ready to go home. After the day I'd had, I couldn't face that cramped, smokey motel unit with my mother in it—my mother, whose moods these days swung between a deluded euphoria about Dylan's fabled return and an inflammatory anger about the way her misplaced happiness was affecting the actual, living people around her. That would be me. And Dad.

I found my way to the section of floating dock where, about a year ago now (or so it felt like, though it was really only this morning), I'd stepped fearfully onto that sweet little boat that had carried me off into a world that had seemed like paradise on earth. I sat on the dock beside my pack and hugged my knees, staring at the gently pulsing water that was rocking me into a hypnotic state.

The way we had flown over the sea! Oh, my God, what a day. Salt spray on my face, yellow sun and blue sea and sky everywhere, and the wind... oh, the wind! Now that I was safely on land—or nearly so, on this dock—I wanted nothing more than to be back out there again. There was no way I could separate the feeling of sailing from the feeling of sailing with Walker. But for now, I'd just take the bundle of feelings and run with it. Fly with it!

I let my mind wander back over the few times during the course of the day's events when it had seemed like maybe, just maybe Walker could get to like me the way I was getting to like him. It was hard, though, to identify very many specifics. Most of that hope, if that's what it was, floated around disembodied images of a look, a smile, a smell. He'd never touched me, unless you count that moment of the tiller hand-off, when I'd been too petrified to appreciate it.

But then there had been that moment in the boat, when we were checking things at the dock, about my dad... Walker had gone so quickly to the idea that what Dad had been about to say, after describing the back story to "Layla," was that he was getting serious—maybe even very serious—about someone. Maybe this should have occurred to me, but it hadn't. But now that Walker had said it, the idea made so much sense. Everything about Dad's behavior, and the way he'd looked when he was describing that story, pointed toward something really personal. And the story behind the song led kind of naturally toward getting married again after divorce.

I grabbed my sun-and-salt-stiffened hair and ran my fingers quickly back and forth on my scalp, trying to stop my mind going around in circles in its attempt to avoid landing squarely on the possibility Walker had suggested. I already had too much to think about: Mom's weirdness over Dylan; having just come out to Dad; the paradise of sailing with Walker, of being with Walker, of the luxury of Walker's life, and the potential hell if he finds out I'm gay; the unsettling contrast of Walker the bold and Walker the weak. Was that the whole list? And wasn't that enough? Did I really have to worry about what Dad marrying someone else would do to Mom? To me? To whatever was left of our family?

To try and calm things down, I did my best to imagine what it would be like to be at the Donnells' for dinner, with

Paige across the table throwing darts of distaste and condescension at me. That I could take. But having her throw them at Walker? Somehow, that really bothered me. I wasn't sure how much of that I'd be able to take before I fought back on his behalf.

Why was he so cowed by her, though? She was a little older than Walker to be sure, but so what? All right, so I'd been intimidated too, but I was convinced that was just because she had come on so strong, and because of Walker pulling into himself like that. He was right to think I wouldn't put up with her slapping me.

But it was the idea of her slapping Walker that got to me.

Maybe you have to pay for paradise, even if you're Walker. Maybe the alternative to paying for it is dying, literally dying, to get it.

I let out an exasperated groan as I stood, sweeping my pack along with me, and headed over to my bike. I was never going to figure any of this out. It was no easier than trying to see into the ocean for sharks.

As soon as I walked in the door at home, I knew things were back to the way they'd been on Sunday night. That is, Mom was sober and in a good mood again. She was in the small living room area, towels and sheets and a bed pad around her, some folded and some waiting to be folded.

She turned toward me with a smile. "I've got all these washed and dried, all ready. Go and wash your hands, and you can help me fold the fitted items. They're always harder."

At least these were the items she'd already bought; I didn't see anything new.

Hands washed, I picked up a corner of the bed pad just as the office bell rang. Mom left to "see what that pesky guy wants now," whoever that was.

She got back in time to see me finish folding the last sheet. "I thought we'd order pizza delivered tonight. You can have whatever toppings you want. How does that sound?"

"Sounds great." Sounded great, yeah, except that it made me wonder what she was up to. This kind of offer didn't typically come without strings attached.

It was a couple of hours before the other shoe dropped.

First, a distraction during dinner: "Did you have fun today, dear? Did you take a lot of photographs?"

As I finished chewing my mouthful of pizza with pepperoni, sausage, green peppers, and caramelized onions, I tried to decide how much I was ready to tell her about sailing, and about the Donnells. I decided I wasn't at all ready. "I have several shots of a dead seagull, and some of gravestones. Wanna see them?"

She laughed lightly, a fake-sounding giggle, really. "Oh, I don't think so."

Maybe a minute later I was glad of my decision; it was obvious to me now that she'd been just pretending to be interested so she could put forth her own agenda.

"I hope you haven't made a lot of plans for Sunday." She didn't wait for me to answer. "Because there's something I'd like us to do together that I think you'll enjoy."

This time she did wait for my response. I went for a neutral tone of voice, struggling against a feeling of *Christ; now what?* "What's that?"

"I was thinking that it would be a shame to have Dylan home and not give you boys the chance to be together. So rather than send you to live with your father, I think we should look for another place to live. A place where we can all three live together. How does that sound?"

I snuck a glance at my watch; I had another hour before Dad would charge over here if he didn't hear from me.

Choosing my words very carefully, I said, "Wow. That would be great. Um, though, aren't we where we are because we didn't have a lot of money to spend?"

She waved a hand in the air before reaching for another slice of pizza. "When I took this job, Micah, it was because there wasn't much I could handle at the time. But I am a trained accountant. Not a CPA, or anything, but there are lots of places I could get work. Probably the most likely would be Hartford, but we wouldn't live there. Then there's Norwich. I'm thinking the farther away from the Sound we get, the less expensive houses will be. And," she lifted her glass of ice water, took a sip, and waved it in the air as she made her point, "as I'm sure you remember, there are loads of little lakes, and there's riverfront, all over the place. So I figure we should drive around in the area sort of half-way between Norwich and Hartford and just get the lay of the land on Sunday. Nick will be in the office all day, so we'll have as much time as we need. How does that sound?"

Lakes... rivers... Christ. I had to pretend to take this shit seriously, because I wasn't prepared for what would happen if I told her how demented it all sounded.

When I was a kid, maybe nine or so, there was a period of time when the four of us would drive around kind of at random, maybe with some newspaper clippings from the real estate section, "just to see." Mom always wanted to live on the water, and she was partial to lakes. I didn't know, during the time we were driving around, whether Dad was really in on it, too, or if he was just humoring her.

Nothing we could have lived in was ever in a price range we could afford, so nothing ever happened. But still, we'd drive. And get lost (which I never minded, really). And walk around the outsides of houses for sale where nobody lived (which I actually really liked doing). We'd inspect the waterfront, kick the supports on any docks we saw, speculate as to how much beach there would be in rainy and dry seasons, or if there was no beach we'd consider how much work it would take to clear out the reeds or trees or whatever. But the houses... It seemed like they were always priced way, way over our heads, or they were not much more than shacks.

Sometimes it was kind of fun as family time, but more often Dylan and I got into an argument, or he'd be pissed because he'd wanted to be with some girl or with his friends instead of driving aimlessly down unmarked country roads that might or might not lead to water, or maybe on a given day Dad just really hadn't been in the mood and Mom had insisted on going.

The point is, it always came to nothing. And now Mom wanted me to go with her. Just the two of us. To find a house. For Dylan. For fucking dead Dylan.

Mom sat across from me, smiling like that would help me see how much fun this was going to be. I decided to say as little as possible. "Okay."

From her enthusiastic response, you'd have thought I'd jumped up and down and waved flags in my excitement.

"Great! I can't go Saturday, what with so many vacation folks checking in. But then, with you out of school right now, I figure we can do some more research during the week. Nick said he could be here all day on Tuesday."

Tuesday... No! That was sailing with Walker. "Um, except I have plans on Tuesday."

That surprised her. "Oh? What plans?"

"I'm meeting a friend. We... um... we're doing some beach combing, photography, that sort of thing."

"Can't you do that another time?"

"Can't there be a different time for driving around? Can't Nick be here Wednesday?"

"We need to get started as soon as possible, Micah, so I can figure out where to apply for work."

"Well... you don't really need me with you all the time, do you?"

She sat back in her chair and glared at me. "Don't tell me you don't care about your brother, either."

I knew that "either" applied to Dad. "Hey, that's not what I said. But you don't need me just to go driving around. If there's something great you want to go back to, that's different." Yeah. Real different. Like, now-someone-needs-to-throw-a-monkey-wrench-into-the-works different. "Um, listen, gotta hit the head. I'll be right back."

In the bathroom I pulled my phone out of my pocket. I couldn't talk to Dad in here without Mom knowing, but I could text him. So I told him I would call him shortly, just to keep him on his leash for a little longer. I waited for his reply: *Call B4 10.* I flushed the toilet, ran the water in the sink, took a few deep breaths, and headed back to the table, thinking maybe I liked Mom better when she was drunk.

I hadn't even sat down again before she started in. "I'm not happy with your not wanting to participate in this, Micah. I thought you'd be delighted. You used to love looking at lakefront houses."

"I never said I didn't want to participate." Thought it, maybe, but I never said it. "And we don't have to decide where to live before you find your job, do we?"

"It's going to be harder to find the house."

She was right about that. We wouldn't find it at all. "Then we could rent for a while, couldn't we?"

Mom crossed her arms over her chest and let out a long breath. "I want your help, Micah. It's as simple as that."

"Okay, but not on Tuesday."

"Wednesday, then."

"Fine." Which still left me committed for however much time on Sunday she could spare, but it was probably better if I had some idea just how crazy she was getting, which meant seeing at least some of what she was doing.

I got away as soon as I could, into the pharmacy parking lot next door again, and called Dad. No surprise, he started frothing as soon as I told him about the house-hunting adventure. But he calmed down again pretty quickly.

"She can look all she wants, Micah. She won't find anything she can afford, and I can't contribute more than I already pay her. If I were you, I'd keep her focused on the house first, like she said. Otherwise, if she gets a job in Hartford or someplace, you'll have to move again, even if she ends up renting something."

"Could she even afford to rent a place big enough?"

"Probably not one with three bedrooms." Silence. Then, "Let me know how it goes, Micah. Has she bought anything else?"

"Not that I know of. Though she said she'd found a bed she wanted to order. I don't think she'll order it until she has someplace to put it."

"Yeah, well, that ain't happenin'. So... how was your sailing adventure?"

How much to tell him? Bare essentials, I decided. "It was fun, actually. My friend really knows what he's doing. We got out as far as Fisher's Island and then turned back."

"What's his first name?"

"Well... Walker, actually. Last name is Donnell."

He was quiet long enough to make me wonder whether he knew I'd deliberately left him with the wrong impression last time we'd talked. Then, "Going again?"

"Yeah. Tuesday."

"You be careful, Micah. And I'm not jut talking about the sailing. Sometimes we get to feeling really dissatisfied with our own lives when we see how much better somebody else has it. Just makes us unhappy."

"It's cool, Dad. Really. I guess if I want a sailboat someday, I'll have to earn it. I'll have to water my own grass. If someone else' grass is greener, maybe that's motivation. For now, I'm just having a little fun for the summer."

For the summer. Or until Walker gets tired of me. Or until he finds out I'm gay.

I nearly asked Dad what it was he'd almost said that day he'd played "Layla" for me, but I chickened out.

Driving around with Mom felt so weird. It was both a lot like when we used to do it, and totally different. We didn't get into any arguments, mostly because I knew better than to contradict her on something that wasn't gonna happen anyway. But it was kind of depressing. With only the two of us in the car, there was none of the banter the four of us used to generate. No teasing, no laughing. Dylan and Dad were both conspicuous in their absence. It didn't help that there was a light drizzle all day. At least Mom let me drive while she navigated, so that was something.

We saw basically the same pattern we used to see: beautiful places way out of our price range, and ramshackle places that needed massive amounts of work. We didn't see the inside of anything, because Mom wanted to decide on an area before she talked to realtors, but we peeked in the windows of a number of the places that were dilapidated enough that nobody lived in them. Mom took lots of notes, and she made me take lots of photos—all for nothing, of course.

For me, not only did it remind me of what I didn't have any more (a family), but also it forced me to withdraw, to turn inside, or risk blurting out something about how crazy this whole thing was. And I worried that maybe Mom was losing it. I just couldn't tell how much of it was a desperate need to believe what this "psychic" had told her, and how much of it meant that she was becoming certifiable.

Sunday night's dinner was take-out Chinese; we didn't have time for anything else, especially since there were a few things at the motel that Mom had to deal with as soon as we got back. I could tell she felt discouraged about what we'd seen.

Reporting to Dad from the parking lot next door sent me into even more of a blue funk, because I'd kind of wanted Dad to suggest that we go someplace together to watch Fourth of July fireworks. And I wanted it to come from him; I didn't want to have to suggest it. But he didn't. I decided he was probably going somewhere with his new lady friend.

I headed toward my room, thinking I'd watch something streaming to get my mind back into its normal working order. The bathroom door was closed, so I figured Mom was in there. Just as I was about to close the door to my room, I heard her voice, obviously startled, talking to herself.

"Oh! My God, what a huge spider."

I heard a smack, which I assumed meant a huge, dead spider. Then I heard a scream. It was the fakest scream you can imagine. I paused, my door half closed. What should I do? For sure, I knew damn well she wanted me—expected me¬—to go rushing in to see if she was all right, to protect her, to help her, to do whatever. In my head, my Dad's words echoed: *Don't you spend your life looking out for her. That's not your job.*

I closed my door all the way without thinking through what the consequences of not pretending to be concerned for Mom's safety might be.

Later, through the closed doors of her room and mine, I heard her crying. That time, I don't think it had anything to do with Dylan's box. Nothing to do with Trapper's missing collar, which I still hoarded. As usual, but maybe for a slightly different reason this time, I felt like shit.

I slept late on Monday, and by the time I got up (eleven) it wasn't raining any more, but it was still overcast. After my shower I was sitting on the end of my bed, still in my underwear and staring unenthusiastically into my bureau drawer (which I can reach from the bed, the room is that small), when my phone text tone went off. Dad, maybe? About going to see fireworks? I fell back and rolled on the mattress to reach the phone, which was on the bedside table.

Walker! It was from Walker!

Feel like dinner and watching fireworks from the water in my dad's boat? No P.

Did I! Mom had said nothing about fireworks, so I figured I was free, and time with Dad was not on the menu.

Sure. I decided "No P" meant Paige wouldn't be there. Good.

Pick u up 3:30.

Here it was. He'd see where I lived. But—what did I have to hide? It wasn't my fault I lived in a motel. The only down side was that Mom would probably want to meet him, but if this friendship (or whatever it was) continued, that was bound to happen, anyway.

I'm in the unit at far left end

Cool

What r u wearing

Jeans polo shirt

Got no polo

There was nothing right away, and then the phone rang.

"Don't worry about clothes, Micah. Do you have another shirt along the lines of what you wore on Friday?"

"I guess. Just don't want to be odd man out. I've never been on a yacht before."

He laughed that fun laugh, no ridicule in it. "You're adorable. Just be neat and clean. Will I get to meet your mom?"

"If she's here. Might be unavoidable."

"I'll charm her. See you!"

We hung up, and I stared at the phone. *You're adorable*. It bounced round and round in my brain. No one—and I mean no one—had ever said anything like that to me. *You're adorable*. What guy says that to another guy? *Is* Walker gay? And how the fuck do I find out?

Mom's car was outside, but she wasn't in our unit. Probably in the unit of some guest with a problem. Quick as I could, I grabbed something to eat that I could take with me, threw that and the camera into my pack, and headed out. I was no longer in a blue funk. I was now flying. I mean, flying! I was going out onto the water in a friggin' YACHT!

Oh, yeah, Dad, the grass is greener. But as long as I get to walk on it sometimes, I can deal.

I barely remember how I got to that rock where I'd thrown nasty words at a gorgeous, wealthy, friendly guy who was fast becoming really important to me, but that's where I went. And it's where I sat, staring out at the water without seeing anything, not looking for Walker's boat, just staring. Staring and fantasizing, remembering that dream where he and I had made out on the floor of his boat, waves gently rocking us. I changed the dream a little, extending the time afterward, picturing us lying side by side, matching our breathing, touching everywhere we could, playing with each others' hands, gazing into each others' faces like moonstruck puppies or something, until I found I had to go a little way into the trees and... you know.

I was home by three, figuring it wouldn't take me long to change. Mom was there, on the phone with someone who needed to come and get something fixed in one of the units. She was trying to get them to come out today, even though it was a holiday, and she was getting angry. I moved as quickly as possible to get to my room.

Pawing through my drawers, I realized that I had pretty much run out of clean T-shirts. In a panic, I pulled all my shirts out of the bureau, laid them on the bed, and shook my head over one option and then another, starting to breathe hard through my nose. I wanted to scream, but I didn't want Mom's attention. Why the fuck hadn't I done this earlier? There would have been time to do some laundry.

I sat on the bed to think, and my eyes went to my closet. I did have a few decent shirts. They were all long-sleeved, but I could roll them up. Frantic now, I dived toward the closet, rejecting three shirts, and finally came up with a simple white cotton shirt. How could you go wrong with that?

Shoes. Should I wear my boat shoes? It seemed like wearing them and not needing to would be better than the other way around.

By the time I was ready to go and tell Mom about my plans, I'd decided that a white shirt with rolled-up sleeves over jeans was a good look for me. I slid Dylan's sunglasses into my shirt pocket so Mom wouldn't see them well enough to identify them, draped my camera strap onto a shoulder, and admired what I could see of my reflected image in the bureau mirror.

Mom must have thought I looked good, too, by the expression on her face when I approached her at the kitchen table. She was off the phone, working at her computer. I didn't see any liquor.

Whatever she thought, she didn't sound happy. "Where are you going, all dressed up?"

I glanced at my watch: three twenty-five. "The friend I'm meeting tomorrow invited me for dinner tonight, and then to go with his family to see fireworks." I decided against mentioning yachts, or even sailboats, and suddenly I wished I had clued Walker in to the lie I'd told Mom about my Tuesday plans.

"What if I want to go see fireworks?"

I shrugged, hoping to play that idea down; I sure as hell didn't want her invited onto the Donnells' yacht. "You hadn't mentioned it before."

Just then I saw a flash of dark red through the front window and heard the sound of a large vehicle's engine shutting off.

"That's him, now. Not sure what time I'll be back, but I have my phone."

"Just a minute!" Her chair scraped as she pushed it away from the table. "Who is this friend?"

I heard a car door slam; I kind of wished he'd just honked. *Think fast, Micah; do you want her to see his brand new Jeep, or would you rather let him see how you live?* I decided on the latter; it would mean fewer questions from Mom this way, and there was no gin on the table. I moved to the door, opened it, and smiled as Walker approached.

"Can I introduce you to my mom?"

"I'd love that." Whether he would love that or not, he sounded convincing. Smiling his wonderful, open, friendly smile, he stepped inside, sunglasses in his left hand. Bless his heart, he didn't look around at all, just went right over to Mom and held his hand out.

"Mom, this is Walker Donnell."

"Mrs. Jaeger," he said, pronouncing it perfectly. "Such a pleasure to meet you! Micah's so proud of what you do here."

I had to stop my jaw from dropping; not only had I not said that, but also I hadn't told him very much about her job.

Her tone told me she wasn't as won over as I'd have liked. "Is he really? How's that?"

"It can't be easy, having to be helpful and friendly to everyone who comes here. I imagine there are some people you'd like to shove bodily into their suitcases and send home in the back of a bumpy delivery truck."

She laughed. She actually laughed. "You have no idea."

"Anyway, Micah's amazed at how well you handle things. And I want to thank you for letting him come with my family this evening. We'll have him home before too late." He turned to me. "You have your phone with you, right? So your mom can call if she gets worried." He turned his smile back toward Mom. "Thanks again."

He turned toward the door and I followed, not daring to sneak even one glance at Mom, who said nothing more. Neither of us said anything either, until we were in the Jeep, doors shut, engine on, air conditioning humming, and pulling out onto the highway.

"Do you do that a lot?" I asked, thinking I'd just seen yet another side of Walker I hadn't known existed. Not that I knew him super well, but what I'd just witnessed was almost another personality. It would be the third one, now.

"Do what?"

I laughed, partly from a heady feeling of escape, partly to let him know I was teasing him. "Lie through your teeth to your friends' mothers."

"It wasn't a terrible lie. You'll notice I didn't actually say that you'd told me anything."

"But you said... wait...."

"How late can you stay out?"

"After that exhibition, till next Sunday."

We both laughed. After a minute or so of nothing but driving sounds, he said, "I'm glad you brought your camera."

"Oh? Want me to shoot something?"

"My dad wants to chat with you about what you've done with it."

My brain bounced back and forth between the intimidating prospect of talking with Mr. Donnell about anything, and the implication that Walker and his father had talked about me. All I could say was, "Right. I remember he has a camera like mine."

"Like yours was, before you enhanced it."

We didn't talk much for the rest of the ride, and I took a minute to text Dad that I was out with friends and might not be able to reach him again before nine.

When Walker pulled the Jeep into a paved spot on one side of his garage, he didn't turn the engine off right away. He turned his face toward me, and I glanced at him.

"Just want you to know," he said, "you look really great." He didn't smile. I allowed myself to believe that a smile would have been just his way of referring to our phone conversation. But no smile? That was serious. That meant he really liked the way I looked. And it meant that it mattered.

Inside, Mrs. Donnell was at the kitchen island, packing things. She looked up as we came in.

"Walker, the caterers are a little late, so we're not leaving quite on time. Shouldn't be long, though." To me she said, "Hello, Micah. Would you like something to drink?"

Before I could say no, thanks, Walker said, "I think we'll go out to the point and wait there. Where's Dad?"

"On the boat, getting everything ship-shape." She grinned. "Or maybe just hanging out, enjoying his dominion until we descend upon him."

I liked these people. I really liked these people. Except for Paige.

Walker led the way past the pool, over the tough, sun-resistant grass and down a gentle slope toward the water, to a spot where there were taller seagrasses and a light coating of sand, high over the rocks at the water's edge. He sat down, and I had to stop myself from sitting as close to him as I wanted to. I set my camera down carefully, and both of us, knees up and arms wrapped around our legs, stared out over the water to the south.

There was a light breeze, and the clouds had moved aside just enough to let some of the late afternoon sunshine find us. The way the seagrasses tickled my forearms was kind of mesmerizing. I didn't dare look at Walker for fear that I'd want to kiss him so badly that I wouldn't be able to stop myself. Instead I marveled at what it would be like to call this view your own, and behind you to have a beautiful house filled, I was sure, with more luxuries than I had seen so far.

After about five minutes of silence, though, I couldn't stand it. Still gazing across the water, I said, "You didn't say anything to my mom about going out on the boat."

He plucked a grass stem and toyed with the seed head that had started to form. "I wasn't sure how much you'd told her. You didn't seem like you wanted me to see where you live, after sailing on Friday, so I decided you might not have told her any more than you had to about me."

"You were right. I should have warned you. But it worked out."

"Are you going to tell her?"

"About the boats? Probably not."

"Why not?"

Good question, to which I gave him a not very good answer. "Not sure. Maybe I'm just not ready to have her ask a whole bunch of questions." I wanted him off of this subject. "So, where's Paige, if she's not coming out on the boat?"

"With her own friend, on her friend's boat."

"I guess this is a thing, then—people who have boats, going out onto the water to watch the fireworks?"

"It is, yes."

There was something odd about Walker, now. He answered my questions, he was talking, but something had come between us that made me uncomfortable. But it had been his idea for me come tonight, his idea to wait out here alone, his idea for everything. Had I done something wrong? I hunkered down against my bent legs, waiting it out for want of a better plan.

Walker turned toward me rather suddenly. "Do you know anyone who's gay?"

I nearly fell over sideways, my arms slipped off my legs that fast. "Um... maybe. Why?"

"How do you think someone knows? That they're gay, I mean."

"Well... Jesus, I don't know. I guess they're attracted to the wrong people." Fuck! What did I just say? "I mean, you know, people they aren't supposed to be attracted to."

He was quiet for so long I nearly died. Then, "That seems like kind of a negative way to see things." I couldn't tell if he was pissed or what, but it wasn't a good feeling.

"Look, that's not quite what I meant. Because, you know, I'm expected to be attracted to girls. But if I'm not, if I'm attracted to boys, that's not what I'm supposed to do."

"By whom?"

Whom? Who says that? Must come from all that homeschooling. Never mind. "By, like, parents, and stuff. Friends. Teachers. Look, don't tell me you don't know what I'm talking about."

"If you were gay, whom would you tell?"

I reclaimed my knees with my arms and looked back out over the water. "Not sure I'd tell anyone."

"Okay, but what if you liked someone? Would you tell them?"

I gave myself just enough time to think about why he was asking all these questions. If I told him about me now, and if he didn't want to hear it, that would ruin the whole evening. He couldn't exactly un-invite me at this point, but things would be way awkward the whole time, stuck on that boat. But he knew that as well as I did. So maybe that would mean he'd be okay if he knew the truth. Maybe he was asking because he kind of already suspected. Though the idea that he might have figured it out made my stomach flip; how would he do that? What might have given me away?

I decided to take at least a little risk. Without changing my position, partly for the protection hugging my knees gave me, and partly because I didn't quite dare look at him, I said, "I'd tell you."

His turn to think for a minute. Then, "Are you saying you're not gay?"

Now I looked at him. "Do you think I am? Is that why you're asking?" My eyes got dry staring into his, but I didn't want to blink.

"Maybe I'm trying to tell you that I am."

I stopped breathing. But I didn't drop my eyes. He leaned toward me slowly, giving me plenty of time to pull away. I didn't.

God, but his lips felt so soft! It didn't last long. And it lasted forever. And during that forever, my brain reeled. *I'm kissing a guy! A guy is kissing me! I never thought this would happen! Am I sure I want this to happen? What happens next?*

The kiss ended, but we didn't pull very far away from each other. His voice faint but heavy with meaning, Walker asked, "Was that an okay thing to do?"

Yes! No! I don't know! Not true; I *did* know. I started to reach for his face, to pull it close to mine again, to make the next kiss last longer than forever, and then his phone rang. I told myself that the reason he pulled away from me so sharply was because of the phone, because even though no one in the house could see us unless they were upstairs, he probably felt like someone was watching. But I worried that it was because he regretted what had happened, and because he was afraid of what might have been about to happen.

"K. Be right there," he told the phone, and without looking at me he shoved it back into a pocket. "The caterers are here. Mom wants us to help carry things to the boat."

He stood, so I did, too, and followed him as he walked quickly back across that tough grass, past the pool and into the kitchen, my mind going six ways from Sunday. Had a guy—not just any guy, but Walker, the guy who comes into my dreams and... well... makes me come—*just kissed me?* And was he or was he not now sort of pretending that nothing had happened? Pretending that the earth hadn't moved, that the sea hadn't changed its course, that everything was the same as it had been before?

Christ!

But all I could do was set my camera into one of the canvas bags that Mrs. Donnell handed me as she smiled broadly, looking quite happy in the work of getting ready for an evening cruise on her husband's yacht.

I wasn't just out of my element. I was out of my world. Out of my universe. Off course, trapped in the doldrums. I'd looked that up; it's when you're sailing and you end up someplace where the winds die, and you can't move in any direction at all. That's where I was. Paralyzed.

Chapter Six

As soon as we stepped on board, Walker said, "Come on up to the bridge. It's the best place to be as we get underway." He didn't stop climbing stairs until we were at the top of the boat, where the steering wheel was (or whatever you call that on a yacht).

I felt really weird. Walker seemed to have forgotten what had happened out on the point of land where, in that beautiful and private setting, he had kissed me. And it seemed he also expected me to act as though it hadn't happened. I didn't know how I was gonna do that. But, for now, I had to try.

At the first opportunity after introductions, curious about where all the money to pay for this luxury came from, I asked Walker quietly, "What do your folks do for a living?"

"Dad's a venture capitalist. Mom helps with that, and she also does illustrations for children's books."

Mr. Donnell didn't look much like I'd expected him to: wavy, light brown hair, a little on the long side; horn rim glasses, though the shape seemed kind of stylish; and, like Walker, slight and not very tall. His face wasn't ruddy or especially crinkled, not like the guy who'd accosted me beside *First Million* at Sailaway.

Evidently the caterers had already been up here. There was a selection of different kinds of foods, beer for Mr. Donnell (there was already a can of it beside him), white wine for Mrs. Donnell (who held a glass of it), and Coke, ginger ale, and bottled water for whoever wanted that.

I let myself fall into one of the upholstered seats, trying to get myself to believe that I was really on a yacht, and that real people actually lived like this. But Walker was standing, watching the shoreline as we pulled away and headed west. I got up and stood beside him, leaning on the railing or whatever it's called, loving the way the air was moving across my face, ruffling my hair, making my shirt catch wind almost like one of the sails on *Dare Ya*.

Mrs. Donnell came to stand on the other side of me from Walker. "Do you go to school in Stonington, Micah?"

"Yes, ma'am." At first I thought she must already have known this, but then I remembered that Walker had a tutor.

"Do you think you'll go on to college?"

"I hope so. Nothing fancy, but I want to study photography."

"An artist! Did Walker tell you what I do?"

"About the children's books? Yes, ma'am."

"Micah," Mr. Donnell's voice cut above the wind and the motor. I glanced at him; he was indicating the seat beside him at the helm, or whatever it's called. "Talk to me about that camera of yours."

I held it up so he could see it while he steered the boat, and gave him a brief description of what I'd done to construct the housing.

"I see," he said, stealing glances at it. "So the housing keeps it open and protected. Much more stable too, isn't it?"

"Yeah. And the tripod mount on the bottom works really well."

"Walker tells me you like unusual subjects." He didn't say *Like dead birds*, but he didn't really have to.

"Oh… well, I mean, yeah."

"Any photographers who inspire you?"

"I saw this special on Vivian Maier, that weird woman who took, like, thousands of shots of New York City. Mostly of people, actually, in the nineteen-forties and fifties, or around then, anyway. I really liked some of the ones where she included something that makes you look twice. Like, there's one where she's standing on the sidewalk facing a window that has a shade pulled down, so the glass reflects the cars outside. Only the shade isn't pulled all the way down, and you can see these rows of cans inside on the windowsill—paint cans, maybe? And right in the middle of the row of cans are these two feet, in leather shoes, and the bottoms of a guy's cuffed trousers. The rest of him is behind the shade. So she shot a bunch of really ordinary stuff, but the way she captured it all together in one photograph was unbelievable."

I stopped suddenly, keenly aware that I'd babbled on, equally keenly aware that both Mrs. Donnell and Walker were listening. At first I felt really self-conscious. But that faded fast, and I kind of got into having all these privileged people hang on my every word.

Plus, Mr. Donnell encouraged me. "Do you look for that kind of shot, yourself?"

I shrugged. "It's harder to find that kind of combination of things around here. In the city, there are buildings and windows and angles and cars, all kinds of stuff to work with. So around here I do things like double-expose a dead bird onto a shot of clear water so you can't tell right away that the bird is dead. It might be swimming."

Mr. Donnell looked at me with an expression that made me feel really good, kind of like he was impressed. Then he laughed. "That's very creative, Micah. A little grim, but very creative."

"Sometimes I go into the Barn Island Marsh and shoot there." It was where I'd been the first time I'd seen Walker, but I didn't want to mention that. Anyway, I felt it was his turn. "What sorts of things do you shoot?"

He shook his head. "I take snapshots a lot. Family, friends, boats. I like seascapes, especially when there are unusual or striking cloud formations. An approaching storm often makes me reach for a camera before I think, 'Oops, better get back to shore before this thing breaks.' So I'm not sure I'd use the more serious word 'photographs' to refer to what I shoot."

"Do you have any other cameras?"

"Not that I use very often. I have a Canon digital SLR when I want to tell myself I'm doing something serious." He laughed, almost like he was laughing at himself. I really liked that. As much as I admired people who could laugh at themselves, I'd never been able to do it. But then, he'd made such a place for himself in the world that he could afford to make fun of himself.

"Food, anyone?" Mrs. Donnell's voice rose above the breeze.

I looked toward her and saw one of the caterers, holding out a tray with all kinds of things on it. Mrs. Donnell handed me a small plate, and I took a few things: a couple of scallops wrapped in bacon; some tiny triangles of white bread with what I think was thin-sliced raw tuna and soft little dark green pods; and little square, white platforms with something yellow swirled onto them and sprinkled with something powdery and red, which turned out to be egg whites under mashed yolks with mayonnaise, and paprika, I'd guess.

"Thanks," I said to the guy, even though I wasn't sure whether you're supposed to thank caterers. It just seemed polite. Plus he was really good-looking.

As Mr. Donnell was selecting some things, I asked him, "Don't you like wine?"

"Love it. But the beer can is less likely to spill. Plus, there's less alcohol in beer, and I'm driving. Same alcohol blood level rules apply on the water as on the road." He grinned at me in a way that made me feel like an insider. Couldn't have said why.

We were quite a distance from shore by now, though I could still make things out. Mostly we headed west, and I was glad of my sunglasses. Dylan's sunglasses.

Walker and I leaned on the railing, facing the shore, while he pointed out landmarks. I asked, "Will we see Paige's boat?"

He shook his head. "Doubt it. And, as she'd say, not if she sees us first."

Behind me, I was aware that Mrs. Donnell had moved over to sit beside her husband in the seat I'd been in earlier. They started up a quiet conversation that I couldn't really hear, though it sounded to me like she was telling Mr. Donnell about something that had happened in church yesterday, as though he hadn't been there. It was an opportunity to say something to Walker that his parents wouldn't hear. And I knew just what I wanted to say. I wanted him to admit he'd kissed me. I wanted to know what it meant. And I wanted to know if it would happen again.

I didn't say it. Walker kept pointing things out, and then there would be a little silence until the next landmark came into view. But then the boat took a hard left turn, increased speed, and we headed farther from shore.

Walker said, "It'll be a while before there are fireworks any place. Hope you don't mind a bit of a ride first."

Now, I thought; *now's the time to say something*. I opened my mouth, but before I could speak, Walker asked, "Would you like a tour of the boat?"

"I—well, sure. Yeah."

It was hard to take in all the boat's features, what with wondering whether Walker would touch me, take my hand, kiss me—or whether I would do any of those things to him. But I wasn't exactly feeling confident enough to take any initiative. It also didn't help that the areas "below decks" all had different names from what they would have had in a house, and I felt like I had to pay attention. There was the galley, which looked like an incredibly efficient kitchen, where the caterers were busy preparing more food; the bathrooms (two, with showers) were called heads; and the bedrooms (three) were staterooms. My mom, plus Dylan, plus me—we could probably have lived together on this boat. I was tempted to take a few shots just to prove to myself later that I was actually here, but I was afraid that would be pretty lame.

We were in the stateroom in the lowest part of the boat when Walker turned toward me and asked, "Are you okay with what I did earlier?"

Amazed at my own bravery, I said, "More than okay, yeah. Are you going to do it again?" I had meant it to be teasing, expecting—well, it's obvious what I was expecting. Hoping. But instead, Walker sat down on some kind of shelf that was built into the side of the boat.

"I'm not sure I should."

I stood there like an idiot, feeling almost like he was having me on. "You're not sure you should? Why *shouldn't* you?"

His scowl looked like it came from pain rather than anything else, but I wasn't ready to believe it.

"I—I don't know—I'm not sure how to tell you." He looked down at his hands, wringing themselves into knots. "I'm sorry."

I picked up on the only part of that I could make sense out of. "Sorry?"

He didn't look up. "That I kissed you."

"What? Why?"

His eyes hit my face like he'd thrown something at me. "I don't want to lead you on. I like you, Micah. I like you a lot."

My brain tied itself into a tangle trying to find a response that didn't sound like a little kid pleading for something he knew he wasn't going to get. What came out was, "Are you saying that you don't know if you're gay?"

"Do you?"

"Yes." No hesitation. "I am."

"How can you be sure?"

"Because I really, really want to kiss you again." I decided to take a risk. "And I think you want me to."

He didn't move, but I did. I wrapped a hand around one of his wrists and coaxed his hands apart, pulled him to his feet, and with my other hand I drew his face toward mine. At first it was sweet. At first it was all about the softness of our lips, the warmth of each others' bodies. But then the kisses grew more intense, and suddenly our mouths were open, and it wasn't just lips that were soft and moist.

I was right, a voice in my head told me. *This is something both of us want.*

We fell onto the bed, on our sides and facing each other, and I ran my hand down his arm, then over the swell of his ass, and then down his thigh. I didn't really know what I was doing, but this seemed kind of natural and easy. We were both breathing hard, the kisses quick and frantic. My dick was hard and ready, and maybe because I was hoping he'd reach for mine, I reached for his.

There was nothing there. Or, almost nothing. Maybe the smallest dick *ever*.

My eyes flew wide open, Walker rolled away from me toward the wall, I moved away from him and stood quickly, and there was a hole in the universe so big I nearly fell into it.

When I could form thoughts, my brain repeated what Walker had said a few minutes ago. He didn't know how to tell me....

At this point, my brain cramped. I felt it. It really happened. I couldn't form thoughts. Words bounced around inside my head at random: girl; boy; gay; transgender; and, finally, weird.

No. That's not quite true. There was another word hiding behind all of that. The word was "freak." I tried to ignore it. That's a mean word, a horrible word, and this was *Walker*.

I got to my feet and shook myself. I hated that word, hated that it had even been in my head.

Walker hadn't moved. My lungs caught air for the first time since the gasp I'd taken when my hand had landed on the spot I'd reached for, the spot I was sure I'd recognize as very much like my own. An image came to me: Walker in *Dare Ya*, thighs pressed against the side of the boat as he faced Fisher's Island, manipulating himself somehow so that he could piss over the side of the boat. No wonder that posture hadn't made sense to me.

But what the fuck did this mean? He was a boy, I was sure of it. So he wasn't very tall, but neither were his parents. Walker's voice was lower than any girl's I'd ever heard. His hair was a little long, but not so long as to make him look like a girl. His bedroom was all boy, despite the gorgeous colors in it. His mother would probably not have let us go up to that room if she'd thought of Walker as a girl.

I strained my brain back to that day; had anyone—his mother or Paige—referred to him using a male pronoun? I couldn't remember.

He had to be a boy. He *had* to. So—what the fuck?

Walker still hadn't moved. He was in pain; I could believe it now. And it was pain that I had caused. Why the fuck did I have to go and grab at him? What had I done? I felt so guilty, like I'd done something horrible.

But—damn it, Walker wasn't the only one who could get hurt. I'd never kissed a guy before. No guy had ever kissed me. I had a lot invested, here. *Was* he leading me on?

I stood there, watching him, waiting for him to say something—anything—that would help me understand what had just happened. Anything that would help me understand him.

But he was silent.

I figured I was gonna have to make the next move, but almost nothing helpful came into my head. *Something you wanna tell me?* sounded mean, and that's not what I was going for. I rejected a few other options and finally came up with this: "Are you okay?"

Slowly, Walker unfolded his body, wiped a hand across his face, and sat on the end of the bed, head hanging. He said nothing. He looked... ashamed? This was not the same guy who had spoken to my mother earlier today with an easy confidence practically oozing out of him. I had to figure this out.

"Look, Walker, you said you didn't want to lead me on. Lead me on how?"

He took a shaky breath and raised his head, but he didn't look at me. "Isn't it obvious?"

My fingers dug into my hairline as though massaging the outside of my head would help my brain. I didn't know what to say. And saying nothing was probably the right approach, because Walker, still staring at empty space, spoke again.

"There's this thing. This condition. It's called intersex. You've probably never heard of it."

"Um..." Intersex... intersex... It bounced around the back of my brain in the same general area as things I'd heard about in one classroom or another, like the number phi and the phrase "The Sun King." Well, maybe not quite the same area, because it had to do with sex, but the common area was classroom lessons. But what on earth did "inter" have to do with sex? *Think, dammit!*

I managed to say, "I think they said something about it in sex ed at school. I just... I don't quite...." My voice trailed off, along with any brain activity.

Walker gave me an odd look, somewhere between *Just how stupid are you?* and *Fine, I'll just tell you and put you out of your misery.* "I could go into a whole lot of shit about chromosomes and how it affects different people differently. I could tell you what they think the incidence is in the human population at large. But I kind of think you don't wanna know any of that."

He shifted his position, sitting taller now, his posture almost challenging. "For your purposes, if you're gay, and if you're interested in me, it means I have a really tiny dick that's not good for much."

My mouth opened and closed a few times. Finally, "I don't know what that means. Beyond the obvious, that is."

"It means I have to get testosterone injections so that I'll at least look and sound like a guy. It means I was fabulously lucky that the surgery they had to do on me down there didn't make me non-functional. But it also means that I have a micropenis that *I* can take advantage of, but nobody else can." Despite his challenging tone, he blushed a bright pink. I couldn't tell whether he was angry or embarrassed. Maybe both.

I shook my head, not in denial but in confusion. "Micro," I echoed, unable to bring myself to add the rest of the term.

Now came the anger. "It's tiny, okay? I have a tiny dick. But what I do have was just as hard as yours a few minutes ago."

So the feeling was there. He had wanted me. "So, are you gay, or what?"

"I don't know." Was he about to cry? "I mean, I wanted to kiss you earlier. Out on the point. And I wanted to kiss you just now. I think about you all the time. I dream about you. I—"

"You dream about me?" He nodded. "I dream about *you.*" We stared at each other a little wildly. "When you dream of me, what happens? I mean, do you come?"

"Sure. But it's just cum. There's nothing in it. I mean, it wouldn't get a girl pregnant."

"No worries. I'm not a girl."

He half smiled, and the whole room lightened, I swear. But then it darkened again. "But, see, I don't know if I'm gay, because sometimes I don't really feel like a guy."

My mind wouldn't focus on that, so I ignored it. "Well... but you have a dick, right? Or, most of one?"

It was the wrong thing to say, even if it was a reasonable question at that point, because tears welled up in his eyes. "Rub it in. Go ahead."

"No! No, what I mean is—fuck. I don't know what I mean."

His voice low and harsh, he said, "What you mean is I'm a freak of nature."

Freak. The very word that had occurred to me. Twice. Otherwise maybe I could have denied it. "I think what I mean is that if you—Jesus. I don't know how to say it without sounding horrible."

"Just say it."

I took a deep breath and let it out slowly. "I'm not saying you're a freak, okay? You're just who you are. You're saying you might not know whether you're gay because you might not know whether you're a guy. But from my point of view, you're a guy, even if—you know, even if you're small."

We both let that hang in the air for a minute, during which my mind bounced around trying to land on something specific. This is what it came up with. "You said that you were hard when—you know. So that means you liked having another guy kiss you. So you're gay."

"In case you failed sex ed, girls get hard, too."

I was ready for that. "Girls have boobs."

"How do I know the testosterone hasn't pushed me in the wrong direction? How do I know I wasn't supposed to be a girl?"

I wasn't ready for that. And I was beginning to wonder if this whole thing had been a mistake. Our eyes locked, as though this idea was at the heart of the matter. Then, suddenly, I realized what *was* at the heart of the matter.

"Let me ask you this. Do you *want* to be a guy?"

"Yes." So fast. That came out of him like a bullet.

"Okay, then."

His voice quiet, he said, "Even so, what good is that?" He raised his arms and dropped them. "Would you want to be with a freak like me?" It wasn't a question; the answer "No" was an assumption.

My voice spoke before I had time to think. "I don't know yet. But I'm willing to figure it out."

That got his attention. Hell; it got mine, too.

And then something else got my attention.

"Boys?" It was Mrs. Donnell's voice.

Boys.... Were we both boys?

Walker jumped up and went to the door, adjusting his clothes. "Down here, Mom."

"Come on up. Your father's attracted some friends."

"K." To me, he said, "Jeez. I didn't even hear the engines stop. Anyway, what she's saying is Dad's been chumming. Let's go see what he's got." And just like that, we were back to "nothing happened."

Following Walker up the first flight of stairs, terrified because I already knew what it meant, I said, "Chumming?"

"For sharks. He's crazy for sharks. And they especially like to feed in the morning and the evening."

My foot landed wrong on the next step, and I slipped, hitting my knee painfully on the step above.

"Micah? You okay?"

"Yeah. You go on. I'll be right there."

I limped my way into the nearest bathroom and sat on the closed toilet. Rubbing my knee almost kept me from focusing on the idea that in this lowest level of the boat, there wasn't a whole lot of material between me and the sharks. Which led me to decide I'd rather be up with the others, even if things between Walker and me were unresolved. Unresolved... understatement.

I expected everyone to be up in the top level. Bridge. Whatever. But they were only one level up, in the back of the boat and not more than a couple of feet above the water, leaning over the edge to watch the monsters. I stopped just inside the door that opened onto this small deck, trying not to shake.

Walker saw me and held my camera toward me. "Here. I fetched it for you. I figured you'd want to shoot some of these."

As I took the camera from Walker, I nearly squeaked, "Some of these?" Ye gods; how many were out there?

Mr. Donnell grinned at me, as though any self-respecting boy would be thrilled at his news. "We have at least five sand tigers out here. A couple of them look fully grown."

I hung onto the side of the doorway. "Fully grown? How big is that?"

"Maybe ten feet. Quite large." He turned back to the sharks.

Quite large... and the one that had taken a piece of my leg had been only about three feet. *Don't be a wuss, Micah.* I could hear my dad's voice. So, with my legs (what I had left of them) shaking so badly I thought I might fall with the rolling of the boat, I moved forward, nearly collapsing against the side. I think the only reason I didn't collapse was because of not wanting to damage my camera.

I peeked into the water, but I didn't see anything. Then Mr. Donnell picked up a bucket full of a disgusting mess and dumped it overboard.

A sudden rush of something massive and gray with its mouth open, nasty teeth snapping only a few feet from me, sent me flying backward. And I fell.

They all laughed. It was in fun—humor, not ridicule—but it didn't matter. I couldn't catch my breath.

Mrs. Donnell stopped laughing. "Micah? Are you all right?" She moved over and kneeled at my right side just as my lungs managed to snatch some air in a kind of gasping pant. I wanted to nod. I wanted her to go away and not advertise my panic. Too late.

Walker was on the other side of me from his mother, and he lifted my camera off the floor. Deck. Whatever. "Micah? What's wrong?"

I still couldn't speak, but I managed to move along the deck until I could lean up against the wall beside the doorway. I waved a hand in front of my face, trying to let everyone know not to worry about me, but it didn't work. Even Mr. Donnell, still over near the edge, had turned to look at me.

Mrs. Donnell had me bring my knees up and lean my arms on them, head down. "Take a slow, deep breath, Micah." It shook my whole body. "Do it again. Slowly. And again." Her voice was even, gentle, unhurried, and after a few more deep breaths I could sit up and lean my head back.

"What happened?" Walker wanted to know.

I turned my face toward him, took one more breath, and pulled the left leg of my jeans up. It made no sense, but the scar was burning, throbbing even. I watched as Walker's eyes took it in.

"Holy shit."

"Walker! Language."

"Sorry, Mom. But look at this. Half of the calf is gone." He reached a hand toward it, and my whole body cringed away from him.

Mrs. Donnell moved around to my left so she could see. "Oh, Micah. How old were you?" She knew what had happened, I could tell.

I had to cough before I could speak. "Twelve."

From his spot where he could look at the sharks, Mr. Donnell called, "What kind of shark was it?"

Mrs. Donnell spoke before I could. "James! The boy's terrified."

I coughed again. I actually preferred Mr. Donnell's pragmatic question to being fussed over. "Young black tip. I still have a tooth it left in me."

Walker said, "You told me you weren't afraid of the water."

"I'm not afraid of the water. I'm afraid of sharks." I started to get up, but I needed Walker's help. "But I don't want to be. Are they still there?"

Mr. Donnell nodded. "They are. Come on over."

Walker handed me my camera, he and Mrs. Donnell moved away to give me some space, and I managed to get myself to the edge of the boat.

And there they were, three of them, circling the mess in the water. Mr. Donnell's steady voice walked me through what I was seeing.

"On most sharks, the front dorsal fin is larger than the back one. You can see that on these sharks, both dorsal fins are about the same size. Given that, and the size, and the fact that sand tiger sharks are native in the Sound, we know that's what they are."

He waited while I watched for a minute and wondered why Shark Week hadn't featured sand tigers. Maybe they weren't as interesting as great whites, or maybe there aren't enough other sharks in the Sound to warrant featuring this area in a show.

Mr. Donnell interrupted my thoughts. "Another difference between sand tigers and many other sharks is that their teeth are always visible. So they look pretty ferocious, even when their mouths aren't wide open."

As if on queue, one of them lifted its head above the water just enough to slurp in some of the bloody goo. I clenched the edge of the boat, but I didn't panic. Or, not as much as before. When the shark was underwater again, I tried to get my camera ready to shoot, but my hands shook too much.

Mr. Donnel said, "If you crouch down a little and lean the camera on the boat, that will steady it."

I knew that. The problem was it would bring me that much closer to those snapping jaws. Defying the screaming in my head, I positioned myself as he'd suggested. I had to monitor the rocking of the boat and try to shoot at the top or the bottom of a surge, but I managed to get several shots of dorsal fins, sometimes two sets at once. And the next time those teeth appeared above water I was ready, and I snapped the shot. After that, I had to back up again and lean on the wall, but it felt so fucking great to know what I'd done. Those sharks—almost twice as long as I was tall— hadn't been any more than six feet from me.

But I was still shaken. Shaking, even, if only a little by this time.

Walker said, "Let's go up a level. We can still see them from there."

I followed him up to a kind of lounge area, also in the back of the boat, where there were white wicker chairs with blue and white striped cushions. Setting my camera safely on the carpeted floor, I allowed myself to sink against the pillows in a chair that faced the sea, and I closed my eyes. I didn't need to see any more sharks.

Walker sat in the chair next to me. He waited a respectable amount of time and then said, "That was really brave. To stand there and shoot them, I mean."

I didn't know what to say in acknowledgement, so I just sat there. Maybe three minutes later, he asked if I would tell him what had happened.

So, eyes fixed on the horizon, I told him the story. I told him about standing in the water in the evening—which I now knew to be a dangerous time to be in the ocean. I told him about the sudden, massive jolt and the shock and the pain and the warm blood. And I told him about Trapper. What Trapper had done. How Trapper had saved me, and how Dylan had carried me to safety. What I didn't say, but what was huge in my thoughts, was that both Dylan and Trapper were now dead. And as I finished, I realized that my eyes felt hot, and tears were about to make their way down my cheeks.

In the quiet that followed, with only the sounds of water lapping gently against the boat, the rolling felt comforting. A few minutes later, I heard the sounds of the engine (engines?) starting up, and we moved slowly away from that spot, that unmarked place in the universe where I'd faced my demons and even captured them to prove it.

I heaved a long sigh, and then I felt Walker take my hand in his. We sat there like that, not speaking, flying through space as the speed of the boat increased and the light faded, and it felt like we could go on like that for a long, long time before I'd want anything else.

We saw lots of fireworks. Somehow I can barely remember them. What I remember is standing there with Walker, leaning on the side of whatever part of the boat we were on at the moment, so close that I felt the warmth of his body, so close that I kept getting these little shivers whenever there was the slightest touch between us. I remember not looking at him directly, and knowing that he was not looking at me directly, and knowing that we were so focused on each other that no looking was necessary; looking might even have taken away some of the magic.

It took me a long time to get to sleep that night, and not because I was afraid I'd dream of sharks. I won't say that those few minutes of facing them down (through the safety of my camera lens) "cured" me, or anything, even though it felt major. But that wasn't what kept me awake.

I was thinking about Walker. I was wondering what it would be like to be a guy and go through life with nothing more for equipment than he'd been given. He'd said they were giving him testosterone. And that was another thing. To be a guy, to know you're a guy, and to have to take male hormones anyway....

And what would it say about me if this turns into something? I mean, if I'm gay, then I want a guy. Right? So what would it say about me to be with a guy who doesn't have what a guy should have? Does that throw shade on who I am as a gay guy?

I reached down to find my own equipment, feeling around more than getting off, testing the size, the heft, the texture. Walker couldn't do that. Or, it wouldn't be anywhere near the same. Maybe one day I'd actually see what he does have, but what must it be like for him to feel himself? Did he and I feel the same things?

I'd never felt anything like pride in my dick and balls; they'd always seemed pretty normal to me, based on what I'd seen on other guys. Not too big, not too small, everything in the right place. But what would it be like to be *ashamed* of what I had? Hey—is that why he didn't go to regular school?

Man. I wouldn't give up what I was born with for all of the Donnells' money, boats included. This realization gave me a feeling of relief—that I was normal, and that money couldn't buy everything.

But relief turned into something else, something I felt about Walker, for Walker. It was a kind of tenderness. It wasn't pity, and it wasn't sympathy. It was actually kind of a sweet feeling, like wanting to let him know I thought he was perfect just like he was.

But was Walker gay? He'd wanted me as much as I'd wanted him. I was sure of that.

And what, if anything, did I want to do about that? I mean, we were all of seventeen. Well, he was. I was, almost. So it wasn't like we were headed for marriage or anything. But what would it be like to—you know—be with him? Did I like him enough that whatever we could (or couldn't) do would be enough for me?

Suddenly it occurred to me that Walker might just be awake, thinking about all this, too, wondering whether my "I don't know yet" might really lead to something for us. I sat up and reached for my phone, staring at the text screen. If I texted him now, it would almost certainly encourage him. Did I want to do that? Would it be leading *him* on?

I leaned my back against the wall and closed my eyes, one hand massaging my balls, and I thought about Walker. Pictured Walker. That curly blond mop. Those gorgeous blue eyes. That smile.... It took about one-point-five seconds for my dick to spring into action-ready formation. Setting the phone down, I gave my mind permission to focus on Walker and my dick permission to do whatever it wanted to do. A few minutes of hard breathing and some light clean-up later, I picked up the phone again and texted him.

U ok?

It took maybe thirty seconds for him to reply.

Y. U?

No sharks here

LOL! Um... thinking about you alot

Me too, you

Still up for sailing tomorrow?

I took a deep breath. *Sure just want to be with you*

There was just enough digital silence for me start to get nervous before I saw:

Me too will text in am

K. Night

Sweet dreams

And just like that, I had a boyfriend. At least, that's kind of what it felt like. But I wasn't sure. I'd never had a boyfriend or a girlfriend. Now, if I had a boyfriend, I had a boyfriend with a micropenis. How special was that?

It took me less than a minute of searching the web to see what a micropenis would look like. The images were... well, kind of funny looking, but also they were cute. I fell asleep thinking up ways to make Walker's hard.

Maybe I wasn't afraid of dreaming about sharks, but I had a nightmare anyway. I was in *Dare Ya*. Walker must have been there, but I didn't see him in the dream. I looked down at the bottom of the boat for some reason—one of those things that make sense in the dream and not otherwise—and that part of the boat disappeared. I went crashing into the water, even though crashing isn't usually associated with going underwater, but that's what it felt like. There were bubbles all around me, and although it makes no sense, I saw my own hair as it moved with that soft, wavy motion that happens under water. My arms and legs thrashed as I tried to get back to the boat, which had completely disappeared. Something from below grabbed me and I started to scream. But it turned out to be a person, not a shark.

Dylan.

He swam upward, holding me, until we were safe on some kind of floating raft. But when he set me down, he wasn't Dylan any more. He was Mr. Donnell.

"Micah! Sweetie, wake up!"

There were arms around me, but they were my mother's.

"You're having a bad dream, that's all."

I wasn't crying, but there was water all over my face, just as though I'd been in the sea. My heart pounded in my ears so loud I almost couldn't hear Mom talking to me. She wiped my face and kissed my forehead.

"There, babe. All better now?"

The light coming through the window barely reflected in her eyes. I looked right into them and said, "Dylan. He's gone, Mom. He's dead."

.

Chapter Seven

My revelation about Dylan's mortal state did not go over well. Mom barely spoke to me over breakfast. Sensing her mood, I busied myself poking around on my phone, killing time until Walker's text arrived. It wasn't until nearly ten that I finally saw it, and it wasn't good news.

Not sure things will work out today after all maybe tomorrow?

My heart sank, but I tried to seem casual. *What's up?*

There was a long pause before his next entry. *Cousin arrived last night. Yuck*

Cousin... cousin... He'd said something about a cousin, and it was another last name/first name thing... Oh yeah. *Cameron?*

The same.

Why yuck

Him. I hate him

An image of Walker's face, of Walker's whole body, shrinking in the presence of Paige hit me. Did Cameron affect him the same way?

Sounds like you need me then

?

Two against one if I'm there. Still sailing?

He'll make me.

Okay, now I was sure. *How soon can you come by? Or should I bike to you?*

Another long pause. *U sure?*

Y. You coming to me or me to you?

Be there soon don't bring yr camera

I didn't have much time to wonder about the camera comment before Walker's Jeep arrived and honked, which made Mom scowl at me. I grabbed my backpack, lighter without the camera, and fled. And once outside, I understood the honk. It wasn't Walker behind the wheel; he would have been too polite to honk. But he was in the passenger seat. And beside him, honking yet again, was a big hunk of a guy with tousled light brown hair and mirror sunglasses. No shirt. He leaned his left arm out of the open window, and I couldn't help thinking that he must have been aware of the effect those incredibly well-defined muscles had on anyone who saw them. There was a big, expensive-looking watch on the wrist. The skin was tan. The jaw was chiseled. I had to stop myself from staring.

He'll make me, Walker had said. That had been about Walker's boat. But it looked like the dynamic applied to Walker's car, as well.

I climbed into the back, and the car was in motion before I had completely shut the door.

I saw Cameron's face in the rear view mirror. I heard his voice, deep and resonant. "You Micah?"

"Yeah."

"Cam."

"I gathered."

His sunglass lenses held my gaze in the mirror just long enough for me to wonder whether he'd make me pay for that comment.

No one spoke again for the rest of the ride. Short as the trip was, I was certain Cam's driving habits made Walker as nervous as they made me.

As Cam jumped out of the Jeep I had to stare at the rest of him, which was just as impressive as his bare arm and shoulder had been. Tall, muscled, tan, and with a walk that said, *I own this. Whatever it is.* I glanced at Walker. Head down, only his eyes flicked toward me and away again. I could almost read his mind: *I told you so.*

Cam headed straight for the dock; didn't even glance toward the house.

Walker said, "Micah?" He jerked his head toward the door to the kitchen, and I followed him in.

No one was in the kitchen. Walker picked up a note pad and wrote something on it. He said, "Letting Mom know we're on the water."

"Walker," I waited until he looked at me. "Who is this guy?"

"I told you."

"Okay, but why does he get to drive your car instead of you?"

"I told you that, too."

"He makes you. But how?"

A sigh of impatience escaped Walker as he turned to look at something, nothing, anything other than me. But I waited, and he had to turn back again. "He's a wrestler, okay? Champion in his weight class for his school's division. The things he can do to you..." He let that trail off into the world of dark imagination.

I had to ask. "What does Paige think of him?"

"Oh, she hates him, too. The one thing we have in common."

I liked her better already. "Does he 'make' her do things, too? I mean, like taking over her things, whatever?"

He laughed without humor. "No way. He tried to take her car once, and she screamed bloody murder. He caught hell from my dad and never goes near her any more."

Just then a woman I didn't know came into the kitchen from the living room, an unlit cigarette in her hand. Her skin was about the color of Cam's, but wrinkled and leathery. She had light streaks in her short dark hair.

She looked at Walker, holding the cigarette up. "Lighter fluid?"

He shook his head. "No idea. Matches are in there, though." He pointed to a drawer beside the fridge.

She didn't move except to look at me. "Who's this?"

Walker sighed almost silently and went to the drawer to fetch matches. I would have held my hand out, but she didn't look as though she had any plans to offer hers.

"Aunt Joanne, this is Micah Jaeger. Micah, my aunt, Mrs. Brock." He walked over to her and handed her the matches, which she took and turned to leave.

"Aunt Joanne," Walker called.

She glanced back at him with what I think she meant to be a conspiratorial look. "You won't tell."

"I will, though."

Her expression morphed into a glare, and she changed direction, walking past me without a glance and into the back yard.

"Mom doesn't want anyone smoking in the house or the guest cottages. And by anyone, I mean Aunt Joanne. No one else who smokes ever comes here."

He moved suddenly to the back door and looked out. "Checking to be sure she didn't just head around the garage to the guest cottage."

"Would you really tell on her?"

"Sure would."

So he wasn't as intimidated by her as he was by her son. Or his own sister.

Walker turned back to me. "Guess we have to bite the bullet."

"Wait." I moved toward him, and he waited as I got closer. And closer. "Here's a little courage."

At first he didn't respond to my kiss, but it didn't take long for us to lose track of where one of us stopped and the other started, even though we were standing in his parents' kitchen. He hugged me hard and then let go, and his smile made me smile back.

"That ought to hold me for a while," he said, just before we both heard Cam's voice shouting Walker's name. And I could tell that the "while" was over.

I followed Walker outside. "What's your problem?" Walker said, sounding braver than I expected. Maybe the kiss had worked after all.

"What's the fucking idea?" Hands on his hips, Cam stood leaning hard on one leg, six-pack abs casting shadows on each other. I glanced toward his mother, who was in one of the lawn chairs by the pool, but I didn't see a reaction to Cam's choice of words.

"Meaning—?"

"The lock! You locked the fucking boat."

"I did. That's right." He walked past Cam while I waited so I could follow behind Cam; I wasn't sure I wanted him behind me. And this way I got to watch the alternating tomato-shapes his ass made in the pale yellow swim shorts he wore. Maybe he was a lousy person, but he did provide some nice scenery.

I didn't remember Walker locking *Dare Ya* the day we'd sailed. He must have done it today to prevent Cam from getting control of it. When I got close enough, I could see that there was a complicated rigging of some kind, a metal chain sheathed in blue plastic, wrapped around various parts of the boat and connecting ultimately to the side of the dock. A combination lock held it all in place.

Dare Ya was floating pretty close to the top of the dock; must be high tide, or close to it. I made a mental note to look up a tide chart, just so I didn't feel like quite so much of a land lubber. Walker descended the couple of steps to the boat and immediately took up a position by the tiller. Cam jumped from the lower step, landing hard.

"Hey!" Walker said. "Cut the shit or you don't sail at all."

Cam looked a little surprised. "What's with you? Here, gimme that." He held his hand out toward the lock in Walker's hand.

Walker didn't respond. He undid the lock and, without moving from where he stood, handed one side of the chain to me. "Micah, can you do the honors?"

I knew he meant to untangle the boat from the chain, and I knew he didn't want to yield the tiller to Cam. But Cam grabbed the chain, right over my hand, as I took hold of it. He glared at me.

I froze. There was no way he was trying to let me know he liked the idea of holding my hand, I was sure of that. What I didn't know was whether he had any reason to think I would want to hold his. I didn't know what to do, so I left it up to him.

He glared at me for a couple of seconds and then thrust my hand away, chain still in it. I detected nothing but irritation from him, with a little contempt to round it out. I heaved a silent, internal sigh of relief

"Fine," he said, still glaring. "I'll take over once we're underway."

I was glad I'd left my camera at home, but I wished I'd brought the canister of pepper spray Mom kept in the box on the counter, the one with loose cash.

Cam fidgeted and complained while I moved around the boat, untangling the web Walker had woven to protect her from Cam, and Walker held fast to his position as captain. I seriously considered suggesting that maybe today wasn't a good day for a sail, after all. The sky was milky with thin clouds; how did we know a storm wouldn't come up? But once Walker had unlocked the chain, there didn't seem to be a good way to lock things up again without Cam getting control. He was obviously more powerful than either Walker or me, and possibly more than both of us put together.

With the motor, Walker got us away from the island and headed west today, instead of east; east would have taken us past the boulder where we met and, eventually, to Sailaway. He cut the engine and started to tell me how to help get the sails open. I was ready to do whatever he told me, and I knew he didn't dare move from the tiller or Cam would take over. But Cam knew what to do with the sails.

"Sit, kid," he said, practically pushing me down onto the seating shelf on the side and causing me to whack my knee painfully in the process. By now, I was so over getting any pleasure out of his beauty, out of watching his muscles ripple under the tan skin, out of admiring the animal strength and coordination of his motions. But he did get the sails unfurled and ready for wind.

Speaking of which, there wasn't a lot of wind today. Walker was hard pressed to keep moving forward, heading the boat first in one direction, then in another so the sails could catch what breeze there was.

Cam got impatient. "You're not tacking right," he said at least three times. And, finally, "Get up, Walker."

Walker glared at him, and I thought we'd have a mutiny for sure, but then Walker shrugged. "Fine. You won't do any better."

Cam thrust the tiller back and forth much more awkwardly than Walker had been doing, swearing a blue streak as he did, and we came nearly to a stop.

Cam was nothing if not adaptable. "Just about where I wanted us," he declared, and stood, sweeping his arms down his legs in one smooth motion to remove his swim shorts.

I gaped. I couldn't help it. His dick was a good eight inches at rest, the balls behind it providing an equally impressive set of pillows. He stretched luxuriously as I watched, fixated, my brain too busy to register that my fascination for large male genitals might be insulting to

Walker, might make him feel inadequate, might make him doubt my interest in him.

In a flash, Cam dived over the side of the boat into the water, and almost as quickly, Walker reclaimed his rightful place at the tiller. My mouth agape, I looked at Walker, whose face showed an odd combination of disgust, envy, and hatred.

Our eyes met, and I shook my head. "Why do you even let him come out here with you?"

"Like I have a choice."

"Why don't you have a choice?"

A shower of water sprayed over us as Cam surfaced and swept an arm toward us, laughing demonically.

"The same fucking reason I don't have a choice about dealing with Paige."

"But—"

"It's called family, Micah. You've heard of it?"

He was hurt. I'd hurt him. But I still didn't understand why Walker had no say about allowing a potentially dangerous person onto his own boat. "He's only your cousin."

I was vaguely aware of Cam out in the water. The boat was hardly moving, and he had no trouble swimming around it, diving down, surfacing, and repeating it all again, punctuating it with splashes that I was sure meant he wanted our attention. I didn't give him any, and neither did Walker.

"I told you not to come today. Remember that."

I was getting pissed by this point. "What you should have done is suggest that you and I do something else. This is dangerous for you, whether I'm here or not."

As if on cue, Cam surfaced beside us, somehow pushed himself high enough to grab the side of the boat, and then he rocked it as violently as he could. I went sliding off the shelf onto the floor—deck?—of the boat, and Cam laughed wildly, rocking the boat hard enough that I had to give up getting back onto the shelf. Oddly, all I could think of was how Walker had insisted that this little boat was exceptionally stable in the water, and I was grateful for that. Walker hung onto the tiller with one hand and the side of the boat with the other and managed to keep his seat in the stern, but I could tell he was furious.

As quickly as he'd appeared, Cam was gone again, underwater.

As I reclaimed my seat, I mumbled, "Maybe a shark will get him."

"No such luck."

We sat in silence as Cam resurfaced several feet away and swam around.

"He's showing off," Walker told me, like I needed to be told. But then he added, "He knows he's hung like a horse." Pause. "And he knows I'm not."

I watched Walker's face carefully. "How does he know?"

Walker waved a hand in the air as if to say it didn't matter, or it should be obvious, or something like that.

Suddenly I heard a yell, frantic, shouting, "Help!" and "Shark!" I wheeled around to see where Cam was, and he was thrashing and screaming. But when I glanced at Walker, all he did was roll his eyes.

"Shouldn't we—"

"If a shark really had him," Walker said, "we'd be seeing some combination of blood in the water, Cam being pulled under, Cam being shaken from side to side. He's just treading water and thrashing, all on his own. Besides, he's done this before."

As Walker described what a real shark attack would have looked like, I realized—from my hours of watching shark documentaries—that he was right.

I looked out toward Cam and yelled, "What kind of shark is it?"

By now he knew we hadn't been fooled, and it seemed he didn't like my challenge. He gave up the pretense and swam back to the boat, hauling himself up and over the side in a way that made me wonder how he didn't castrate himself in the process.

"You fuckers would have let me die!"

Walker shrugged as if to say, *You got that right.* "It's not like you haven't pulled that one before."

Cam laughed. "I had you going that time, though, didn't I?" which made me conclude that it had been me he'd wanted to fool this time. He nearly had.

He had his shorts back on now, and I thought he might try to dislodge Walker from the captain's spot again, but he dropped heavily on the shelf across from me, spread his legs wide, draped his arms along the sides of the boat, and let his head hang back. By now I knew he wanted me to admire him, but I looked at Walker instead, and I smiled. He smiled back.

The wind had begun to pick up, and the cloud cover had thickened. Walker headed us back toward Jasper Island and the safety of the dock, even though we'd been out only about an hour. By the time we were at the dock, large, heavy drops of rain were falling, lots of space between them but almost certainly gearing up for more. Cam jumped to the dock and left Walker and me to finish tending to the boat, which included locking her up again. We were both drenched by the time we climbed onto the dock.

I thought Walker would make a B-line for the house, but instead he sat on the end of the dock. I sat beside him.

"I like to sit here when it's raining," he said. "And it's worlds better than being anywhere Cam is."

I laughed. "For sure. What a jerk." We watched the raindrops hit the water or splash on the wood of the dock or off of our bodies. "So, did you tell me not to bring the camera because of Cam, or because you knew it was going to rain?"

"I didn't know it would rain. The forecast was only a slight chance of that. But Cam always wants what other people have, and I know what that camera means to you."

I nodded. "So he'd want my camera like he wants your boat."

"He wants control of my boat, that's for sure. But he'd never be bothered with caring for her."

"Does he live near here?"

"Not very, thank God. His folks are divorced, and he and Aunt Joanne live in Tarrytown."

"Where's his dad?"

Walker turned toward me for the first time since we'd sat here in the rain. "Prison. Insider trading." And he grinned.

"You don't like the guy?"

"No, but what's great is that Cam's ashamed of him. So he might have a big dick, but my dad's a great guy with lots more money than Cam's family ever had."

"That watch he wears..."

"Knock off. Got it from some street vendor in the city."

"Okay, so there's still something I don't get. Don't get pissed at me, but if your folks won't let him take over Paige's stuff, how does he get away with taking over yours?"

"I didn't scream bloody murder."

"There's gotta be more to it than that."

He shrugged and looked down at the weathered, gray boards of the dock. "I think they feel sorry for him. Because of his dad. I don't know, Micah! Can we change the subject, please?"

I decided I wasn't likely to get a better answer.

The rain began to let up a little, but of course by this time we were beyond caring how much wetter we got.

"Here's a thought," I said, picking at a splinter of wood between us. "If you can get into your room and grab some dry clothes without picking up any hitchhikers—that would be Cam—we can take your car, go to my place where I can change, and then grab some lunch out someplace. Wha'd'ya say?"

I looked up at his face in time to see him grin. We jumped up, and as we headed toward the house he said, "Go around the front of the house to the car. He'll be in the kitchen, stuffing his face. Get in the driver's seat, just in case. I'll bet Cam's still got my key fob, but there's a spare. Be there in a flash."

I hated to sit on the cream leather in my wet clothes, but there didn't seem to be any help for it. Watching nervously, expecting to be found out and thwarted, I let out a long breath of relief when I saw Walker trotting toward me. He got into the passenger seat.

"You can drive, right?"

"I can. Not legally yet, without—"

"Just get us out to the main road. I'll take it from there. Hurry!"

He had to show me how to start the thing, with one of those keyless ignitions, but after that I was fine. And I loved loved loved driving that beauty!

Mom wasn't at home when we got there. I hadn't given any thought to what this process of changing into dry clothes would look like, so Walker and I just headed for my room and shut the door. He dropped his pack and grabbed me almost before the door clicked into place.

It's challenging for two people to strip while they're kissing, but we did our best, almost giggling as difficulties arose. They weren't all that arose.

Without speaking, we both kind of slowed down when it was Walker's turn to drop trou.

"Are you ready for this?" he asked.

"I was gonna ask you that."

He gave me a light kiss and let his jeans go, underwear inside them. But it felt too weird to stare at his crotch, so I kept my eyes on his.

He smiled. "It's okay. You can look. Here." He flopped onto my bed, knees bent and feet on the floor, eyes closed, exposing himself to me completely.

That feeling of tenderness came over me again. I felt like I wanted to be so gentle, so—I don't know, maybe loving is the best word. I sat beside Walker on the bed, the leg nearer to him bent under me so I could turn toward him. And I looked.

It was as he had said, and pretty much like what I'd seen on the internet. The little head nestled in the soft folds of his foreskin, close up against his body. There were more folds of skin behind it, which I figured were the ball sacks with nothing much in them.

I spoke without thinking. "It's kind of cute."

He opened his eyes and I watched his face. He grinned. "Yeah, it is, isn't it?"

"You know," I started, wondering how I was going to finish; I'd been about to say that I'd really like to take some photographs of him, of that part of him, and—not knowing what kind of a response I'd get, I hesitated just long enough to hear the unit door open, and I jumped up. "Shit. Mom's home. We're just changing, right?"

He got off the bed and grabbed the pack with his dry clothes, trying not to laugh.

"Micah?"

"In here, Mom. Walker and I got drenched in the rain. Just changing into some dry clothes. Be right out."

In a hoarse whisper, Walker asked, "Does she know you're gay?"

I shook my head. "Only my dad knows."

"And me." And he grinned at me as he fastened his waistband, making me want to strip those jeans off him again and nuzzle my way toward that adorable little dick.

The rain had stopped, so we headed to the Angry Gull at Walker's suggestion; it was a fun place, and we could put lunch on his dad's account. Most of the outdoor tables were available; probably people had been chased in by the rain and were settled inside by now. We'd just placed our orders (fish and chips again) when his phone sounded. He glanced at the screen and let out one loud Ha!

"Cam." He grinned at me. "Wants to know where I am."

"Is it your job to entertain him, or something?"

He shrugged. "Almost." He pocketed the phone and grinned. "But not this afternoon."

"How long is he staying on the island?"

"They'll be here through the weekend, unfortunately. I didn't even know, or I'd have warned you."

"Sounds like we might want to come up with a few things to do that don't involve sailing. He scares me out there."

Walker tilted his head, teasing. "Oh, really? So you're inserting yourself into my plans to quite an extent, are you?"

I think I blushed. Can you tell when it's you who blushes? "Not tomorrow, though. I have to go driving with my mom."

He picked up the glass of Coke Toni set before him. "You don't sound thrilled."

I started to shake my head, then shrugged, then decided to tell all. I mean, if the guy let me see his micropenis, coming clean about my wacky mom seemed only fair.

So I told him more than I had before about Dylan (skipping the part about how it was my fault Trapper had died), and about my folks splitting and selling our house and forcing me to change schools and live in that peculiar motel unit.

"But when I was younger—maybe eight, nine, even ten—we used to take these trips into the county, all of us. Dad always drove, and Mom would have a map and maybe some newspaper clippings, and we'd go all over the place. Mom had this fantasy about having a house on a lake, but of course waterfront property is expensive. The places that weren't as much money were either total shacks or they were what you call fixer-uppers. Like, roofs caved in, or foundations coming apart, or fire damaged."

"Was it fun, though? Driving around all together like that?"

"Yeah, it kind of was. Most of the time, anyway. Dad would play CDs and sing along with them, and we'd make fun of him. I don't remember trying to get out of going more than a few times. Dylan tried, sometimes, but he was older. And he was always a good sport once we were on the road."

"I wish I had a brother instead of Paige."

"Yeah, well, some sisters are nicer than Paige, y'know."

Toni placed our plates on the table (including Walker's extra tartar sauce), asked if we wanted anything else, smiled, and left us alone.

"It's a low bar," he said, his voice quiet. "She..." He stopped like he'd thought better about telling me something.

Maybe I could encourage him. "Why is she so mean to you, anyway?"

He lifted one shoulder and dropped it. "It's partly my fault, actually. I found out she was adopted when I was about seven. I overheard something my folks were talking about. And the next time she made me mad, I told her. I said it like it was a bad thing. And—well, she hadn't known."

"No shit! How old was she?"

"Eleven. Old enough for it to hit her like a ton of bricks."

"And she's been taking it out on you ever since, sounds like."

"She…" Here we were again, him falling into silence in mid-sentence.

"She what?"

"She found out about me. About my size. You know. It was maybe a year later, in the back yard. We'd been in the pool, and Cam was there. He pantsed me."

I almost said *No shit* again, but it seemed wrong to say anything.

"So they both found out at the same time." He took a shaky breath, eyes on his hand where it toyed with his fork. "She laughed so hard. They both did. And then she said she was glad she was adopted, because she'd never want to be a freak like me."

I wanted so much to reach over and take his hand. But the table was just big enough that it would have been awkward. And I was pretty sure it would have been the wrong thing to do.

But maybe I could distract him. I hadn't finished my own tale of woe, though it seemed less woeful than his. But I dived back in.

"I wish I could be with you tomorrow. Those jerks might not be as shitty to you if there was someone else around. But I have to do this thing." I heaved a sigh, kind of a bridge to the next part of my story.

"Like I said, my folks split after Dylan died. My mom started drinking a lot. She went with gin. Looks like water, and she doesn't like vodka. Anyway, sometime last winter she started seeing this psychic. This medium. She wanted to contact Dylan."

Walker sat up straighter. "Did she?"

I blinked. "You believe in that stuff?"

"Maybe. I don't know."

"Anyway, yeah, this person—Madam Alberta Halliday—has been telling my mom all kinds of crap, delivering messages from Dylan. And recently she changed her tune. Now she says he's still alive. And Mom's convinced he's coming home. So we're on this hunt to find a bigger place, preferably the dream lakefront house, and Mom wants to get a better job. She's been buying stuff for him, like she thinks he's gonna show up any day."

Maybe fifteen seconds of silence later, Walker said, "And you don't believe it. So you have to help her find this place that you know you won't need for a brother who's really dead but who your mom thinks is coming home?"

"You got it."

"Oh, Micah." I was pretty sure it was his turn to wish he could reach across the table to me. "What does your dad think about all this?"

"He thinks she's crazy. I have to call him every night to let him know if there've been any developments, or if she's spent some huge amount of money on something for Dylan."

"How often do you see your dad?"

"Kind of depends. Every other weekend, more or less. I'll see him this coming weekend. Hey," and I looked up. "Maybe you could come, too! Oh—wait. There's only one bedroom. I sleep on the couch." It was a dumb idea, anyway; why would Walker want to go to Warwick for anything?

"Does he know about me?"

"He knows you have a sailboat. That's about it. When I mentioned you, it was last week. Before we went sailing. I told him we were just friends." And that was another reason Walker couldn't go with me; "just friends" had been true at the time, but now I didn't know how well I'd be able to maintain that impression, or if both Walker and I would be willing to prove it wrong.

He asked, "And what are we?"

152

His phone sounded; another text from Cam, by the look on Walker's face. He turned the ringer off.

I held his gaze. "You tell me. You're the one who's not sure you're gay."

"Well, whatever I am, I really like you."

"Okay, but I *want* you. That's different."

He grinned. "Not that different."

"I've never had a boyfriend."

"You do now, if you want one."

I tried to subdue the grin that wanted to spread all the way across my face. I failed. "I just might."

After lunch, we went out onto the floating dock to the slip the Donnells rented; no boat there today, so we sat on the weathered boards and dangled our legs over the water. The tide was going out, so the dock was hanging low with it.

A few minutes of sweet silence went by. Then I asked if he was doing anything this weekend, while I was in Warwick.

"My mom wants to drive up to visit my grandmother, and I'll go with her. Gramma's living on her own, now, because Gramps died last year. In New Canaan. Actually, it's on a lake. Your mom would like it." He grinned at me.

"Something tells me it would not be in our price range."

He laughed, and at first I was pissed, but then I thought, you know, he's accepted me for who I am. He's seen where I live. And the laugh wasn't *at* me.

"Probably not. It's a teeny, tiny lake, but it's not a teeny, tiny house. Anyway, it's kind of too bad you already have plans, too, because Cam and Aunt Joanne will still be on the island. I mean, they're not going with us, and I'd love for you to meet Gramma. She's—she's just kind of cool. It's like she gets me, you know? I couldn't say what it is about her, but somehow I think if I told her about you, about you being my boyfriend, she wouldn't be at all surprised. I mean, maybe she wouldn't have been thinking I was gay. It's more like she hears what you say and accepts it. Accepts you. You know?"

"I'd probably like her." Wouldn't meet her this weekend, though. I needed to be with Dad; I needed to be with somebody sane who knew the truth about Dylan and Madam Alberta and even about me. I wanted to tell him about Walker.

My gaze landed on a nearby boat that looked a lot like Walker's, and all the fun of being out on the water with him came back to me. I asked, "What do you like best about sailing?"

"Depends."

"On?"

"For one thing, on whether I'm alone. With you, it was a blast seeing you out there for the first time. I loved sharing that with you." He sighed and wrapped his arms around bent knees. "But when I'm alone, I get this feeling that doesn't feel right anyplace else, but that feels perfect out there. It's knowing that the sea doesn't care about me as a person. No interest at all. If I have a great sail, I have a great sail. If a storm catches me, then it catches me. If I drown, then I drown. Makes no difference to the sea."

"And you like that?"

"Shit, man. I fucking *love* that."

"Why?"

He thought for a minute. "Maybe because it puts things in perspective. I mean, when I'm with other people—think 'Paige and Cam,' here—and they're picking on me or ridiculing me? Everything's all wrong, and it's huge. It takes over. And because it's wrong, I feel like it ought to be different, but I don't know how to make it different. Short of killing them, that is, but of course that brings other problems. But even when I'm alone in my room or something, and I'm feeling like the freak Paige says I am, and like I'll never be able to live a normal life, I almost want to end it all."

"You mean—" I couldn't bring myself to say the word "suicide."

"It gets real bad sometimes."

"But out on the water...."

"Out there?" He nodded toward the open water. "Out there, everything gets reduced to sun and sea, wood and sail and rope, life and death. Everything gets equalized. Out there, it's like I don't have an identity. I'm just part of the whole."

To lighten the mood a little, I said, "So on land you're like a fish out of water." No response; evidently he wasn't feeling lightened. Then, suddenly, I got it. "It might be a little like when I'm shooting."

"Yeah?"

"That day you saw me, with the dead seagull, the reason I was so rude to you was because you'd interrupted. You'd made me lose the zone I get into when I'm shooting. It's like nothing else exists."

"I get that."

After that, we didn't talk much, just gazed down at the water or off into the distance. At some point Walker moved to sit closer to me, and he took my hand in both of his. I watched as his fingers stroked mine, teased my palms with tiny movements and sweeping circles, followed the crease lines of my wrist. It was the most marvelous sensation. Several times I felt shivers all over.

I was almost but not quite hard when it all came to a crashing halt.

A voice behind us said, "Oh. My. God."

Our hands yanked apart, and Walker wheeled around to stare at Paige, towering over us, one hand on her hip, the other dangling a green-and-white striped bag gathered with a string, sunglasses pushed up onto her head.

Walker jumped up as she repeated, "Oh. My. God."

His voice tight, he said, "What are you doing here?"

"What am I doing here?" She laughed. "The question is, what are you two doing. Here, or anywhere else."

I got to my feet, trying to look confident, telling myself not to be intimidated. "Walker asked you a question."

She tilted her head at me with the kind of gaze she might have given an unfamiliar but non-threatening sea creature. "It speaks."

"Are you stalking me?" Walker tried again.

Slowly she allowed her gaze to drag itself away from me and toward Walker. "Don't flatter yourself. Ashton will be here any minute." She turned back to me, but she didn't seem to be speaking to me. "So. This is interesting."

"Yeah, well," I said, turning away from her and sitting down on the dock again, "you aren't."

"I suppose it makes sense that you'd want to be with a boy." I wasn't looking at her, but I could tell she was talking to Walker. "You must have wanted to know what you should look like."

That hung in the air just long enough for me to jump to my feet again. "Leave him alone!"

To Walker she said, "You have a knight in shining armor, then?" And to me, "You do know he's got no equipment, right?"

"Can you swim, Paige?" That made her blink stupidly at me. "Just checking before I push you off the dock."

As I took a step toward her, and as she took a step back, I heard the sounds of a motor coming toward us over the water. In my peripheral vision I saw this long, skinny boat coming closer. It cut its engines enough to coast up to the dock behind me. I didn't look at it. Neither did Paige. Neither did Walker. I took another step forward, and Paige side-stepped and went around me toward the boat.

I turned to watch Paige, who was looking a little less confident than usual. This made me gloat a little, until I got a good look at the boat, which was mostly pure white with cobalt blue along the sides and in jagged patterns all over the deck or whatever you'd call the covered section in front of the steering wheel. I saw the word "Cigarette" in stylized gray lettering. The guy driving was one of those blond guys with blond teeth, tan skin over lean muscles, a "Fuck you" attitude toward everyone but his favored few. In other words, the blond counterpart to Paige. And the perfect owner for that boat.

She got into the boat and said, "Let's get out of here." The guy managed to maneuver away from the slip, and as the boat sped off, Paige raised a hand behind her head with the middle finger prominently erect, like she knew we'd be watching. Walker's voice broke the moment.

"You've made an enemy, Micah. A dangerous one."

"Well, fuck her! Who the hell does she think she is, anyway? I can't believe you let her get away with this shit."

As though I hadn't spoken, he said, "There will be consequences. I hate to think what they might be."

We stood there looking at each other, not touching, not speaking. I played out a few scenarios in my head: she tells Cam what she saw; she tells her parents what she saw; she tells Walker's friends what she saw, given a chance. And then—what?

"Given who she is," I told Walker, trying to sound sure of myself, "whatever the consequences are, they would have happened anyway, no matter what I said."

"Maybe."

Chapter Eight

Several times after Walker dropped me off, I texted him. *Any fallout?* and *U ok?* and *C U Thurs?*

I got short, non-descriptive responses that tempted me to call, but something stopped me.

When I called Dad later, he was not happy that Mom and I would be driving around again for part of the day Wednesday, even though I'd already told him it was happening.

"Does she really think she'll find something?" he wanted to know, as if I had an answer. He might as well have asked, "Is she really sure Dylan is coming home?" It was almost as though he thought I should have done something to stop her.

Wednesday was dreadful. The weather was great, but that didn't help at all. Mom still hadn't forgiven me for what I'd said that night I'd had the dream, about Dylan being dead. But at least it meant I didn't have to pretend any more.

We weren't on the road five minutes when, her voice dripping sarcasm, Mom said, "It's very nice of you to come along today, given that you consider it a wasted effort."

I shrank down in the passenger seat; she wasn't letting me drive today. "I said I'd come, so I'm here." My voice sounded tiny. Where was that bravado I'd shown Paige yesterday? Was it just that I had the guts to stand up for someone else but not for myself?

Like last time, Mom made me take pictures of some of the properties while she made sarcastic comments like of course we wouldn't need such a big house because it would be just the two of us, or it didn't matter that Dylan wouldn't like the color of some house because he'd never see it. I just let her drop these bombs; didn't retaliate; didn't stand up for myself. It didn't seem worth it.

If I thought the day had been awful already, well… it was about to get much worse.

We'd been home maybe fifteen minutes—just enough time for me to text Walker and start to worry when I didn't hear back—when a blue Lexus drove up.

Mrs. Donnell.

I dashed to the door before Mom could get there and watched my boyfriend's mother approach, looking like— I'm not sure what, but it wasn't good.

She didn't smile when she saw me. "Micah." We stared at each other a few seconds. Then, "Is your mother home?"

"Who is it, Micah?" Mom came up behind me.

"Mrs. Donnell."

"Walker's mother? Don't leave her standing there! Come in, please."

The three of us stood in the tiny living room like we were waiting for something to happen. Finally Mom said, "Won't you sit down? Would you like something? Coffee?"

"No, thank you." Mrs. Donnell looked at me a moment as if unsure how to proceed. Then she looked at Mom. "I'm sorry to have to do this, but I need to ask Micah not to spend time with my son from now on. It's a very complicated situation, and I can't go into my reasons in detail. Let it be enough that Micah's influence is confusing to Walker."

Mom turned toward me, her own confusion showing, then back to Mrs. Donnell. "What did he do?"

Mrs. Donnell waved a hand vaguely. "It's not that he did anything. I'm sure he's a fine young man. But Walker is in a very vulnerable time of his life, and—oh, this is so difficult." She looked at me as if I could help her.

So many things went through my mind. My heart. My soul.

First, gay. If Mrs. Donnell hadn't already known I was gay, she knew now. This was no doubt one of those consequences Walker warned me about after I confronted Paige. I felt sure Paige, either in some direct and accusatory way or in some passive aggressive manner, had made sure that her parents knew what she'd seen on the dock yesterday.

Second, gay. She doesn't know whether my mom knows, and she's decent enough not to out me this way.

Third, gay. Walker had told me that his parents might be conservative financially, but that that they're politically more progressive. Which means that whatever Mrs. Donnell feels personally about gay people, she wants to be seen as being accepting.

Fourth, intersex. In the time it took me to blink, I wondered whether Walker might have had a conversation or two with his folks about his orientation before we met, when he was confused about how he felt. So now that he's met me, he's not confused. And now they don't want him to decide he's gay?

Fifth, Walker. Were his parents, in fact, the ones who had confused him? Do they really think being gay is a *decision?*

Sixth, me. I'd been wondering when, how, and why I would tell Mom the truth about me. My thoughts, vague though they'd been, had centered on having Dad prepared before I told her, so he could be on my side, because I had no idea how Mom would react to the news that her only surviving son was gay.

Seventh, Walker *and* me. I wanted Walker. And he'd told me he felt the same about me. And for me, this—the two of us as a couple—was the clincher. This was the most important point of all.

Both women were staring at me as though I held the answer to universal secrets. In a way, I did.

I looked at Mrs. Donnell as directly as I had looked at Paige on the dock yesterday. "How does Walker feel about your decision?"

She looked taken aback, but she recovered. "I'm not going to discuss that with you. I just want to be sure you understand the need to do as I ask."

So many things came to me, things I didn't say. Like, *Oh, I understand, all right. I understand you want to push your only natural child down a path that's right for you but wrong for him.* Or, *The only need here is for your own selfish comfort, which you can have only if you force your son to be something he's not.* Or, *Have you taken Walker's phone away from him? Because otherwise he wouldn't be ignoring me.*

That last one, about ignoring me, pushed back at me. Because if anyone had taken my phone away so that I couldn't communicate with Walker, I'd have found another phone, or I'd have been on my bike in a flash to get to him. But he hadn't done those things.

I wasn't ready to give up, but I didn't want to make enemies of the Donnell parents just yet. So I softened my response, and my tone of voice. "I'd like to hear it from him."

"I'm sorry, Micah. I can't do that."

"*You* can't do that?" I think my tone slipped a little on that one.

"I mean, he's in too fragile a position."

"Are you aware that I know about him? About that fragile position?"

She was getting impatient, I could tell. "Yes, yes. He told us you knew. That's not the point."

"So—what is the point?"

She let out a long breath. "The point is that he needs more time than he's had to think things through without the influence of a personality as strong as yours. I don't suspect you of anything ill-intentioned. But you seem so sure of who you are."

"You say that like it's a bad thing."

"It's a bad thing for him."

"Knowing who I am is bad for Walker? Or is it that *what* I am is bad for *you?*"

Mom had had about enough. "Micah! Have some respect. And will someone please tell me what's going on?"

Mrs. Donnell still guarded Walker's secret and, indirectly, mine. "I've said all I can say. I'm sorry." And she walked out the door.

Mom stared at me. I stared at the door. The Lexus drove away.

"Micah? What on earth is going on?"

I closed my eyes, and then opened them when I felt my whole body sway dangerously. I grabbed at the arm of a chair. Probably I should have sat down. But I didn't want to. I wanted to say what I had to say standing up. Somehow it gave the information more dignity, and also I might want to leave quickly.

This shouldn't be happening. None of it. Walker and I should be together. He should want to be with me enough to fight his family's resistance. And I shouldn't have to tell my mother I'm gay before I'm damn good and ready to do that.

Sometimes life turns on you like a shark. It was doing that to me now.

"What's going on, Mom, is that Walker is not just a friend. He's my boyfriend. I'm gay. So is he. And his parents obviously don't want him to be."

"I—you—but—you're *gay?*" Her face slack with shock, she nearly fell as she lowered herself onto the couch behind her. When I didn't speak, she asked, "Does your father know?"

"I told him the last time I was in Warwick."

"What did he say?"

"He said there are gay people everywhere, and they're all related to someone. I'm related to him, and he's getting used to that."

If possible, she was more shocked by Dad's response than she'd been by the news itself. I shouldn't have said this, but I was in a state. "Madam Alberta didn't tell you?"

The sharp jangle of the office bell interrupted whatever might have happened next. I couldn't read Mom's face as she got up and moved to the door that led into the motel office; I was just relieved. Not only did I wish I hadn't sent that last barb at Mom, but also I wanted her so focused on my being gay that she'd forget to ask why Walker was so "fragile." So "vulnerable." Because mad at Walker or not, I wasn't going to tell anyone about his "equipment," as Paige had put it so crudely.

Angry with Walker... was I?

Yes. I was. Like I said, if my folks had told me not to see him, then seeing him would have been the next thing I'd have done.

Kind of automatically, I grabbed my camera before Mom could come back and demand any more information. I rode my bike out to Sailaway Marina. It wasn't that I expected to see Walker or any other Donnell there; it was just someplace I didn't think anyone in my family would look for me. In the parking lot, I turned off the *Friends and Family* app and the locator feature. I didn't want to be found before I was ready, this time. I also turned off the ringer.

I found an empty slip far out on a floating dock and sat there watching the sky change color as the sun set. At first, the few puffy clouds caught the light and turned bright peach. Then the blue deepened, and the clouds darkened. Then I saw just one star appear.

Ever since that shark attack, I'd thought of myself as a bit of a coward. No one ever exactly called me that, but being told not to be a wuss, not to be a sissy, having people—that is, Dad and sometimes Dylan—tell me to buck up, to be brave... those things all added up to one thing, and that thing was that it wouldn't be necessary to say all those things to someone who wasn't a coward. And, for sure, I would *never* have signed up to go to Afghanistan.

I'd avoided other kids at school; I hadn't wanted them to know I was gay. And I saw that secrecy as part of my cowardice, even though I'd pretended to myself that I hadn't needed friends. That I hadn't needed anyone. At some point I think this avoidance had registered in my subconscious as just more cowardice.

But I'd been wrong about that. Otherwise, why would I have been so quick to agree to meet up with a strange kid— a kid with whom (that one's for you, Walker) I obviously had nothing in common, a kid who'd thrown a wet rag at me to get my attention? Why would I agree to show up at a marina, a place I'd never been? A place I'd never wanted to be? A place where the uncomfortable differences in our living situations were highlighted to an extreme degree?

Hell, no coward would have done that.

Right?

And then... and then! And then I'd not only let him talk me into agreeing to go out sailing in shark-infested waters with him, but also I'd actually done it!

And I'd loved it!

Just once. We'd done that just once (the ill-advised, brief sail with Cam didn't count), but I'd loved it. I'd loved the freedom, the wide open horizon, the potential for opportunities—opportunities I couldn't name, even now—a potential so real I could almost taste it. Hell, I did taste it! It tasted like salt and sea spray and wind and Walker.

Walker.

I leaned my arms on my bent knees and hung my head, fighting tears, his beautiful face smiling at me from the insides of my closed eyelids.

Did I love him? Is that why I felt so fucking horrible right now? I wanted him, but was that the same?

That tenderness I'd felt when he'd told me his secret, and again when I'd seen him naked, washed over me yet again now. The words his mother had used floated in my brain: fragile... vulnerable....

But was he a coward? With this new demand from his folks, he hadn't come to me, like I'd have gone to him. He'd sure looked like a coward in front of Paige, and in front of Cam. He couldn't stand up to either of them.

But he'd approached me that day, the day of the dead seagull. And he'd thrown that wet rag at me. He'd invited me to lunch, and then he'd invited me to sail alone with him in his boat. He hadn't known the first thing about me before any of that.

I'd been brave in front of his mother, but he'd been brave in front of mine, too. And I'd been brave on Mr. Donnell's yacht, even if I'd needed a little encouragement to creep up on those feeding sharks.

I picked up my camera and scrolled to those shots. I pulled up the last one, the one where the hungry shark's open mouth and terrible teeth were right there, and I stared at it for several minutes. I felt no fear.

So if neither of us was a coward, why were we at the mercy of people trying to control us? Or was each of us brave in his own way and afraid in his own way, too?

What was I afraid of?

Well... I'd just run from my mother. But, really, that was more from a need to sort things out for myself, not fear of her. I think.

So was I afraid of something else? Other than sharks, and other than admitting to my mother that I'd confiscated Trapper's collar, I couldn't think of anything specific beyond the general anxiety I think anyone my age feels about what the next year holds. I was gonna have to go back and let Mom yell at me, but anyone would want to avoid that.

So I *wasn't* a coward. Not really.

And like a rubber band that had been pulled hard away from the stick it was nailed to, my mind snapped back to Walker.

Did I love Walker?

The word "potential" occurred to me again. The potential for love was there. It was powerful. Not only could I taste it, but I could smell it. If I closed my eyes and pictured Walker, brought him close to me, I could smell the wonderful, musky rope smell of him. I could smell the sea water on the little rocks near the dock at his house. I could smell the sunlight on the air around us as we sailed through life.

And I could feel the potential. It was in the softness of Walker's lips and mine as they touched, in the warm, soft-hard feeling of our deeper kisses, in the searing heat of my crotch as my dick reached out for him in my dreams.

Did I love him? Given half a chance, I would. And that chance had just been ripped away.

I picked up my phone to see if Walker had tried to contact me. Nope; just a text from Mom, from over an hour ago, in all caps: *WHERE ARE YOU???*

I called Dad. As he answered, I could hear laughter in his voice. I could also hear a woman laughing in the background.

"Hey, son. What's up?"

I almost hung up. This was not going to be a fun conversation, and I didn't even want to know who was with him.

"Micah? You there?"

"Yeah. Yeah, I'm here, Dad." And I stopped. No more laughter. "Everything okay?"

"Mom hasn't called?"

"No. Micah, spit it out. What's going on?"

Deep breath. "I had to tell her. About me. Got kind of pushed into it."

"About you... oh. That." Not the tone of voice I would have liked.

"Yeah, 'that.' Do you have a problem with 'that' again?"

"No, Micah, no. I'm sorry. Didn't mean it to sound that way. So you told her? How did she take it?"

"Is this a bad time?"

"Hang on." He tried to muffle it, but I heard him say, "Gotta take this, Sharon. I'll just step inside for a minute." So they were on the balcony.

Sharon. Not Layla. But it might was well have been.

"Okay, so what did she say?"

"She asked if you knew. I told her yes."

"That's it?"

"The office bell rang. And I left."

"Wait... so you didn't actually talk about it? You just dumped and ran?"

Something in me burst. "Yeah, Dad, I ran. Like the coward I am. Like the coward you've always told me I am. Like I ran after I told *you*."

"Micah, that's enough."

"I don't think so. Wouldn't you like to tell me how else I'm a coward?"

"Where's this coming from?"

"From you! All my life! 'Don't be a wuss, Micah.' 'Buck up, Micah.' 'Just fucking go into the water, Micah.' 'Just ask some girl out, Micah.' All my life!"

The silence was so big I felt dizzy. I swayed forward a little toward the water that slurped around under the dock. I fell back and down on the weathered boards, feet propped on the edge, and held my breath—partly to shut myself up, partly to keep the tears at bay.

When Dad spoke again, he seemed very calm. "Micah, son, I don't know what's going on, but I want to help. Is there anything I can do before you come out for the weekend?"

I held the phone at arm's length so I could get control of my breathing. Then, "No. I just called to let you know that Mom knows about me. In case she calls you. See you Saturday." And I rang off.

Sharon.

Layla.

Dylan.

Walker.

On my feet again, I faced the water, jumped up and landed hard and felt the dock move, jumped again, felt and heard the water's reaction, jumped again, and again. Every time I jumped and waited, the water did the same thing it had done the last time. It was predictable. It was consistent. It made sense. I jumped until I couldn't jump any more. Then I stood there as darkness wrapped itself around me, watching as lights appeared on the water where someone was still out there in a boat. The water surged up and down, predictably, sensibly, and lights that were farther away seemed to flick off and then on again as the boats they were on rose and fell above what I could see of the horizon.

It was close to nine o'clock when I pulled out my phone again, and there were two more message from Mom: one text and voicemail, both demanding to know where I was. I texted back.

Gathering my thoughts. Back soon.
I didn't want her calling the police on me.

Mom was sitting on the couch, smoking a cig, her usual gin glass beside her, when I got home. I couldn't read her face, but she watched me as I came in and set my camera down. On the ride back from Sailaway, I had decided to face the music. Take the bull by the horns. Pick a metaphor. I sat in the only upholstered chair we owned—no room for more than that in the tiny living room.

She didn't exactly stare at me, but her eyes stayed on my face as she took another puff, blew the smoke sideways, picked up the glass and took a sip. She said nothing. So I did.

"Haven't seen you drink in a while." I hoped she wasn't going to blame this relapse on me. I wouldn't let her.

Another several seconds of watching later, she said, "It's water. Try it if you don't believe me."

I blinked. "It's in your gin glass, though." Why would she do that? "Wait—you wanted me to think you were drinking gin?"

"I wanted to make a point. If I can give up gin, you can give up this boy."

I wanted to stand, wave my arms wildly, yell and scream. Instead, I threw myself against the back of the chair and laughed.

Mom was not amused. "You think this is funny?"

"I think it's absurd. You've told me before that you're not an alcoholic. That means you drink by choice. I'm not gay by choice. It's who I am. And it's not a disease or a sickness, either. I don't need to be 'cured.' I don't need a twelve-step program or an AA-style support group."

"You finished?"

"Depends on what you say next."

"I didn't tell you to stop being gay. Personally, it seems very unlikely to me that you are, and in fact I'm pretty sure you'll grow out of it. But I don't see it as an argument I can win with you, so I'm not arguing. But Mrs. Donnell wants you to stay away from Walker. So that's what you'll do."

"You don't even know why—"

"I don't need to know why."

Despite my intentions, my voice got very loud. "She just doesn't want him to be gay!"

"I don't want *you* to be gay, either, but that's not the issue. If I needed to tell someone to stay away from you because they were a bad influence—"

"Being gay is not a bad influence!"

"… because they were a bad influence or for any other reason, I would expect that person to stay away from you." She stopped, like that said it all.

"Well, both of you can say it as much as you like. But if Walker wants to see me, he will. And *I* want to see *him*."

"Have you heard from him?"

I sank into the chair, arms crossed, hurt all over again. "No."

Her voice was gentle as she said, "And yet he's had plenty of time. So it looks like he doesn't want to see you."

I came close to yelling more objections, to calling out the wild injustice being inflicted on me and on Walker, but just in time I realized two things: Not only would it get me nowhere, but also the more of a fuss I made, the more watchful Mom would be, reducing my chances of connecting with Walker.

But I couldn't just slink away to my room, and I didn't want to consider why I hadn't heard from Walker. So I attacked on another front. "So you don't want me to be gay? What's that supposed to mean? Because I'm not going to grow out of it."

Another drag on the cig, another smoke cloud sent sideways. It was like she was willing herself to remain calm, and smoking helped. Maybe it did. Maybe I should try it.

"What it means, Micah, is that your life will be a misery if you try to live that way. Legal advances like marriage equality aside, and in fact because of them, there's more pushback all the time. Look at all the madness around the bathroom issue. Someone actually bombed a Target bathroom."

"That's a transgender issue. It's not about being gay."

She stubbed out the cig and sat forward. "Micah, it doesn't matter. Look at what happened in Orlando. I don't want you to be a casualty of hatred. To these people, the people who pass laws against trans people, and nutjobs who use AR-15 rifles to mow down a whole crowd just because they're gay, it's about fear. And it's about sex. And I'm sorry, but when most people hear 'gay' or 'LGBT' or 'transgender,' their minds go directly to sex. It wouldn't matter who you are as a person. It would matter only that you're gay. You could even be chaste, and for those people it would still be about sex. They'd still want you dead."

I had never thought about it like that. Hell, I hadn't really *thought* about it at all; I'd just felt it, and I'd known it was right. I was gay. "You can't ask me to change who I am."

"That isn't what I'm doing. You wanted to know why I didn't want you to be gay, and that's the reason. Well... that, and the fact that I don't understand it at all. I want you to have the same chance your brother will have, to marry and have kids and have just as normal a life as you want."

I noticed that she mentioned Dylan in the future— referring to what he "will" have.

Her voice started to crack a little, and tears stood in her eyes. "I want you not to have the problems we've had, your father and I. I want you to be happy and loved. And if you try to do that with another man?" She shook her head.

"People will throw things in your way all the time. Maybe even throw things like bombs."

She covered her face with her hands. I sat there, stunned, and waited.

"Micah, the thing is," and she grabbed a tissue from the box on the table beside her, and blew her nose. "I don't want to have to think about another son being blown apart for no good reason. So, no, I don't want you to be gay. I don't understand why you think you can't be normal. But I'm not focusing on that right now. All I'm saying to you right now is to leave Walker alone, like his mother asked."

I'm here to tell you, it's not easy to be mad and yell at someone who's crying because they don't want you to get hurt. But I had to try and explain myself.

"Mom, I know you don't want me to get hurt. But telling me I can't see someone because it makes someone else uncomfortable is hurting me. Can't you see that?"

She blew her nose again. "Micah, you're not even seventeen yet. You'll have the rest of your life to meet someone and fall in love. You've known this boy all of—what, a few weeks? If that? It's not like you'd been together for a year. You barely know him."

I knew there was a problem with this thinking, but I couldn't land on what it was. My brain raced, scrambled around, until it hit on this. "If Walker were a girl, no one would have a problem. And you can't tell me that you don't know that if I met a boy in school I liked, we'd catch hell from classmates and maybe teachers, too. It's actually a very good thing that I met someone outside of school"—my voice rose a little here—"so we're not catching hell at school, but now we're catching it from our families! You're telling me there's no place that's safe. You're telling me I can't be with anyone, anytime!"

"I'm telling you that you can't be with this boy, at this time. That's all. Don't make this out to be some massive attack on your personhood."

I had no more words. Or, none I wanted to give away. I stood, snatched up my camera, and went into my room. I dug Trapper's collar out from its hiding place and sat on the side of my bed holding it, meditating on the cracks and gouges and rough spots, and I cherished the fact that she didn't know I had it.

Chapter Nine

I spent all day Thursday alone, trying to distract myself from being pissed at Walker. He hadn't called, he hadn't texted—nothing. I had sent him a text shortly after midnight when I couldn't fall asleep, thinking maybe he'd see it when he was alone and be able to reply. It said, *Are you ok with this cause I'm not.* There was no reply.

To hell with him. So, to be sure I stayed away from the shore on Thursday, I biked to the inland section of a favorite haunt, the Barn Island wildlife area, camera and tripod in my pack along with enough food and ginger ale and water to see me through the day. I could wander around there for hours and never go near the shoreline.

With my bike locked to a tree near the Palmer Neck Road entrance, I set out on foot toward the tiny fingers of water that creep in from the Sound. I shot the reflections that grasses and bushes and trees made in the water. I shot a white clover flower that I'd placed in shallow water beside a stone with markings that made it look a lot like the clover blossom. I shot other stones through shallow water that was sometimes still and sometimes rippling. Lying on my belly, I took shots of different subjects through long grasses, or I changed my focal length and shot the grasses themselves. As the sun got lower, I shot just the shadows that grasses and rocks made.

And I kept checking my phone for a message from Walker. Nothing came.

Around six o'clock I called Dad. When he answered, I was pretty sure he was alone. Good.

"Dad, did Mom call you?"

"Haven't heard a peep."

"Because we had it out after I got home. She hates that I'm gay. Oh, also, she doesn't believe it. So I just thought she might have phoned you."

"No. Are you okay?"

"Yeah. But—listen, is there any way I could come out early? Maybe Friday night?"

He paused just long enough for me to think he was gonna turn me down, and I pictured him with Layla. I mean, Sharon. In my mind, she was in her twenties—isn't that the kind of woman who attracted middle-aged men? She had blue hair cut in different lengths, lots of eye makeup, and a silver ring right through the middle of her nose that hung down in a way that made me want to tie her up like a bull to a fencepost someplace.

"Sharon will be here. I'd like you to meet her. I was going to suggest it for Saturday dinner, but if you really need to get away we could do it Friday instead, if your Mom's okay with the idea. Would that work for you, son?"

Before I could stop the words, they escaped. "Will she stay overnight?"

His answer was just as quick: "Probably."

I froze, just for a second. "Does she know about me?"

"She does. She's very supportive, actually."

"Really."

"Are you at home?"

"No."

"I'll call your mother now and see if she has a problem with giving you up a day early."

"She'll be glad to see me gone."

"I doubt that, Micah. I'll call you back in a sec."

I sat on the ground leaning against the trunk of a wide, tall tree—maple, I think—resting my arms on my upturned knees and staring into space, facing the direction of the ocean that I couldn't see from here. Walker might be out there right now, I was thinking. He might have managed to escape Cam's clutches and taken *Dare Ya* out so he could be alone. Alone, like he'd said he liked. Getting things into perspective. Arranging the priorities in his life.

I wasn't a priority, evidently.

Christ, but I was pissed at him! What the fuck? I would have found my way to him *so fast* if our situations were reversed. Did I mean so little that one word from his mother would convince him I didn't matter? But how could that be? Wasn't I the only person he'd chosen to shown himself naked to?

Hell, maybe I wasn't. Maybe this whole time he'd been having me on. Maybe he actually uses his—what was it, a disadvantage? A disability? Deformity. Maybe he uses his deformity to gain sympathy. Maybe he's done this before. And so maybe, just maybe, Mrs. Donnell wasn't protecting Walker. Maybe she was protecting *me*.

This idea stunned me. And it made me realize that I'd fallen for this guy awfully quickly. Okay, so I didn't know a whole lot of other gay guys (that is, none) who might be interested in me, and vice versa. So he was the first guy who'd been interested in me that way. So what? Did that mean I had to lose my own perspective? Did that mean he could use me like some kind of puppet?

I couldn't sit still, so I got up and headed back to where I'd left my bike, hoping Dad would call before I got there. He did. I kept walking as we talked.

"Friday's fine, Micah. Sharon's looking forward to meeting you. Your mom will drive you out to meet me around seven."

"Will Sharon be with you?"

"In the truck? No. She'll be getting dinner ready, here at my place."

So we'd have a few minutes alone. Good. "Okay. And, Dad? Thanks. I gotta get away, that's all."

"Got it. See you tomorrow, Micah."

By the time we hung up, I was maybe fifty feet from where I'd left my bike. I could see it waiting there. And I could see something white on it that wasn't anything I'd left there.

I broke into a trot to close the distance faster. The white thing was an envelope with my name written on it.

"What the fuck?" My own voice startled me a little. I glanced around to see if anyone was nearby, watching to see me pick up the envelope, or running away so I wouldn't see who'd left it, or whatever. No one. I tore it open and found a short letter.

Micah —

Please don't be mad at me. I know you sent messages, and I'm sorry I couldn't answer.

It's like I told you on the yacht that night. I'm really confused about who I am and whom I want to be with. I didn't lie about liking you. And when I said we were boyfriends it felt right at the time. But now I'm not so sure. I'm not sure about me, that is.

Mom really wants me to pray about this. She's Catholic, and she wants me to talk with the priest at her church. She says he understands issues like being gay. And I need to know what he has to say, because I'm so confused.

Mom says I have to let you get back to your life for your own good. She's probably right. You don't need someone in your life whining about not being sure who they are, bringing you down, leading you on. Remember, I said I was afraid of that.

So I guess that's all I can say. I hope you have a really wonderful life.

Sincerely,
Walker Donnell

I had to sit down. I leaned against the tree my bike was locked to and just breathed for a minute. I wasn't sure whether I felt more upset at the letter or weirded out by the fact that Walker had been able to find my bike here, that he'd known where I'd be.

"Sincerely?" "Walker *Donnell?*" Like I knew anyone else named Walker who'd blow me off.

Christ!

I ran back into the park, furious, desperate not to cry, until I came to a place where I was sure no one would hear me. Then I yelled and screamed and howled.

How could he do this to me? Because of him, I'd found out I loved sailing, and I'd never have another chance to do it. Because of him, I'd come out of my shell and admitted that I wanted someone. Because of him, I'd had to tell my mom I'm gay long before I'd felt ready to do that. Because of him, I'd figured out that I'm really not a coward.

Not a coward. And if I'm not a coward, what do I do about this? Do I honor his wishes—or, not his, but his mother's—and stay away? Or do I come up with a way to get him alone and find out what the fuck that priest is saying to him?

That priest! I knew religion could be really bad about gay people. I'd heard about places where they do terrible things to try and convince people they aren't gay, or trans, or anything other than some limited, antiquated version of humanity.

I hadn't even known his mother was Catholic. But— there'd been that snippet of conversation I'd overheard on the bridge of Mr. Donnell's yacht, when Mrs. Donnell had mentioned church. Maybe I could get to Mr. Donnell! He either wasn't Catholic, or he didn't take it seriously enough to go to church. He might not want that priest telling Walker who he should be.

I didn't know what I was going to do, but I knew I had to do something. Partly it was because I didn't want to give

Walker up. But even more, I didn't Walker to give up on himself.

At first, on my way home, I pedaled really fast; had to release some energy. But then I slowed down; I didn't want to actually *be* home. Also, I wanted to think.

In a way, I felt like a creep, being angry with Walker. Hell, being angry enough that in my head I'd called him deformed. What a jerk. Here was this kid nature had played a nasty trick on, making him feel so close to being male that he wanted to be male, but not letting him feel male enough that he'd know he was gay when he liked another guy.

Then along comes his religious mother, who thinks gay is a sin, and she takes the poor kid off to be brainwashed by some narrow-minded bigot to make him think he isn't gay. Taking it to the next step, and pedaling so slowly that I had trouble maintaining balance, I pictured a contrite Walker, trying to convince himself he wasn't gay, still wanting to be male, trying to feel about a girl the way he felt about me, not being able to do it—Jesus Fucking Christ. What would happen to him then?

Suddenly I stopped pedaling, one foot on the ground, and stared ahead into space, Walker's words echoing in my head: "I'll never be able to live a normal life... I almost want to end it all... It gets real bad sometimes."

It felt like something inside my chest was caving in. My breath came in sharp, shallow gasps, and my eyes burned with tears that didn't fall.

Walker was going to kill himself. Maybe not today, maybe not this weekend, maybe not this month. But that's what would happen if I didn't do something. It might happen anyway. But knowing what I knew, I couldn't do nothing. I was just going to have to figure out what.

As soon as I opened the door to our unit Mom said, "Where've you been all day? I could have used your help around here." She was at the counter in the kitchen area, no doubt putting something together for dinner, and she didn't even turn her head toward me.

It was a huge effort to sound calm, to push back on the thoughts that were front-and-center in my mind. "You never said anything—"

"A lady in a wheelchair took a room, and I had to help her with her luggage."

"Okay, well, sorry, but that doesn't seem like a lot."

"And I needed some groceries." She stopped chopping, or whatever she was doing, and turned part-way in my direction. "If you're not going to have a summer job, then you can jolly well be some help to me around here."

I opened my mouth to say that I'd need some advance notice for these little tasks, that I wasn't about to hang around here all day and wait to see if she needed something, but a voice in my head told me to tread softly. So instead, I asked, "Anything I can do now?"

That took her aback, I could tell; she was probably as surprised as I was that I didn't push back. She waved a hand vaguely. "You can set the table. We're having tuna casserole and corn on the cob."

She turned back toward her task, and as I set about to do mine, she said, "Your father tells me you want an extra day with him."

How to respond? "I didn't think you'd mind. Anything you need me to do tomorrow during the day?"

She looked at me oddly, and I couldn't help wondering if she was getting suspicious. "Were you with that Donnell boy?"

"Walker, Mom. His name is Walker. And no. I was shooting all day. Alone. In the marshes." I let my voice rise just a little so I'd seem like the old version of me. And when I realized I had done that, it gave me a shock: Was a new version of me emerging?

"Your father isn't helping the two of you get together?"

I was surprised that she'd even think that, followed closely by fury at Mrs. Donnell that I didn't want Mom to see. Then came the temptation to distract her by mentioning Sharon. Did Mom know about Sharon? Dad hadn't said.

"Dad doesn't even know about Walker."

"But you said you'd told him."

"No, I said I'd told him I was gay. That's all."

She scowled just a tiny bit. "So—you thought you were gay before you met Walker?"

"I *knew* I was gay. I've known for a long time."

She waved a hand and turned back to the counter. "Whatever."

After dinner I texted Dad. *Does Mom know about S?*

I got an answer almost immediately. *No. Pls don't say anything.*

K

Whew. Maybe Mrs. Donnell had forced my hand so I had to tell Mom about me, but I really didn't want the responsibility of forcing Dad's hand about Sharon.

I spent as much time as I could after dinner doing research. There was lots of information about this lie called "ex-gay therapy," or "reparative therapy." There's no way those terms are anything you can take seriously. The whole thing is a fraud. There was this huge organization, Exodus International, that had been lying to gay people, trying to make them become straight, since 1976. Three years ago, it closed its doors with some pathetically inadequate apology, saying they hadn't changed anyone, and they'd ruined countless lives—including lots and lots of suicides. And there was no research I could find that showed any other effort had succeeded, either, though some gay people said they'd managed to change their behavior. But not their nature.

Next I looked into Catholicism. I guess I already knew how that church feels about gay people, and about how sinful homosexuality is to them. But I hadn't focused on the details.

The Vatican doesn't officially endorse "ex-gay therapy," but it does take exorcism seriously. (This confused me; the two seemed equally stupid.) I saw a few posts quoting Pope Francis saying he doesn't judge gays who "seek the Lord in good faith." He also made some comment about how Christians should apologize to gay people and ask forgiveness for treating us badly, though it wasn't clear to me how that was going to play out.

At first I thought maybe the pope wasn't such a bad guy, and maybe the Catholic priest wouldn't actually push Walker toward suicide. But when I thought harder, I realized Catholicism would still condemn gay people who weren't chaste, so they'd never be able to have sex. And there were issues like marriage, and adoption, and a whole host of other stuff we weren't allowed to take part in. All of which made me wonder just what made Pope Frank think we'd forgive him for anything, if he ever actually did apologize. Maybe he wouldn't judge us, but it was obvious he still expected God to.

Mom had me running around doing things all day Friday, no doubt as punishment for disappearing on Thursday. And, probably, to make sure I wasn't seeing "that Donnell boy." This pissed me off; I wasn't so much planning to see "that Donnell boy" as I was hoping to bike over and somehow sneak onto the property just to see if *Dare Ya* was at the dock or not there at all. If it wasn't

there, then probably Walker was sailing, I hoped without
the dreadful company of Cam. But as it was, I barely had
time to pack for the weekend.

For once, we were right on time to meet Dad, though
the journey hadn't been fun for me. Mom was back on the
topic of Dylan. "I'm seeing Madam Alberta this weekend,"
she told me. "I'm sure you won't care to hear about any
news, so I won't bore you with it."

Oh, boy.

Once I was in the safety of Dad's truck, he told me
Sharon was at his place making dinner, and the next thing
he said to me was, "You didn't say anything about her to
your mother, did you?"

"Nope. You planning to?"

He started the engine and we headed out. "Soon. Kind
of hard to know how to approach things, with this business
about Dylan hanging in the air."

I didn't tell him about my dream where Dylan got
replaced by Mr. Donnell, but I did tell him I'd spilled the
beans about Dylan. That is, about how I didn't believe what
Madam Alberta had told Mom. I said it had been a moment
of weakness, and Dad chuckled. "Bet that didn't go over
well."

"Not at all. So, Dad, how serious is this thing with
Sharon?"

Maybe a quarter mile later, he said, "Kind of. We're not
engaged or anything. Not sure it will come to that. But it
might." He grinned and glanced at me briefly. "Men like
me, we're not great on our own."

"Will I like her?" It was out before I could stop it.

But he grinned, so it was okay. "I think so. I hope
you'll show her some of your work. Photos, I mean."

Oh, man, was I glad I hadn't had time to snap a pic of
Walker's... you know.

I asked, "What does Sharon do?" If she had blue hair
and a nose ring, I'd have guessed she was a tattoo artist, or

maybe a sales clerk in a comic book store, something like that.

"She's an HR consultant. Sorry; human resources. She helps companies with things like interviews, but her favorite thing is working through problems when an employee and a boss have a conflict."

Brakes squealed on inside my head. "How old is she?"

"My age, plus a year or two."

I did not see that coming. Not that, and not the next thing Dad said.

"In her work, she specializes in issues around L... T—whatever those initials are."

No way. "Are you talking about LGBTQ?"

"That's it. Can't remember what they all stand for."

"Lesbian, Gay, Bisexual, Transgender, Queer. Sometimes there's I and A, which are Intersex and Asexual." Intersex. Hell; I'd known that. But until this moment I hadn't connected it with Walker.

"Right. I've asked her what makes 'queer' a separate category. Not sure I got it. Intersex has me confused as well."

My brain was firing on all thrusters, though not all in the same direction. I started with the topic of my own revelation to Dad. "So, that night I told you about me... that was only two weeks ago. You were already seeing her, right?"

I'd hit a nerve, and he cringed a little. "Yeah. Why?"

"Did you call her after you ran out on me? After you found out I'd run out on you?"

He was trying not to grin. "You're too smart for your own good. You know that, right?"

I leaned back against the seat and stared out of the windshield, seeing nothing, reconstructing that night in my mind. At the time, I'd been a little too preoccupied to focus on how quickly Dad had seemed to turn around in his thinking. Now that I knew Sharon had coached him, it made more sense.

"She's not gay, obviously, if she's your girlfriend. Why did she specialize in LGBTQ issues?"

"She had a gay son. He committed suicide when he was fourteen. She's never actually said this, but I think she blames her ex-husband. He was pretty hard on the kid." A few seconds went by. "You probably shouldn't bring that up unless she does."

I tried to imagine what it would be like to talk with this Sharon lady. Was she the type who'd convinced herself she knows all about gay people but really has most of it wrong?

"Micah," Dad's voice yanked me out of my thought stream, "you haven't ever... you know. Thought of doing that. Have you?"

"What, offing myself?" Walker's voice in my head told me that would hurt, that it was way, way too casual. "Sorry. That's a bad way to put it. No, Dad. Not so far, anyway." At least, not seriously. I kind of think everyone has the idea in their head at some point in their life.

Probably goes without saying that Sharon didn't have blue hair. Or a nose ring. Though her brown hair was short enough for me to see that she had a second hole in one of her earlobes, with a tiny diamond stud in it. She wasn't fat, but she was not exactly slim, either. What shouldn't go without saying is the jolt I felt when I saw her, normal hair aside.

When Sharon had existed as an idea only, and given the way I was feeling about my mom this week, it hadn't hit me that Sharon was filling a gap that maybe I didn't want filled. Maybe, in the way-back part of my brain, I'd held onto the hope that my family could be a family again. Maybe I'd thought that my parents would somehow reconcile, maybe even (imagination running wild) over their efforts to accept their younger son as gay.

Maybe, this hope had suggested, we'd live in a real house again. Maybe we'd get another dog. Maybe it could be that the only reason I would feel marginalized at all would be that I was gay, and not that the rest of my life was so pathetic. And it was pathetic; my mother and I lived in a sad, cramped motel unit, and my dad went home alone every night to his Spartan bachelor apartment, and I didn't get nearly enough time with him.

I hadn't even known I'd had this hope. And given the way I felt when I saw Sharon, it must have been huge. Because as soon as my eyes took in that normal-looking woman in my dad's kitchen, working at the counter as if she belonged there, as if she had every right to be there—all I can say is that I froze.

Sharon moved away from the counter, wiping her hands on a towel, as Dad and I came in.

"Hello, Micah." Her voice was low but not soft. She held her hand out, and I took a few wooden steps forward to give her mine. I wasn't ready to cause a scene. Hell, I don't know what I was ready for. She added, "I'm glad you could be here a day early this week."

I had imagined this meeting ever since Dad had said she'd be here. I'd pictured her all wrong, of course, but also I'd imagined her saying things that were predictable, like *Your father's told me so much about you.* Or *I've been so looking forward to meeting you.*

Somehow, something in her voice, something about not feeling forced to answer, made me take a mental step back from hating her. I said, "Me, too. Smells good in here." And it did.

But then bad feelings crept in again when Dad washed his hands and asked Sharon what he could do to help.

He never helped Mom in the kitchen without being asked.

Do people get smarter about relationships after they've had one fail monumentally? And if that was true, why hadn't Mom's life improved? Why hadn't mine?

Sharon half turned toward me. "Micah, please help yourself to a snack by way of appetizer. I'm afraid I don't talk and cook at the same time very well, and your father is worse!" She grinned and turned back to her work. But then she proceeded to chat with Dad, tease Dad, flirt with Dad.

I hadn't wanted to hate her. Or maybe I had. In either case, as I stood there watching them, a line from "Layla" came to me, sung by a man desperately in love with a woman: "Layla, you've got me on my knees." I couldn't picture anyone, let alone my dad, feeling like that about this woman. And yet I was now positive that he'd had Sharon in mind when he'd played that song for me weeks ago.

Dinner turned out to be something I've never had before. There were these long, curly spaghetti-like strands mixed with really small pieces of raw veggies and chopped hard boiled eggs, all tossed together with this red sauce that was room temperature and just slightly spicy. There were salads on the side with more stuff in them than Mom had ever put in a salad. Dessert was ice cream floats.

Sharon asked about my photography, but she didn't just ask what kinds of things I shoot. Instead, she asked what inspired me. At first I didn't even want to respond; why should this interloper be treated as if she had the right to know that about me? Or, the right to know anything about me? But I had to say something.

"I guess I like shots that appear to be one thing at first, but when you really look, it turns out not to be about that thing after all." *Like right now,* I wanted to add. Because if someone looked through the window at us, we'd look like a family. We weren't. And anyone who took a good look at my face would know that.

She nodded. "I think we have that in common. When I'm working with people in conflict, the things that seem at first to be on the surface usually turn out not to be the real source of the disagreement." She laughed. "Sometimes it's just a question of one person not realizing they were coming from a set of assumptions that the other person doesn't have. It can be a challenge to know what our own assumptions are until we bump into someone with a different set of them."

She laughed and added, "It's like that scene in *Fiddler on the Roof.* Tevye's friend Lazar asks him over for a conversation and says, 'I suppose you know why I wanted to talk to you.' Tevye thinks he does know and says that there's no point in talking. Lazar says, 'But you have others.' They go back and forth like this until Lazar says, 'This is very important to me. I get lonely.' Tevye says, 'How can a cow keep you company?' Lazar asks how Tevye can call her a cow, and Tevye says that's what she is, his new milk cow. That's when they figure out that it wasn't the cow Lazar wanted. It was Tzeitel, Tevye's oldest daughter."

Sharon grinned at me. "That's what I like to do. Figure out how people are talking at cross purposes and help them get on the same page."

She hadn't mentioned her specialty. Maybe that was to her credit, or maybe she wasn't brave enough to bring it up in the first meeting with her boyfriend's gay son. So I did.

"Like, 'gay is bad.'"

She didn't miss a beat. "That's a conclusion based on a whole spread of assumptions that someone might not even know they have. But whether someone knows they have them or not, the assumptions are incorrect."

"And you tell people they're wrong?"

"There's usually a less confrontational way to do it. What I try to do is talk them through things until they come to that conclusion themselves."

Dad said, "Like you did with me the night Micah told me about him."

"Oh, Gus, I think you would have realized most of that yourself. I just gave you some facts and asked a few questions that pointed you in that direction."

They smiled at each other in a way that made me hurt for Mom. And for me.

I didn't sleep well. No surprise, with Dad and Sharon in a bed together on the other side of the wall at my feet. If they did anything in there, I didn't hear it, but that didn't make me any more comfortable.

Lack of sleep was my excuse for being grumpy at breakfast, or at least that's what I said when Dad asked why I wasn't joining in the conversation. Truth be told, I was trying not to say aloud that the french toast Sharon had made (she even declared "Pain perdue!" in a French accent as she set my plate down) was the best friggin' french toast I'd ever had. And I was even grumpier when I realized that if I'd been friendlier, if I'd watched what she was doing, I might have been able to make it like that, myself.

I did my best to moderate my reaction when Dad announced that the three of us were taking a ferry ride to Block Island, and that we'd all take beginner lessons in paddle boarding on one of the ponds on the island. It was hard, because it appealed powerfully to my sense of righteous self-pity to know that Walker was away, not sailing, and I wouldn't even see him from a distance. Dad didn't help matters, though I'm sure he thought he would, by assuring me that this outing was Sharon's idea.

Bathing suits on under our clothes, we boarded one of the ferries that take cars as well as people, even though we weren't taking a car. Sharon said she thought the longer ride out would be fun, and that we'd take the catamaran back; that's only half an hour, and with our wet suits we might appreciate the shorter ride home. Way too thoughtful. She was just way too thoughtful.

I spent most of the sunny, hour-long ride out to Block Island with my arms resting on the side of the boat, squinting against the glare despite Dylan's sunglasses, watching for any sign of a Cape Dory Typhoon. Anyone's would do; I just wanted to see the boat, to imagine myself on it, to feel that freedom again.

No joy.

The taxi driver on the island let me sit in front rather than squash in the back with Dad and Sharon. I opened my window all the way, but as soon as we were moving Dad told me to close it; too much wind for Sharon.

Okay, I have to admit I really enjoyed paddle boarding. At least, on a pond. I wouldn't want to have this board I was standing on be the only thing between me and those sand tigers that I now knew for a fact were out there. Mr. Donnell wasn't here to rescue me today.

At first I was glad to see that Sharon wasn't very coordinated. But she was so fucking good-natured about it, and she laughed at herself so honestly, and Dad (who was really good at it) paid so much attention to her and tried so hard to help her, that even her failure annoyed me.

The good news was that the teacher, Porter, had more time for me, with Dad helping Sharon so much. There were four other people there for lessons, but they were all friends, and they entertained each other fooling around. So I was the only single person there who wanted to learn. And Porter, I was sure, was gay. He looked more real than Paige's boyfriend. Ashton had looked as though he'd been put together by a focus group. Porter had the kind of face that was homely in an adorable way, the kind of face that makes you want to smile.

I watched him anytime he wasn't helping me, admiring the way the muscle definition became more obvious as he worked an arm or a leg. I realized, with a pleasant shock, that I was kind of into thighs. Not only was it fun to watch the lines showing where one muscle group ended and the next one began, but also the back of the thigh leads the eye right up to the ass. And Porter, whose swim shorts were wet because he'd already fallen in while demonstrating what not to do on a board, had a very nice ass.

There was one awkward moment when I was standing on my board, just floating, watching Porter work with one of the other beginners, and I noticed that both Dad and Sharon were watching me watch. In my embarrassment, I moved too quickly, and I fell off the board. I was in a kind of deep area, so I went completely under. I wasn't afraid; like I've said, I'm a good swimmer. But I let go of the paddle.

That had a silver lining, though, because after Porter retrieved my paddle and swam over to me, he used me to demonstrate to the group how to get back on a board if you fall off in deep water. His hands, where he touched me to support my efforts, felt like the best possible combination of strong and gentle. I was terrified, though, that I'd get a hard-on that everyone would see. Thank God that reaction waited until Porter left me to demonstrate on his own board, so no one was watching me any longer.

As we were leaving, I looked for Porter once more, delighted that he was looking at me. I thought he'd smile, but maybe that would have been considered inappropriate. Instead, he tilted his head just a little and gave me the kind of nod that told me we knew something important about each other. I nodded back.

We had lunch in a place near where the boat had docked. Dad and I had hamburgers and fries. Sharon, it seemed, had a fondness for onion rings, which she ordered to go with her turkey club. She declared them substandard, but she ate every one.

Sharon had our day all planned, and right after lunch we grabbed another taxi out to the Southeast Lighthouse. We all took the tour, which was actually kind of fun. Oh, except there was this girl, about my age, who kept looking at me. If Dad or Sharon noticed, they didn't say anything, but I kept trying to get out of the girl's line of sight.

I was pretty tired by the end of the day, but I still wanted to sit in the front of the upper level on the catamaran. Dad and Sharon went to find seats in the back, which suited me just fine. I sat quietly, eyes mostly closed, and let the wind buffet my face. I loved the way the catamaran moved over the water, with a speed and power I hadn't felt in the boat we'd taken earlier. It was different from the sensation of flying that Walker had achieved in his little boat, but I let it remind me of him anyway.

As soon as I got back to the apartment, I changed clothes and then collapsed on "my" couch (the one I sleep on). I think Dad and Sharon went out to the balcony. I didn't care what they did; I just felt dead tired, but in a good way. As I drifted off, I thought that maybe I didn't actually hate Sharon.

We went out to a Chinese restaurant for dinner, and Sharon taught me how to eat with chopsticks. I did okay. Dad confessed that he'd tried to learn and had failed, so he used a boring old fork.

Falling asleep later, I had to admit to myself that I'd had a good day. It still didn't compare to my day of sailing with Walker, but then I wasn't sure what would. And if there was anything truly fucked up about this weekend, it was that I knew that missing him at this moment was nothing to how it was going to feel once I got home.

Mom totally freaked me out on the drive home, after she picked me up at the usual spot on Sunday afternoon.

She used to be cheerful, I think. It had been a while. Anyway, Sunday I could tell right away, as soon as I got in the car, that storm clouds had gathered and were about to start spitting lightening and yelling thunder.

My brain not being my best friend in circumstances like this, I said, "What did I do now?"

She let a good thirty seconds go by. "Did you enjoy yourself?" The tone was all wrong for a question, like she already knew the answer. Or like the real subject had nothing to do with my enjoyment.

I let out a quiet but exasperated breath and pretended the question had been genuine. "Went out to Block Island yesterday. Learned how to paddle board. Toured a lighthouse. Had Chinese for dinner." I didn't mention the chopsticks; Mom might know I didn't know how to use them as recently as last week.

"Just you?"

"Well, no, of course not. It was a 'Dad' weekend."

"Mmm-hmmm. Dad and who else?"

Shit. "Whaddya mean?"

"Don't lie to me, Micah. I know your father is seeing someone."

Fuck! Did I do something to give it away? I was searching back through everything I'd said since last Wednesday or so when Mom's voice, pointed and with ice around the edges, interrupted that effort.

"You recall, I hope, because I hope you hear what I have to say *sometimes*, that I saw Madam Alberta yesterday." She waited.

"Yeah, though I don't recall a specific day."

"It was yesterday. I saw her yesterday. And she told me the truth, about your father's new relationship, which is more than you and your father have done."

"I didn't lie!" It was all I could think of to say, when what I wanted to say was, *You mean that charlatan got something right for a change?* What I was thinking was, *OMG. How did she know?*

"You don't think deliberately not telling me that your father has a girlfriend is lying by omission?"

Think fast, Micah. "It's not my job to report back to you on what he does." Man, but that was the coward's way out. I regretted it immediately, although I didn't know what else I could have said.

"How long have you known?"

"Not long." Truth was that at that moment I couldn't recall when Dad had told me. Eric Clapton's song two weeks ago had been only a hint. It was everything I could do not to pull my phone out and text Dad to give him a heads-up.

"And when is he planning to let me in on this little secret?"

"Look, Mom, I'm sorry no one told you, okay? But maybe he hasn't told you yet because he's afraid you'll be hurt. That's why I hadn't said anything." Not true, but I was willing to see if it would buy me any credit.

Another long pause. "Well, it's just too bad that you had Chinese food last night, because we're getting it for take-out tonight. I haven't felt much like cooking since this bombshell was dropped on me yesterday."

Fine with me, actually, though I considered making disappointed noises to give her some sense of satisfaction. But as I sat there, feeling sorry for myself, this sad feeling came over me, but not for me. It was for Mom. I remembered how antagonistic I'd felt watching Sharon make herself at home in Dad's kitchen Friday night. I'd almost hated her. But that bad feeling hadn't been on my own account. It had been for Mom's sake.

"Do you... Did you... Were you thinking you and Dad might get back together at some point?"

A kind of barking laugh escaped her. "Wouldn't take him back if he crawled all the way from Warwick to beg." But there was a false note in there. So I didn't believe her. Which really did make me feel bad for her.

"You haven't met anyone else you like?"

"Oh, for God's sake, Micah. Where would I meet someone? When? How?"

I shrugged and decided to keep quiet for the rest of the ride. For the rest of the night. For the rest of the summer.

It was maybe half an hour after midnight. I was supposed to be asleep, but a phone and a good set of earbuds can make faking that easy enough. What I'd been watching had ended, and I pulled the earbuds out. I hadn't been able to pay attention very well, obsessing on the phone call I'd made to Dad, after that additional Chinese dinner.

I'd gone over to my customary spot in the drug store parking lot, despite a light drizzle, not so much to hide from Mom as to spare her having to hear about this again. But he needed to know that she knew about Sharon.

"How?" he demanded. "You said you hadn't told her!"

"It wasn't me. She saw Madam Alberta yesterday. That's who told her."

Silence. Then, quietly, "What the fuck?"

"I know, right? But that's what Mom said. She told me in the car on the way home. She didn't say anything about a name, and I didn't, either." I repeated most of what Mom and I had discussed.

He said, "Shit." Then, "Sorry; I shouldn't be saying these words."

Like I didn't? Parents…. "She's not any too happy that I didn't tell her, or that you didn't."

"Well I guess I'd be mad, too, if some medium had told me something important I thought should have come from my family. I don't blame her." I heard a few breaths. Then, "This is on me, Micah, not you. You know that, right?"

"I guess."

"But—good God, how did that woman know? Well, whatever the case, I'll call your mother tomorrow. Meanwhile, I hope she doesn't take it out on you."

I assured him I was fine, and we ended the call.

And this whole mess ran through my mind as I tried to watch a movie in my room, overwhelming the movie plot, dialog, music, all of it. I was wondering if maybe I should get at least a little sleep, when I heard the familiar sound of Mom crying.

I heaved an exasperated sigh and pictured her in there with Dylan's box. Then it dawned on me that as far as I could tell, she hadn't cried over that thing since Madam Alberta had said Dylan was alive. Which made me wonder what Mom *would* be crying about.

I got up, stood in my now open doorway, and listened. Yeah, it was her, all right, crying in her bedroom as usual. But the crying seemed different this time. Less forlorn and more… I don't know, more present somehow. Like she was crying over something going on now, not something that happened in the past. Was I imagining that?

I told myself to go back to bed and find something to distract myself on the phone, but I didn't move. I told myself it was like that time with the spider, when she'd wanted someone (the only someone around—me) to rescue her from the beast. But I knew that wasn't true. Still, I didn't move.

When I finally did move, it was toward her door. I knocked lightly; no answer, more crying. A louder knock made the crying stop.

"What do you want, Micah?"

I opened the door. She was on the floor, legs folded as close to her body as she could get them, leaning against the side of her bed. The only light was what came through the window from the parking lot outside, but it lit the room up fairly well.

"Are you okay?"

She swiped her hands across her face in a sudden, impatient gesture. "Since when do you care?"

I decided to ignore that, sure that she didn't expect a direct response. Sitting on the floor in front of her, I said, "Can you tell me what's wrong?"

She let out a rasping breath and dropped her head back against the mattress. "What *isn't* wrong?" She lifted her head again and looked at me. "My youngest child has told me he's gay, and I don't have a clue what that's going to mean. My older son is God knows where, maybe hurt, maybe worse, and my husband—sorry, *ex*-husband—has a new girlfriend, and they have the time and resources to take you out doing fun things like paddle boarding. I have this God-forsaken job that I hate that doesn't earn me enough money to provide a home for Dylan if he ever shows up and that doesn't provide you with a very good one now. I have no prospects and no one to help me." She lifted a hand and let it fall to the floor. "Who wouldn't cry?"

I wanted to point out some good things, but I couldn't come up with any. It felt horrible, knowing she was in real pain, knowing there was nothing I could do about it. I wanted to tell her I hadn't liked Sharon, but that wasn't true; I'd just hated seeing Sharon with Dad, and telling Mom that might make things worse. Then it occurred to me there was one thing I could do. It might make things worse, or it might make things better. I had to try.

"Hang on." I went back to my room, fished Trapper's collar out from its hiding spot in the back of my closet, and returned to Mom's room. She was still on the floor, blowing her nose.

"Mom, I, uh, I have something you were looking for once. I took it because I felt so guilty, and I didn't give it to you because—I'm not sure why. I guess I wanted to have my own little piece of Dylan, and you had all his other stuff."

I had her attention, that was sure. She watched my face as I held my hand toward her, the fastened circle of a collar clasped loosely in my fingers. I both wanted to snatch my hand back, to keep this painful token, and I wanted to give it to my mother, who seemed to need it more than I did.

She looked down at my hand, took a few seconds to focus in the faint light, and gasped. But she didn't take it right away. For maybe ten seconds she just stared at it. Then, slowly, her hand shaking, she reached for it. Her grasp was soft, as if in reverence. For a few seconds we both held it, our hands on opposite sides of that circle that held so much meaning.

And then I let it go.

Now there were tears in my own eyes. I didn't weep, but my eyes watered with tears of guilt, of tragedy, of regret, and of love. It was love, but it hurt because it had nowhere to go.

There was nothing in Mom's look or actions that seemed to be accusing me of anything, even though she could reasonably have accused me of a number of things. She held the collar in front of her, eyes taking in every detail the low light would reveal. She turned it around and around as though there might be a beginning and an end to that circle. Or maybe she just wanted to make sure there was no end.

"I'm sorry." Speaking those words released something in me, and I started crying for real.

The next thing I knew Mom's arms were around me in an awkward embrace, and we were crying together. When Mom finally let go, she began to laugh through her tears.

"Aren't we a pair, eh?"

She handed me a few tissues, and we both blew our noses. Then she leaned back against the mattress again, and I resumed my position across from her.

"Micah, talk to me about this boy. Walker."

Whoa. That was out of left field. "Like, what kind of things do you want to know?"

"Well... I asked Madam Alberta about you. Now, I know you don't take her very seriously. But when I asked if she could tell that you're gay, she said, 'Oh, yes.' It was like she thought I'd already known. Certainly, it was as though *she'd* already known. So I asked her about Walker."

She blew her nose again, and I took advantage of the pause to ask, "Why?"

"When Mrs. Donnell was here—I'm ashamed to say this, Micah, but I was a little intimidated. And because of that, I didn't respond in the way I should have as your mother. I didn't protect you. I should have."

This made no sense to me. "Protect me how?"

"I mean, who does she think she is, telling my son he can't be friends with hers, and not giving me a damned good reason why?" She waved a hand in the air. "Oh, I know she thinks she gave me a reason. I've been going over in my head what it was that she did say. She used words like 'vulnerable' and 'complicated.' She said you were too strong an influence for him in his 'fragile position.' But, damn it, that's not enough."

She took a breath, and I reminded her, "She doesn't want him to be gay."

"Right, and that's another thing. I didn't react very well to that, either. And maybe, after she left, the shock of finding out that you're gay sent me in another loop, but here's the thing." She took a deep breath and let it out

199

slowly. "I got the distinct impression that she thinks of you as somehow not good enough for her son."

Wow. Like, wow. "Well... I don't know. She was nice enough to me the couple of times I was with her. I didn't really get that impression." I didn't want Mom to feel bad about something that wasn't true.

"Did she know you were gay then?" I shook my head. "So is it really as simple as not wanting him to be gay? Doesn't she know that's not something either of them has any say about?"

I wanted to hug Mom all over again. She got it! She understood! This is who I am. This is not a choice or a decision. The only decision was whether to come out, whether to be fully myself, whether to live life as I am. I felt almost giddy. And once that giddiness combined with the anger I was feeling toward Walker, any reluctance I had about revealing his secret to Mom disappeared.

"I think she's afraid he's making a mistake in *thinking* he's gay. Which is also very silly. But she might be afraid of that because of his condition. He's what they call intersex."

She blinked hard; I could tell, even in that low light. "What on earth..."

It took a nanosecond for me to realize that in all my research—looking for images of a micropenis, investigating "ex-gay therapy" and Catholicism, I hadn't researched what it meant to be intersex. I told Mom all I could remember from Walker's explanation.

"It has something to do with chromosomes."

"You mean the X Y chromosomes?"

"Must be, yeah. I keep meaning to look it up. He has to take testosterone, because he knows he's a guy, but I guess there might be some question..." My voice trailed off as I realized I knew nothing. *Nothing.*

"If he has to take testosterone, maybe he has an extra X in him. But what's that got to do with being gay?"

"Nothing, as far as I know. He happens to be gay." I wanted to add, *He can tell by the way he feels about me*, but that seemed a little too personal despite this new-found togetherness. "But his mother's Catholic, and Catholics think there's all this sin gay people fall into just living our lives."

She watched my face for a few seconds. "Are you telling me that she's trying to make him straight through religion?"

I didn't want anyone to know that Walker had left me a note, so I shrugged to cover my lie. "I don't have a lot of information. Maybe she wants him to talk to her priest, or something."

She reached out and gave me another hug, a quick one. "Micah, I promise you, I would never do anything like that to you."

Chapter Ten

Mom and I sat for a while over breakfast on Monday, talking on and off between interruptions from the front office as a couple of early rising guests checked out. She wanted to know about Sharon, and at first I was suspicious. But I decided it didn't seem like she was asking questions out of sadness or even jealousy. It was more that she just wanted to know how things stood.

I gave her a brief description and repeated what I could remember of Sharon's job, though I left out the part about how she specializes in gay issues. That just seemed like too much for Mom to take in right now. Maybe another time.

"Did you like her?"

I lifted a shoulder and dropped it. "I guess. She was nice enough. Decent cook."

Mom switched gears and asked for more details about what we'd done on Saturday. I'd gotten about as far as learning to use chopsticks, which was almost everything, when the office bell rang again.

"For God's sake!" Mom said under her breath as she headed toward the office yet again.

I went to the fridge to see if there any more chocolate milk and stood there with the door open, considering how long it would take for Walker to see the full extent of what his mother was expecting from him, at which point I would step in and burst her bubble. There was no more chocolate milk; I could go get some later. As I was closing the fridge door, I heard Mom cry out. I dashed toward the office.

She stood there, frozen, a hand over her mouth, staring bug-eyed at two uniformed Army officers, hats in their hands. I couldn't tell a damn thing from their expressions about what was going on, but it was eerily like when they'd come to tell us Dylan had been killed. I didn't have any other siblings to kill, so what the fuck?

Mom realized I was there and turned toward me, her free hand reaching out for support. She wrapped both arms around me and squeezed so hard I couldn't breathe right away, but she didn't say anything. I looked over her shoulder at the two men, who hadn't moved a muscle.

"What is it?" I wanted them to say something, anything, to explain.

One of them said, "We've just given your mother the good news that her son Private First Class Dylan Jaeger has been found alive."

Between Mom's ecstatic wails and my own shock I barely heard what else he said, but I gathered that Dylan had escaped from the wreckage we thought had killed him and had managed to evade enemy fire and make his way into the hills. He'd been there for several months, now, helped by a local Afghani family.

Mom still couldn't speak, so I did. "Why are we just hearing about this now?"

"We just heard from him. He was in a remote area were there's been a lot of Taliban activity, and it wasn't safe for him or for the family to get word out until now. We've just reclaimed the territory he was in."

"But—we have his dog tags. We buried him."

At last, a break in their robot-like expressions. "It, um, it seems likely that you buried someone else. We'll be in touch with you about that as we know more."

My ears rang. The blood pounded in my head. My eyes burned. I felt as though I would fall.

One of the men came over and led my sobbing mother away from me and toward a chair. I grabbed the edge of the reception desk, determined not to cave, not to look like the wuss I knew I wasn't.

I coughed a couple of times and then managed, "What happens now?"

"He's in an army hospital in Germany getting checked out. He'll phone you here in just over an hour."

I did a calculation in my head that took longer than it would have at another time. "Can he call in two hours?"

"Why?"

"I think my dad would like to be here, too, and he's in Warwick. He's on a construction site. I'm not sure how long it would take him to get here."

As the two stepped outside to discuss this request, a family of four stepped into the office to check out. Mom was still a mess, so I forced myself to focus. She'd taught me to do this, but I hadn't had to check anyone out very often.

The woman—mother, I assumed—in the group looked toward Mom. "What's going on? Is she all right?"

"We've just had some surprising news," I told her. "She'll be very happy once she calms down." I almost added that I, too, might be fine after I calmed down, but I wasn't falling apart visibly the way Mom was. Just internally.

By the time I'd finished the checkout process, including making sure they didn't need help with luggage, the army guys were back. One of them said, "We'll return in two hours for the call."

I pulled my phone out of my pocket so fast it nearly went flying across the room. My text, with the subject 911, didn't have to wait long for Dad's response. Mom and I watched each other's faces as I talked to him.

"Micah! Is everything all right?" He must have been up on a building somewhere, overcoming his fear of heights; I could practically feel the wind through the phone, and he was shouting.

"We're fine, Dad. Before I say anything else, are you someplace safe? Like, where you won't fall?"

"Hang on… okay. Spill."

"Dad, two army guys were just here. They found Dylan. He's not dead after all." It was so hard not to blurt out everything I knew, even though it wasn't much. But I waited, letting that sink in, through maybe ten seconds of nothing but the sounds of wind and distant traffic noise.

"What did you say?"

"Dylan's alive, Dad. He's coming home. Is there any way you can be here in two hours? That's when he's going to call from Germany."

Even as I said this, I could tell Dad was moving. "Leaving now. I'll call you from the road." And he hung up.

I called Nick and asked him to come man the office, and I went over to sit in the chair beside Mom. She grabbed my hand, but she didn't look at me. I could tell she still wasn't ready to speak. So I did.

"I guess Madam Alberta was right."

She didn't reply; she couldn't, she was sobbing so hard.

Mom and I waited in our tiny living room. She sat on the couch, wordless, wringing her hands and starting up every time the office door opened even though Nick was there. Dad arrived almost in time for the original plan for the call from Dylan. That was good, though, because it gave us a little time, the three of us, to be together— something that hadn't happened in I couldn't remember how long. I'd told Dad everything I knew when he'd called after getting on the road, so there was nothing new to say about Dylan.

As soon as Dad stepped into the room Mom flew to him. She'd quieted down after I'd called him, but now she was crying again. Dad reached an arm toward me for a group hug, something I couldn't remember doing since I was little, and by the time we let go we were all teary-eyed.

They sat on the couch and I took the chair, and it seemed like none of us knew what to say. We repeated what the officers had told us and then speculated on what it must have been like for Dylan, hiding in the hills, supported by a sympathetic family, unable to let us know he was all right, with the Taliban roaming around. Dad said Dylan had probably been in a cave, there were so many. Mom wondered how skinny he was and whether he was sick. I wondered if he had a beard.

No one said anything about Madam Alberta.

Only one of the Army officers, Colonel Atherton, returned, about ten minutes ahead of the expected call. He pulled a kitchen chair closer to us and explained that an officer in Germany would initiate the call, Colonel Atherton would answer the phone, and then we could speak with Dylan.

It was the longest ten minutes I could remember.

We all jumped (except the colonel) when the phone rang. He exchanged a few words with whoever was on the other line, and then he put the phone on speaker. We waited.

"Hello?"

I think all three of us shouted, "Dylan!" at once. Then Dad took over; Mom held her hand over her mouth, tears streaming from her eyes. I think I might have heard her say, "Oh, my God! My baby!"

Dad said, "Dylan, son, this is unbelievable! How are you? Are you hurt? Sick?"

Dylan chuckled, a sound so familiar to me that I nearly started bawling. "I'm fine, really. They're giving me an overhaul, make sure everything's in working order, before they send me home."

Mom found her voice. "When?"

"Probably leave here in a couple of days. So I should be home by the weekend, anyway."

"Were you wounded?" Dad wanted to know.

"Well, yeah, but not horribly. Broke an arm in the explosion, took a few rounds getting away. All in the past."

He sounded like himself, and he didn't. Fighting the enemy overseas, getting shot, living in a cave for months—maybe all that changes you. Plus I hadn't seen him since he'd enlisted, and that was long enough ago now that I wondered whether he'd recognize me.

Mom finally found her voice and asked a bunch of questions, and either Colonel Atherton or the officer at the other end would interrupt when they didn't want Dylan to say something they thought shouldn't be said over the phone.

Finally I had a chance to ask my question, which I knew was silly, but I wanted to lighten things a little. "Do you have a beard?"

"I do, as a matter of fact. Been growing it ever since the explosion."

"I knew it!"

Colonel Atherton stepped in at this point. "Folks, it's great you had a chance to talk. We'll be in touch when we have the specifics about PFC Jaeger's return." And that was the end. The colonel said a few more things I don't remember, mostly just to end the visit, and left the three of us alone again.

Dad had stood to see the colonel out, and he didn't seem able to settle again. He paced back and forth in that small space until Mom told him to stop.

"Gotta go for a walk, then." And he was gone before I knew whether I wanted to go with him. But probably he wanted to be alone.

For the first time that day, I wondered about logistics. Would Dylan move in here, like Mom had been planning? Would I have to go to Warwick? And was there no scenario in which Dylan and I could live at the same address?

Sure. If my folks got back together.

Was that on the table at all? Might it happen now? If their grief over Dylan's supposed death was what tore them apart, might they get together again? I looked at Mom, who'd about killed the box of tissues she'd been carrying around with her. I fetched her a new box and sat beside her on the couch.

"Mom, can I ask you something? Promise not to get mad."

She chuckled and blew her nose again. "I'm not sure what could make me mad right at this moment."

"Once Dylan's home again, what are the chances you and Dad might—"

"Stop." She held a hand in front of her, palm out. "I'm sorry, Micah. There's too much water under the bridge for that."

"But we could all live together then."

She let out a long breath. "Chances are that Dylan won't want to move in with his parents. Either of us. I confess I feel a little silly now, with all my preparations and hopes. I went a little crazy." She smiled at me and shook her head. "Oh, I suppose he'll stay with one of us for a short time, until he can get his feet under him. But Micah, he's a young man, now. Twenty-one years old. He's survived war. I doubt he'll want to go back to living with Mommy *or* Daddy."

Good point. "What do we do now?"

The door opened, and Dad walked in. So what we did was make some decisions. It was the calmest discussion I could recall my folks having in a long, long time. They decided that Dylan would move in with Dad, because if he wanted to find a job his chances were much better in

Warwick. Or he could easily go into Providence from there. Dad was going to see if there might be a job for him with the construction crew, in case Dylan was interested. We all agreed Mom and I would stay put for my senior year and then see where things lay.

And suddenly there was nothing more to do. Dad said he was heading back to work, and Mom wanted to call Madam Alberta to give her the news. I had to stop myself from saying she ought to know, if she's so powerful, but— damn. The woman had known about Sharon. She had known about me. And she had known about Dylan.

I decided to bike over to Jasper Island. It was a free country, right? And I'd see if I could find a place with a view of the dock without being seen, myself—and a place where I could be alone and let my feelings about Dylan settle at least a little.

It was not quite two miles to the bridge that crossed over to the island. Once across it, there was another mile to get to the far end where the Donnells' house was. As I pedaled, I grew more and more anxious that one of them would be driving either to or from the house, and they'd recognize me. I knew all their cars, so maybe I could take evasive action of some kind. But I made it without running into anyone who might know me.

There was a large area with trees between the Donnells and their neighbors. I couldn't tell which house the land went with, but I looked around one more time to be sure I wasn't seen, lifted my bike, and made my way into the trees. I found a good spot to lay the bike down where it wouldn't be visible from the road or from the houses, and I moved quietly toward the water.

The shore here was narrow and rocky, and it faced east—not the sort of shore where anyone would spread out a towel. And although it curved inward, forming a slight bay, the houses were situated so that no one from either house could see me. I moved cautiously toward the

Donnells' dock. When I could see it clearly, the only boat there was *Magic Spell*. So Walker must be sailing.

Immediately a longing came over me, and I had to sit on a large rock near the trees. I so wanted to be out there with Walker, ocean air buffeting my face, salt spray stinging my arms, feeling the joy of that little boat as we flew over the water, free and boundless for at least a while. My chest hurt, and—still feeling vulnerable after talking with my not-dead-after-all brother—I almost wanted to cry. To distract myself, I focused hard on the little lapping sounds the water made on the stones a few feet in front of me. The trees I had come through were right behind me, shading me. I could sit here as long as I wanted, dreaming of flying in *Dare Ya* with Walker. Walker, at the helm, in control. Walker, at peace and not being told who he was or how he should feel.

Wait. Was I telling him who he was or how he should feel? Was his mother right, and was I influencing him in a particular way, pushing him in a direction that was mine but might not be his? Well, if I was, the direction was a hell of a lot better than what she wanted her church to do to him.

But—what was the difference, exactly?

Well… well, he'd kissed me before I would have had the guts to kiss him, so that speaks to his being gay. And there was the memory of those few seconds in the lower stateroom on *Magic Spell*, when we'd both wanted each other. He'd told me he'd been hard. And there were those sweet moments after the sharks, after I'd told Walker about Dylan, when we'd sat there quietly, holding hands, just being together. He'd trusted me with seeing him naked. He'd kissed me passionately and declared us boyfriends. That was a lot!

And what did his mother have to go on? As far as I could tell, all she knew was that Walker's condition gave him reason to proceed cautiously. But that didn't mean he couldn't proceed! At seventeen, he wasn't ready to commit himself for life to me or anybody else. Okay, so he felt confused. The only way out of that was to pick a direction and see if it was the right one. So all his mother had to go on was that she didn't want him to be gay. Tough shit.

And if I was wrong about him? If he wasn't gay? What were the consequences? I couldn't see anything truly terrible coming out of that for Walker. So maybe he'd spend part of a summer making out with a guy. If he decided, by September or so, that it had been a delightful summer of love that he wouldn't repeat, what did he lose? If anything, he'd *gain* something. Because if he thought he might be gay but he never tried it, he might be haunted by the question for a long time. Maybe for the rest of his life.

And if she was wrong about him, and her priest had his way with him, and if they did something really terrible like put him in one of those horrible places, and if he got through it and realized he really was straight, that would be the only possible good outcome. Because the other consequences were either that he'd only *think* he was straight and proceed down a path that would lead to grief, or he'd kill himself. The biggest grief of all.

I pictured Mrs. Donnell in my mind. She and Walker looked so much alike, it wasn't difficult. She had seemed so nice, both the day I'd met her when she'd fed me that pasta dish, and again on the fireworks cruise. But now she wanted to keep me away from her son. It was almost as though some graceful fish had lifted its head out of the water and opened its mouth to reveal ferocious teeth.

Mrs. Donnell was a shark.

My phone startled the hell out of me. I nearly dropped it in the sand. It was Dad, calling from the road, from the sounds on the line.

"Micah, I just wanted to make sure you're okay. I'm sorry I couldn't stay any longer, but I had to get out of there."

I snorted a kind of laugh. "Guess how the place makes me feel." It was a stab, and I knew it. I was saying, *It's not my fault I don't live in a real house. And guess whose fault it is.*

He paused a second or two and decided to ignore that poke. "I hope you're really okay with staying put for the school year. It seemed like the best thing for you."

"Yeah. That's fine. I don't really want to change schools again. And I want to go to college. Photography." I couldn't remember if I'd ever even told him that.

"I didn't know that." There was a pause, like maybe he wanted to say something about choosing a practical course of study, but then he said, "Anyway, I expect Dylan will move into Providence or someplace. I'm not sure what your mother will do, but she's a free agent."

So he felt the same as she did. No chance for reconciliation.

"If Dylan stays with you, what about Sharon?" This time the pause was lengthy. "Dad?"

"I'm here. Yeah, um, I'll probably let Dylan have the apartment to himself."

When he didn't go on, I prompted, "You—you're moving in with Sharon?"

I could almost hear him shrug. "At least while Dylan needs a place. After that, we'll see."

"You called her, didn't you? Before you phoned me."

"Micah, don't take it personally."

"I'm not. I just would like to know what's going on."

"And I'm telling you. Is there anything you don't know, anything you think I can tell you?"

So many things. But they weren't things he could tell me. "Not right now."

"I'll be in touch, Micah."

I was sure he was feeling the same thing I was: it was so fucking amazing, confusing, wonderful, painful, and joyful that anyone would be making plans that involved my living, breathing, bearded brother.

Waiting for Walker, watching for that joyful little boat to head home from it's adventure, I had plenty of time to think about Dylan. On the phone, he'd sounded both like himself and different from the Dylan I'd known. What did that mean? Would he be too old, now, and too experienced, too world-weary to be my big brother again? And what would it mean to me, now that so much time had gone by— now that I wouldn't let anyone ever again tell me to buck up or not to be a wuss—to have a big brother again? How did grown men handle this relationship?

I stood, shook myself back to the present, and went into the trees to pee. It was maybe three o'clock, and I'd had no lunch. But I figured I could come back here anytime and be better prepared. And maybe disguised, somehow, at least on the road. Maybe I could grow a beard....

Back at my rock, I stared as far past the dock as I could, trying to decide whether to sit and wait some more or not. Maybe two minutes went by, and then the bow of *Dare Ya* appeared from around the point of the island. I watched, frozen, as Walker maneuvered the boat into place, secured her sails, and moored her safely. It wasn't until he'd climbed onto the dock that he turned in my direction, and he saw me.

His turn to freeze.

We stared at each other, neither of us moving at all, until he lifted an arm. One wave, and he turned and walked slowly toward his house and disappeared.

I didn't wave back, just stared at the spot where I'd lost sight of him. If there would ever be a reunion, it would have to come from him. And everything about his body language told me that was not going to be today.

As sure as I was about him, I wanted him to be sure as well, and I didn't want to push him. I didn't want him to be more confused than he already was.

I did want Walker. But I'd take my time, and I'd let him take his. I'd wait. Aloud, still staring at the spot where he'd disappeared from view, I said, "I'll wait as long as it takes."

I made it off the island again without being spotted by any Donnell, but I wasn't ready to go home. Feeling nearly faint with hunger, I stopped at a gas station and picked up something to eat from their odd selection of food items, along with a ginger ale, and then headed toward Wilcox Road, to the entrance of the Knox Preserve. I hadn't been down there in a while, and I knew where there was a spot on Quiambog Cove where people could launch a small boat. A large boat couldn't have made it under the railroad bridge, but a boat like *Dare Ya* could make it out to the Sound. There wasn't really any place to go from the launch on foot. If you wanted to get to the tiny strip of sand on the Sound, you could cross the railroad tracks. But there were some nice places to sit right there on the cove, so I headed there.

The tide was just beginning to go out, so there wasn't a whole lot of sandy area to sit on. I took my shoes off so I could wade out to one of the larger rocks. I was perched there, sitting a little awkwardly, having finished most of my ginger ale, when I caught sight of something moving in the water. The water wasn't very clear here, and probably the tide going in and out had stirred up some silt, so I couldn't really make out what that shape was, though I have to say it made me really nervous.

Don't be wuss. Master your fear. Buck up.

It moved away from me, out into deeper water, and I lost sight of it. I had polished off my drink and had just tucked it into my pack with the shape reappeared.

This time it came closer—so close that it was just a foot or so from my rock, and my rock was only about a foot above the water. I stared hard, and then harder, and then my breath caught and I smelled the sharp pang of my own terror.

It was a shark.

It was a shark, and it was a bigger shark than the one that had chewed my calf. But this water was only brackish, not salt water, because of the fresh water flowing into the cove from the river. I wracked my brain: What sharks can survive in brackish water? There are a few river sharks, but they wouldn't be anywhere near here. There was the spear tooth shark, but again, not around here. So it had to be a bull shark.

Bull shark. Carcharhinus leucas. The only shark in this part of the world that can tolerate fresh water. Seen far north up the Mississippi River. Seen far, far up the Amazon. Seen well inland from almost any shore they feel like prowling. Heavy, aggressive, extremely dangerous. They take what they want, period. And this one wanted me.

It wasn't a mature bull; it was only about four feet long. But I knew, from my years of watching *Shark Week* on television, that it could take me, all of me, no sweat. I couldn't move, even to glance behind me to see how much water was still between me and the shore; the tide had been going out, but there were probably still five or six feet of shallow water to get through, and bull sharks are just fine with shallow water. They're known for attacking the legs of people standing in the water, fishing, people who think they're safe because they're in a river. They're not safe.

Breathe, Micah. No, seriously. Breathe. Breathe again.

Could I distract it? Moving slowly and carefully, eyes on that dark shape swimming back and forth so close to me, I picked up my drink can, crushed it with my right hand, and heaved it as far away from me as I could.

The shark took off after it! It worked!

I don't think I've ever moved so fast, and I scraped one of my feet in my haste, but I made it back to shore with no new shark tooth souvenirs. I stood on the narrow spit of sand, breathing hard, staring at the water to make sure that thing couldn't follow me onto the shore, wondering if I should call someone to let them know what I'd seen.

The only person I could think of to call was Mr. Donnell. And I wasn't about to do that.

Chapter Eleven

The rest of that week was pretty crazy. Mom and Dad talked a lot on the phone, and after quite a bit of arguing they agreed that Dylan's homecoming dinner should be at Dad's apartment. And, of course, Dad's plan to move in with Sharon couldn't be kept secret. I didn't get any more time to spy on Walker's dock, because Mom really needed me to be around. Sometimes it was to go and fetch stuff for Dylan's homecoming, and sometimes I think it was just so she could reassure herself that she still had one son willing to live with her, and maybe to distract her from thinking about Dad's living arrangements.

On Wednesday of that week, she did something that surprised the hell out of me. She had Nick come over for a few hours, she went out, and when she came back she was a brunette again. I had the presence of mind to tell her she looked great.

"Well, you know, I went blond while Dylan was overseas, after—well, after we thought he'd died. I guess I want him to see the mother he knew."

One thing I did make time for was looking up information about intersex on my computer after dinner. And what I found was something between an alphabet soup (XY, XX, XXY, AR) and the most incredible frustration.

People who are intersex had the worst level of frustration, but their families and friends—people who cared about them, like me—felt it, too.

Walker had told me so little about the medical details: chromosomes; testosterone injections. So I went through website after website, some of them so medically technical I could follow only a little of what was there, and stories— some so personal that they had me near tears. It seemed like Mother Nature had fucked with some people big time, and they were left with this monumental task of having to figure out who they were with little or no help from anyone around them. Part of the reason there was no help was because the condition is kind of rare, and it's not something you advertise when you shake hands with someone, so intersex people usually feel very much alone. But the other part was how horrible some other people's reactions were if they found out.

As for my own purposes—that is, being with Walker the way I wanted to—I realized that while I'd been willing to give him some time to figure out whether he was gay, I'd been thinking of it all wrong. That is, I was thinking he needed to figure out who he was in that area pretty much the same way I'd figured it out about myself. I was way off base.

Because being intersex has nothing to do with sexual orientation, one way or another. If Walker was attracted to me because he knew he was a guy, he was gay; but if he was still struggling with being sure he was a guy—and he'd already told me that he was—then as a girl, liking me would mean he was straight, but of course it wouldn't help me at all, unless I was willing to be more flexible than I had ever even considered. And it seemed there were lots of intersex people who identified as neither male nor female, not gay or straight. What the fuck was I supposed to do with that?

I took a short break to watch a few shark vids, but even the gory ones didn't distract me enough, and my mind kept going back to intersex.

If Walker's parents had been different people, or his doctors had had outdated ideas, Walker might have been one of those people who were castrated at birth and raised as a girl, no matter what they might come to feel about themselves. Supposedly when this was done, it was "for the good of the child." But I think it was more like the parents just couldn't deal. A lot of these babies grew up into people who killed themselves.

The idea of Walker possibly committing suicide even though his parents and doctors hadn't mutilated him gave me an idea of just how little I had understood how deep this thing could go, and how profound the confusion and frustration could be.

On YouTube, I watched several vids of intersex teens and adults explaining what they'd been through, how they felt, how other people had reacted. There were two things in particular I heard them say that I knew would stay with me:

1. *Too often, trans people can't get the surgery they need. Intersex kids get surgery they don't want.*

2. *Why did God make me wrong?*

What the fuck could Mrs. Donnell's priest say to Walker that would help him?

But the real question, the question for me, was whether I would feel the same about Walker the person as I did about Walker the gay guy. Would I feel the same if he didn't end up as either a guy *or* a girl? Or if it turned out Walker was a she?

I had to go back to the sharks. At least they didn't confuse me.

As I was falling off to sleep later, after another imaginary, intimate scene with Walker the gay guy, I realized that from the time I'd started my research that evening until just that second, I hadn't once thought about the size of his dick.

We were in the visitors' waiting area at Fort Hamilton in Brooklyn, New York by eleven o'clock Friday morning. Dad did his best to appear calm. Mom didn't even try. I tried and failed. I thought I'd prepared myself for the sight of my brother. No way did I succeed.

We weren't the only ones meeting a returning soldier, so when the door to wherever they arrived opened, everyone in the room turned and moved that way. I watched as the soldiers came in—tall black guy; short white guy with shaven head; woman with lanky blond hair; short woman with dark skin and a huge smile; skinny guy with shaven head and a dark beard; medium guy with—hey! That bearded guy was Dylan!

Oh my god. Oh my god.

I couldn't move. Mom could, and she went flying toward him. Dad grabbed my arm and we walked toward them and then stood while Dylan worked his way free of Mom's embrace.

"Micah. I hardly know you." His slow, warm smile seemed to pull me forward, and we hugged. He was skin and bones, but his grip was strong. He was only about an inch taller than me, now.

Dad's turn next. They clasped right hands and then hugged. I thought it would be one of those straight-guy hugs, but it was more emotional than that.

Then Mom had another go at him until she had to release him to blow her nose.

There was some paperwork before we could all leave, but as we headed toward the SUV Dad had rented for the occasion, Dylan had a request.

"I am so friggin' hungry. Any place to eat around here that isn't Army food?"

Dad started to say something about how it shouldn't be hard to find something, but I'd done some research. "There's a Pizza Uno not far from here, right on Fourth Avenue."

"Great!" Dylan, as I had suspected, was up for pizza.

It was super easy to find, or it would have been if we hadn't all been asking Dylan questions the whole time we were driving. By the time Dad found a place to park we knew that yes, Dylan had been living in a cave; yes, he had been helped by a local family; yes, the Taliban had been roaming and causing trouble, and often Dylan couldn't have a fire going. Somehow we managed to be inside the restaurant by one thirty.

The waiter started to lead us to a table, but Dylan asked if we could have a booth. "I've sat on enough hard surfaces for a while."

Dad and I both laughed, but it sounded forced and nervous to me.

Mom was glommed onto Dylan, so they sat on one side of the table. Dad sat directly across from Dylan, which was fine by me; gave me a chance to look at him from a slight distance, which was all I was ready for at first.

Dylan's order surprised all of us. He'd always been a serious sausage fan when it came to pizza, but today he ordered a custom pizza with chicken and green peppers.

"Chicken?" Mom asked. "Since when do you like chicken on pizza?" She laughed. Dylan didn't.

As soon as the waiter left with our order, Dylan had something to say. Something huge.

"I wasn't going to hit you all up with this right away, but you've already asked so many questions about where I've been that—well... I guess what I'm trying to say is that it would be easier if I just give you a fuller picture."

He had our attention. Even Mom, who practically hadn't stopped asking questions or telling him things since we'd left Fort Hamilton, sat silently watching him.

"See, the thing is, I don't eat pork any more." He let that sink in, looking from one of us to the other as though he hoped we'd figure out for ourselves what that meant.

Only Dad hit on it. "You're kidding."

"What?" Mom asked. "What's he kidding about?"

Dylan leaned both arms on the table and watched his fingers twisting around each other. "I've converted to Islam."

Dad's back hit the booth behind him so hard I thought we'd both go over backward. I fought the urge to ask, "Madam Alberta didn't 'see' this little tidbit coming?" But I'm not sure I could have spoken, anyway.

Mom was the only one who could speak. Or maybe the only one of us who dared. "Why?"

"Yeah, that's another part of the story." He looked at Dad, an almost-smile on his face like he was asking not to be punished. "I'm married."

Conversation after Dylan's bombshells waned a bit, to say the least. We still had lots of questions. Or, at least, I did. But I think we were all too stunned to be able to frame them. And they weren't at all the kinds of questions I think we had expected to be asking him.

Mom was braver than Dad or me, and because of her questions we had learned a bit more by the time we left. His wife's name was Darya, which means ocean in Pashto, whatever that is. I mean, it's a language they speak there, but I hadn't heard of it before. Her father's name was Abdul Bashir Samim, and then some other name at the end having to do with his tribe that I didn't catch. As a young man, Abdul Bashir had once seen the ocean, and he'd been so impressed that he'd decided to name a daughter Darya, if he had one.

It seems Abdul Bashir was pretty progressive; Dylan had figured this out as soon as he knew that Darya, who was eighteen, had not yet been given away or sold as a bride. Abdul Bashir's son, Ali Fareed, had been the one to discover Dylan hiding in the cave, nearly dead with exhaustion and pain. His mother and Darya, having dealt with injured soldiers from their own village, had enough medical knowledge to deal with the through-and-through bullet wounds and to set Dylan's arm, and although there was an odd bump on the bone now, it was healed well enough to satisfy the Army doctor who'd examined it.

Of all of us, I think Dylan was the only one who actually tasted his meal. And he had, indeed, been ravenous. I offered him a piece of mine, which had no sausage, but he said the pepperoni had pork in it.

Mom still wanted to hang onto Dylan, so she sat in the back seat with him on the drive home. We got more information during the ride, though the exchange had an odd feel. It was still hard to know what to ask and how to ask it, and there were lots of awkward silences that Dylan broke by coming up with something he thought we might want to know.

For example, he'd converted to Islam because otherwise he wouldn't have been allowed to marry Darya. Or, she wouldn't have been allowed to marry him. She wore traditional women's garb at home, but she had already decided that when she came to the United States, she wouldn't. Dylan said that it was a very courageous decision, one that she'd need a lot of support for.

Then he said, "Her mother used to come to the cave with her so we could be together but not alone. And she'd bring these long, flowing, cotton dresses in bright colors. She and Darya would disappear into the back of the cave to change, and then they'd dance around together to recorded Afghani music while I watched. Very taboo."

I had turned to look at him while he was talking, so I saw him smile and shake his head, like he was picturing the scene.

"It was so amazing, watching them, for so many reasons. But the most stunning one was the contrast between the way they moved when they were inside those burkas and the joy in their dancing, free of those restraints." He pinched the bridge of his nose, and it looked like he was trying to control his emotions. "One day, after we were engaged, Darya started crying while she was dancing, and then her mother started, and they hugged each other and wept. It took me a minute to realize that it was probably because once Darya left to come here, her mother would have no one to dance with."

We were all silent for a few minutes, letting that sink in. I drew pictures in my mind of what it would look like, two women free of heavy, black fabric, twirling wildly in light, colorful, flowing dresses. I felt so sad for Darya's mother.

Dad asked, "So the only reason you're Muslim now is because of marrying her? Are you changing back now that you're home?"

"Back to what?" Everyone let that hang in the air. Because although we could be said to be Christians, no one observing us would ever know that; we didn't go to church, we didn't pray (at least, as far as I knew), and the only reasons we might go to a church now would be for baptisms, weddings, and funerals.

Dylan had more to say. "No, I won't change. I've learned a lot about Islam, and I like the emphasis on being kind and peaceful."

He would have said more, I think, but Dad interrupted him. "Are you fucking kidding me?"

I thought Mom would object to the language, but she said nothing.

"I know what you're thinking," Dylan said before Dad could go on. "But it's only the most radical groups within Islam that cause the problems. They've latched onto phrases in the Holy Quran that have more to do with how people had to live in the desert hundreds of years ago. Most Muslims today are peace-loving and gentle and kind. Darya's parents are like that, and no one questions their religious sincerity."

"What about Darya's brother?" As Dylan's brother, I had to ask. And the question was met with silence that lasted several seconds.

"Fareed. Well, he, uh... No. He's not especially peaceful. I'm actually very lucky that he didn't decide to turn me in. I think the only reason he didn't was because it would have meant death for the rest of his family." He chuckled and added, "I'll say this for Fareed. He plays a mean Rubab, which is this really complicated stringed instrument. And when Bashir gets going on the tabla, his drums, no one can sit or stand still."

"And Darya," I asked. "When will we meet her?"

"There's scads of paperwork and forms and testimonials she'll have to work through, and her father needs to be involved. It was dangerous, for me and for her family, for me to stay with them while this is going on. So it might be a few weeks, or it might be a few months."

I wasn't sure whether I heard relief in Mom's voice when she asked, "What's she like?"

Dylan chuckled. "She's a hot ticket. You know, there are a lot of Muslim women who are under the thumbs of the men of their families. But Darya and her mother, Faiza, are not. Again, Bashir is pretty progressive. And I gather that in families where the women aren't emotionally subjugated, they tend to rule the roost. That's Darya. She and Fareed used to argue ferociously. Once there was an honor killing in the village, where a woman was accused of adultery, and no men stepped forward in her defense, so she was stoned to death. Darya was beside herself, but she didn't dare speak up to anyone but her family, and me. She insisted that honor killings would not be considered part of Islam except that the tradition had been brought forward from the tribal customs before The Prophet, blessings be upon him, appeared on the scene."

The sounds of tires on the highway was the only thing I heard for maybe a minute. It was like all of us at once, including Dylan, realized that wishing for those blessings so automatically, so necessarily, and so audibly, brought us smack into the wall that represented this change in Dylan—this change that was so unexpected, so radical, and so mysterious.

As though he knew the best thing at that point would be to change the subject, he asked, "How much farther to the house?"

And then it was everyone else's turn to break some news.

I heard Mom say, "Oh, Dylan." Dad cleared his throat. I sank down into my seat.

"What? What is it? Did something happen to the house?"

Dad cleared his throat again. "We don't live there any more, Dylan. In fact, your mother and I split." He stopped, maybe waiting for Dylan's reaction.

"You—you're divorced?" His voice was high, strained.

"I live in Warwick now. Actually, we should probably talk about arrangements."

It felt like a bit of a reprieve, describing practical logistics instead of telling shocking personal revelations. Dylan mostly listened without comment as Dad explained the plan for Dylan's immediate future. He finished with, "You can stay in the apartment as long as you need to. It's not huge, but you can decide if it's big enough for you and—your wife."

"Darya."

"Right; just couldn't remember her name." Which I took to mean he hadn't tried hard enough; it wasn't a hard name to remember.

And we were back to personal stuff again. I decided to deflect the topic. "The officers who told us about you didn't give any explanation about how come they thought you were—y'know. Dead."

At first I didn't think he was going to answer my implied question. He cleared his throat a few times, though, which made me keep expecting him to say something. I even turned around once to see whether he was even thinking about it. He was gazing out of the window. As I watched he coughed, a hand curled into a fist at his mouth. I turned around again, feeling like I'd said something wrong but not having any idea what.

Then Dylan spoke, but I didn't turn around again. Didn't want to risk it.

"It was an IED. An improvised explosive device. It blew up the truck I was in. The guy next to me, Arnie Tollman, was the only one besides me who wasn't killed outright, but he was trapped under the truck. I leaned over him to see if he was alive, and he grabbed at my clothes. He must have grabbed my dog tags."

He took a few deep breaths while we waited. Then, "There was another explosion—from what, I don't know— and it threw me off to the side. The truck caught fire and blew up, and I couldn't get to Arnie. He must have had my tags in his hand still, because that's about all they could have found. The fire—" Dylan coughed and took another couple of breaths. "The fire consumed everything so badly that no one could tell what was burned, or who had been there. But they found my tags. No one knew I'd been thrown free. And I'd had to run immediately, because there were insurgents shooting at anything that moved. The only direction I could go was toward the hills. I got lost and walked for almost two days before finding the caves."

I was about to ask how Darya's family had found him, but before I could do that, his voice thin and tense he said, "I need to stop talking about this now."

When we got to Stonington, Dad parked the car alongside Mom's sedan. We'd been on the road, driving through nasty summer Friday traffic, for over four hours. Mom had anticipated this, which is why she'd had me help her plan for it. We sat around the tiny kitchen table, snacks and drinks in front of us, and tried to think of things to say that wouldn't be too much for Dylan, who kept looking around the place like he couldn't quite believe Mom and I lived there.

Dylan himself offered a subject: Me. "So, Micah, what are you up to these days?"

I gave him the easiest answer. "Photography. I've decided to study it in college."

His look told me he was impressed. "That's pretty cool. What do you shoot?"

So I told him about my recent projects, and I mentioned Vivian Maier's work and why I liked it. "And I've been sailing." I waited, wondering what he'd make of that.

"Sailing? Like, on the ocean, sailing?"

I knew he was thinking about my phobia. "Yup. I met this guy who has a Cape Dory Typhoon. He's been sailing since he was a little kid. I really like it."

"Wow. Think he'd give me a ride sometime?"

Shit. Busted. "Well… I've sort of lost track of him for now. But if things change, I'll ask, for sure." I was determined that they would change, but for right now I couldn't say more than I had. I also couldn't say anything about the nature of my relationship with "this kid," and it hit me suddenly that Dylan would have to be told about me. Soon.

There was a joyfully tearful moment when Mom went and fetched the box with those items of his she'd been holding onto. He started to go through them, but I think he decided he needed to do that in private, because he stopped and said, "This feels so weird." He had to stand for another hug from Mom before setting the box aside.

Nick was a little put out that he'd have to mind the store until we got back from Warwick, but he couldn't exactly argue about it; he had agreed, and Mom had a very good reason for being absent. Plus she was paying him an extra fifty bucks.

Dad drove off with Dylan in the SUV, and Mom and I followed in her sedan. I wanted to drive, but she was concerned about the heavy traffic. "Maybe on the way back, Micah."

They beat us to Warwick by a good ten minutes, and they were at the dining table. Dad had a beer; Dylan had a ginger ale. And I thought, *Right; no alcohol.*

Within minutes, a delivery guy was there with Chinese food, and it occurred to me that I was having an awful lot of that cuisine lately. But there were chopsticks in the bag, so I got to show off my new skill.

Halfway through his Kung Pao chicken, Dylan turned to me. His elbows leaning on the table, he waved a fork in my direction and asked, "Got a girlfriend yet, Micah?"

OMG. This was exactly what Dad had asked me, that evening out on his balcony a few weeks ago. Word for word.

I opted for discretion. "Not yet, no."

He nodded. "Just as well, I suppose. You'd only have to break her heart when you head off to college to become a famous photographer." He laughed lightly, the first time I'd heard him do that all day. I didn't want to do anything to mar that, so I let the subject drop. Or I tried to.

I almost didn't know I was speaking. "Dad knows someone who specializes in solving gay issues in the workplace. What does Islam think about LGBTQ people?"

Dad had stiffened before I'd finished the first sentence. By the end of the second, I thought Dad would jump out of his skin. But he must have been trying not to give anything away—like, that the "someone" was, in fact, his own girlfriend.

Dylan asked, "What's the Q stand for, anyway? I've been wondering that."

"Usually queer, meaning gender-nonconforming. Sometimes it means questioning.

"But—queer? Isn't that offensive?"

"The community is reclaiming the term queer."

"What on earth for?"

I shrugged like it was nothing to me, though even I had learned more about the abbreviations while doing my research about intersex. "It's better than LGBTQQIAAP. That all stands for lesbian, gay, bisexual, transsexual, queer, questioning, intersex, asexual, allies, and pansexual. That's too much to say. So, even though it leaves out allies, queer is a good catch phrase meaning other than cisgender straight. You just have to be careful when you use it. And you have to use it respectfully."

All that, and what Dylan's mind caught on was, "Allies?"

"Yeah. Straight, cisgender people who support queer rights."

"Cisgender?" His tone was odd, and I couldn't quite tell where he might come down on this issue.

"You know, people who really are what they look like. I mean, they're the same on the inside as they are on the outside. Everyone here is cisgender. It's the opposite of transgender. And different from intersex." I didn't dare look at my folks, so I just watched Dylan.

He shook his head and poked at a piece of chicken with his fork. "Well, I can tell you that the military is changing. Sometimes it seems like the rules change faster than the troops, and sometimes the other way around, but we're getting better." He chewed thoughtfully, watched my face, swallowed, and asked, "And you brought this up why?"

"Like I said, I want to know about Islam. I mean, you can't eat pork, you can't drink alcohol. Are you allowed to talk to gay people?"

He took a deep breath and let it out slowly. "There are so many different paths within Islam." I noticed for the first time that he accented the second syllable more than the first—not the way I'd ever said it, but more like I'd heard Muslims on news programs say it. "Scripture is clear that it's a sin punishable by death. But those of us who follow a more compassionate philosophy are more accepting. If I were to go back into the Army, for example, I would be fine with having gays serve with me. They even allow transgender people now. But I'm still learning about how to live as a Muslim here at home. So I don't think I'm a good person to ask."

He took a sip from his glass of water, his eyes on my face. "But I'd still like to know why you're asking about it."

I looked at Dad and then Mom, trying to get a sense of whether they'd curl up and die if I came out to Dylan right now. I'd found out what I'd needed to know: He wouldn't stone me to death on the spot. On the other hand, I couldn't say how much shade my revelation would throw on our little reunion. But—damn, it! Dylan had dropped a bombshell or two. Why couldn't I be honest about my own life?

I didn't speak quickly enough. Dylan looked at Mom, and then Dad, and asked, "Any idea what's going on?"

Mom glanced down at her plate. Dad must have come to a decision, one that Sharon would approve of, and he held Dylan's gaze. "Yes. I think Micah is trying to find out where you stand, personally. You say you'd have no problem in the military. Would you have a problem in your own family?"

Dylan's eyes snapped back to me. "No girlfriend?" No one spoke, no one moved. "Are you gay, Micah?"

It was so hard—so fucking hard—to keep my eyes on his. But I did. I'm no coward. "Yes."

He glanced down at his plate. I held my breath. He set down his fork. He looked back up at me. "Okay, so do you have a boyfriend yet?"

Nervous laughter has a special sound to it. Kind of too high, kind of too loud, kind of strained. But it was laughter, though in my case it was the kind of laughter that's so close to tears it was almost the same thing.

"I really like the guy with the sailboat."

Dad's head turned my way; I knew this would have come as something of a surprise to him, but he didn't say anything.

Dylan took it in stride. "In that case, I definitely want a ride." He grinned at me and then dug back into his food.

The weekend was an odd collection of times with Dylan and times back in Stonington. I really wanted to stay in Warwick Friday night; after all, I was used to sleeping on the couch. But when I'd said something about it after dinner Friday, Dylan had looked down at his hands, and Dad had said, "Let's give Dylan a little breathing room, Micah."

Mom convinced Nick to babysit the front desk again Saturday, so we drove back to Warwick to take Dylan shopping. When Mom and Dad had sold our house, they'd given away or thrown away his stuff. After all, they weren't saving it for him, Mom hadn't yet started visiting Madam Alberta, and no one had space to store it—not that his old clothes would have fit him now, anyway. So he needed just about everything.

During the expedition, Dylan kept disappearing. Sometimes he went into the rest room and didn't come out for, like, fifteen minutes, until Dad went to look for him. Other times he wandered off on his own or went outside "for some air."

I suggested Red Robin for dinner, thinking Dylan would really like a good, juicy burger, but he said he'd rather just get something to take back to the apartment. So we got burgers; that much was a good idea.

It was a very different meal from Friday's. Dylan was really quiet, almost like he was depressed. He went out onto the balcony alone at one point, giving me a chance to ask, "What's with him, anyway?"

Dad said, "He's going through a huge adjustment, Micah. He's been living in a cave, don't forget, and although it sounds like he had company sometimes, and visited Darya's family sometimes, he spent hours and hours by himself, with only the wind for music. He's not used to noise, or crowds, or indoor air."

Mom added, "And I'm sure he misses Darya."

We all looked toward the sliding door, Dylan's silhouette barely visible against the darkening sky.

Dad added, "It could take him a while. Give him some time."

Sunday Dylan drove the SUV, which Dad had rented for him for a few weeks, out to Stonington. Nick wasn't working today, so Mom couldn't go anyplace, and after she fed us all lunch (interrupted a couple of times by guests with problems), Dylan stood, looking a little awkward.

"Is there a good place to walk around here?" He looked from Mom to me.

When all Mom said was, "Well..." I jumped on this golden opportunity.

"There's Barn Island. It's a wildlife sanctuary with lots of ocean frontage. Some great views."

"Sounds perfect. How do I get there?"

I had to risk it; I almost didn't care if he wanted to be alone. "I could show you."

Our eyes locked for a second or two, and then he smiled. "Sure. Can we go now?"

Mom smiled and nodded, though I could tell it hurt her to let him out of her sight. She was a trooper, though; she even made sure he had the special foot blister patches she'd bought yesterday, in case he had trouble with his new shoes. I grabbed my camera, and we were off.

I would have taken my bike if I'd been alone, so as I climbed into the driver's seat I wracked my brain for the best place to go with the car. I really wanted to take him to that rock where I'd been the day I'd met Walker. It was a beautiful spot, no one else was likely to be there because it was hard to get to, and it had a gorgeous view of the water.

We left the car as far into the park as we could and then started walking, me in the lead along the narrow path and then through a patch of woods. Dylan was quiet, and I didn't try to get him to talk. Dad's description of what his life has been like for months was still fresh in my brain.

We sat side by side on the rock for maybe ten minutes before Dylan spoke.

"This is a great spot." Silence. Then, "How did you find it?"

"I'm always on the lookout for places to shoot. I've been all through most of the wildlife areas around here. Everything else is highway, marinas, and boring old beach."

It was so tempting to talk about Walker, to laugh with Dylan about the way we'd met, to complain about the way his mother was treating him and, by extension, me. But I didn't think he was ready for that. Instead, I asked about Darya.

"I hope Darya can come over soon." I thought that might get him talking, even though I was nervous about meeting her. But he said nothing. So I went on, "How did you get to know her? I mean, with you not knowing her language. Does she know English?"

I watched the side of his face, and there was a small grin there. "We managed. Actually, I had learned some Pashto and a little Farsi. Plus, her father had traveled before returning to the village to marry, and he'd picked up some English, which he'd taught his family. So we did okay."

"I suppose not everything gets said in words, anyway."

There was another longish silence before he said, "It might surprise you to know that we've barely touched each other. We haven't made love yet."

"But—you're married!"

"That happened right before I left. And we weren't sure—hell, we still aren't sure—what to expect, time-wise, about when she'll be here. There's no way I wanted her to get pregnant and have to deal with that process, and leave her family and everything she's ever known, all at the same time. Plus," and his voice got a little strained, "if for some reason she changes her mind and wants to stay in Afghanistan, I didn't want her to feel as though she had to come here just because of being pregnant. As it is, she's still a virgin. She could marry someone else."

He changed the subject rather abruptly and asked about our parents, about the split, about why it happened. He seemed to want the whole story. I told him as much as I could without giving him the impression that the breakup had been because of him, which it kind of had been.

When he had no more questions, and I'd stopped babbling, he got up and walked toward the water, stopping right at the edge of the rock. The tide was pretty high, so I knew he wasn't seeing that little spit of sand that's sometimes visible. As quietly as I could, I took a few shots of him standing there, sea and sky behind him, his form almost just a dark shape. I was going for mysterious, deep, maybe even spiritual. At some point, though, he heard the shutter and turned around.

"Let's see." He sat back down, and I showed him what I'd shot.

He sat quietly and let me take a few head shots, dappled sun on part of his face while the rest of it was in shadow. Then he asked, "What else do you have in there?"

I nearly giggled; this was the second time I was glad I hadn't captured Walker's privates. At least, not in the camera. But the shots right before today's were those sand tiger sharks.

"Micah." Dylan's voice had wonder in it. "I can't believe this." He looked from the screen to my face. "Where were you?"

"Well..." Shit. I decided it was time to tell him the story about Walker. "Friday night, you asked if I had a boyfriend. I do, and I don't." I pointed to the edge of the rock. "Just there, I was shooting a dead seagull, and this kid appeared out of nowhere in a sailboat."

Without mentioning Walker's special secret, I gave Dylan an abbreviated version of how things with Walker had progressed, right through to the fireworks cruise on *Magic Spell*.

Dylan threw back his head and laughed. It was an open, honest laugh, and it surprised the hell out of me. "So it took a love affair to get you over your fear of sharks! That's great."

Love affair. Maybe a little overstated. Maybe not. "Well... but then his mother decided I shouldn't see him any more."

"What? Why not?"

"She doesn't want him to be gay." There was more to it, of course, but I didn't want to go there right now.

"And he's going along with that?"

I shrugged and gazed out over the water. "For now. I'm giving him a little space. He's gay; I'm sure of that. And he'll want to see me again. Meanwhile, I'm letting him know I'm here. Some afternoons, I go to a place where I can see the dock at his house, and if his boat isn't there, I wait for him to come back, and he sees me. One of these days, he won't be able to keep his distance. Or he won't want me to."

Dylan was silent, but I could tell he was watching me. Finally, he said, "Little brother, you're becoming a man."

He couldn't have said anything nicer.

Chapter Twelve

We went to Warwick for dinner on Tuesday, and Dylan came to Stonington for dinner on Wednesday. Sometimes there were long silences that felt awkward to me. One minute Dylan would seem depressed, and then five minutes later he'd be telling us some funny story about what things had been like, living in the cave.

I'd been doing some of my own thinking, wondering how much of the regard Dylan felt for Darya had come from the fact that he really didn't see anyone outside of her and her family for months. He must have been lonely, and they—Darya in particular—must have seemed like a light in the darkness. Would he have developed the same feelings for her if he hadn't been so alone?

All week, I could tell Mom didn't want to be alone, though I knew she would rather have had Dylan with her than me. But he wasn't there, so I stayed as much as I could, listening to her talk about Dylan, about what his wife would be like, about how it would be for him to live here as a Muslim. Sometimes it felt like Mom was hoping Darya would change her mind and stay where she was, and sometimes it seemed like Mom really did want to meet her, like she couldn't wait to see what kind of woman had captured Dylan's heart.

But there were times when I couldn't take the speculation any more, and I'd done everything she'd asked me to do for the day, and I had to get away. These were the times when I biked out to Jasper Island. I hadn't figured out a good disguise, so I just wore a baseball cap and hoped it would be enough.

Sitting on that rock I'd found, which high tide never covered, I watched for *Dare Ya*. She was out a lot, which I took to mean that Walker needed to be alone, to feel that sense of perspective he'd told me about, to get to a place where the ocean didn't care, a place where he felt free. I sat through a thunderstorm on Thursday, which I really liked, except that it wasn't great that Walker was sailing in that. Plus, I got all wet. So I took my shirt off after the sun came back out, and I was standing, pacing a little, starting to worry about Walker, when I saw the little boat round the point of the island and head for the dock.

This time, when Walker saw me, there was something different about him. From this distance, it was impossible to be sure, but he seemed anxious, or unhappy, or maybe even a little frantic. He paced on the dock, stopped to stare at me, paced some more, going on like that for maybe a minute. Then he trotted off the dock and onto the grass, turned in my direction, stopped, turned away, and ran toward the house.

I told myself not to be hurt, or mad, or even disappointed. Because this change in his behavior told me he was reaching some kind of decision, or some kind of breaking point.

But Friday, he didn't sail. *Dare Ya* sat at her mooring, waiting with me for someone we loved who didn't come.

I'd hoped to spend Saturday with Dylan, but when I got home for dinner Friday, Mom told me he'd disappeared.

"What does that mean, Mom? Didn't Dad give him a phone?"

"Calls are going to voicemail, and the only text he sent was to your father, saying not to worry about him, that he just needed some space."

Yeah. A whole mountain range full of space.

"So," Mom went on, "I've told Nick he doesn't need to be here this weekend. I just hope that if Dylan reappears soon, I'll be able to talk Nick into coming in after all."

I almost wished Mom had taught me enough about manning the office that I could do it when she wasn't there, so that if Dylan did reappear, she could be with him. But then, I wanted to be with him, too, so there was that.

I tried not to be angry with Dylan. It wasn't easy. And I knew I'd fail completely and would get pissed off if I stayed in the unit Saturday. This would have been a weekend with Dad, but everything had been so out of sync lately that he'd begged off. And now I couldn't see Dylan, either. So as soon as I could get away, I grabbed my camera and left.

I headed toward that rock, the seagull rock, the Walker rock, now also the Dylan rock. But this time as I approached, there was a figure there, someone sitting near the edge and gazing across the water.

Dylan?

No. It wasn't even a man. It was a woman.

Who else had the nerve to use this rock the way I used this rock? Who dared take over like that? I stood, trying to come up with another destination for my own alone time, but—damn it, who *was* that?

I approached the mystery lady slowly but not trying to be quiet; I didn't want her to think I was sneaking up on her. When I was maybe ten feet behind her, she turned suddenly, no doubt startled.

Paige!

OMG, it was Paige Donnell. What the fuck was she doing here?

"You." She spat the word out as though it tasted like shit.

"You." My reply was no sweeter.

"What are you doing here?"

"What are *you* doing here? This is where *I* come to think."

"Since when? I come here all the time." We stared at each other, and then she added, "Well... I used to, anyway."

She looked odd, and it took me a minute to realize that it was because she'd been crying. "You used to? Before what?"

She turned her back on me and resumed her original position on the rock, knees up, long arms wrapped around her bent legs. I couldn't have said why—maybe it was because she seemed so vulnerable—but I moved forward and sat on her right, assuming the same position, both of us now looking out over the water.

Finally, she said, "Before I met Ashton."

A quick calculation brought me to this conclusion: "Did you guys break up, or something?"

She sighed a shaky sigh. "I hate blonds."

I laughed; I couldn't help it. In three words, she'd told me her boyfriend had thrown her over for someone who looked nothing like her. "Sorry; I know it's not funny. It's just the way you said it."

"Don't you hate blonds, too?"

"You mean, because I can't see your brother?" Her silence said that was it. I knew there was a good chance it would be a stupid move, but I decided to take a risk. I wanted to know whether she really was my enemy, or if I might be able to use her to get to Walker somehow. So I said, "I'm hoping that will change."

She turned her face toward me, and we looked at each other intently. Facing the water again, she said, "You might have reason to hope. He's not getting on all that well with Father Gaffney."

"That's the priest your mom's having him talk to?"

"My mom... yeah."

"She is your mom, isn't she?"

Paige turned her nearly-black eyes on me in a hard stare. "Didn't Walker tell you?"

"About being adopted? Yeah, he did. But Mrs. Donnell's still your mom, I think."

Paige stood so suddenly I thought she might go over the edge of the rock. Arms crossed over her chest, she stood there, her back toward me, long enough for me to wonder if I should leave. Then she turned her head just enough for me to hear her words.

"My 'mom,' as you put it, robbed me of my true heritage." She wheeled around to face me. "I've had more than a few talks with Father Gaffney, myself."

She threw her head back and laughed, but it had no joy in it. "You know, I never thought I'd have anything meaningful in common with Walker. We've never gotten along. He never had the slightest bit of empathy for my situation, so I haven't exactly turned the other cheek. But thanks to you, we now have a common enemy." She smiled, but it wasn't a warm smile. It was almost evil.

I decided to take another risk. "So is the enemy of your enemy now your friend?"

She chuckled, again with no humor. "That might be going a bit far. And I don't think Walker's ready to say that, either. But I'm watching. I'm waiting for him to rebel."

"Thanks to me."

She cocked her head. "You are an unusual person, aren't you?" Not really a question.

I shrugged. "So, what heritage did you lose?"

She took a breath so deep her shoulders rose nearly to her ears, and she let it out slowly. Then she sat back down, and we both watched the water again.

"My mother was Muslim. Her family were living in Detroit when my father, may his soul rot in hell, who is not Muslim, raped her. She was sixteen. Rather than bring disgrace on her family, she ran away, but as you can imagine she was ill-equipped to manage on her own. She ended up in a shelter, where she died giving birth. To me."

Wow. It was hard to know what to say about that. Paige's tone had been pretty flat, no hint in it of expecting sympathy. So I went to practical matters. Deciding it was too invasive to ask how she knew all this about her mother, I asked, "Detroit? So how did the Donnell's find you?"

Paige stood again, arms crossed once more, eyes on the ground at her feet, and walked back and forth as she talked. "My 'mom' was determined to bring a heathen child into the light, and she went hunting for just the right one. Mind you, she's never used those words, but that was her intent. She got me baptized into Catholicism, made me go to catechism lessons, made me get confirmed. I was just a child; what did I know?"

She paused in her walk and her speech, stood watching the water for a minute, and then paced again. "It wasn't until I found out I was adopted—thanks to you-know-who—that I started to wonder seriously about things. Like, how different I looked from everyone else in the family. And I started asking questions."

She stopped again, her back to me once more.

"What kind of questions?"

She wheeled around to face me, towering over me. "The kind of questions that told me the truth about myself. And when I said I wanted to know what it would mean to be Muslim, my 'mom' forced me into conversations with the good Father G. So I have some idea what Walker's going through."

"My brother's Muslim." That tidbit flew out of me on its own.

"What?"

She'd told me so much about herself. I figured it was my turn. "He was sent to Afghanistan. In the Army. There was an IED, and he escaped, but he had to run into the hills, and the Army thought he had died. That's what they told

243

us. But he wasn't dead. He found some caves, and a local family helped him stay clear of the Taliban. He fell in love with the daughter, Darya, and he converted to Islam," I said that word the way I'd heard Dylan say it, "and he married Darya. He was sent home last week, and Darya is supposed to follow as soon as it can be arranged."

Paige stared at me so long, I began to worry about her. Then, "Your supposedly dead brother is home as of last week? Are you shitting me?"

I shook my head. "Nope. He's having a little trouble adjusting. Living in a cave for so long is a lot different from cities and highways and things like, you know, running water and electricity. And just having people around all the time. People who expect him to talk, to tell everything that happened to him, and explain his conversion."

It was as though Dylan's spiritual representative were speaking through me, so that those things I said about him to Paige poured out of me. I'd never thought about his situation quite like that, never felt patient when he seemed distant so often, or why he needed to disappear. But it made so much sense.

Her next words surprised the hell out of me. "Can I meet him?" When I didn't respond right away, she added, "Does he know about Walker? Hell—does he know about you?"

I nodded. "He does. And he's cool with it. Um, I guess I could ask him. About meeting you, I mean. And maybe you can help me with Walker?"

One half of her mouth lifted in a smile. "What strange bedfellows we are." She sat down again and pulled out her phone. "What's your number?"

In another deja vu moment, this one imitating the way Walker had asked me the same question, I told her, and she texted me with her email address. "There," she said, "now we're joined forever. So. What do you want to know about Walker?"

We both turned a little more toward each other, sitting there on that rock, and she talked about the daily morning sessions with Father G that Walker was being forced to undergo. He hadn't confided in her—no surprise—so he hadn't actually told her what he was thinking or feeling. But she was getting the impression that although Walker had been on board in the beginning, at least enough to see where his mother's approach might lead, he was seeming more and more jumpy in the last few days. She said he was even snapping at his parents, which was unlike him.

"Walker's always been such a goody-goody little boy. Never talking back, never being disobedient in any real way. Now? Not so much. I think he's gonna crack any day."

There was no way I believed that Walker had ever told Paige about his suicidal thoughts, but I asked, "What do you think that would mean? Cracking?"

"You know, explode. Dig his heels in and scream."

I was dying to ask whether she thought that would mean he'd fully accepted that he was gay, but just the idea made me feel too vulnerable. "If there's any way for me to see him...." I let that trail off.

"Yeah, I figured that's where you were going. What you wanted help with, I mean. Maybe. I'll think about it, about whether I could help with that. Especially if you can put me in touch with your brother, but maybe just as much so I can stick it to my 'mom.' What's your brother's name, by the way?"

"Dylan."

We were silent for a bit, Paige looking out at the water, me poking with a bit of twig at the rough spots on the rock. Suddenly I realized she might be looking for that Cigarette boat, and Ashton. I asked, "Do you wanna talk about the blond you hate so much?"

Eyes still on the water, she said, "Don't misunderstand me, Micah. We're not friends. We're co-conspirators."

"Fair enough." I watched her watch the water for a few seconds, and it hit me how fine her facial bone structure was. I reached for my camera. "Do you mind if I take a few shots? The way the light's falling on your face is really interesting."

She looked at me, shrugged, and faced the water again.

She didn't move as I took shot after shot, from different angles. I moved to different spots around her, farther away, closer in. I shot from above and then while lying on my back and looking up. She was the perfect model. Something about her face made it possible for me to capture several different moods without her changing her expression in any way. It was fascinating.

When I'd shot all I wanted, I showed her the results. She examined them closely, taking her time, almost as though she were looking at portraits of someone she didn't know.

"You're good." She handed me back the camera. "I'd like a few of those."

I had no problem with that. "Do you want me to choose?"

She considered this for a moment. "Sure. A representative sample."

"K. I should probably get back, now. My mom will go a little crazy if I leave her alone too long. She's kind of unsettled, what with Dylan and all."

"You'll let me know about Dylan?"

"Yeah. I'll ask him as soon as he reappears. He needed a little space today."

She nodded and turned her attention back to the water. I said, "See you," but I got no response. Yeah; not friends. But I'd take a co-conspirator.

By the time I got home, I couldn't remember anything about the trip, with all the thoughts and feelings whirling around inside me. My sympathy with Dylan's adjustment issues, the confirmation from Paige that Walker was leaning more and more my way, my new-and-improved relationship with Paige... and if all that wasn't enough, I couldn't wait to load the shots I'd taken of her on my laptop, and see if they were as great as they'd seemed when I'd shot them. Unless, of course, Mom seemed okay, in which case I was gonna bike out to Jasper Island; maybe today would be the day Walker would come to me. I knew enough to know that it needed to be like that. I mean, he had to come to me, not the other way around.

Dylan was at the motel when I got back, at the kitchen table with Mom, and they were chatting like old buddies. Honestly, I might have gained some sympathy for Dylan this afternoon when I'd made his case to Paige, but these mood swings were annoying. I went into my room; if they wanted to be such close friends, let them.

I'd just gotten my shots of Paige into my laptop photo software when the office bell rang. I heard Mom get up, and then I heard Dylan's voice.

"Whatcha up to, little brother?"

He leaned in my doorway, arms crossed loosely, a light smile on his face. I didn't even know I was going to get up, but suddenly I was across the room, my arms wrapped around him and his around me, and we stayed in that tight hug while I felt the beating of his heart—that heart that was, after all, still beating—feeling his chest expand and contract with breaths I had thought had left him forever.

When we finally let go of each other, I turned quickly so he wouldn't see the moisture in my eyes. "I just took some shots of Walker's sister, Paige."

He sat in my chair and scrolled through them, saying nothing, until he'd seen them all. Looking up at me, he said, "Micah, these are gorgeous. I can see why you want to keep going with photography. Do you have the ones you took of me?"

I brought those up, and he liked them a lot.

"And that girl... Who is she, again?"

"Walker's sister."

"That's what I thought you said. But she looks Indian."

Here was my chance to keep my promise to Paige. "Her mother was Muslim, from Pakistan. But Walker's family adopted Paige as a baby when her mother died giving birth. The father disappeared." That was enough for Dylan to know, I decided. "By the way, I mentioned you to her. She was raised Catholic by the Donnells, but she's not in that church any more. She wants to know more about Islam."

I watched his face carefully. It seemed unlikely he'd volunteer to meet with her, but I gave him the space. He was thoughtful but silent. So I said, "She wanted to know if she could talk with you about it." Pause. Nothing. "Too soon?"

He leaned back and rubbed his face. "No, not too soon. I'd be happy to talk with her." His eyes were now back on the screen as he moved from one image of her to another.

"I promised to send her a few of these shots. Any suggestions?"

He picked out two that he thought were among the best, then he gave me my chair back, and I added a few more. Dylan watched as I composed a message to Paige saying he'd be willing to meet with her, and I attached the shots we'd selected.

Just before I hit *Send*, Dylan said, "This is assuming you'd be with us, Micah. Ideally, she should have a female friend with her as well, but we can be flexible if we meet someplace that isn't too private."

"Sure." As I sent the message, it occurred to me that I very much wanted to hear what Dylan would say to Paige.

The meeting was Sunday afternoon. Paige had suggested a picnic, and the idea of her putting all that together seemed odd; but when she got to the motel, and Dylan transferred everything from her BMW to the SUV Dad had rented for him, I saw that a caterer had put it together—probably the same one who'd prepared the food for my *Magic Spell* cruise.

Paige started to get into the passenger seat, but Dylan stopped her. "I don't exactly follow the more extreme requirements," he told her with a smile that said it was an understatement, "but it would be better if Micah sat beside me. I hope you don't mind being chauffeured."

He opened the rear door behind what was to be my seat, and bowed gallantly for her to enter.

She shrugged. "Guess I might as well start learning now." And she climbed without protest into the back, which wasn't exactly a hardship in that big vehicle.

Paige didn't say anything about the photos of her I'd taken, and neither did I. She directed Dylan to drive east along the coast and then out on a long access road, past some huge homes, to a point I'd never known was there. It was all massive, table-shaped rocks, no beach. It was just a little past high tide (I now had an app that tracked tides on my phone; quite the sailor, eh?), and the surf was splashing up onto the rocks closest to the water, but there were a lot of rocks. We found a good spot to spread out.

I half expected Paige to have beer or wine, despite the illegality of it in public, but either she didn't want to risk arrest or she already knew Islam's official attitude toward alcohol. She busied herself getting everything laid out, looking so much more domestic than I would have thought she could (let alone more than I'd have thought she would have been *willing* to look), and with a bit of a shock I realized she was also dressed much more modestly than I'd ever seen.

The food was great—lots of little things as well as a chicken pasta combo, and baklava for dessert. Nothing with pork. We filled our plates, and then Paige opened the discussion topic for the day.

"Has Micah told you the circumstances of my adoption?"

I was impressed with how matter-of-fact she sounded. Dylan said yes but asked her to tell him herself, so she did.

Then he said, "Micah tells me you want to know more about Islam. I hope you know I'm no expert. My knowledge is limited to the experiences I had in Afghanistan—a little before the explosion that sent me into the hills, and more from my wife and her family. I know enough to have converted, but I'm still a total beginner. What is it you want to know?"

"First, I want to hear about the place of women in Islam. I want to know about Sharia law. And I want to understand how Islam can be peaceful. I keep hearing peace is what it's supposed to be about, but then there are all the attacks, and the Islamic Sate, and all that."

Dylan chuckled and shook his head. "You don't want much, do you? I'll tell you what I can. But, like I said, I'm no expert."

I sat silent in my role as chaperone and listened as Dylan did his best to respond to Paige. I have no way of knowing how well he did, but at least he was clear enough for me to follow along. The first thing he said was that the term "Sharia Law" is redundant, because Sharia means law in Arabic. After that, what he said made it sound as though everything hinged on how each Muslim, or maybe each Muslim community, interprets Sharia.

Dylan said the law covers belief and faith, and then it goes into how people should approach life and each other, and then it describes specific things to be done. I got the sense that across all of Islam, there are conflicting ideas about whether government and Sharia are the same. Where they're the same, the government enforces religious law. But there are Muslim communities that believe compliance is between the individual Muslim and God. Allah.

By the time Dylan stopped talking, he'd barely eaten anything, and I'd learned some stuff I hadn't known, for sure. Like, there's controversy about how much the circumstances—for example, living in a Western society—should be taken into account to decide how (or even if) a law should be followed. There's controversy on the dress code for women, with some Muslims saying that the law's intent was merely to encourage modesty for both men and women—something that definitely varies from one society to another, and from one time period to another.

The controversy around peaceful vs. violent, though, was tougher for me to follow. I had always assumed the Holy Quran, as Dylan referred to it, was like the Bible, telling a story. But the way Dylan described it, there are over a hundred chapters, and lots of verses within them, and there's no strict chronology to the order they appear in. He said something about Meccan verses and Medinan verses and how sometimes they're mixed together in a chapter and sometimes they're not.

I think the most important part of what he said had to do with the circumstances around the start of the religion. That is, it was a violent time—lots of conflict, lots of people trying to kill other people—and defense of your own community was hugely important. Also, though it wasn't clear to me what the difference is or why there's so much disagreement between them, there's always been war between the Sunni and the Shia branches of Islam, ever since the death of Mohammed.

Dylan said he believes that Mohammed wanted his own society to be peaceful, but that the way the scripture is organized makes it possible for some Muslims to point to the verses that say defense against attack makes violence necessary, now as much as hundreds of years ago. And it also depends on what someone thinks "attack" means.

"I'm going to eat some of this great food now," he said finally, "so let me just say this. The violence is perpetrated by only a small percentage of Muslims. There are many others who adhere strictly to Sharia in terms of their own behavior but aren't violent when someone else doesn't. These people focus on the revelations about being kind, and being humble. It seems to me that Muslims who believe in peaceful coexistence with non-Muslims follow the more peaceful and loving verses. And, Paige, there are an awful lot of us who do that."

Paige had let him talk, not asking questions, not trying to direct what he said. She gave him a few minutes to eat before she asked, "So what does all that mean for women?"

"Where would you like me to start?"

"Clothes."

"The Holy Quran requires all Muslims to behave and dress modestly. I have my own ideas about why women once had to cover themselves, and it has to do with interpreting Sharia—and the definition of modest— according to different times and different societies. Today, many Muslims don't believe that the only modest woman is a covered woman."

"Does your wife wear a burka?"

"In her village, yes. It's required, and she and her family would be in serious trouble otherwise. But once she comes to live here, her plan is not to do that. She's determined to find contemporary, Western ways to behave and dress modestly. And her decisions will be between her and God."

"You don't get to tell her what to do?"

Dylan laughed. "I wouldn't dare."

Paige smiled but didn't laugh.

"Paige, you need to understand that my wife's family is unusual. Her father traveled quite a bit before he came home to take over his late father's farm. Both he and his wife hold pretty progressive views—most of which they need to be quiet about, given where they live. My wife, Darya, agrees with them, but her brother, Fareed, does not. So I got to see both sides represented. That is, the progressive and the strict sides. I agree with my wife and her parents, and I'll support Darya however she wants to appear once she's in the U.S."

Up to this point, Paige had been unlike herself, or the self I knew her to be. But suddenly she reverted. Her voice took on more of the edge it usually had. "How can you be sure that Darya didn't marry you just to get out of Afghanistan? Just to live someplace where she doesn't have to cover herself up any more?"

Dylan finished chewing a mouthful of pasta, his eyes on Paige. He seemed thoughtful rather than pissed off, which I would have been. Hell, which I was already, on his behalf. I wanted to push back at Paige, but something about Dylan, something calm, made me sit still.

He swallowed, took a sip of lemonade, and said, "Something in your life has taught you to distrust. I'm sorry that happened to you." He went back to his pasta salad.

I think I learned more in that response than I'd learned from everything else he'd said, put together.

Lying in bed that night, trying to sleep, it occurred to me that it was July twenty-fourth. Not an important date in and of itself, but it had been June twenty-fourth when I'd been shooting a dead seagull, and a gorgeous, boat-shoe-shod guy had tried to make friends with me. I'd rejected him, then dreamed about him, then watched for him for days until he'd reappeared. And now I couldn't get him out of my mind.

I felt a little guilty, actually, like I should be thinking about Dylan and about how great it was that he wasn't dead. It *was* great. And it still freaked me out in a very good way. But a little mind worm was always there, always bringing me back to Walker.

Boat shoes.

I fetched my own boat shoes and actually brought them into bed with me. Then I allowed myself a few minutes of... we'll call it pure physical pleasure while I pictured Walker, pictured us in his joyful little boat, pictured us kissing and happy and together.

Together. That was huge.

I'd been insisting to myself that as long as he knew I was there waiting, he'd stay alive. But what if that breaking point he was approaching, the one even Paige could see, actually broke him? What if being pulled from both sides—mine and his mother's—tore him apart?

God damn it to hell, but this horrible situation was going to change. I would change it.

Chapter Thirteen

Monday morning it was raining. Hard. So much for my plan to wait on that strip of beach for Walker to come home from sailing, make my way toward him, and see what he'd do. I tried to think of where he'd go in this weather and came up with nothing other than sitting at his PlayStation in that huge blue and orange room. And maybe struggling through another meeting with Father Gaffney.

Mom told me Dylan was job hunting in Warwick and Providence, so I couldn't hang with him. I was at my laptop playing with images when an idea hit me. I went to find Mom, who was doing the motel's books at the kitchen table. I took the chair across from her and waited for her to look up.

Barely lifting her head from her work, she said, "Did you want something, Micah?"

"How busy is the place today?"

She looked back at her laptop screen. "Probably will be a number of complaints, what with this weather. When folks hang out in the rooms, somehow things break. Very mysterious, I'm sure." She lifted her head all the way up. "Why?"

"I wasn't very nice to you about Madam Alberta. But she knew about Sharon, and she knew about Dylan." I stopped.

"What's your point? Are you apologizing?"

Not what I had intended, no. But— "Yeah. I'm sorry I was so skeptical."

She leaned back in her chair. "You should be skeptical, Micah. That wasn't the problem. The problem was that you disrespected me, and I'd be willing to bet you and your father said some less than complimentary things about me because I believed her."

"I'm sorry I disrespected you. And I'm sorry I doubted you."

"And?" She was trying to sound mad, but I could tell there was a smile struggling to get out.

"And for maybe saying a couple of things that weren't entirely understanding."

She actually laughed at that one. "Fine. Now, anything else?"

"Yeah, there is. Um, you know how I told you what Walker's mother is making him do? I mean, meeting with that priest to pray the gay away?"

I could tell it bothered her as much to hear that now as it had when I'd told her, the night I'd given her Trapper's collar back. "I remember."

"I'm kind of worried about him. Because of the intersex thing. He's told me there've been times when he felt like he was at the end of his rope."

Mom sat up straight. "Are you talking about suicide?"

"That's what I'm worried about. And I was wondering whether you thought Madam Alberta would be able to— you know, get a sense of things, or whatever it is she does."

Mom was thoughtful for a minute. Then, "For the sake of argument, let's say we ask her, she says something like yes, he's in danger. What would you do about it?"

Hmmm. A reasonable question. And not one I'd thought about, so I had no answer. "I guess I don't really know, other than try to reach out to him. You know, like, maybe if he knew I was still here, he wouldn't feel so alone. Or maybe Madam Alberta would have a suggestion."

Mom was thoughtful again, and then she picked up her phone. I listened as she spoke to an answering service;

perhaps Madam Alberta was in session. Mom asked to have her call back. Then she called Nick and asked him whether he'd be available today if she needed him. He would.

I went back to my laptop, leaving Mom to her finances, until I heard her phone ring. Standing in the doorway to the kitchen, I listened as Mom described Walker's situation much better than I'd have thought she could. There was some back and forth, and when Mom hung up she looked in my direction.

"She had a cancellation for one o'clock today. I'd need to be in the session with you. And," and she chuckled here, "you'll need to turn off your phone. Are you game?"

"Yeah. Let's do it." What did I have to lose?

Madam Alberta didn't look anything like I would have expected. Instead of a woman with long, dark hair and black clothes sitting in a room draped with purple velvet, she was a short, chubby lady with a shock of curly red hair, and she had on khaki slacks and a bright green sleeveless blouse. She looked just like somebody you might barely notice if you saw her at the grocery store.

After a few minutes of comments like, "So this is young Micah!" we all three sat at a small, round table under a hanging lamp shaped like a slice of kiwi or something. It gave off a bright green light that, surprisingly, didn't make everyone look sick.

"Spring green is my favorite color," she informed me. "I inhale spring green when I need to exhale muddy colored energy. All right. So, Micah, your mother has told me what you're concerned about."

Good; she wasn't pretending that it was something she'd already known.

She fetched a white bowl and a white pitcher with water in it. She put the bowl directly in front of her, and she poured water into it from the pitcher, watching the flow intently. No one spoke.

She sat back in her chair. Her voice now softer, smoother, she said, "Micah, can you say in a few words what it is you'd like to know? I imagine it would be something that would help you understand whether you could or should take any action."

"Mom and I talked about this on the drive over. Here's my question. Two parts, really. Is Walker being pushed by his mother or by Father Gaffney in a direction that's wrong for him? And whether he is or not, is he in any danger?"

Madam Alberta nodded. "That's clear enough. Good. Now, I'm going to ground myself. We don't all have to hold hands, or anything, in case you were wondering. Just follow me as best you can into a place of security and calm. And Micah, if you can hold Walker in your thoughts in a general kind of way, that would be helpful."

She folded her hands in her lap and closed her eyes. I watched her, curious to know whether anything weird would happen. It didn't. She inhaled deeply and let her breath out slowly, sat quietly for maybe ninety seconds, then opened her eyes on the bowl. A hand on either side of it, she gazed into it. Her face was soft, and she seemed to be listening to something I couldn't hear. She sat like that for maybe two minutes, while I focused my thoughts on Walker. They went to sailing, and boat shoes.

Suddenly her hands jerked, and some of the water slopped onto the table. She closed her eyes and, with a voice that sounded distant, she said, "It's all right, Micah, don't worry. I'll tell you more in a bit."

Mom and I sat silently as Madam Alberta seemed to come back into the room, even though she hadn't left it. She mopped up the water and took the bowl and pitcher into another room. When she came back she had a white plate and some flowers. She plucked at the flowers until the plate had a light layering of purple, yellow, pink, and white petals on it.

She took another deep breath, let it out, and said, "Grounding again."

This time when she opened her eyes and stared at the petals, about ten seconds went by before tears started rolling down her cheeks. She didn't seem to be crying, and at the same time she did. I got worried; was she seeing Walker in trouble? Or dead, even? Why didn't she say something?

Her closed eyes squeezed out tears, and then more tears, and then she took a deep, shuddering breath and slumped a little in her chair. Another minute or so later, she opened her eyes, blew her nose, and then looked directly at me.

"Micah, I'm glad you came to me with these questions." She sat up a little straighter and went on. "First, I do not get a sense of your friend in danger of dying from his own hand or another's. That doesn't mean it couldn't happen, just that I don't see it. I do see that he's in a good deal of emotional distress. I think he loves his mother very much. I get the sense that she's been a kind of champion for him in the area of his intersex condition, but I don't see that a champion has been needed. That is to say, I don't see anyone opposing Walker or standing in the way of his mother's support. This leads me to think that she might be driven by something inside herself, rather than solely by Walker's need. This can be concerning, because if I'm right, she's not fully aware of her own motivation and is convinced she has only Walker's needs in mind."

Mom interrupted, which surprised me. "Wouldn't it just mean she's being protective? Isn't she just being a good mother?"

Madam Alberta turned to Mom and smiled. "She's probably a very good mother. Sometimes, though, even good parents conflate their own needs and those of their children."

I took the opportunity to ask, "What made you cry?"

She smiled. "Oh, that. I always cry when I use flower petals as a medium. It says something about me, not about the message. So, let me tell you a little more about what I learned. I think Walker is very torn, and it's between his mother and what she wants from him, and you and what you want from him."

"I don't want anything from him!" It was out before I could even consider whether it was true.

Her smile made it look like she knew something I didn't. "Oh, we all want something from each other. This is particularly true of people we love. And there's something he wants from you." She paused and leaned back in her chair a little. "Walker wants to fall in love. I can't say why. Maybe he thinks that if he can fall in love with someone, it will tell him something he needs to know about himself. He believes he's in love with you. I'm not qualified to say whether he is, just that he thinks he is. He might be right. And, of course, he wants you to love him. He reads as rather needy to me, which is understandable, but also he seems to be a person of great depth. I can't tell you whether a relationship with him would be deep and meaningful for you, or worth facing the challenges of it, but I do think *he* is worth it."

She paused, maybe to see if I had any questions, but I was too busy organizing my own thoughts. My own feelings.

Then she said, "As to whether he's being pulled against his nature, it seems to me that he's allowing himself to be pulled in order to find out who he is. It's a plan that has some risk. And I'm seeing a lot of fear in him right now. But also a lot of courage."

This wouldn't settle in my brain. "Wait—how can there be both?"

"Courage, Micah, isn't the absence of fear. It's facing that fear. And one can't overcome a fear until one faces it."

Sharks. *Magic Spell*. Mr. Donnell calmly talking me through photographing the sand tigers. And here I'd managed to convince myself, that evening when I'd bounced up and down on the dock at Sailaway, that I was courageous. On my own, without a Mr. Donnell, without someone to walk me through my fear, was I still a coward?

Madam Alberta's smile disappeared quickly. "Micah, are you all right? I'm getting some troubled energy from you.

"Yeah. Fine. I'm fine. So what should I do about Walker?" I desperately wanted to redirect the focus, get back to Walker. No way was I going to talk about my cowardice in front of Mom or anyone else. And, oddly, I deliberately avoided looking at those flower petals in case they'd have the same effect on me as they'd had on Madam Alberta.

Madam Alberta didn't look convinced, but she said, "He knows you're watching him, correct?" I nodded. "As long as you're willing to take whatever comes—and by that I mean accept Walker's decision, whatever it is—my reading of you tells me you need to keep doing that, for your own sake, at least until one of you needs to stop. You or Walker, that is."

"Should I approach him?"

She thought for a few seconds, shook her head, and said, "I can't advise you, there. I'm no psychologist, and I didn't learn anything that points toward or away from that idea."

Mom had another question. "Isn't Micah's spying something that goes against Mrs. Donnell's wishes?"

"Oh, no doubt. But I'm not concerned with her wishes, and I didn't hold any intent for her in my listening. That said—and this is my personal feeling only—I think Walker's best interests are more important than her wishes.

I read that he's doing everything he can to honor those wishes, but in the end if they don't match his needs, I vote for him."

I was with Madam Alberta, of course. "And if he tries to meet her wishes and fails, he has to go against her or he can't go anywhere at all. That won't be easy."

"Very astute, Micah."

I liked this lady better every minute. But she hadn't answered one of my questions thoroughly enough. "And is he being pulled in the wrong direction by Father Gaffney?"

"If you're asking me whether Walker is gay, I can't tell you that. Only Walker can. And here's my last advice for you, Micah. It's possible, given the different forces inside him and around him, that he could change his mind a few times about who he is in more than one respect. This could be very painful for you, if you've allowed yourself to love him." She smiled kind of a sad smile. "You might need a lot of courage."

Mom had let me drive on the way to Madam Alberta's, but it was raining harder than ever as we left, and she wouldn't let me drive home. "Besides the rain, Micah, I imagine you have some serious thinking to do. Best not to do that behind the wheel of a car."

She was probably right. We didn't speak for the whole ride, and between the rain pounding on the roof of the car and the feelings rising and sinking and rising inside me, I barely noticed anything about the drive home.

Fear. Courage. Love. Need. Pain. These words hammered and pounded in my head louder than the rain on the car. So I should keep "spying," as Mom had put it. And then what? Even if I convinced Walker to reject Father Gaffney's exhortations and his mother's expectations, even if he turned to me, Madam Alberta had said he might not stay. He might change his mind. And change it again. And again.

She'd said he was worth it, but that the relationship might not be worth it for me. She'd said I'd need courage.

Did I have enough of that? Did I have any? I couldn't exactly go to Mr. Donnell, a proven source of courage, and ask for him to talk me through loving his son. Daughter. Child. So where would I get this courage I'd need? Where would it come from? Walker had courage, according to Madam Alberta, but if he couldn't be sure about himself, how could he help me be sure of what I was doing?

Round and round and round. And round again. It felt like being trapped in a whirlpool smack dab in the middle of the doldrums.

Back at the motel, Mom mumbled something about turning her phone on again, and I headed toward my room for more round and round, unless I could think of something to distract myself. But I'd just turned my laptop on when Mom appeared in my doorway, phone in hand.

"There was a message from your brother." Her voice was odd; was something wrong? "I'm about to call him back. He says Darya will be here late Thursday afternoon."

I nearly said, "So they'll finally be able to have sex." Almost had to clamp a hand over my mouth. Almost. Mom called Dylan's number, put her phone on speaker, and sat on the end of my bed.

"Dylan? I have you on speaker. Micah's here. I got your message, honey. About Darya? You must be thrilled." Mom was smiling for all she was worth, but it looked fake to me. Couldn't have said why.

Dylan's voice, tinny and thin, came through the phone. "You have no idea. I'm, uh, going to pick her up on my own. I think it would be better that way."

"Of course, honey, whatever you like. When will we get to meet her?"

"What I'm thinking is to have a kind of family dinner here, in Warwick, on Friday. We won't be ready to cook for everyone, so I'll order something."

"Sounds lovely. But how about if I bring the food? I can dig up some of your favorite recipes from—"

"That's very generous, Mom, but no. I think it would be better if I plan things."

I got the sense that Dylan was feeling the need to protect Darya from us, or at least from too much Western culture all at once. I watched Mom's face as she ended the call. It was still all smiles, until it wasn't.

Tuesday afternoon I was back at the Jasper Island beach. I saw Walker dock his boat, I saw him look directly at me like he knew I'd be there, and I saw him stand there like a statue for maybe thirty seconds before he headed toward his house.

Wednesday I almost missed the docking, because it happened sooner than usual. And Walker wasn't alone. Cam was with him.

Walker glanced my way, kind of sideways like he didn't want Cam to know I was there, so I moved back toward the trees. I could hear Cam's stupid howling laughter, no doubt at some lame "joke" he'd made at Walker's expense.

I left as soon as I was sure I wouldn't be seen and then headed—for no reason that I could say—toward Quiambog Cove, where I'd seen the bull shark a couple of weeks ago. Part of me wanted to see it again. Part of me wanted to condemn all bull sharks to hell.

I sat there on a rock high enough that I could watch the water for a gray, threatening shape. But I didn't really care if I saw it. Knees up, I rested my arms on them and my chin on my arms and wondered what the fuck I was doing. There was not much more point hanging out on that Jasper Island beach and watching for someone who wouldn't talk to me than there was sitting here scouring the water for sharks. When I saw Walker, he still wouldn't talk to me. And if I saw a shark, there would be no contact, no communication there, either.

Another line from "Layla" came to me: Like a fool, I fell in love with you—turned my whole world upside down.

It pissed me off royally that that asshole Cam could spend time with Walker, sail with Walker, and I couldn't. In my frustration, I did a stupid thing. I took off my shoes and waded into the water, past that rock I'd sat on last time. Even the fucking shark was avoiding me.

But Thursday, frustrated or not, pissed off or not, there I was again at my spot on the Jasper Island beach. *Dare Ya* was at the dock, all tied up with locking cables, the same way she'd been the day I'd met Cam. Evidently, Walker wasn't sailing, no doubt because he didn't want Cam in the boat with him, and he didn't want Cam sailing, either.

This time, as I was on my bike and on my way off of the island, I was spotted. And it was that jerk, Cam, who saw me. He was driving Walker's Jeep back from someplace. I didn't see anyone else in the car as Cam slowed, his muscled arm hanging out of the open window, sunglasses covering his eyes, a grin that said, "You're busted!" on his stupid face. He came to a stop just before our paths crossed and threw the Jeep into reverse, tracking with me, going backward on the empty road. I refused to look at him.

"Well, look who it is! I know you didn't get to see your sweetheart, because he's at his nanna's. Boo-hoo for you-hoo." His cackling laugh and sudden braking happened at the same time, and he took off toward the Donnells' house.

The rest of the way home I worried. I didn't care if he told Walker he'd seen me. But what if he told Mrs. Donnell? Did he know I'd been read the riot act and told to stay away from my "sweetheart," as he'd called Walker? And did he really have any idea how close that was to accurate? What would Mrs. Donnell do if she knew I'd been here? She wouldn't necessarily know I'd been coming here a lot, but even once would be in direct opposition to what she'd told me she expected. If she confronted Walker, would he be unable to hide the fact that I'd been there several times already?

Fuck. Fuck Cam. Fuck Mrs. Donnell. Fuck Father Gaffney.

I was in a foul mood by the time I got home, so I didn't respond very well to Mom's latest acquisition. As soon as I stepped through the door, I was greeted by a frolicking, over-friendly puppy. He was darker than Trapper had been, but he did look like he might be part shepherd. His feet were quite large, which I'd heard was the sign of a big dog in the making.

He emitted little yelping barks as he pawed up my shins. I glanced at him and then looked for Mom. She was at the kitchen table, watching, grinning.

I tried to be nice. Really, I did. "Who's this?" I asked, walking into the dog's embrace so he'd back off.

"Isn't he adorable? I gave him a bath, but I didn't want to name him. Calling him Trapper seems a little too on the nose. So I'll leave that to Dylan."

"Dylan?"

"Well, it's going to be his puppy." She grinned as though she'd figured out exactly what he wanted for his birthday and had finally found it.

"Are you sure he wants one?"

"Why wouldn't he? He loved Trapper! You both did. Why wouldn't he want another dog?"

"Well, gee, how about that he hasn't even got his own feet under him yet, and as of this afternoon he's got his wife alone with him for the first time, she doesn't speak much English, she doesn't know how to drive, she might never have seen some of the things in Dad's apartment before in her life, she doesn't know anybody but Dylan—"

"She doesn't speak English?" All that, and it was the language that caught Mom's attention. "How will we communicate with her?"

I didn't even try to answer, so Mom laid into me for my attitude. "Micah, how can you be so cruel, making it sound like this gift is a mistake?" I didn't try to answer that one, either, so she said, "And I'm pretty sick and tired of everything being about Darya. Darya this, Darya that. Honestly!"

"I don't think it's so much about Darya. I think it's about Dylan."

"Do you think I don't know that?" She was practically shouting at this point. "Do you think I don't care about my own son, delivered back to me from the grave? Who do you think I got the dog for? Me? You? It's for Dylan!"

I tried to throw a little oil on the roiling water. "Okay, okay. Maybe the dog will be good company for both of them. Dogs are great, and this guy is adorable, you're right."

Mom's expression started to change, but then she caught sight of that adorable puppy squatting over the floor, conspicuously not over any of the the doggy pads Mom had scattered around the place. She jumped up, lifted the dog in mid-stream as it were, and plunked him down on the nearest pad.

"Micah, fetch some paper towels and a plastic bag, will you?"

Oh, this was going to be fun. So much fun. (Sarcasm alert.)

I spent a good part of Friday with the puppy. We were calling him that—Puppy—so Dylan (or Darya, I supposed) could name him.

The motel was just down Route 1 from one of the many inlets of water that feed into coves. They aren't quite fresh-water rivers and aren't quite sea water. Camera at the ready, I took Puppy along the highway to one of these areas and walked him around, peering into water whenever we got close enough in case there was a bull shark lurking. Didn't see anything, so I let Puppy splash around a little, keeping a firm grip on the leash attached to his collar.

It was difficult to keep my mind from going back to Cam and the possibility that Mrs. Donnell would find out I'd been going to Jasper Island, but there was nothing I could do about it. And once Puppy was tuckered out, it was fun taking shots of him—nothing artistic, just fun shots.

After a quick run for a few groceries Mom asked me to get, I went alone to Quiambog Cove. Before I left the motel, I grabbed the binoculars I'd swiped from Dylan's box. I'd never returned them, so when Mom had given him the box, these hadn't been in there. Maybe I could see that shark with them.

The tide was lower today in mid-afternoon, and I didn't see anything of interest with or without the binoculars. I lost interest in this effort and decided to find a place where I could climb up and over the railroad tracks between the cove and the Sound. And once I'd done that, I had a shock.

It shouldn't have been a shock, given who was involved. As I looked out over the open water I saw a boat that looked just like *Dare Ya*. At first I thought I must be wrong, because it sure wasn't Walker at the helm. Plus, he was supposed to be at his grandmother's. I lifted the binoculars and took a closer look.

Cameron.

That asshole must have taken Walker's own Jeep to a hardware store, bought some wire cutters, and cut the little boat loose! I watched as he seemed to be struggling to catch wind in the sails, which I was sure Walker could have done, no problem. Cam wasn't looking my way at all, so I just kept watching him, which wasn't hard; he wasn't exactly sailing out of sight.

Watching Cam struggle, I had to laugh. Maybe he'd have to call the Donnells and get rescued by *Magic Spell!* I'd sell tickets to that.

It got boring very soon, watching him go nowhere, and if he did anything horrible to Walker's boat, I didn't want to see it. I packed up the binoculars and headed home.

Saturday night's dinner marked a major shift in my family dynamics. Like, a major rift. And I couldn't see how we were going to get past it.

Mom let me drive to Warwick, even though it was raining off and on. Neither of us said a word, really, for most of the trip, other than Mom repeatedly telling Puppy to settle down. She had him tied to a fastened seat belt in the back, surrounded by doggie pads which he proceeded to chew. Beside him was was a pile of paraphernalia Mom had bought—things every dog needs. She wasn't about to get blamed for not equipping the young married couple properly to take care of this new baby.

As I pulled into a parking spot a few slots away from Dad's pickup truck, Mom found her voice. "Oh my God. You don't think… He isn't bringing *her*, is he?"

"Her? Oh, you mean Sharon? I kind of doubt it. I think this will be interesting enough without that complication."

We left Puppy in the car and headed up to the apartment. And in fact there was no Sharon. Dad was at one end of the couch looking distinctly uncomfortable, a glass of what looked like water held in both hands as he leaned forward, elbows on his knees. In a chair more or less facing him was a woman covered in black cloth, head to toe. Her face was exposed, and I could see her hands clasped in her lap, but that was all. She might have been pretty, but I was so taken aback by her costume that I mostly saw that and not her.

It was everything I could do not to turn to Dylan and ask where Darya was. I mean, okay, there's this woman hiding under a tent, but hadn't he told us Darya wasn't going to wear this thing once she got here?

Dylan made the necessary introductions. Darya mumbled something as she was introduced to Mom, but she said nothing to me. She looked distinctly uncomfortable shaking my hand, eyes down. Was it because I'm male, or had Dylan already told her I was gay? Either one might have been the problem; Islam as it's practiced in places like Afghanistan has a rather nasty reputation when it comes to people like me.

There was some back and forth as Darya offered lemonade to everyone and then sat down again, silent again, perhaps lacking the appropriate English phrases. Hard to know if that was the only reason for her silence.

Dylan made a little speech about how wonderful it was to be home and to have his wife and his family meeting for the first time. He seemed sincere, but he sounded kind of formal and anxious. I didn't blame him for that.

As gently as if she were made of glass, he pulled Darya to her feet and held her hand. "Darya is looking forward to preparing customary Afghani dishes for us all to share at a future dinner. For now, she's made the lemonade, and she's laid out the food I bought."

Dad was the bravest of us. He said, "Welcome, Darya."

She nodded, and in halting and heavily accented English, she said, "Thank you very much. I love to be here."

I had begun to feel rather sorry for her; I wouldn't have wanted to be in her place. I'd have been willing to bet that she was afraid of appearing inadequate, not being able to prepare a meal for her new husband's family. Still, I couldn't help hearing Dylan's voice in my head, responding to Paige's question about whether Dylan got to tell Darya what to do: "I wouldn't dare!" Where was that woman?

She smiled, and it looked like an effort. "We shall eat now?"

"Sounds good," I said, and I led the way to the table to set my lemonade down at one of the place settings.

The counter was covered in a spread of cold cuts (no pork, I was sure), cheeses, tiny tomatoes, sticks of various vegetables, pickles and cocktail onions, lettuce, condiments, some sliced rolls, and pita bread. There was a pasta salad of some kind on the side. I picked up a plate, helped myself, and went to my chair.

Once everyone was seated, I made a point to praise the lemonade, which really was very good. Darya had evidently gained a little courage; she looked directly at me and thanked me. Then she bowed her head, eyes closed; I guessed it was some kind of prayer, like some Christians say grace before a meal. Dylan did the same thing. The rest of us waited, unsure about what to do, until the two of them raised their heads again.

To say conversation was strained would be an understatement. I was curious to know whether Dylan had mentioned anything to Darya about his conversation with Paige, but I didn't feel like I should say anything about it. Dad asked about leads from Dylan's search for work, and that discussion took a few minutes. Mom asked Dylan if there was anything he or Darya needed that she could help with; he said he'd let her know. No one asked Darya anything, which on one hand was reasonable, but on another bothered me.

So I said, "Darya, have you ever seen the ocean before?"

Her dark eyes sparkled at me, I swear. "Only here." She smiled, more naturally this time, and I assumed Dylan had made sure she'd seen it already. "It is my name."

"Dylan told us," I said, glad she'd understood enough of my question to answer. Perhaps she understood English better than she spoke it? That's how it was for me in French class.

Dylan told us about having taken Darya to see the water, and it sounded a lot like where Paige had taken us. Then he said, "I'm thinking about getting her a burkini so we can go to the beach, but that's a little progressive just yet. Maybe next summer." He popped a grape tomato into his mouth, swallowed, and added, "By the way, in case you're wondering, she's decided to make the transition from burka to western clothes gradually. She started by not wearing her niqab, which—"

Mom said, "Niqab?"

"Yeah, that's the piece that covers her face. Anyway, she felt more comfortable like this today, meeting everyone for the first time, even though you are family now."

Mom had another question. "What's family got to do with it?"

"Ordinarily, she wouldn't wear the full burka at home unless there were men unrelated to her there."

"I see. Well, I suppose gradual change is sensible. There's so much to get used to here, I would think." Mom's smile was almost natural, though her tone made it clear she wasn't entirely convinced.

The awkwardness at dinner was undeniable. And yet it was nothing compared to what happened before dessert, which Dylan said was ice cream.

"Oh, I have something for you both," Mom said, grinning shyly. "Maybe this would be a good time to give it to you? Micah, would you fetch it from the car?"

"Me?"

She leaned to my ear and whispered, "Just bring the dog in on his leash; none of the rest of it yet." She handed me the car key.

It wasn't raining when I got to the car, so I decided to let Puppy take a piddle first. I walked him around for a couple of minutes until I felt relatively sure that he wouldn't embarrass himself and us—at least not right away.

The apartment door had locked behind me, so I had to knock to get back in. Dylan opened the door, saw Puppy, and his eyes went wide. But not with joy. It was more like horror.

Immediately, Puppy dashed into the room and jumped around, acting just like you'd expect a puppy to. I had released the leash, thinking it was safe to do that in the apartment, but Dylan shouted at me. "Micah! Get him!" But Dylan didn't wait for me; he dashed for the dog.

As Dylan chased Puppy, Darya jumped up from her chair with a little screech. She stared wide-eyed at the dog, waved her hands, and shouted, "No! No! Out! Out!"

I looked at Mom, at a complete loss; I mean, it's true I'd thought it wasn't the best plan, handing a puppy over to someone who wasn't expecting it, and I'd told her so. But I hadn't expected this kind of reaction. Mom looked as confused as I felt.

Dylan managed to grab the leash, and he held it in my direction. "Micah, you have to get rid of this, now."

Too shocked to echo, "'*This?*'" I took the leash from him and headed toward the door. Behind me, I heard Mom say, "Dylan, what is it? What's wrong? I thought you'd love to have another dog!"

I waited in the open doorway, with Puppy in the hall and trying to get back into the apartment, wanting to hear what Dylan had to say. Darya still stood, transfixed, her huge eyes on the dog.

Dylan fumbled for words. "It's just—look, um... you have to understand that in Afghanistan, dogs are not considered household pets. They're animals, and they're kept outside the way we might keep chickens or a goat outside. They often live in packs, and sometimes they're aggressive. Bringing a dog into the house is unheard of. Darya will feel like she has to clean the apartment very thoroughly now, and she just cleaned it thoroughly before you came."

At the mention of her name, Darya had turned toward Dylan, a look of frustration on her face. Dylan turned toward me and, slowly, shut the door, leaving me in the hallway with Puppy.

I had no choice but to lead the little guy back outside. He didn't know he'd been rejected, of course, but I did. Poor thing! He hadn't done anything wrong. And he wasn't dirty. I'd been prepared to be patient with Darya, but her reaction to a sweet little puppy—even one she hadn't expected—had pissed me off. And it was an insult to my mother, as well.

I mean, why the hell did Darya even want to come here? Just to see the ocean? She was going to have a lot to get used to here; having a dog for a pet seemed like the tip of the iceberg, and she hadn't handled that any better than she'd handled her wardrobe decision.

Even though I'd walked Puppy just a few minutes ago, I didn't want to go back into that apartment. I didn't trust myself to be civil. Let everyone else argue this out. Besides, I figured staying outside with the dog was sending the message that I'd rather be out here with him.

I was standing beside the car, thinking maybe I'd sit in there with Puppy for a while, when I saw Mom heading out of the building. Fast. I waited as she approached, and when she got close I could see she was crying.

"Mom?"

She shook her head and climbed into the passenger seat. She managed to say, "You'll have to drive home, Micah. I'm too upset."

I settled Puppy in the back seat, and just before I shut the door I said, "I'll be right back."

Dad opened the apartment door this time. He looked worried, and kind of like he didn't know what to do with himself. But I knew what I wanted to do.

"Dylan, what did you say to her?" I was barely aware that my hands were clenched into fists at my sides.

"Look, Micah, it's going to take some time, okay? We have to do things slowly. We can't assume something's good for everyone just because it's good for someone."

"You know, I wasn't sure the dog was a good idea, either. But for God's sake, Dylan, it was a gift! She got you a dog that looked as much like Trapper as she could find, and you threw it back in her face! She got you something she thought you'd love."

"I know, I know. But Darya"—

"Darya," and I pointed right at her, "had damn well better make some adjustments, and she'd better make them fast. Is being rude to your new mother-in-law something you would do to *her* mother? I don't think so."

"Micah—"

Again I interrupted him. "Where is all this progressive attitude you told us about? Where are the colorful scarves she had, dancing for you? What about—"

"Micah!" He shouted my name, and I stopped talking. "This is my wife you're talking about."

"And that was your mother you just sent out of your house, crying! She thought you were *dead*! She cried over that fucking box of your stuff almost every night, even after a psychic said you were still alive. She was the only one who believed it, but boy, did she believe it. She lived for it!"

I turned to Darya. "Don't you ever treat my mother like that again!"

I'd said all I needed to, and I turned toward the door to leave. Dylan grabbed my shoulder and spun me around, his fist raised. I held my jaw up.

"Go ahead. Make yourself feel righteous."

"Dylan!" Darya shouted, and he lowered his fist and let go of me.

Now I had something else to say. "Why did you come home at all? Why didn't both of you stay where you were?" I practically ran down the hall.

As soon as I was behind the wheel, door slammed shut beside me, I knew I'd gone too far. And yet I hadn't said anything I hadn't meant at the time I'd said it. Why *did* he come back? Why didn't he stay there with his Afghani bride who was invisible beneath a tent, keeping all dogs outside, speaking whatever they speak there, hiking up to hidden caves when she wanted to wear colorful silks and dance?

Mom and I sat still, then she blew her nose, and I asked, "Are you all right?"

She let out a long sigh. "I don't know. What did you say in there?"

"What didn't I say? I said too much, I think. But, damn it, Mom! That was a terrible way to treat you."

Several seconds went by, and then she said, "I think I can still take him back."

"Back?"

"To the shelter. He's young enough. He'll get adopted by somebody else."

"No." My voice surprised me, but my tone surprised both of us.

"No? What, you think I want a dog?"

"I think we need a dog. I think we need *this* dog."

I expected more pushback. I was sure she'd dig her heels in and make noises like how expensive a pet is, how I wouldn't be around for most of the dog's life and she'd end up taking care of it forever, that sort of thing. But all she said was, "Why?"

"Because it's like Dylan coming home again." I was mad at Dylan, but there was no denying the joy at having him home, of having him alive and well after being sure he was dead, mutilated beyond recognition in a far-off land I couldn't even picture in my mind.

There was something else there, too, in my protest. Something besides Trapper and Dylan reincarnating. Puppy had a sweetness, an innocence that was both joy and pain for me. He trusted us. He didn't know any better.

Mom was quiet for a few miles, and then out of nowhere she said, "Rondo."

"Rondo?"

"The dog's name. Because he's come 'round again."

Chapter Fourteen

I didn't get much sleep Saturday night. Partly it was because of what had happened at Dylan's apartment. But it was also because I wanted so much to talk with Walker about it.

Not having any real friends, with a few rare exceptions, hadn't bothered me much in the past. But now, now that there was someone I really wanted to be with, someone I would love to have talked this situation over with, I missed Walker like mad. Jerking off—twice—with him in bed with me (in my imagination, at least) didn't help. It wasn't sex I wanted badly right now. It was friendship.

Sunday after breakfast I tucked Rondo into my backpack, secured him so he couldn't scramble out, and I biked over to Jasper Island, to my hidden beach. I knew I wouldn't see Walker. I was watching for Cam, to see if he took the boat out again.

I had to say, Rondo's name fit him somehow, and he was smart enough that I think he'd already figured out it referred to him. I threw sticks for him back and forth on the beach and sometimes into the water, but never far, in case of sharks. And, sure enough, eventually I saw Cam stride out boldly to the dock, untie the boat, and head out.

I found myself wishing I could use my knowledge of his transgressions to keep him from saying he'd seen me, but really that wasn't likely to work. After all, it would be obvious to Walker that Cam had cut the boat free; he wasn't hiding anything, and he didn't think he had anything to fear from me or anyone else.

With Rondo tucked into my pack again, I headed back to the motel to see if Mom needed anything, including company. When I was maybe a couple hundred feet away, I saw Dylan in an unfamiliar car turning into the parking lot. Stopping far enough away to avoid being seen but close enough for me to see them, I watched as Dylan and Darya got out and headed toward the motel. She wore that tent and a head covering, but evidently she'd also felt the need for that other piece—the niqab—to cover everything but her eyes.

Dylan knocked on the door, and I moved forward enough to see Mom open it. She did not look happy to see them. I could barely hear her say, "What do you want?"

"Mom, can we come in, please?"

Mom didn't look at Darya. "Aren't you afraid the place is filthy from that horrible dog?"

Dylan pinched the bridge of his nose and then dropped his hand. "Please?"

Mom stepped back inside, and her son and daughter-in-law followed. As quietly as possible, I walked my bike around to the back and freed Rondo from the pack but not from his leash, keeping clear of the open windows. Rondo, no doubt tired from running back and forth after sticks on the beach, settled quietly onto the ground beside me as I positioned myself close to one of the living room windows to listen. I couldn't tell whether anyone inside sat down, but they probably did. Mom didn't offer them coffee or anything, though.

Dylan spoke first. "We want to apologize for the way we reacted to your gift."

"To the dog."

"Yes, the dog. I've explained to Darya that here in the U.S., people are very fond of dogs and keep them in the house."

"Are you saying you want to take him after all?" Her tone made it sound as though it wasn't likely she'd let him.

"Well, no. The apartment complex doesn't allow dogs."

"Isn't that lucky for her."

"Mom, please. We're sorry."

I heard Darya's faint voice: "Yes. I'm sorry."

"What did you say? I can't hear you."

Oh, shit. Mom was obviously not letting Darya off the hook so easily, and she was pretending not to be able to understand her from behind that face curtain.

Dylan must have figured this out as well. "Mom, stop it. You heard her."

"I thought you said this—all this cloth—wasn't necessary when you're just with family. I don't qualify, evidently."

"Can't you understand how vulnerable Darya feels? She's outside of her homeland for the first time in her life. She doesn't know a lot of English. She's never seen so many cars before. Everything's different for her, Mom. The burka helps her feel less vulnerable."

"Yes, well, I guess it would. That's what it's for, isn't it?"

"What?"

"I've been doing a little research this morning, as it happens. This religion of hers—"

"Of *ours*."

"Whatever. It tells her that if she gets attacked by strange men, it's her fault. It tells her that her safety is her own problem. And, by the way, it implies that men are such animals that they wouldn't be able to control themselves if they got a glimpse of her shoulders. Darya, why are you shaking your head? You know I'm right."

There was a low conversation between Darya and Dylan that I couldn't have understood even if I could have heard it better; what I could tell was that only some of it was in English.

Dylan's voice got louder as he spoke to Mom again. "Okay, I'm going to try to explain this right. First of all, the burka frees women from feeling like they have to measure up to someone's idea of beauty. Second, it allows women to participate in society in a way that's based on their important attributes, like intelligence and piety, rather than on whether they're pretty or smiling or whatever. Third, it advertises a wife's virtue and honor, which allows her to help society by maintaining the integrity of the marriage, avoiding the temptations of things like adultery."

Darya's voice now had a tone more in keeping with the way Dylan had described her in the past: direct, fearless, uncompromising. "Purdah... it is our tradition. I was the honor of my father. Now I am the honor my husband."

This must have confused Mom as much as it confused me. "You mean, you honor your husband? And you wouldn't do that without the burka? "

Dylan took up the baton. "That's not what she's saying. She's trying to tell you that this tradition gives her a really important role in maintaining honor."

Mom was getting angry. "You can't convince me that a man who forces a woman to dress like that will let her 'participate in society' in any meaningful way just because she's hiding in that tent."

In my mind, I saw Mom wave a hand in the air, dismissing their explanations as she added, "I don't see how what you two are telling me is different from what I just said. And anyway, this costume is more a cultural requirement than a religious one. From what I can tell, there's no Islamic law that requires her to hide away like this."

Dylan's voice got louder. "Look, even if you're right—and I don't know that you are—what makes you think a cultural norm is something she can toss over her shoulder just because she got on a plane? If you had to move someplace where everything was different, everything was strange, don't you think you'd get some comfort from whatever familiar things you could bring with you?"

Suddenly I felt horrible because of the way I'd reacted to the burka. Dylan was absolutely right.

Mom wasn't fazed. "Well, you better believe that she's going to get stared at and avoided around here. That thing's not going to give her much comfort."

"She sure isn't getting any comfort from you."

"From me? From *me?* Dylan, I don't even know what I'm looking at." Her voice changed a little, and I thought she might have been about to cry. "I can't see her face. I can't read her expression or her body language or communicate with her in any way that makes me feel like there's someone in there! I don't know how she's reacting to anything I say, so I can say anything."

There was some kind of shift; I think it was Dylan, standing. "Or you can say nothing. We came here in good faith to apologize to you, and you've done nothing but criticize. Darya can't respond to what you say because she can understand only some of it. But I understand all too well."

I heard the motel phone ring, and Mom answered it. More shifting; pretty sure it was Dylan and Darya moving toward the door. I picked up Rondo's leash and planted myself directly in their path.

Dylan's tone almost made me take a step back. Almost. "Micah. Your turn to be nasty, is it?"

"I heard what you said. About the pet policy. And about apologizing. Mom's just hurt, that's all." I turned to Darya. "I accept your apology."

I watched her eyes—which was all I could see of her—and they softened, I was sure. She reached a hand out, slowly, toward Rondo, who was smiling at everyone, and she stroked his forehead with just one finger. She pulled away when he tried to lick her hand, but the gesture had been real.

She said, "I hope he accept, too."

It was odd—I had to agree with Mom about that—to hear Darya speak and not be able to see it happen.

I grinned at her. "He's a dog. He loves everyone. Doesn't hold grudges. And—I'm sorry I yelled at you."

Her eyes crinkled up, and I knew she was smiling. "I accept. Good. We go now."

Dylan wrapped an arm around my neck and let go. I watched as they moved toward the car, and just before Darya got in, she waved at me.

Mom appeared beside me and heaved an exasperated sigh as the car drove off. "I blew that, didn't I?" Another sigh. "God, but I wish this weren't so hard."

"Time."

"What?"

"Give it time. I'm gonna walk Rondo a little."

Rondo and I walked back and forth more times than I could count, in the little strip of trees and bushes behind the motel. He didn't seem to mind that we kept covering the same ground; it was like he knew that things would change, and he was willing to wait for that.

Things do change. Over time.

Time. It affected me, too.

I was waiting for Walker, waiting for him to realize who he was, waiting for him to tell me. He'd once said that he wouldn't pretend he was someone he wasn't just to get a new friend. Or a new boyfriend, I assumed. And he'd been as honest with me as he could.

But how long was I willing to wait? And what would happen if I tried to hurry him? I still couldn't shake the possibility that showing up on the beach, having him see me over and over, might be pushing him rather than letting him know I was there. I'd been over this ground as often as I'd paced that beach, and the repeat journeys hadn't helped.

Christ, but I wanted to talk to him! That's all I asked for, at that moment, all I wanted to push for. Just to talk.

Just to find out where his head was, just to know what he was thinking, how he was feeling. And, okay, to know how he was feeling about me.

But this wasn't about me. I had to keep reminding myself of that. I was already pretty sure I knew who I was, and what I wanted in life, at least in a general sort of way. But Walker wasn't sure of something so very fundamental to how he saw himself that he didn't know how to ask others to see him.

I leaned my back against a tree and sank to the ground, Rondo beside me, his tongue hanging out, patient grin on his face. Then he wandered slowly away, not testing the length of the leash, just looking under the leaves and sticks on the ground for whatever might catch his attention.

At first all I did was look up, up at the green leaves and the bits of blue I could see between them, noticing the tiny shafts of sunlight that slanted more every day as we moved toward August.

Waiting.

Time.

I've read that time is an artificial construct that we give meaning to only when we divide it into seconds, minutes, hours, days. Sitting there, with nothing happening, no one speaking, I could almost believe that. Live for now. That's what people keep saying, as though repeating it makes it possible. But how long is "now?" A nanosecond? An hour? What?

What makes waiting so hard? Is it just that we know something's coming, something's changing, and we want to be ready for it or avoid it or stop it or make it be something else before it gets here?

So what was it I wanted, in that now, or in that waiting for Walker to come to some realization? Did I want to influence him? Or did I just want him to make the best decision for himself, to find his way out of what must be a dark, painful, shrinking cave, whether he came toward me when he saw light or not?

Of course, I wanted him to be happy. But I wanted to be happy, too. And right now, in that now, in that waiting, I wanted him. So I asked myself if that meant I was willing to try and influence him, pull him toward me.

No. I wasn't.

But—fuck! Why couldn't this be easier?

Easier. Hadn't Mom just said that, or something very like it? And I'd told her to wait. Was there some connection between her waiting and mine? Between her "now" and mine?

Mom needed to give Darya time and space to make a huge transition that she had already said she would make. I needed to give Walker time and space to decide whether he'd stay as he was—that is, how he'd presented himself to me—or not. The difference seemed to be that Mom at least knew what to expect. All I knew was what I wanted.

When Mrs. Donnell had shown up with her demand, I'd been totally pissed at Walker for not defying her, for not running to me immediately like I would have done in his place. Why had I changed my attitude? What had softened my anger?

Oh, yeah; I was afraid he'd kill himself, caught between the pressure from his mother's priest and my insistence that he be who I want him to be. And—all right, I admit it—it's also because every time I dream about him, about being with him, I want the real version even more. But what was the real version?

This phrase echoed in my brain, in Walker's own voice: "Sometimes I don't really feel like a guy." And as I remembered that, it hit me hard that Walker had trusted me with so much. Had trusted *me* so much.

Rondo, bored with nosing about in the dirt, came over to me, a puppy smile on his face, and as he lay down beside me he rested a paw and his chin on one of my feet. Immediately my eyes teared up.

I leaned my head back against the tree, partly to trap the tears and partly to avoid looking at that innocent, trusting, foolish puppy. Because wasn't it foolish to trust that someone who's supposed to take care of you, supposed to have your back, will actually be there when you need them? How do you know they wouldn't just take you back to the shelter or—worse—take such lousy care of you that you end up getting smashed in the road by something you can't protect yourself against?

Trapper had trusted me. Dylan had trusted me. I had betrayed that trust. There was nothing I could do to change that. But I knew that whatever the outcome, I would not betray the trust Walker had in me.

The tears overflowed my eyes and rolled down my face. I felt Rondo shift, and when I glanced at him, through the mist in my eyes I saw that he'd lifted his head and turned to look at me. I hadn't made a sound. All that had changed was that my tears had increased. How had he known?

Maybe, when you trust completely, you leave yourself open to the pain of someone else.

That first week of August was more of the waiting game. Mom went to see Madam Alberta. I don't know that the psychic said, but Wednesday evening Mom called and apologized to Dylan and Darya. From my room, door open, I heard her say she understood about wanting to maintain some sense of familiarity with what Darya had left behind, to retain something that made her feel a little safer than she otherwise would in this foreign environment. Usually I didn't let on that I was aware of what Mom was doing— like shutting out the sounds of crying, or ignoring that fake terror at a little spider—but after she hung up I went to her and hugged her. She hugged back kind of hard and then let go. She went back to her computer and I went back to mine.

And I had kind of a brainstorm. It occurred to me that Darya, in her burka and niqab, presented a photographic subject I wouldn't have access to anywhere but with her. I scoured the internet for images of women in traditional Muslim dress and began to get some ideas for how to shoot Darya, if she'd let me.

But I wasn't sure how to reach her. Did she have a cell phone? Would she have been allowed to have one before coming here? Would she even know how to use one? And would she expect me, her brother-in-law, to ask for her husband's permission to meet with her?

I picked up my phone and called Dylan. He didn't answer until the fifth ring; maybe his phone had been in another room? And his voice sounded tense. Had he not reacted well to Mom's call? Whatever. I had already apologized to Darya; we were good. So I told Dylan about my idea.

He wasn't enthusiastic. "I don't know, Micah. It seems kind of weird to me."

"It's not weird. If you think it's weird, maybe you have a problem with the way she's dressing." Dumb. That was dumb. Dylan had already been on edge.

"Don't be an ass."

"Sorry. So will you ask her?"

"The thing is, I'd need to be there."

"Is that a problem? I mean, you don't have a job yet, do you?"

Silence, except I could hear him breathing. "Hang on."

He was gone at least a couple of minutes, and when he got back on the line he didn't sound any more relaxed than when he'd answered my call. "Darya wants to know if it can be at the ocean."

To be honest, I hadn't given any thought to the environment, which is really dumb for a photographer. But

I liked Darya's idea. "Sure. What are you doing tomorrow?"

"Tomorrow's not good. I have a job interview. It'll have to be Friday. I'll call you in the morning." And he hung up.

Just as I was about to get ready for bed, Mom knocked on my door.

"Micah, I need to let you know about something that's coming up. I just got a final email from the Tollmans. Do you remember—"

"Yeah. Of course I do. It was Arnie Tollman who grabbed Dylan's dog tags. And probably we buried his remains." I almost said "bits and pieces," because that's about all we'd be given, just enough to fit into a small coffin-like box.

"Okay. Well, they live in Maine. I've been trying to work out the best time for all of us to be at the cemetery at the same time when they come to fetch the coffin."

It shouldn't have shocked me; after all, that wasn't Dylan's bits and pieces buried nearby. But I'd thought of it as his grave for so long that the idea of digging it up hit me hard. On the other hand, it made perfect sense that the Tollmans would want the coffin. I shook myself mentally and said, "And?"

"And–well, it looks like it will be Saturday, August 13. The day before your birthday. I tried to push it out, but their schedule was pretty full, and it needs to be a weekend so your Dad can be there without missing work."

I shrugged. "Okay." Not great timing, but what are you going to do?

"You're not upset?"

"I'm just glad it isn't Dylan's remains in there."

She smiled. "That's my boy."

Chapter Fifteen

I didn't get to shoot Darya on Friday. Instead, she called me, frantic, at eight in the friggin' morning.

"Micah! I am sorry. Dylan is not here."

"What do you mean he's not there? Where is he?" Even in my sleepy state, it occurred to me to wonder whether she should be calling me; was she allowed to call a guy who wasn't her husband?

"I do not know!" Her voice was high and squeaky. "He is not here at night."

"You mean he's been missing since last night?"

"Yes! I do not know where."

"Okay, well, don't panic." Don't panic! I was panicking already. "Um, did he leave any kind of note? Any writing?"

If he'd left a note, would she have been able to understand it, even if part of it was in Pashto? And could Dylan write in Pashto? Were the letters different? Fuck! I felt like a total ignoramus.

"No. Nothing. Just not here."

"Do you know if the car is there?"

"Not here."

"Okay, so he took the car. Let me call my Dad. We'll try and find him. I'll call you soon."

"Yes."

Should I tell Mom and worry her? I didn't have much choice; she was already up, and she'd heard me on the phone. So I told her what I knew and then together we called Dad at work.

"Christ! How could he—Micah, do you have any idea where he might be? Because I sure as hell don't."

"How would I—wait. There is one place I could look. Maybe two. They're near here. Let me try them first, and I'll let you know."

We hung up, and Mom said, "Let's go."

"No, wait." We stood there, staring at each other. She was waiting for me to say something else. But what? I knew she shouldn't go; I'm not sure how I knew it, but I did. "I'm going on my bike."

"But—"

"This way he won't feel outnumbered. If I find him, I'll do my best to get him to come here, Mom."

She nodded. "Call me!"

I threw clothes on, ran a hand through my hair, and I was off.

One of the two places was the rock where I'd taken him just after he'd come home; the other was the rocks near the ocean where we'd had that picnic with Paige. The first was closer, so I went there.

I saw Dylan's car, the one from the other day and not the SUV Dad had rented. I leaned the bike against the car and walked into the trees. It was eerily like when it had been Paige sitting there. I was maybe twenty feet away when he turned and saw me.

"Go away!"

"I can't. Everyone's worried about you."

He faced the water again. "Tell them I'm fine."

"Okay." So I pulled out my phone and called Darya first. "I found him. He's okay. I'll call again soon." I hung up before she could speak. I texted Dad and then Mom with the same message.

I sat beside Dylan, much like the last time we'd been here together. And I waited. Maybe ten minutes passed in silence, and I thought, *Fuck. Here I am again, waiting for someone who won't talk to me.* Then it occurred to me that maybe it was as hard for Dylan to know who he was now as it was for Walker to figure himself out, even though it would be in a totally different way. So I waited some more.

Finally, he said, "It's like—it's like I was on hyperdrive before that last IED, with bombings every day and someone getting shot and bleeding and even dying every so often, and it could be any of the guys at any time. It could be me dying at any time. You sort of get used to the constant presence of that."

Again I waited.

"And then, after the IED, there was a lot of pain, and a lot of fear, and I had to crawl up high into the hills toward—God, toward I didn't know what. Just away from death."

More waiting.

"I don't remember what it was like in that cave before Fareed found me. I was barely conscious."

Still more waiting.

"After that, there was the constant threat that I'd be found by the Taliban, or that Fareed would report me, or that someone in the village would figure out what was going on and report the whole family. The fear was constant. It—it kind of took the place of the tension from before the IED."

He stood so suddenly, so forcefully that it scared me. As he stared out over the water, his fists clenched and unclenched. Then he stomped over to a tree and pounded it several times with the side of his fist. When he turned back to me, he looked like someone else. Some*thing* else.

His voice was so loud I swear people in boats on the water could have heard him: "Now there's nothing! Nothing!"

Head bent, he covered his face with his hands. Then he dropped his arms to his sides, and his voice was quiet. "But I'm still listening. I'm still watching. I'm still expecting that any minute, any second, something's going to happen.

Something that I'll have to respond to. Something that will mean life or death. But *nothing happens*."

I searched through my mind for words, for anything I could say. I came up empty.

"Sometimes... sometimes I'm in a place where there's other people around. Could be the whole family. Could be in a mall. And it's like I'm all alone. So, *so* alone. And I hear about other guys who've come back, and they get together with their brothers—I mean, the other guys they served with—and everything feels normal, when they're all together again. And I—" Dylan's voice cracked so badly I could barely understand his next words. "I don't have that. I can't have that. Not even that. No one else in my troop survived! There's no place I'm normal."

He clenched at his scalp, turned away from me, turned back again. "When I was there, every second I wanted to come home. Now that I'm home?" He made a sound, a kind of barking laugh. "Now that I'm not there any more, all I want is to be back, back before the IED, when everyone was still alive, when we were all together."

He took a couple of shuddering breaths. "I don't know what to do." Tears streamed down his face. "I don't know what's expected of me. I don't see how I can just get a job, go quietly to work every morning, joke around with people at work just for the sake of it when joking around had come to mean a distraction from the possibility of death every moment, go quietly home, and be nice to my sweet wife who deserves a real husband. She deserves someone who can help her with the mundane things that I took for granted in a former life. Things that I should be able to explain, but that now seem so trivial to me that they don't deserve explanation. So I get mad at her for even asking."

He lifted his arms out sideways and let them drop again, his face crumpled and shining with tears.

I had to subdue the hurt that had come up when he'd said that, about being home and getting together with brothers, and he hadn't meant me. What I said next might have sounded like a challenge. "You want things to be life and death still?"

"No!" And the fists were clenched again. I cringed. "No! I don't! That's not the point! The point is that I can't get used to things *not* being life and death."

I tried again. "So it's like stepping off a step that isn't there. Or maybe swinging at a punching bag that disappears before you can hit it. Is that what you mean?"

He moved forward so fast I nearly fell over backward. "Yes! Well... it's very much like that. I'm spending every minute looking for trouble, for a crisis that never comes." He squatted in front of me, his face now full of desperate hope that he was getting his message across, that someone—me, though I don't think it mattered who it was—understood.

I asked, "Does Darya understand this feeling? Doesn't she have at least some of it?" Much of what Dylan had described must have been true for her, too.

He sat down hard and let out a long, deep breath. "Darya is affected by not having her family with her. And she's overwhelmed by new things. By being able to count on electricity whenever she needs it, to have hot water any time night or day, to have access to a huge variety of foods. She's figuring out new kinds of foods, how to use appliances. She's working hard on her English." He held his arms out in a helpless gesture. "She's busy. She's occupied. I'm not."

We stared at each other for a moment. Then he added, "She wants me to teach her to drive. I can't do it, Micah! I can't! It's not her fault. It makes me absolutely wild with fury to have to explain things! It's not fair to her. *I'm* not fair to her."

"Would it be better," I began slowly, feeling my way, prepared for Dylan's fury to be aimed at me, "for someone else to help her with some of these things?"

He looked blank, so I added, "I'm talking about Mom. And before you blow up, she feels really bad about how she treated both of you when you came to apologize. I know she apologized since then. She's been teaching me to drive, and believe it or not she's calm and easy to learn from. She knows about appliances and all the other things Darya's not used to dealing with."

I watched Dylan's face carefully. So far, so good; I pushed on. "And I think she would love to be helpful." And then, another brainstorm: "And you know who else might like to help? Paige Donnell!"

Something in his face changed. And I waited.

He nearly whispered, "That would be so much better for Darya."

"And Mom and Paige would have a chance to learn something about Islam, and being Muslim." This was such a great idea, now that I thought of it, that I was actually a little jealous that I wouldn't be the one learning, and helping Darya learn. But it had to be women.

Dylan nodded, and he smiled, but it was a sad smile. "That would be great. Now maybe you can figure out how to help *me*."

"I'll see what I can do."

We sat there together, side by side, watching the water, looking at nothing. It felt right. It felt good, even though we really did need to figure things out for Dylan, too. I was about to say something about PTSD and therapy, working out in my head how to do that as delicately as possible, when I caught sight of a certain Cape Dory Typhoon sailing past. I sighed quietly, wishing I were out on the water with Walker. Then, even from here, even from this distance, a closer look told me it wasn't Walker. It was Cam. Alone. I was staring hard at him when Dylan spoke again.

"I've been thinking I should get some help. For Darya's sake as much as mine."

My mind snapped back to my brother. "That's probably a really good idea."

Dare Ya had disappeared from sight, and as if on cue Dylan stood.

"Thanks for coming to find me, Micah. I'd like to get back to Darya. Can you get home on your own?"

"Sure. I do it all the time."

And he hugged me. Hard.

"Say, Dylan, whose car is that?"

"Mine. I couldn't afford to keep renting that SUV, and I sure didn't want Dad footing that bill as well as paying my rent. I had enough to buy a used sedan. So that's what I'm driving now."

At first, Mom didn't seem thrilled about the idea of spending time alone with Darya, but we talked it out, and she warmed to it. Sitting across from her at the kitchen table over eggs and toast, I told her about my idea concerning Paige.

"Walker has a sister named Paige. I don't think I've mentioned her before."

Mom looked at me from under her eyebrows, like she thought I might be wrangling to see Walker. "Not that I recall. Why bring her up now?"

"She was adopted. Her father disappeared before she was born, and her mother died in childbirth. But the important thing here is that her mother was Muslim. And now Paige wants to learn more about Islam."

"And you know this how?"

"I met her before, at the Donnells'. Then I bumped into her recently when I was out shooting, and we got to talking. She, um, that is, I told her about Dylan and his conversion to Islam. She asked if she could meet him and ask him some questions. I went with them."

Mom leaned back in her chair and stared at me. "When did all this happen?"

"Couple of weeks ago, maybe? Or almost."

She shook her head, more in confusion than anything else. "Okay, and why mention her now?"

"Well, maybe she could help Darya, too, and learn some things in the process. Kind of a win-win."

"Interesting. Let me think about that, will you, Micah? Don't talk to her yet."

"Okay, well, I won't say anything to her, but I did mention it to Dylan."

She nodded and then looked so thoughtful for a moment that I could almost hear the wheels in her head turning. Then she bent down to scratch Rondo's head, and as she sat up again she looked right at me. "So you can see Paige but not Walker, eh?"

I just nodded and started to get up. Mom said, "You need to walk Rondo. And again this afternoon. Having a dog is a responsibility, Micah."

I almost protested that it had not been my idea to get a dog, but I grabbed Rondo's leash and he followed me to the door. I guess, after all, it had been my idea to keep him.

I tried to let the clownish behavior of what was becoming my dog distract me, but visions of Cam out there sailing in Walker's boat kept throwing themselves into my mind's eye. There was nothing I could do about it, of course, but it made me restless. I decided to go look for sharks. I pulled something mysterious from Rondo's puppy mouth and headed home.

There was no particular reason for me to go back to Quiambog Cove, unless I wanted to continue my journey away from cowardice and challenge a truly dangerous bull shark again. Maybe I did want to test myself, just a little.

296

But I'd seen that thing only once, for all the times I'd been down there.

As I got close to the tiny beach area, to that spot that was really more of a launch for a rowboat, I saw something through the trees that made no sense to me. It was white, much too white to be a rock, too big to be a person. The closer I got, the more it looked like a sailboat.

"Oh my god." My own voice startled me almost as much as the sight of *Dare Ya* did. She was pitched at an odd angle, slightly propped up on a rock in the water, and beside her was a bare-chested Cam, in the water up to his armpits, evidently trying to wrestle the boat free.

He didn't see me right away, so I leaned my bike against a tree, pulled my camera out of my backpack, and got off several shots of Cam looking like a helpless idiot, with expressions on his face ranging from frustrated to furious. But they were nothing compared to the expression on his face when I walked out onto the beach and he knew he'd been seen.

He tried to cover his embarrassment with his usual arrogance. "What are you staring at, fucker?"

I laughed. "You look ridiculous. How did you get yourself into that jam?"

"Shut up! Get out here and help."

I shook my head, not in refusal but in puzzlement. Setting my camera and my phone back into my pack and placing that on the ground, I took my own shirt off, then my shoes, and I waded out toward him. I was so distracted by the absurdity of the scene that it wasn't until somewhere near the half-way mark that it occurred to me to look around for sharks; didn't see any.

"I'm doing this for the boat and for Walker," I told the idiot Cam, "not for you. It serves you right that this happened."

"Shut the fuck up and start pushing."

It wasn't entirely clear to me how the boat was lodged, and I wasn't convinced that what Cam had been trying to do would have freed it. I swam around the boat once, moving in close in a couple of places to see what was going on.

"What the hell are you doing?"

"I can help you better if I understand how it's caught. I think if we—"

My breath caught in my throat. Just behind Cam was that dull, gray, oblong shape that I'd seen here before. And the dorsal fin—that ominous triangle of my nightmares, the shark's version of a sail—was riding well above the water. My mouth opened and shut a couple of times as though I were a fish.

"What?" Cam was nearly shouting.

"Shark!"

Time slowed nearly to a halt as I saw the nose of the shark lift above the water line. I saw the eye nearer to me roll back, as I'd seen so many times on shark documentaries, which it does as the animal is about to attack. I saw the jaw open, teeth thrusting forward in that distinct way some sharks have.

I heard Cam say, "Knock it off and—"

And then I heard Cam scream as the shark closed its jaws around his left arm.

After that, everything happened very fast. I threw myself forward toward Cam and, as I'd seen Chris Fallows do so many times during Shark Week, I thrust the heel of my hand out hard and fast, hit the underside of the shark's nose, and it opened its mouth.

Blood and Cam's screams swirled around us. I didn't take my eyes off the shark. It started to move forward again, but it was close enough that I was able to punch its eye, hard. It swam away, not far away but far enough that I knew this was my only chance to get both Cam and myself out of the water.

WAITING FOR WALKER

Cam never stopped screaming as I pulled him by his right arm toward the shore, leaving a trail of swirling red in our wake. Once my own feet were on the beach, I heaved as hard as I could to get Cam completely free of the water, panicking as I saw the shark's dorsal fin heading our way. With one final heave and a grunting scream, I hauled Cam fully onto the sand.

He lay there on his back, his face white, eyes staring sightlessly toward the sky, his quiet groaning the only sound I could hear other than my own panicky breathing. One look at his left arm told me he wasn't likely to die here, but it was gory; the muscle above the elbow wasn't all there any longer. I had to fight the urge to upchuck. In a giddy moment, a voice in my head told me Cam's wrestling days were over.

He was still bleeding a lot. I knew enough to look for something to make a tourniquet with. I had no belt on, and neither did he, but his swim trunks had a thick cord in the waist. I pulled that out and tied it around his upper arm, trying not to look at where the muscle was torn from the bone. Irrationally, I was thinking that his beautifully muscled arm, which I'd first admired where it had rested on the open window of Walker's Jeep, would never be beautiful again. That thought took my mind off the gore and helped me do what I had to do.

It must have taken me much less time than it seemed to dig my phone out of my pack and call 9-1-1. And it took much longer than I could believe for me to communicate that an ambulance wouldn't be able to make it through the woods. In the end, I had to say I'd meet the ambulance at the intersection of Wilcox Road and Route 1.

It was there within a few minutes that seemed like hours, and I led the EMTs to where Cam lay, nearly unconscious. I watched in a kind of stupor as they settled Cam onto a stretcher, hefted him up, and stumbled away through the woods toward the road.

It hadn't occurred to me until that moment that I should probably call someone and tell them what had happened. On my phone, I tried to find a land line for the Donnells, but either they didn't have one or it wasn't listed. I called Walker's number, but it went to voicemail; he probably had my number blocked. But I had Paige's number.

"Are you fucking kidding me?" were the first words she said after I told her what had happened. "Where did they take him?"

"Lawrence Memorial. Not many choices, really."

"Um... are you okay?"

"Yeah." No. Yes. How the hell did I know? There was so much adrenaline coursing through me that I didn't know when I'd ever feel normal again. My head felt like it wasn't correctly attached to my body, I couldn't quite catch my breath, and I had to fight the urge to run. Not to run anywhere in particular, just to run.

"So, can you hang out there for just a few minutes?"

"What for?"

"Can you or not?"

"Yeah. Sure." What the fuck....

I ran. I ran up to the road, and back down to the beach. I jumped onto a rock and looked for my shark.

There it was, still out there, circling near the boat, probably trying to slurp up as much blood as it could, robbed of any more Cam meat than it had already swallowed.

I have no idea how much time had gone by before I heard a vehicle approaching. Walker's Jeep!

It couldn't get all the way to where I was, so I sprinted toward it and then stopped: It wasn't Walker inside. Mr. Donnell was behind the wheel, and Paige sat beside him.

Mr. Donnell got out so fast he didn't close the door. He ran toward me, taking my shoulders in his hands and looking hard at my face and then down my body.

"Micah, son, are you all right?"

My knees chose this moment to give way. If Mr. Donnell hadn't been there, I would have landed on the dirt. He walked me to the Jeep, opened the back door, and helped me into the car. I nearly fell over, just managing a graceful descent into a lying position along the back seat. For the first time since going into the water, I realized I had no shirt on. I closed my eyes and breathed long, deep breaths.

"I'm okay," I managed to say, though my voice sounded weak and thin. "I'm fine."

"Take your time, son." Calling me "son" twice in the space of a few minutes nearly made me cry. A few more deep breaths calmed me a little, and slowly, almost painfully, I managed to sit upright.

Mr. Donnell stood at the open door to my right, and Paige was at the other door. I closed my eyes, breathed a couple more times, and opened my eyes again.

In that calm, matter-of-fact voice he'd used to get me to photograph sand tigers, Mr. Donnell asked, "Can you tell us what happened?"

I stared forward, afraid that if I looked at Walker's father I might break down.

"I come here sometimes, just—you know, just to hang out." Somehow it seemed ridiculous to say I came here specifically to look for bull sharks. "I saw Walker's boat, stuck on a rock or something, and Cam was in the water trying to work it free. I went in to help. But then I saw the shark."

I rubbed my face hard, took another couple of breaths.

"It bit Cam's arm. So I punched the underside of its nose, and then I punched its eye, and it swam far enough away that I could get Cam out of the water. I tied his trunks cord around his arm and called 9-1-1. I guess that's about it."

A motion in my side vision made me look toward Paige. She had covered the lower part of her face with a hand, and her eyes were huge.

Mr. Donnell's voice made me turn toward him. "You saved his life, Micah."

"I guess."

He laughed, and that got me laughing, and we laughed until our faces were wet with tears. My belly hurt, and I couldn't stop. Somewhere in the back of my mind I registered that a phone was ringing. It was Mr. Donnell's.

He could barely answer it through his laughter, but he managed. He stepped away to talk, and I looked at Paige, who had obviously been laughing as well.

Wiping tears from her face, she said, "I have no idea what we're all laughing about. Just the tension, I guess. Anyway, Dad's right. You saved that idiot's life." She chuckled. "I'm not sure we should thank you for that, but maybe his mother will."

His call over, Mr. Donnell reappeared. "That was my wife. She's at the hospital. Cam's mother is golfing and isn't answering her phone. Anyway, Cam's going to be fine, other than missing some muscle on his arm. It will probably look a little like your leg, Micah."

"What about his leg?" Paige wanted to know. So I had to tell that story again. Then she said, "What is this with you and sharks? Some kind of weird karma?"

"Must be. Think I'll have to move to the Rockies or something. Can't be any sharks there."

Mr. Donnell slapped gently on the top of the Jeep where he was leaning on it. "I think we ought to get you home, young man. Let's go fetch your bike. I think it will fit in the back of the Jeep."

I didn't especially want Mr. Donnell to see where I lived. "Um, I'm okay, really. I can bike home."

"Oh, I don't think so. You're not wounded, but you're suffering a kind of shock nonetheless. If anything happened to you on your way home, no one would forgive me, including me."

So I showed up at home in that cherry-red Jeep once more, and Mr. Donnell insisted on seeing me inside. "I'd like to be sure your mother knows what happened today. I have the feeling you'd downplay your role, if you even mention it."

We sat there in that tiny living room, me in a kitchen chair and Paige looking around from time to time (in distaste, I was sure), while Mr. Donnell sang my praises to Mom. He was interrupted once when Mom had to respond to the office bell, but he didn't let that distract him.

Mom couldn't stop saying how proud she was of me, and nothing I said seemed to call an end to that. Finally, Paige said something about the time and then stood, so we all moved toward the door. As soon as we were alone, Mom hugged me.

"Micah. Micah. You are a brave, brave boy." She laughed and held me at arm's length. "And an intrepid shark hunter!"

"Oh, no, I don't go looking for them. They just find me."

The office bell rang again, and I went into my room to lie down, to be alone, to breathe deeply again. Mom appeared at the door long enough to say, "Now that I've met Paige, perhaps I'll ask her about helping Darya. I decided I like that idea. I'll get her number from you later."

I pulled out my camera, found the shots I'd taken of Cam, and sent them to Paige. Then I fell asleep and didn't wake up for two hours.

When I woke up, Mom had called Nick to have him office-sit, and she took me out for a fun dinner. Burgers, of course. And fries. And ice cream.

Somewhere in the middle of the ice cream course, Mom got serious about something that had never occurred to me.

"I talked to Dylan on the phone while you were out hunting sharks. Something he said to me got me thinking. I gather that before Darya left home, she hadn't heard much about Donald Trump and all the anti-Islamic sentiment that's been stirred up. But she's been reading news online and listening to TV news, partly to find out what's going on here and partly to improve her English, and she's just found out about this Muslim registry idea."

OMG. I hadn't given any thought to what all the antagonism from this wild and crazy presidential campaign would mean for my brother and his wife, just what it would mean for me and for Walker.

"But—that's not going to happen, is it? I mean, really, Mom. That guy? Elected president?"

She shrugged. "You never know. People are unpredictable." She sighed. "Anyway, I told Dylan to assure her that if it came to that, if they require all Muslims to register, that your father and I would register, too. And there would be a lot of non-Muslims across the country who would register for the same reason. That is, if we get enough false registrations into the database, the thing will be meaningless."

Wow. Like, holy shit. "You'd do that?"

"Of course we would! Dylan is our son."

"Can I do it, too?"

She looked hard at me. "It remains to be seen whether they'd want only adults on it. And I'm not sure I like the idea that you might possibly mess up your future. You know, get put on the no-fly list, or something like that."

"But—"

"We'll see, Micah."

Later that night I got an email from Paige. She loved the photos of Cam. I replied and asked about Walker's boat, and she said it had already been rescued. People from Sailaway had gone out in motor boats and pulled it off the rock it had been stuck on. It didn't have any punctures, but it would need about a week's worth of repairs before it was seaworthy again. Her message ended, "You better believe Cam will never again get anywhere near that boat."

I did a search for Cape Dory Typhoon and found lots of stories about people who sail them, love them, even adore them. I especially loved one vid I found that showed brilliant white sails flashing as they caught the wind. When I saw that flash, this feeling of joy went through me in a warm gush. I couldn't stop from laughing out loud. Walker's sweet little boat was going to be okay.

Saturday afternoon, I took Rondo to the Jasper Island beach again. I had taken a bit of a break this week, and I hadn't gone at all until then. Let Walker wonder, if only a little. And then, of course, there was my courageous rescue of his cousin to keep me on his mind.

When I got to the beach, there was already somebody there.

Walker. Waiting for *me*, this time.

Joy. Fury. Pain. All of that and more shot through me.

As soon as he saw me, he was on his feet. "Where have you been?"

He was angry; good. That meant he'd missed me. And though I wouldn't have expected it, he wasn't the only one who was angry.

From my backpack I freed Rondo, who was already a little too big for this mode of transport, and settled my bike. I found a suitable stick and heaved it for Rondo, who raced as well as he could, still pretty awkward on those big feet. Then I looked at Walker.

"You know where I live," I told him, my tone cutting despite efforts to flatten it. "You know how to text me, or call me, or find me." We stared at each other a minute, and I added, "The real question is, where have *you* been? No— scratch that. Where are you *now?*"

More staring. Then he picked up a stone and threw it into the water just as Rondo returned with his stick. I threw the stick again. I was dying to repeat my question, but I knew that, yet again, I needed to wait for him. Plus, I was feeling a little guilty; it had taken very little to make me forget, if only momentarily, what I'd learned recently about intersex, about the hell Walker had been going through.

He gazed at nothing, facing the water. "I miss you."

I couldn't breathe. "Yeah, well, I miss you, too. Are you ready to do something about that?"

"Yeah." But he kept facing the water.

I was done waiting. "And what is it you're ready to do? Are you still seeing Father Gaffney? Have you decided whether you're a guy or a girl?"

Man, that sounded mean. Where was that coming from? But I knew.

I hadn't been able to answer that question I'd asked myself recently, about whether I'd feel the same about Walker the girl or Walker the not-girl and not-guy as I did about Walker the gay guy. And something in me, something I was ashamed of but couldn't deny, resented Walker for putting me in the position of having to answer it. Or of even having to think about it.

For most of my life I'd been aware that people treat each other differently based on how we perceive each other, and the perception of male or female seemed like the very foundation of that. But the fact that people treat boys one way and girls another had been something I'd picked up on without thinking about it. And it had nothing to do with idiots who think girls aren't as smart or as capable as boys. That's not it. We're just different. Or we see it that way, and we act accordingly. I'd treat a female like a female whether she was Paige or Walker's grandmother. And I'd treat my dad and my brother a certain way because they're male.

And, damn it, I wanted to treat Walker like I'd treat any other guy. Except, of course, that I wanted him in a way I hadn't wanted another guy before. And here I was treating Walker as though the confusion I felt—and the potential for disappointment—was his fault.

"Walker, I—I'm sorry. That was a terrible thing to say."

Rondo returned with his stick, and Walker took it and threw it. Then he said, "I told my mom I wouldn't meet with her priest again. I told her I wouldn't pretend I was someone I wasn't. I even told her it was her fault that I had any doubts about who I am."

That stunned me. "What? Why? What's she done?"

He stabbed the toe of his shoe into the sand, watching the hole get bigger. "She's always been protective. Too protective. All this home schooling, keeping me where she could see me, where she could control what happens to me. I think she sees it as love, but it's made me afraid of the world outside. And then there were the doctors."

"Doctors? Plural?"

"Lots of them. Poking and prodding and prescribing. Trying to turn me into a 'real' boy." He kicked hard, and a spray of sand went flying. "I *am* a real boy!"

At least that much was decided. And I had to agree; he seemed male to me, in all the right ways. But there was one more thing I had to know. Keeping my voice soft, I asked, "And are you gay?"

His blue eyes drilled into me. His hands grabbed my face and his mouth grabbed mine, hard and insistent.

Oh... my... *God* but I wanted this. I'd been *waiting* for this. And yet there was resistance coming from deep inside me, someplace where I kept anger and hurt and betrayal.

And fighting that resistance was an intense desire to be with Walker like this, a deep thrill, deep enough to pull through me all the way from the soles of my feet, a thrill that maybe he had finally cast aside all the questions about himself and about us and had chosen me.

Even so, there was resistance. It surprised me.

What was wrong with me? Was I one of those pathetic people who don't want to be with someone who wants them? I couldn't believe that. I *wouldn't* believe that. So—what was it? Why was I resisting? What had changed?

And it hit me suddenly: *I* had changed. It was almost like I used to be in a rowboat, and I'd been forced to go wherever the current pushed me or else pull like hell on the oars to work against tides that weren't taking me where I wanted to go. Now I was in a sleek sailboat, and I could go in any direction I wanted by merely adjusting the sails. And now that this was true, all that was left was to decide what direction I wanted to go in.

I held Walker at arms' length.

"What?" he asked, obviously confused. "You—you don't want to be with me any more?"

I sat down hard on the sand, and he sat beside me but facing me. "Micah?" His voice had something insistent in it, but something painful, too.

I leaned back on my elbows, facing the water, silent for another few seconds. Then I sat up straight and turned to face him so suddenly he pulled back a little.

"You need to understand something. This isn't just about you. It's about me, too. I think you owe me a little more of an explanation. I've been waiting for you, waiting for you to—I don't know, decide about your life, which would translate into a decision about mine. I waited, even though I was dying to talk to you. I've been in a kind of hell, you know. Okay, it's different from yours, nowhere near as bad as yours, but I didn't know where the fuck your head was at. Or if you might—you know. Hurt yourself."

"You were worried about me?"

"Of course I was worried about you! You'd already said sometimes life wasn't worth it. You'd already said how confused you felt. All I knew was that I wanted to be with you, and you'd told me to have a nice life."

"That's because I needed to be sure of who I *am*! Can't you fucking understand that?"

"No. I can't. I've tried, and I can't even imagine what that would be like. That's not your fault," I added quickly, seeing that he was ready to yell something at me. "I know that. I've done enough research to get at least a vague idea of what you've had to go through. But can't *you* understand why that made waiting for you so hard? And I didn't even know whether the waiting would come to anything! I didn't know what direction anything was going in! God!"

I took a few breaths, but I wasn't done. "There were so many questions I wanted to ask you. And I had so many questions I had to ask myself, too. You once said something about leading me on. I'm not saying you did that, but I am saying that I've had a lot of thinking to do. This isn't exactly how I saw my first relationship going, y'know. I thought it would be with someone who might have a few questions about whether he was gay, but who wouldn't have any doubt about being male."

"I don't doubt that now!"

"Okay, but while you took time to figure that out, I've waited. And I've thought about a lot of things. And I'm—I guess I'm a little different, now. I feel like a lot has happened."

It was almost like we were speaking different languages and there was a massive amount of meaning being lost as a result. Irrationally, my mind went to Dylan and Darya, speaking English and Pashto. They had some words in common on both sides of that barrier, but how sure could either of them be that they understood each other?

Somehow, though, they had risen above those differences because they cared about each other. Why *that* was true, I couldn't have said, but the question I had to answer was whether I wanted to be with Walker enough to do something like it.

We stared at each other as though our eyes could communicate something our words couldn't. And maybe they did. Because what he said next helped me decide how to trim my sails.

"Micah, I'm sorry it took me so long to figure things out. But even though I felt like I had to let you go, I never stopped wanting to be with you, whoever I was. You pull on me. It's like—you know how the moon pulls the ocean? It's what makes tides. That brilliant thing in the sky has so much power that it forces all the oceans on earth to surge. That's how it is for me. With you."

The only other times in my life when I'd been so aware of my heart were when we'd heard Dylan was killed, and then when we'd heard he wasn't.

Slowly, almost experimentally, I reached a hand toward Walker's face and wrapped my fingers around the back of his neck, pulling him gently forward as I leaned toward him.

And we kissed.

The experiment was over. We kissed and kissed until we fell together onto the sand. I kneeled over him, knees on either side of his hips, and we kissed until Rondo had dropped three different sticks beside Walker's head and then tried to climb onto his belly.

Laughing that kind of laugh where you're not sure whether you might not be able to breathe or you might cry or you might float into the air, we lay side by side, Rondo nearby, gnawing on a small piece of driftwood.

"So, do you still want to be with me?" There was some amusement in his voice; after all, what had we just spent the last few minutes doing?

"I never stopped." I let a beat go by. "But what about your mother? When you pushed back to your mom about Father Gaffney, did you push back on seeing me, too?"

He moved into a sitting position, facing where I now sat on the sand. "Funny thing about that. Seems Dad hadn't understood what was going on with all these visits to the good Father Gaffney. He'd thought the whole thing had been my idea. But after you saved that idiot Cam's life—no thanks from me for that, by the way—you sort of became a topic of conversation. And at some point Dad figured out that it hadn't been my idea to stop seeing you."

"Okay. And that helped how?"

He laughed. "Dad was ripshit. He told Mom in no uncertain terms that I was the only one who should make that kind of decision about my life. Whether I'm gay. Or a boy. And he said he'd rather see me with you than some kid—girl or guy—whose character he didn't know."

We gave that some space, and then Walker said, "Since when do you have a dog?"

Dog. Right. As my mind searched for an answer to that question, it occurred to me how many things had happened since his mother had laid down the law. I told Walker about Dylan coming back from the dead, now a Muslim, with a new bride who wore the full regalia, at least for the time being. I told him about Mom getting Rondo and why, which didn't make a lot of sense until I also told him about Trapper. Somewhere in there I managed to let him know he'd been right about my dad having a girlfriend. And then I stopped to breathe.

"Good God, Micah. I can't leave you alone for a minute, can I?"

I grinned. "Well, you sure as shit shouldn't leave me alone for a whole month. By the way, how is Cam?"

"He'll recover, unfortunately. You really should have left him there. He's never setting foot on my boat again."

We lay back, side by side, listening to the small waves that made it as far as this protected beach, for maybe ten minutes. His fingers teased my palm, then gave me shivers as his hand moved up the inside of my forearm.

Walker's phone broke the mood. "It's Mom," he said to me, and then, into the phone, "Yeah?" Pause, then, "I'm with Micah. We're throwing sticks for his dog."

I held my breath as I listened to his side of the conversation, and it didn't seem like she was giving him any grief about being with me.

He rang off and told me, "I have to go home. We have company coming for dinner, some business people. I have to make nice." He slid the phone into a pocket. "Hey, you wanna get together tomorrow?"

"Yeah!"

It felt so good, so fucking *right* to hold him in my arms, to be in his, as we stood there, kissing good-bye. Or kissing see-ya-later, which I now knew it would be.

I watched him walk away, grinning as he turned several times to smile at me, and I was flying so high that when I got ready to leave, I almost left Rondo on the beach.

The only thing that could have made this day any better happened when I told Mom that Walker was allowed to see me again. She hugged me.

Chapter Sixteen

Sunday was overcast but not rainy. Walker picked me up, and we bought some sandwiches and stuff. He knew the place where Paige had taken Dylan and me, and that's where we headed.

I gotta say, it was kind of a rush being out on those huge, flat rocks with him, the nearest house barely visible, and anyone passing by in a boat would be unlikely to see us very well. After we ate, we stripped down to our swim shorts which—I'm here to tell ya—give pretty easy access to private parts. Walker seemed really shy about letting me touch him, so I said maybe we should just lie back on our rock for a bit.

At first, I just relaxed so he would, too. With every inhale I got the soft smell of raw granite that had been through eons of being warmed by the sun and washed over by salty water and warmed again. I turned my head to look at it and noticed little flecks of my namesake—of mica—in the stone underneath us.

Moving slowly, I found Walker's hand with mine, and I lay there, eyes closed, teasing his wrist and forearm with my fingers. Gradually, I moved my hand until the back of it was on his chest, and I stroked up and down oh, so gently. Then a little farther down. Then a little farther. I decided not to go under his swim shorts. Instead, I rolled my hand slowly over his belly, and then lower, and lower.

His gasp and my awareness of a small, hard bump happened at the same time, and I knew I'd struck pay dirt. I let my hand rest there, thinking the bump would soften and his breathing would calm, but—no. The sweet little thing poked at me, and Walker's breath caught with every intake of air.

I watched the side of his face as he strained his head back, chin pointing to the heavens, eyes crunched shut, mouth open.

In a flash I positioned myself over his body and reached deep into his open mouth with my tongue, loving the way my own dick was responding, barely aware that his hands were on my upper arms, fingers digging in hard.

I lowered my body, allowing most of my weight to rest on him, gently feeling with my dick for that matching spot on him. He groaned and clenched his ass to press even harder against me, and kind of instinctively I moved my hips slowly, grinding us together. Without thinking about it, I held my breath. It was only a few seconds after that when I felt a familiar rush of warmth leave me, and even through our swim shorts I could tell Walker had answered my warmth with his own.

I rolled off and lay beside him, his hand in mine, and we let our breathing calm as the rest of our bodies did the same.

And then he laughed. Walker's whole body shook in a kind of hysterical joy until I couldn't help but laugh along with him.

Maybe a full minute later, when the laughter had calmed to the occasional chuckle, he said, "I have never come so hard before in my *life*." He turned his head to look at me. "I wasn't even sure it could happen like that."

"But you said—"

"Yeah, I know what I said. That I could come. That was true. It was just never this—" he took a deep breath, looked at the sky, and shouted, "fucking fabulous!"

We kissed for a long time after that, and I inhaled the smell of granite and the sweet/salty smell of Walker with every breath. My cum spread itself around inside my damp shorts, cooling everything in a really fun way as it dried. The little bit of breeze from the water made it feel cooler still, until all that was left was a thin, dry film on my thighs and balls.

Finally Walker sat up, arms around his knees, and stared across the water. I sat up, too, admiring the smile on his beautiful face, the smile I'd put there.

"Don't move," I told him, and I fished my camera from the pack I'd brought.

I positioned myself in various ways around him while he looked out to sea, eyes focused on nothing, hair tousled and wavy, a mysterious smile on his face that would have made Mona Lisa jealous.

"Okay, now look at me." He did, and I took several close-ups. I couldn't wait to load these onto my laptop and see what increasing the saturation would do to the blue of his eyes.

"Can I see?"

This time I handed my camera to him without hesitation.

He gazed at the screen and swiped. "Wow. These make me look—" He lifted his eyes to me. "I'm beautiful!"

He was beautiful. But that's not a word I would have expected a guy to be happy about, applied to himself.

"Micah? You look worried, or something. Yeah?"

"Depends. I can't help wondering…." Christ, how to say this? "How does it make you feel to know that?"

He scowled like he wasn't sure where I was going with that. Then he smiled. "I get it. You think there's a girl inside me." He handed back the camera. "There's something you need to understand, Micah. There will always be at least a little something of a girl inside me. Don't get me wrong; I'm a guy, and I want to be a guy. But I'm a guy with some… added attraction, maybe?" He grinned.

I grinned back. "Yeah. That's a good way to think of it." And it was. I could live with that. I could definitely live with that.

Monday afternoon, I did a tiny bit of enhancing on some of the shots I'd taken of Walker, and then I sent them all to him. Maybe half an hour later, my Mom knocked on the door and then opened it.

"Micah? I have Mrs. Donnell on my phone for you. She wanted to make sure it was all right with me if she spoke to you."

To Mom, I whispered, "Mrs. Donnell?" I took the phone. "Hello?"

"Hello, Micah. Walker has shown me the shots you took of him out by the water today. My husband and I were very impressed."

"Um... thanks."

"There are three of them in particular we'd like to buy. Not the rights, just the use of them for framing here at home."

"Buy?"

"Yes. This is going to be your career, as I understand it. And these shots are very, very nice."

I blinked. I blinked again. "Um, well, sure, I guess. But, well, I don't know how much..."

"Why don't you talk with your parents about a fair price?"

"Okay." I was about to thank her and hang up, still stunned, when from nowhere I heard myself say, "I have some of Paige, too."

"You do? Really? May we see them?"

"I'll email them to you. She has copies of some of them already, but I'll send all of them and you can decide."

"That's wonderful." There was something in her voice that made me wonder whether she really wanted any shots of Paige, but after we hung up I decided it was just surprise. Maybe she was even shocked that Paige would have let me shoot her at all. I gave Mrs. Donnell the benefit of the doubt; after all, even if she hadn't apologized, it seemed she'd let me see Walker again.

Mom was thrilled. "These must be really good photos, Micah. Show me?"

I brought up the shots of Walker and then Paige on my laptop. Mom ooh-ed and ahh-ed pretty convincingly. And then I brought up the shots of Dylan.

"Let me sit there." She nearly pushed me out of the chair, transfixed as I moved from one photo to the next. Then she wanted to see them all again.

When she looked up at me, there were tears in her eyes. "Oh, Micah," was all she said at first. Then, "Do you know how to get them enlarged? And printed?"

"Sure. Just need a credit card. Do you want to order something now?"

She did.

Over dinner, Mom asked, me, "Have you thought of taking any pictures of Darya?"

"Actually, I asked her if I could. We were planning to do that Friday, but then Dylan disappeared. We can reschedule."

"Good."

I let that hang in the air for a minute; she'd sounded like she'd meant it, and I gave her the benefit of the doubt, just like I'd given Mrs. Donnell.

"By the way," Mom added, "Darya and Paige are both coming over tomorrow. We're going to work through some recipes of things Dylan used to like."

"Darya *and* Paige? Wow."

"I spoke to Mrs. Donnell while you were out yesterday, and then Paige. I think this could be fun."

"She's—she can be a little edgy. But I'll bet she'll be fine." I almost wanted to hang around and watch the three of them together, but Walker and I had already arranged for him to come get me to hang out at his place. Maybe we'd use his PlayStation.

I did see one snag for the Darya Day. "What are you going to do with Rondo while Darya's here?"

"Dylan and I discussed that, actually, and she was with him at the time. We decided to see how it goes. If he keeps getting in the way, I'll tie him up outside, or shut him in your room, something like that."

It sounded like progress. It sounded like amazing progress. I just hoped to God it would all go well.

Tuesday Walker texted me just before the cooking session was going to start to say he had a flat tire and could I bike out to his house. I was a little bummed, because it was overcast and threatening rain, but I'd already had a wonderful dream about what it would be like, alone in Walker's bedroom.

Mom had me walk Rondo before I left, and when I got back Paige had arrived. She was at the kitchen table, a laptop that must have been hers in front of her. She grinned at me as Rondo and I came back in, which surprised me.

"So that's the famous Rondo," she said, nodding toward the puppy.

"Are you looking up recipes?" I moved to where I could see her laptop's screen.

"Nope; Pashto. I have e-copies of a phrasebook and a beginner's guide."

Mom left whatever she was doing at the sink, toweling her hands, and stood beside me where she could see the laptop screen. "What a great idea."

We all watched as Paige opened one of the books. Then Mom said, "Micah, why don't you put Rondo in your room for now? And lay down a couple of pads. Once Darya gets here, we can bring him out carefully."

Another great idea, as far as I could see, as long as he used the pads if he needed to; his history in that area wasn't great. I was proud of Mom; she honestly wanted this thing with her new daughter-in-law to work. Dylan's issues were different, but helping Darya was definitely something Mom could do.

I was surprised when Mom followed me into my room and shut the door.

"Micah, I just wanted to let you know that Dylan will drop Darya off, and then he has an appointment with someone who might be able to help him... well, help him adjust."

"Like, a therapist?"

"Something like that. I think it's more of an assessment today. I have his permission to tell you, but I wasn't sure I wanted to say that in front of Paige."

I nodded. "Makes sense. Oh, by the way, about my photos. I checked online for what people get paid to let someone else use their photos. It depends on how many places someone uses the image, so I'm thinking that for a single portrait, around twenty-five dollars. The printing and framing would be up to them. What do you think?"

I didn't really expect her to have an opinion, and she didn't. "Oh. My. Well, if that's the going rate. If they offer less would you do it?"

I grinned. "Probably. This is my boyfriend's family."

Dylan hadn't arrived yet by the time I left, rain poncho in my backpack but no camera, just in case.

In the Donnells' kitchen, Mrs. Donnell and Walker were talking about a visit they'd just made to Cam in the hospital. He was going home tomorrow, and I wasn't happy with myself at the little glow I got when Mrs. Donnell said his arm was somewhat disfigured.

I let Mrs. Donnell know I thought twenty-five dollars was my going rate for prints of my photos, and she agreed. "That's reasonable, Micah. I'll get back to you with a list of which shots."

I'd half expected that Walker and I wouldn't be allowed to be alone in his room, but the only admonition we got was that Mrs. Donnell called to us as we left the kitchen. "Door open, boys."

We managed to do quite a bit with the door open. Walker put some music on, and then he took my hand and led me to the bed. We kneeled on that gorgeous orange and blue bedspread, the boat sailing into the sunset on the wall setting the mood. For some reason I couldn't figure out, I felt nervous. WTF? I hadn't been nervous out on those rocks on Saturday, where we were out in the open. But now, here we are in Walker's room, and I'm nervous?

He wasn't. He smiled at me, his hands on either side of my face, and he leaned in for a kiss. An oh-so-sweet kiss. And then another.

The third and fourth kisses were not so sweet, and they got more insistent and more invasive with five and six, and I lost count. Then he pulled away, grinning, and fished a small towel out from someplace.

"For clean-up. Now, lie back."

I did. And what he did to me next will be in my memory forever.

He must have done some reading, or watched some porn, or something, to know what to do with his lips, his tongue, his teeth, his breath. I wasn't aware of his fingers until I felt a sliding pressure between my balls and my ass. I groaned.

"Shhhh!" Walker lifted his head from my dick long enough say that and to giggle. "I don't want anything to interrupt this."

I had to clamp a hand over my mouth, but then I had to grip the bedspread with both fists, so I think a little sound escaped me. Thank God it was not enough to attract the attention of anyone other than us.

At some point I grabbed one of the pillows and covered my face with it, just in time to stifle a screaming groan as I came into the towel Walker held. Walker adjusted my clothes while I panted and gripped the pillow like it would save my life. When I'd recovered well enough to set the pillow aside, I opened my eyes to see his smiling face.

Pulling my jeans back on, I said, "You look very pleased with yourself."

"Oh, yeah. And I think you're pleased with me, too."

"And do I get to reciprocate?"

"I have a different idea. Where's your phone?" I handed it to him. "I know my folks are buying some photos from you. I'd like you to take some they'll never see."

"You mean… of you naked?"

"Mmm-hmm. In case it's escaped your notice, I have a really unusual dick. Very special. You'll probably never see another one like it."

I laughed. "Probably not."

"So, I know this is hardly the same as your real camera, but I trust you have the skill to take some really nice shots."

He stripped slowly while I watched, getting hard all over again. He lay down beside me and struck pose after pose while I shot. Then I got as close as the phone would let me, shooting first his tits, then a small, reddish birthmark near his navel that I'd never noticed before, and then I moved farther down.

Walker held his thighs apart and used his fingers to expose as much of that adorable dick as possible. After a few shots I set the phone aside without taking my eyes off of his body. Gently, tenderly, I leaned over and kissed him. And again.

His voice was husky as he said, "It's okay. You can…you know."

"I don't want to hurt you."

"I'll let you know."

I used my lips and my tongue, flicking lightly, sucking gently, and finally taking everything I could inside my mouth. I heard Walker groan and gasp, and I felt his whole body shake as his hands gripped that bedspread. I didn't reach for the towel. I took it all in. He tasted like ocean.

I nearly flew home, partly because I was still high after being with Walker, and partly because I was afraid it was going to rain.

I was maybe a quarter mile from the motel when I heard the screech of brakes, and then a white SUV went flying past me, barely staying in its traffic lane. I nearly went off the road to get out of its way.

"Fucker!" I shouted at the back of the thing as it disappeared down the highway.

As I got close to the motel, I could hear a woman's voice, somewhere between shouting and screaming. It was my mother's voice!

I sped forward, and what came into view froze my blood. I saw Mom first, on the side of the road, hands flying uselessly in the air where she stood. At her feet on the side of the road was Darya, in slacks and a blood-stained white blouse, nothing on her head. And on her lap was Rondo, on his side, head dangling. She was wrapping a piece of cloth around his front left leg.

In that weird state that happens in a crisis, I noticed that the cloth was a flowered pattern, and somehow I knew it had been on her head. She was using her hijab to help a dog, a dirty farm animal as she saw him, and she had exposed herself in a profound way to do it.

I nearly threw my bike aside and then ran to Darya. She looked up at me, her eyes calm, and in a flash of realization I knew she had done this before. Maybe not to a dog, but how many bodies—men, women, and children from her village—had she bandaged before?

She didn't speak, and neither did I. I ran into our unit, grabbed Mom's car keys, and dashed back out. I lifted Rondo, who whimpered in pain, and Darya stood and went to Mom's car. She got into the back, and I laid Rondo across her lap while an old image—of me, in the back seat, with Trapper's dying body bleeding onto me—flashed through my brain. Oddly, Darya's calm seemed to have disappeared; her eyes were wide and a little frantic, and her hands shook. I put this down to the fact that we were venturing out farther into the world, and she was dressed in a way that made her uncomfortable.

There was a vet clinic just over a mile down the highway, where Mom had taken the new puppy to get the required shots. Rondo whimpered a few times when we hit a pothole or when a loud vehicle passed on the other side of the highway, and Darya made tender, comforting sounds. At one point I glanced in the mirror to look at her. Her eyes were on Rondo, the look on her face rather like what you'd expect on a mother soothing her ailing child to sleep. She didn't seem nervous any longer.

At the clinic, she shook her head when I tried to take Rondo, and she carried him in.

Someone took Rondo into an examination room very quickly and told Darya and me to wait. We sat side by side in the reception area, saying nothing at first. I found myself wondering how many rules she had broken today: her outfit (no burka); removing the hijab; riding in a car with her husband's brother; holding a filthy dog on her lap, his blood on her hands and blouse. What was she risking? Hellfire and damnation? And for what?

And what about Rondo? Would this be a repeat of how Trapper's life had ended? Was this somehow my karma, to be involved in—and sometimes responsible for—dogs' deaths?

I wanted to ask Darya how it had happened, why Rondo had been outside and not on his leash. I looked at her once, ready to see if she had enough words in English to answer my questions, but her eyes were closed, almost squeezed shut, and her breathing seemed shallow. Then I noticed her hands, clasped tightly in her lap. Had she lost the calm I'd seen as she'd wrapped Rondo's leg, or was it really more to do with her outfit, her bare head, and maybe sitting here beside a non-mahram man—someone whose company she could not be in alone? If I spoke to her, would that make it worse?

I was just taking in how young the receptionist looked when my phone rang: Mom.

"Micah! What's happening? How is he?"

"Don't know yet. They think he got a concussion, and then of course his leg is broken. He's in with the vet now. They had us wait out here. Reception area."

I decided against asking what had happened; it didn't matter right now, and I was sure there would be some discussion later. I told Mom I'd let her know more when I did.

I closed my eyes, and to my complete surprise a tear squeezed its way out and ran down my cheek. And then, another surprise: Darya took my hand.

"Darya—"

"Yes?"

"Thank you."

"You are welcome." And, a moment later, "Thank you, too."

"Me? For what?"

"Your—what is word—to do this, today. With your mother."

"My idea?"

"Yes. Idea. It is a good one."

"I'm glad."

"I like Paige."

I turned to look at her; her eyes were open now, staring straight ahead. "Really?"

"You do not?"

"I wouldn't say that. I just think she's not easy to like."

"She is kind."

Okay.

"I will see her again, I am think."

"I am thinking. Or I think." I wasn't sure I should correct her, but she wanted to learn.

"Thank you."

Silence for a few minutes. Her hand pulled away from mine, and then she said, "I think we move to Providence."

"You and Dylan?"

"Yes. Closer to mosque."

That made sense; Warwick wasn't far from Providence, but I'd have been willing to bet it didn't have a large Muslim community. I nodded.

I decided to take a risk. "Have you met Sharon?"

"The woman with your father. Yes." There was something in her voice, not exactly a warning, but an edge.

"You like Paige better?"

"I do."

"Do you mind if I ask why you don't like Sharon?"

Darya took a quick breath in and let it out slowly. "Sharon try—tries hard. Too hard."

"You mean she makes you uncomfortable?"

"Yes."

Interesting. So the woman who consults in employee relations loses to abrasive, edgy Paige. I was tempted to ask how Darya was getting along with Mom, but that seemed like a risk I wasn't emotionally prepared to take at the moment.

Instead, I said, "You seemed to know what you were doing. Bandaging Rondo's leg, I mean."

She continued to stare straight ahead. "Not to dog."

"No. But—"

"Micah, Afghanistan is amazing country. We do for ourselves. We stay—apart?—from attackers. Alexander... the big?"

"The great?"

"Yes. Alexander the Great. Arab nation. Genghis Khan. United Kingdom, two times. Russia. And now, you. Sometimes we lose, but a little while only. Always, we chase out attackers. Always, we remain. And always, we fight. I have seen much blood. I have seen much death. I do not like death. Blood I can take."

That about said it all. And it drew a stunning picture for me of her country, and of her life. Of her.

I was relieved of the need to respond when someone came to bring us in to see Rondo. And in yet another turn in her behavior, Darya seemed to be hugging the wall, staying away from the examination table where Rondo lay.

The vet, a tall woman with very little facial expression, stood beside the table, softly stroking Rondo's side.

Her monotone voice matched her face. "I think he stands a very good chance. We'll watch him overnight because of the concussion. The bones in the left foreleg are badly crushed. I think we'll need to remove it."

My eyes must have gotten big at that, because she went on before I could speak. "Many dogs manage to get along pretty well on three legs, especially if both hind legs are intact. It's particularly hopeful because he's still young, so the adjustment should be easier."

"He looks unconscious."

"I've given him a sedative to keep him calm."

"So should we come get him tomorrow?"

"You should call tomorrow. Now, the receptionist will talk with you." She held a stiff arm toward the door.

I turned as I was about to go through and saw her lean over Rondo, stroking his head tenderly. She wasn't great with people, but it sure looked like she loved animals.

The receptionist wanted to talk to us, all right. She wanted to know who was paying the bills. Rather than give them Mom's phone number, I called first to soften the blow. I'm not sure it helped; evidently, vet bills are not small.

Out in the parking lot, Darya started to get into the back seat, but then she changed her mind and sat in front beside me. I knew she'd broken yet another rule.

Darya said, "Before you start car?"

"Yes?"

"I will show you."

She moved her seat back a little and leaned over her legs. As she pulled the cloth of her slacks up along her left calf, I had to stop myself from gasping. The calf was a mass of scars, and whatever had caused them had removed about as much muscle as that shark had bitten from me.

Darya didn't look at me, just waited maybe ten seconds or so and lowered the cloth back down to her ankle. "I should not show you leg. My leg, I mean. But you are husband brother." I saw a smile spread across the side of her face that I could see as she added, "And you are not for women."

"Darya, did—did a dog do that to you?"

She nodded. "I was young girl. And my leg got—sick? How do you say?"

"The wound? Do you mean it got infected?"

"Infected," she echoed as if learning a new word. "Yes. Almost had to cut off."

OMG. No wonder she didn't like dogs. "Why didn't Dylan tell us about that after we tried to give you a puppy?"

"He protect me."

"You mean, it wasn't his story to tell?"

"Yes."

So she was terrified of dogs, and she'd just given first aid to a dog whose leg had been injured.

"Darya, I will show *you* something, too."

She watched as I got out, propped my left leg onto the side of the car, and pulled the leg of my jeans up.

"Oh! Dog do that?"

"No. Shark. In the ocean."

We locked eyes for a couple of seconds, and then she started to laugh. She laughed, and laughed, and I couldn't help but join her. I leaned against the car door frame and watched her as I laughed, delighted as much by her laughter as by the ridiculousness of our similar limbs. I don't know whether it occurred to her, but when I'd said "in the ocean," the meaning of her name had come into into my mind.

Everything's connected.

Halfway back to the motel, Darya said, "You spend much money on dog."

"That probably seems silly to you."

She seemed thoughtful, and then, "I must learn to understand."

"You took care of him. You got blood on your clothes. And was that your hijab?"

"Yes! It is gone. I feel—what is word?"

"Free?" But she shook her head. "Exposed?"

"Yes, I think exposed."

"Do you want to call Dylan and tell him to bring you another one when he comes to pick you up?"

"Yes."

I pulled my phone out and walked Darya through calling Dylan on speaker, and his voice came into the car with us. "I'm already most of the way there. Why do you need another one?"

Darya looked at me, probably because an explanation would be so difficult for her. To the phone, I said, "Never mind, then. I'll explain when you get here."

When we got to the house, I was in for yet another surprise. I expected the first thing Mom would do would be to talk about what had happened, about what the vet had said, all that. But no; the first thing she did was hand Darya a scarf.

Maybe the events of that afternoon had softened everyone; anyway, Darya hugged Mom with tears rolling down her face. Then we talked about Rondo until Dylan showed up, when we talked about him some more. Dylan seemed even more protective of Darya than usual, and I suspected it was because he knew about the dog attack she'd suffered and wanted to make sure she was okay.

Dylan had some news, too. He was going to see a therapist, and as soon as it could be worked out, he wanted to be trained as a counselor for returning vets. Meanwhile, he'd look for some kind of work to augment what he'd gotten from the army, and once he and Darya moved to Providence they could see if the Muslim community there could help Darya figure out if she could do something to earn money. Evidently, she did embroidery and made jewelry.

We sat there in the living room, silent at last and rather exhausted, when Darya spoke up. "I think we get—apart? apartment?—where we can have dog."

I smiled at her, a big smile, and she smiled back, radiant under Mom's brightly colored scarf. This was all working out! Rondo was like a wounded vet. Darya knew how to take care of wounds. And if Dylan really did end up counseling vets, he'd be with people who understood what he'd been through; they wouldn't be the only ones who'd be helped.

They stayed for dinner. After all, Darya had spent a good part of the day learning to cook some of Dylan's favorite recipes. It was almost like being a family again.

The only thing missing was Dad. But he'd chosen Sharon. I didn't blame him, but that didn't stop me wishing that he'd come back.

Chapter Seventeen

For the first time since I could remember, everything in my life seemed like it was all working for me. Mom was getting along with Darya, Dylan had found a direction, Rondo was a great dog (even though I'd be glad when he went to live in Providence and someone else had to walk him and clean up after him), and—the best part of all—Walker and I were together. My birthday this year was going to be the best one ever.

The only wrinkle in this layout was that Mom and Dad weren't getting back together. Or that *was* the only wrinkle until Dad called on Wednesday evening to say that Sharon was inviting all of us, Dylan and Darya included, to her house in Coventry, Saturday night for dinner. A birthday dinner. For me.

Dad had asked Mom to put him on speaker so I could hear everything, and when he said that about Sharon's house, my eyes snapped to Mom. I'm not sure how many emotions flashed across her face in the span of two seconds. Surprise? Shock? Pain? Anger? Resistance?

What went through my mind like a flash was that Sharon was ruining my birthday. Mom had never even met her. Maybe didn't want to. Why would Sharon do this? Wasn't she supposed to be all sensitive to people's emotions?

Mom opened her mouth to say something, but Dad spoke again. "Before you say anything, Abbie, I know this is a lot to ask. But with everything that's happened in the last few weeks, Micah and I haven't had time together. Plus, I think it would be great for you to meet Sharon. You're the only one in the family who hasn't. And this way you wouldn't have to lift a finger; Sharon will arrange everything.

"Oh, Sharon will arrange everything? Sounds like she already has."

"Abbie, wait. Please see this for what it is. We just want everyone to get along. We want everything to be out in the open."

My turn to speak up. "Yeah, but why do we have to do this on my birthday? What if I don't think it's a good idea?"

"Your birthday isn't until Sunday."

"But you said—"

"You and your mom can have whatever celebration you want."

"Great. What I want from Mom for my birthday is a weekend road trip. Starting Friday. I'm driving. Maybe we'll look for houses for sale on lakes." I knew the Tollmans would be here on Saturday; I just wanted to make a point.

"Micah, knock it off. And actually, Sharon's house is on the water. The Flat River Reservoir."

Mom and I locked eyes at this point.

I asked, "Is Sharon with you now?"

"Yes, of course. You know I'm staying with her these days."

Too bad; I was dying to tell Dad that Darya didn't like Sharon. But even though Dad wasn't on speaker, it didn't seem fair to Darya to say that with Sharon right there. Or, I guess, fair to Sharon, either.

Mom asked, "Whose idea was this?"

"Both of ours."

"Yeah, right." I didn't even try to keep the sarcasm out of my voice.

"Look, why are you both pushing so hard against this idea? We're just trying to be friendly."

I was ready to say something more, but Mom held her hand up. "Gus, if this woman is important to you, then I suppose at some point I will have to meet her. But this weekend isn't about her. Or you. Or me. It's about Micah. And I'm not putting him in the middle of this situation, birthday or no birthday. So please thank Sharon for her offer, but Micah and I will not be going to Coventry this weekend."

Mom ended the call before Dad could say anything else. Then she looked at me. "You agree?"

"Yeah. I mean, I'd like to see Dad at some point this weekend. But not like that." And by "like that," I meant Mom having to meet Sharon for the first time, in her waterfront house, and probably at other distinct disadvantages I could only imagine.

"Did you want to see Sharon?" There was an edge to her voice, even though I think she tried to hide it.

I shrugged. "Wouldn't have been my first choice." I grinned. "Has Darya told you she doesn't like her?"

Mom's eyes got big, and then she started laughing. What she said next felt really good to me. "I think Darya has too much class to tell me that."

In my room a little later, I got a text from Dad. It would have been better as a phone call, but I think he didn't want to risk Mom overhearing my side of the conversation.

Sorry if that was weird. It was actually my idea.
I figured
Do you really not want to come?
R U kidding? Mom's never met S. Awkward for everyone. Not a great birthday.
OK so what do you want to do?
Will talk to mom and get back to you

After that I went out to find Mom, who was reading a book. She looked up and spoke before I could say anything.

"So what would you like to do for your birthday, Micah?"

"I'd like to see Dad on Saturday, after the trip to the cemetery, just for the day. He doesn't know that yet. And Sunday, could you and I have dinner here and invite Walker? Um, *he* doesn't know *that* yet, either."

She smiled. She actually smiled. "I like that idea, Micah. Why don't you ask Walker tonight? And you can work things out with your father however you want."

"Thanks." I started to head to my room, but first I turned back to Mom. "If you and Dad had to split, I'm glad I'm living with you."

I left the room before she started to cry, which I was pretty sure she'd do. Only this time, it would be for a good reason.

With her hijab the only traditional garb she wore, Darya arrived with Dylan at eight thirty on Saturday, and then they followed Dad, who drove Mom and me to Stonington Cemetery.

As we approached the grave where we thought we had buried Dylan, Dylan said, "This feels really weird."

The cemetery staff had already dug the grave open, and there was a small coffin—bigger than it would be for an infant, but not large enough for an adult—out of the ground and on the grass. The sexton waited nearby, hands folded in front of him.

We all stood there, staring into the hole or at the coffin, until three other people joined us: The Tollmans, and the young woman who was Arnie's widow. They'd driven down from Maine the day before, evidently staying somewhere other than The Afterdeck.

Immediately, Dylan went to them. He shook Mr. Tollman's hand, and then he hugged first Arnie's mother and then his widow. Both women were trying not to cry and failing. Mom pulled out a tissue, and I almost wanted to ask for one as well.

Dylan spoke to the Tollmans for a few minutes about Arnie, about his courage, about how much he'd talked about his family, and then there were introductions all around. No one seemed to know what to do after that, until someone else joined us. He was from the cemetery where Arnie's coffin would be buried; it appeared he was going to take control of the little box.

It felt so awkward, standing there at what had been my brother's supposed grave with these people whose own relative's bones were leaving the hole we'd dug for Dylan. I didn't even try to join in the conversation, which was spotty and difficult.

A feeling came over me; not a bad feeling, but an unsettling one. At first I figured it was being in the cemetery, and under weird circumstances. But it made me look around. And I saw a woman, at a distance, leaning against a tree and watching us. She had short red hair.

Madam Alberta.

I glanced at the group and knew I could back away without being noticed, so I did that. I walked toward Madam Alberta, who smiled as I approached. When I got close enough, I almost asked, *How did you know?* But that would have been silly.

"Micah. You look happy. I mean, aside from the solemnity of this occasion. You and Walker are together, right?"

I grinned. "Yeah. You were right. He is worth it."

"I hope no one minds that I came here today. After working with your mother for months, and channeling Dylan for her, and then realizing—oh, my God, but it was so thrilling!—that he was actually alive? Well, I just couldn't resist seeing him and his lovely bride." She laughed. "The bride was one thing I didn't see!"

"But why today? Why not just ask to meet him?"

She half grinned and shrugged, and I think she might have been a little embarrassed. "It's not completely ethical to contact one's clients out of the blue without a reason that pertains to the reason they came in the first place. Of course, I suppose it might be argued that it's not much better to spy on them in the cemetery!" She laughed again.

"But—today?"

"Ah. Well, this was what came to me. I didn't get an image of another time."

I watched her face for a second. "You really do see things, don't you?"

She winked at me. "I do. I know a lot of people find that difficult—even impossible—to believe. But I do."

But there was something nagging at me, something that didn't make a liar out of the lady but that still seemed fake. "So you didn't know at first that Dylan was still alive. But you still kept telling my mom that he was talking to her. What was that about?"

"Talking to her?"

"Yeah. She'd come home and tell me what Dylan had said to her, through you. She said he was in heaven, looking over us, looking out for us."

Madam Alberta blinked and pulled her head back a little, like she was surprised, or confused. But then she nodded. "I think I see. This happens a lot. I was picking up on Dylan's energy, and of course a lot of his thoughts were of home. Sometimes, Micah, when someone dies suddenly, and especially if it was violently, they leave a powerful energy behind. They have difficulty—How to put this...."

She lowered her head and massaged her temples for a minute before she spoke again.

"Okay, so here's the thing. Think if it like a soul, though I don't really like that word because it carries so much baggage, but it'll have to do. If Dylan really had died in that explosion and fire, it would have been sudden and violent, and his soul would very likely have had a hard time finding its way to the next plane of existence. I was trying to guide what I thought was that soul, and I did relay to your mother the thoughts and feelings I picked up as I did that. To be honest, I couldn't figure out why he was hanging around as long as he was, because after a few sessions, he hadn't seemed lost. Now I know that what really happened was that his living energy was fearful and in pain, and then his wife's family began to care for him. So what I thought was his soul refused to move on."

She grinned at me. "That's when I figured out that it wasn't ready to move on because he was still alive!"

"So you weren't just having her on? Trying to get money out of her?"

"Oh, Micah, I'm so sorry that it looked like that to you. It must have been so difficult for you to hear your mother talk about Dylan."

I shrugged and looked down at the toe of my shoe, digging at the grass.

She looked over toward the grave and nodded in that direction. "Looks like your family is leaving the Tollmans alone with their son's remains."

I turned and saw that Mom was headed right for us. Dad, looking confused, began to follow slowly, Dylan and Darya behind him.

Mom and Madam Alberta hugged long enough for the others to gather around, and Mom introduced everyone.

Dad surprised the hell out of me. He stepped forward, took Madam Alberta's hand, and said, "I want to thank you. And apologize. Abbie was the only one who believed you about Dylan, but here he is."

"You are so welcome," she said. "It's such a pleasure when I can tell a family someone is actually still alive instead of focusing on someone's death."

Then she turned to Darya. "My dear, I know you've struggled with this transition. Please take your time to find your way in this strange new world. And Dylan!" She hugged him without saying another word.

Dylan gave Mom a ride home so Dad and I could start our day together. I hadn't brought my camera, but my plan was to show him my favorite shooting spots. We hiked all over, including the place where I'd seen Walker for the first time. We drove out to Jasper Island and past the Donnells' (though we didn't stop), and then I directed him to the Knox Preserve, where we parked the truck and then walked in to Quiambog Cove. This was where I wanted to give myself a very special birthday present.

We stood on the little strip of beach where I'd taken photos of Cam looking ridiculous as he'd tried to free *Dare Ya* from the rock that had damaged the little boat. I pointed toward the water.

"If you look closely, you might just see a friend of mine swimming around out there."

Dad turned his gaze from the water to me. "I don't get it."

I kept my eyes on the water. "I don't actually know whether it's a girl or a boy, and there's no name I can give you. But out there someplace is a four foot bull shark with a dent in the side of its head where I hit it."

Dad turned fully toward me. "Micah, what on earth are you talking about?"

Rather than answer him directly, I pulled out my phone. I'd sent the photos of the sand tiger sharks from my camera to my email account last night so I could bring them up right here, right now. Careful to avoid the intimate shots I'd taken of Walker, I brought the sand tiger series to the screen and swiped slowly through them.

Dad's eyes got huge. "Who took these?"

"I did. They're sand tiger sharks."

"But you said bull shark."

"That's here." I pointed to the water in front of us. "The sand tigers were off the end of Mr. Donnell's yacht."

"Yacht?" He stared at me. "You said Walker had a sailboat."

"Walker does have a sailboat. A Cape Dory Typhoon. His father has a yacht."

It seemed to me as though Dad wasn't sure whether to be more startled that I'd been able to get so close to the sharks or that I'd been on a friggin' yacht. So I decided to redirect his attention where I wanted it to go.

"And out there," I pointed to the water again, "is the bull shark that attacked Walker's cousin Cam. I pushed the shark's nose up so it would let go of Cam's arm, and then I punched it in the eye. So I guess we're not exactly friends, the shark and I."

Dad took a step back, staring at me as though he wasn't sure who I was. "Micah, when did all this happen?"

"The sand tigers were from the Fourth of July. Mr. and Mrs. Donnell took the yacht out into the Sound to watch the fireworks back on land, and Walker and I went with him. I guess you were with Sharon." I almost but not quite wanted to rub it in that I'd been hoping to see him on the fourth, but I decided I didn't need that; I had so much else going on for me right then.

I said, "And the bull shark incident was last Friday. A week ago." Dad didn't look like he knew what to say, so I talked about arriving here and seeing the boat, and Cam, and how I'd gone to help. "The shark took a bite out of Cam's left arm. Kind of a match to my leg. He spent a couple of days in the hospital. I didn't have a scratch."

"So—so you just swam out," and Dad turned back to the water before looking at me again, "knowing there was a shark right there?"

"I swam out to help with the boat, before I knew the shark was there. You don't go swimming just to go into the water if there's a bull shark in residence. Those things are killers. Very aggressive." A glow went through me as I played up the ferocity of bull sharks; my description wasn't overstated, but I did get a kick out of highlighting the danger. Take *that*, Dad. Take that, anyone who ever said "Buck up" or "Don't be a wuss" or "Master your fear" to me. Take that, anyone who would ever be tempted to say those things to me again.

"Micah—I don't know what to say."

I shrugged. "You don't have to say anything. I just thought you might like to know what I've been doing with my summer."

"Look, son, I know we haven't seen a lot of each other. There's been a lot going on."

"Oh, yeah, for sure. I'm not accusing anyone of anything. Just letting you know. I figured, you know, since I hadn't seen you, and with Dylan and Darya and all that, there hasn't been a good time to tell you. So that's what I'm doing now."

I couldn't read the expression on his face, but he was watching mine with an intensity that made me uncomfortable. Then he wrapped his arms around me.

Sunday dinner was a little awkward at first, with Mom and Walker both trying to figure out how to respond to each other. Their introduction on July fourth had been very short. This was different.

Mom pulled out all the stops, menu-wise. She makes the best lasagna I've ever had, and she knows it's my favorite. And the cake—devil's food with butter cream frosting—topped everything off.

Walker's present for me was a gorgeous windbreaker, bright orange (not yum-yum yellow), that he said looked great with my dark hair and would look even better out on the water, which we had plans to do the very next day. When I tried it on it seemed a little large.

He said, "You'll want it a little large so it will fit over a layer or two when we sail in the fall. It gets super cold out there." He grinned at me. I grinned back.

Mom's present didn't take much unwrapping. She handed me an envelope. Inside was a piece of paper with handwriting on it:

When Micah Jaeger heads off to college, this note entitles him to one car to be purchased with whatever amount is then in a savings account started for him twelve months ago today.

Love,

Mom

August 14, 2016

And just like that, it was back to the best birthday ever.

Walker arrived in his gorgeous cherry-red Jeep, no Cam in sight, at nine o'clock Monday. The sun was up, the sky was blue, and I was ready in my boat shoes, my pack holding Dylan's sunglasses, my hat, and my new orange windbreaker. No camera today; I wanted to see everything through only my own eyes.

"Have fun!" Mom called as I headed for the door. "Be safe!"

It gave me a huge thrill when, sitting in the car with the engine purring but not in gear, right there in front of the motel, Walker reached for me and planted a long kiss on my mouth.

Yes!

Dare Ya waited for us at Sailaway Marina, all fixed after her encounter with that rock, fully seaworthy once again. I couldn't wait to get out into the Sound. And it didn't escape me that I wasn't afraid. Partly it was that I had some idea what to expect this time, whereas the first time I'd approached this boat I'd known nothing. But also it was that I'd changed. Oh, I'd probably always be afraid of sharks, at least a little; I'd at least regard them with a healthy respect, preferably from a safe distance. And I couldn't predict what might happen the next time I was on a beach at the ocean; would I go in, and would I be afraid? Yes, and maybe.

But for years there had been some other kind of fear, something that had lived inside me in a dark curl ready to lash out in ways I couldn't control, a fear of—what? I couldn't have said. But it had probably encouraged me to think of myself as a coward.

It was gone. Or it was disappearing fast. Something about this summer—Walker? Dylan? Darya?—something I couldn't identify had let that dark curl relax and release its hold on me.

I jumped on board the boat without instruction this time, and Walker fired up the outboard motor to navigate away from the docks. He had me help unfurl the sails and run through the safety check, and we were off!

If I'd thought my first ride, just over six weeks ago now, had been fun—well, this one was a blast. Even though I knew what to expect this time, I was so much more prepared to let the thrill of flying over the water lift me out of everything else in my life. Only this time, the thrill included being alone with the beautiful Walker Donnell, not as some unusual guy who had thrown a wet rag at me to get my attention, but as my boyfriend—a very special and unusual kind of person—who smelled like salt and clean rope and who wanted to be with me as much as I wanted to be with him. It was a dream come true. You know the dream I mean.

Walker had brought sandwiches and potato chips and cookies and water, and *Dare Ya* bobbed gently, sails at rest, while we ate.

At one point, Walker asked how Dylan and Darya were doing. I told him about the plan to move to Providence and take the dog (who now had only three legs but was mending well), and Walker laughed.

Then he said, "Paige really liked Darya."

"She liked Paige, too. Better than she likes my dad's girlfriend."

"Yeah? How's that going?"

I told him about the rejected dinner invitation. "It was Dad's idea. I think he's just really anxious to have everyone accept that he's with Sharon now. He and Mom talked later, and I think she agreed to meet Sharon, just not yet."

"So your folks won't get together again?"

"I haven't seen any signs of it. And then there's Sharon."

"Back to your brother, though. That was a really great thing you did, Micah. Getting Paige to talk to Dylan. And was it your idea to have her meet Darya?"

"It just seemed to make sense."

We finished our sandwiches, and as Walker handed me the bag of cookies, he said, "You don't know the whole story with Paige. In fact, I didn't know it until recently."

"The whole story?"

"Something about that conversation with Dylan, and learning about Islam, has changed her somehow. She's more interesting, and she's nicer to be with. No picnic, still, but nicer."

He swallowed a bite of cookie and went on. "I told you once that the reason my folks adopted her at all was because they thought they couldn't have kids of their own."

"Right... and then you came along."

"I hear it happens a lot. A couple can't conceive, they adopt a kid, and suddenly the wife's pregnant. It's a thing, evidently. Anyway, there's something I found out very recently that I want to tell you. It helped me understand why my mom got so weird about the whole gay thing, and why she was kind of afraid of you."

"Of me? She was afraid of me?"

"Well, maybe not of you, exactly. But here's the thing. The reason my folks had trouble conceiving was because of her, not my dad. I can't remember the term, but it meant she'd probably never conceive. So when she finally did, and I came along, and I was... you know, different, she blamed herself."

"You mean, being intersex?"

"Yeah. She saw it as some kind of judgment on her that she'd somehow contaminated me with."

"But that doesn't make sense."

He waved a hand in the air. "Catholics. Don't talk to me about sense. I'm just lucky my folks wouldn't let anyone cut off what I've got between my legs and raise me as a girl. Even so, I guess the whole intersex thing threw my folks for a loop."

"I kind of like the loop it throws me into."

He gave me a grin that made me want to do delightfully unmentionable things to him.

"Anyway, so she felt it was her fault I was born like this. Which is why she's always been so protective. And it kind of explains why she wanted to channel me into being as normal as she could. Normal as she saw it, that is."

"As in, not gay."

"Right."

We coasted along quietly for a few minutes, and then he said, "Normal. It used to be something I wanted so badly. Something I thought I never could have."

"And now? Are you normal?"

He laughed. "Hell, no. And that's okay with me now. But—well, it was like—Okay, picture this. My folks and I, usually without Paige in the last few years, would drive together to see Gramma, and Gramps, before he died. Sunday afternoon was usually the time. And when we'd

344

drive back, it would either be really dark, or it might be twilight. There's this one section of road where the side across from us was pretty close to a rock face. At the top of the rock face was this house, really contemporary, with huge windows, surrounded by tall trees. Must have had amazing views."

He paused, like he was waiting for me to see it in my mind. I closed my eyes.

"I'd be in the back seat, and Dad would usually have soft jazz or something playing. Maybe Pat Metheny's *One Quiet Night* album. *Another Chance*; that was the number that really got to me. Solo guitar, gently strumming this tune that's almost but not quite a melody, more a progression that's kind of melancholy. And I'd look up at that house."

When he didn't go on, I looked at him. Even with his sunglasses on, I could tell he was staring off into the distance, focused on nothing that was actually there, seeing only that house. I'd gotten pretty good at waiting for him by now, so that's what I did.

Finally, he spoke again. "That house. Nearly dark outside. Light coming through the huge picture window. The house is positioned in a way that I can just see inside well enough to know there's a couch along the window. I had this dream that someday I would have a house like that, full of elegance and grace and soft jazz, and I would be so happy. I would be so normal."

I waited through another pause.

"Then one evening, I think it was last May, as we drove past I looked up as usual. And this time…" I watched as he shook himself a little. "This time there was a woman sitting on that couch. And a man walked over to her, leaned over, and gave her the sweetest kiss. And in that moment, I gave up. I gave up my dream. I gave up being normal. I gave up being happy."

He reached a hand up and removed his sunglasses, and he waited until I'd taken mine off.

"And then, Micah, then I met you."

The little boat rocked gently with the surge of the sea, but our eyes didn't break the gaze that held us in place. What broke the gaze was both of us moving at the same time, getting down onto the deck of the boat.

I pulled Walker's head against my neck, and he curled against me as well as he could, and we lay like that for maybe ten minutes, gently rocking, no words, nothing but peace and love.

Where would this end? I wondered. How long would this feeling last?

If we broke up next month, it seemed unlikely that either of us would jump into another relationship right away; I didn't even know any other gay guys, and Walker—well, he didn't meet many guys at all, and it seemed likely that some of the guys he did meet would be more put off by Walker's condition that I had turned out to be.

But if we stayed together all year, and if I went away to one college and Walker went someplace else, would we wait for each other?

Waiting. I'd spent so much time waiting for Walker. Or that's what I'd thought. But maybe it wasn't Walker I'd been waiting for. Maybe it was me.

Author's Note

As with most of my novels, *Waiting for Walker* includes subjects about which I knew little or nothing before writing the story. In this case, I still feel remarkably ignorant about three of them: sailing; intersex; and Islam.

I relied upon experts in sailing and intersex to represent those subjects well enough for credibility and respect. However, I did not find a subject matter expert on Islam to guide me.

While my own research into comparative religion has brought me to a limited understanding of Islam and its history, I admit to a deep ignorance of what life is like for Afghanis in general and Muslim people in particular. If in representing Islam and Muslims in this story I have offended anyone, please accept my abject apology. I welcome correction and will create space on my website for comments from readers willing to instruct me in good faith.

WAITING FOR WALKER

Robin Reardon

ABOUT THIS GUIDE

The suggested questions are included to enhance your group's reading of Robin Reardon's novel, WAITING FOR WALKER.

DISCUSSION QUESTIONS

Note: The questions below contain spoiler information. It is recommended that you finish the book before reading through the questions.

1. Even before Micah knew what he felt for Walker, he was fixated on the image of Walker's boat shoes. What do you think it was that caught Micah's attention? Or was he focused on the shoes to distract himself from what he might feel for Walker? Have you ever experienced a similar kind of fixation?

2. Micah has created a special housing for his camera that allows him to look down at the focusing screen rather than facing whatever subject he's shooting. He sees his camera as a kind of passport, or permission slip, to venture into areas he might not otherwise feel he could go. What did he need to be protected from? How much protection does the camera really give him?

3. After losing part of the muscle in his left calf to a shark bite, Micah became terrified of going into the ocean. It didn't help that watching many seasons of Shark Week had taught him how seldom people are attacked by sharks, or how few of these animals actually consume human flesh. Can you imagine what it would be like to experience the kind of terror Micah felt going into the ocean? Has anything in your life made you react in a similar way?

4. What do you think it was about sailing with Walker that allowed Micah to set aside his intense fear of sharks?

5. For months, Micah had to listen to his mother talk about the connection she had with Dylan through Madam Alberta. How do you think he was able to maintain his patience, even through looking for houses and the purchasing of household items in anticipation of Dylan's return, which Micah was certain would never happen? How patient do you think you would have been with her?

6. When Micah joined the Donnells for the yacht trip on July Fourth, he was initially unable to face the group of sharks that had collected behind the boat. What was it about Mr. Donnell's approach that helped Micah recover as well as he did? Did his camera—his protection, his permission-giver—help him in this situation?

7. Were you surprised that Dylan had converted to Islam? Do you think your initial impressions of Darya would have been similar to Micah's? Do you know people who would have reacted as Micah's mother did? Do you know people who would have reacted even more negatively? If so, do you know why?

8. Recall what had just happened in the dynamics of Micah's fractured family just before he returns Trapper's collar to his mother. What do you think moved him to do that? What does it say about where Micah's loyalties lie? And do his feelings at that moment conflict with his feelings about his father?

9. Remembering the guilt Mrs. Donnell felt about Walker's condition, and keeping in mind her religious background, could you understand, or sympathize with, the need she felt to keep Micah from influencing Walker? What do you think her fears were? If Walker had been your son, do you think you would have felt the need to try and protect him in the same way?

10. Do you think accepting his own homosexuality made it easier for Micah to tolerate Walker's indecision about his own identity? If you fell for someone who was intersex, and if that person was in any doubt about their gender identity or their sexual orientation, how might that affect your relationship?

11. Micah struggles throughout the story with the idea that he is a coward. Do you see him as a coward? Why or why not?

12. When Walker tells Micah he's made a decision about himself, Micah is torn between joy and resentment. Do you understand the resentment? How do you think the process of waiting for Walker, and all the events that took place during that time, might have changed Micah, or might have made him see things differently?

Please note that at the end of the Foreword by author Cody Kennedy, there is a list of resources for anyone who would like more information about intersex.

About the Author

Robin Reardon is an inveterate observer of human nature, and her primary writing goal is to create stories about all kinds of people, some of whom happen to be gay, transgender, or intersex—people whose destinies should not be determined solely by their sexual orientation. Her secondary writing goal is to introduce readers to concepts or information they might not know very much about.

Robin's motto is this: The only thing wrong with being gay is how some people treat you when they find out.

Interests outside of writing include singing, nature photography, and the study of comparative religions. Robin writes in a butter yellow study with a view of the Boston, Massachusetts skyline.

Robin blogs (And now, this) about various subjects that influence her writing, as well as about the writing process itself, on her website.

If you enjoyed this book, please consider posting a review on the online sites of your choice. This is the best way to ensure that more titles by this author will become available.

If you would like to be notified when new titles are released, you can sign up for Robin's mailing list at robinreardon.com/contact.

Other Works by Robin Reardon

Novels
THROWING STONES
(IAM Books)
EDUCATING SIMON
THE REVELATIONS OF JUDE CONNOR
THE EVOLUTION OF ETHAN POE
A QUESTION OF MANHOOD
THINKING STRAIGHT
A SECRET EDGE
(Published by Kensington Publishing Corp.)
* * *

Essay
THE CASE FOR ACCEPTANCE: AN OPEN LETTER
TO HUMANITY
(Published by IAM Books)
* * *

Short Stories
GIUSEPPE AND ME
A LINE IN THE SAND
(IAM Books)

www.ingramcontent.com/pod-product-compliance
Lightning Source LLC
Chambersburg PA
CBHW051120120726
47905CB00005B/1356